Harriet Beecher Stowe

Collection of british authors: Oldtown Folks

Volume II.

Harriet Beecher Stowe

Collection of british authors: Oldtown Folks
Volume II.

ISBN/EAN: 9783742830937

Manufactured in Europe, USA, Canada, Australia, Japa

Cover: Foto ©Andreas Hilbeck / pixelio.de

Manufactured and distributed by brebook publishing software
(www.brebook.com)

Harriet Beecher Stowe

Collection of british authors: Oldtown Folks

COLLECTION

OF

BRITISH AUTHORS.

TAUCHNITZ EDITION.

VOL. 1020.

OLDTOWN FOLKS BY H. BEECHER STOWE.

IN TWO VOLUMES.

VOL. II.

OLDTOWN FOLKS.

BY

H. BEECHER STOWE,

AUTHOR OF "UNCLE TOM'S CABIN," ETC.

IN TWO VOLUMES.

VOL. II.

LEIPZIG

BERNHARD TAUCHNITZ

1869.

CONTENTS

OF VOLUME II.

OLDTOWN FOLKS.

CHAPTER I.

Eastor Sunday.

For a marvel, even in the stormy clime of Boston, our Easter Sunday was one of those celestial days which seem, like the New Jerusalem of the Revelation, to come straight down from God out of heaven, to show us mortals what the upper world may be like. Our poor old mother Boston has now and then such a day given to her, even in the uncertain spring-time; and when all her bells ring together, and the old North Church chimes her solemn psalm tunes, and all the people in their holiday garments come streaming out towards the churches of every name which line her streets, it seems as if the venerable dead on Copp's Hill must dream pleasantly, for "Blessed are the dead that die in the Lord," and even to this day, in dear old Boston, their works do follow them.

At an early hour we were roused, and dressed ourselves with the most anxious and exemplary care. For the first time in my life I looked anxiously in the looking-glass, and scanned with some solicitude, as if it had been a third person, the little being who called himself "I." I saw a pair of great brown eyes, a face rather thin and pale, a high forehead, and a great profusion of dark curls,—the combing out of which, by the by, was one of the morning trials of my life.

In vain Aunt Lois had cut them off repeatedly, in the laudable hope that my hair would grow out straight. It seemed a more inextricable mat at each shearing; but as Harry's flaxen poll had the same peculiarity, we consoled each other, while we laboured at our morning toilet.

Down in the sunny parlour, a little before breakfast was on the table, we walked about softly with our hands behind us, lest Satan, who we were assured had always some mischief still for idle hands to do, should entice us into touching some of the many curious articles which we gazed upon now for the first time. There was the picture of a very handsome young man over the mantelpiece, and beneath it hung a soldier's sword in a large loop of black crape, a significant symbol of the last great sorrow which had overshadowed the household. On one side of the door, framed and glazed, was a large coat of arms of the Kittery family, worked in chenille and embroidery,—the labour of Miss Deborah's hands during the course of her early education. In other places on the walls hung oil paintings of the deceased master of the mansion, and of the present venerable mistress, as she was in the glow of early youth. They were evidently painted by a not unskilful hand, and their eyes always following us as we moved about the room gave us the impression of being overlooked, even while as yet there was nobody else in the apartment. Conspicuously hung on one side of the room was a copy of one of the Vandyck portraits of Charles the First, with his lace ruff and peaked beard. Underneath this was a printed document, framed and glazed; and I, who was always drawn to read anything that could be read, stationed myself opposite to it and began reading aloud:—

"The Twelve Good Rules of the Most Blessed Martyr, King Charles First, of Blessed Memory."

I was reading these in a loud, clear voice, when Miss

Debby entered the room. She stopped and listened to me, with a countenance beaming with approbation.

"Go on, sonny!" she said, coming up behind me, with an approving nod, when I blushed and stopped on seeing her. "Read them through; those are good rules for a man to form his life by."

I wish I could remember now what these so highly praised rules were. The few that I can recall are not especially in accordance with the genius of our modern times. They began:—

"1st, Profane no Divine Ordinances.

"2d, Touch no State Matter.

"3d, Pick no Quarrels.

"4th, Maintain no ill Opinions."

Here my memory fails me, but I remember that, stimulated by Miss Deborah's approbation, I did commit the whole of them to memory at the time, and repeated them with a readiness and fluency which drew upon me warm commendations from the dear old lady, and in fact from all in the house, though Ellery Davenport did shrug his shoulders contumaciously, and give a sort of suppressed whistle of dissent.

"If we had minded those rules," he said, "we shouldn't be where we are now."

"No, indeed, you wouldn't; the more's the pity you didn't," said Miss Debby. "If I'd had the bringing of you up, you should be learning things like that, instead of trumpery French and democratic nonsense."

"Speaking of French," said Ellery, "I declare I forgot a package of gloves that I brought over especially for you and Aunty here,—the very best of Paris kid."

"You may spare yourself the trouble of bringing them, cousin," said Miss Deborah, coldly. "Whatever others may do, I trust *I* never shall be left to put a French glove on *my* hands. They may be all very fine, no doubt, but English gloves, made under her Majesty's sanction, will always be good enough for me."

"O, well, in that case I shall have the honour of presenting them to Lady Lothrop, unless her principles should be equally rigid."

"I dare say Dorothy will take them," said Miss Deborah. "When a woman has married a Continental parson, what can you expect of her? but, for *my* part, I should feel that I dishonoured the house of the Lord to enter it with gloves on made by those atheistical French people. The fact is, we must put a stop to worldly conformities somewhere."

"And you draw the line at French gloves," said Ellery.

"No, indeed," said Miss Deborah; "by no means French gloves. French novels, French philosophy, and, above all, French morals, or rather want of morals,—*these* are what I go against, Cousin Ellery."

So saying, Miss Debby led the way to the breakfast-table, with an air of the most martial and determined moral principle.

I remember only one other incident of that morning before we went to church. The dear old lady had seemed sensibly affected by the levity with which Ellery Davenport generally spoke upon sacred subjects, and disturbed by her daughter's confident assertions of his infidel sentiments. So she administered to him an admonition in her own way. A little before church-time she was sitting on the sofa, reading in her great Bible spread out on the table before her.

"Ellery," she said, "come here and sit down by me. I want you to read me this text."

"Certainly, Aunty, by all means," he said, as he seated

mself by her, bent his handsome head over the book, and,
llowing the lead of her trembling finger, read—

"And thou, Solomon, my son, know thou the God of thy
thers, and serve Him with a perfect heart and a willing
nd. If thou seek Him, He will be found of thee, but if
ou forsake Him, He will cast thee off for ever."

"Ellery," she said, with trembling earnestness, "think of
at, my boy. O Ellery, remember!"

He turned and kissed her hand, and there certainly were
irs in his eyes. "Aunty," he said, "you must pray for me;
nay be a good boy one of these days, who knows?"

There was no more preaching, and no more said; she
ly held his hand, looked lovingly at him, and stroked his
·ehead. "There have been a great many good people
rong your fathers, Ellery."

"I know it," he said.

At this moment Miss Debby came in with the summons
church. The family carriage came round for the old lady,
t we were better pleased to walk up the street under con-
y of Ellery Davenport, who made himself quite delightful
us. Tina obstinately refused to take his hand, and insisted
on walking only with Harry, though from time to time she
it glances at him over her shoulder, and he called her "a
le chip of mother Eve's block,"—at which she professed
feel great indignation.

The reader may remember my description of our meeting-
use at Oldtown, and therefore will not wonder that the
:hitecture of the Old North and its solemn-sounding chimes,
ugh by no means remarkable compared with European
irches, appeared to us a vision of wonder. We gazed
h delighted awe at the chancel and the altar, with their
ssive draperies of crimson looped back with heavy gold
·d and tassels, and revealing a cloud of little winged

cherubs, whereat Tina's eyes grew large with awe, as if she had seen a vision. Above this there was a mystical Hebrew word emblazoned in a golden halo, while around the galleries of the house were marvellous little coloured statuettes of angels blowing long golden trumpets. These figures had been taken from a privateer and presented to the church by a British man-of-war, and no child that saw them would ever forget them. Then there was the organ, whose wonderful sounds were heard by me for the first time in my life. There was also an indefinable impression of stately people that worshipped there. They all seemed to me like Lady Lothrop, rustling in silks and brocades; with gentlemen like Captain Brown, in scarlet cloaks and powdered hair. Not a crowded house by any means, but a well-ordered and select few, who performed all the responses and evolutions of the service with immaculate propriety. I was struck with every one's kneeling and bowing the head on taking a seat in the church; even gay Ellery Davenport knelt down and hid his face in his hat, though what he did it for was a matter of some speculation with us afterward. Miss Debby took me under her special supervision. She gave me a prayer-book, found the places for me, and took me up and down with her through the whole service, giving her responses in such loud, clear, and energetic tones as entirely to acquit herself of her share of responsibility in the matter. The "true Church" received no detriment, so far as she was concerned. I was most especially edified and astonished by the deep courtesies which she and several distinguished-looking ladies made at the name of the Saviour in the Creed; so much so, that she was obliged to tap me on the head to indicate to me my own part in that portion of the Church service.

I was surprised to observe that Harry appeared perfectly familiar with the ceremony; and Lady Lothrop, who had

m under her particular surveillance, looked on with wonder
d approbation, as he quietly opened his prayer-book and
:nt through the service with perfect regularity. Tina, who
od between Ellery Davenport and the old lady, seemed,
tell the truth, much too conscious of the amused attention
th which he was regarding her little movements, notwith-
.nding the kindly efforts of her venerable guardian to guide
r through the service. She resolutely refused to allow him
assist her, half-turning her back upon him, but slyly watch-
; him from under her long eyelashes, in a way that afforded
n great amusement.

The sermon which followed the prayers was of the most
ming and sleepy kind. But as it was dispensed by a
gularly ordained successor of the Apostles, Miss Deborah,
ugh ordinarily the shrewdest and sharpest of woman-
id, and certainly capable of preaching a sermon far more
the point herself, sat bolt upright and listened to all those
mberous platitudes with the most reverential attention.

It yet remains a mystery to my mind, how a church which
ains such a stimulating and inspiring liturgy *could* have
:h drowsy preaching,—how men could go through with
: "Te Deum," and the "Gloria in Excelsis," without one
ill of inspiration, or one lift above the dust of earth, and,
cr uttering words which one would think might warm the
zen heart of the very dead, settle sleepily down into the
ctest commonplace. Such, however, has been the sin of
ialism in all days, principally because human nature is,
ve all things, lazy, and needs to be thorned and goaded
those heights where it ought to fly.

Harry and I both had a very nice little nap during ser-
u-time, while Ellery Davenport made a rabbit of his
:ket-handkerchief by way of paying his court to Tina,
o sat shyly giggling and looking at him.

After the services came the Easter-dinner, to which, as a great privilege, we were admitted from first to last; although children in those days were held to belong strictly to the dessert, and only came in with the nuts and raisins. I remember Ellery Davenport seemed to be the life of the table, and kept everybody laughing. He seemed particularly fond of rousing up Miss Debby to those rigorous and energetic statements concerning Church and King which she delivered with such freedom.

"I don't know how we are any of us to get to heaven now," he said to Miss Debby. "Supposing I wanted to be confirmed, there isn't a bishop in America."

"Well, don't you think they will send one over?" said Lady Widgery, with a face of great solicitude.

"Two, madam; it would take two in order to start the succession in America. The apostolic electricity cannot come down through one."

"I heard that Dr. Franklin was negotiating with the Archbishop of Canterbury," said Lady Lothrop.

"Yes, but they are not in the best humour toward us over there," said Ellery. "You know what Franklin wrote back, don't you?"

"No," said Lady Widgery; "what was it?"

"Well, you see, he found Canterbury & Co. rather huffy, and somewhat on the high-and-mighty order with him, and, being a democratic American, he didn't like it. So he wrote over that he didn't see, for his part, why anybody that wanted to preach the Gospel couldn't preach it, without sending a thousand miles across the water to ask leave of a cross old gentleman at Canterbury."

A shocked expression went round the table, and Miss Debby drew herself up. "That's what I call a profane remark, Ellery Davenport," she said.

"I didn't make it, you understand."

"No, dear, you didn't," said the old lady. "Of course ou wouldn't say such a thing."

"Of course I shouldn't, Aunty,—oh no. I'm only con-erned to know how I shall be confirmed, if ever I want to ic. Do you think there really is no other way to heaven, liss Debby? Now, if the Archbishop of Canterbury won't epent, and I do,—if he won't send a bishop, and I become . good Christian,—don't you think now the Church might pen the door a little crack for me?"

"Why, of course, Ellery," said Lady Lothrop. "We elieve that many good people will be saved out of the 'hurch."

"My dear madam, that's because you married a Congre-ational parson; you are getting illogical."

"Ellery, you know better," said Miss Debby, vigorously. You know we hold that many good persons out of the 'hurch are saved, though they are saved, by uncovenanted iercies. There are no direct promises to any but those in ie Church; they have no authorized ministry or sacra-icnts."

"What a dreadful condition these American colonies are i!" said Ellery; "it's a result of our Revolution which never :ruck ine before."

"You can sneer as much as you please, it's a solemn fact, :llery; it's the chief mischief of this dreadful rebellion."

"Come, come, children," said the old lady; "let's talk bout something else. We've been to the communion, and eard about 'peace on earth and good-will to men.' I lways think of our blessed King George every time I take ic communion wine out of those cups that he gave to our lurch."

"Yes, indeed," said Miss Debby; "it will be a long time

before you get the American Congress to giving communion services, like our good, pious King George."

"It's a pity pious folks are so apt to be pig-headed," said Ellery, in a tone just loud enough to stir up Miss Debby, but not to catch the ear of the old lady.

"I suppose there never was such a pious family as our royal family," said Lady Widgery. "I have been told that Queen Charlotte reads prayers with her maids regularly every night, and we all know how our blessed King read prayers beside a dying cottager."

"I do not know what the reason is," said Ellery Davenport, reflectively, "but political tyrants as a general thing, are very pious men. The worse their political actions are, the more they pray. Perhaps it is on the principle of compensation, just as animals that are incapacitated from helping themselves in one way, have some corresponding organ in another direction."

"I agree with you that kings are generally religious," said Lady Widgery, "and you must admit that, if monarchy makes men religious, it is an argument in its favour, because there is nothing so important as religion, you know."

"The argument, madam, is a profound one, and does credit to your discernment; but the question now is, since it has pleased Providence to prosper rebellion, and allow a community to be founded without any true Church, or any means of getting at true ordinances and sacraments, what young fellows like us are to do about it?"

"I'll tell you, Ellery," said the old lady, laying hold of his arm. "'Know the God of thy fathers, and serve Him with a perfect heart and willing mind,' and everything will come right."

"But, even then, I couldn't belong to 'the true Church,'" said Ellery.

"You'd belong to the Church of all good people," said the old lady, "and that's the main thing."

"Aunty, you are always right," he said.

Now I listened with the sharpest attention to all this conversation, which was as bewildering to me as all the rest of the scenery and surroundings of this extraordinary visit had been.

Miss Debby's martial and declaratory air, the vigorous faith in her statements which she appeared to have, were quite a match, in my own mind, for similar statements of a contrary nature which I had heard from my respected grandmother; and I couldn't help wondering in my own mind what strange concussions of the elementary powers would result if ever these two should be brought together. To use a modern figure, it would be like the meeting of two full-charged railroad engines, from opposite directions, on the same track.

After dinner, in the evening, instead of the usual service of family prayers, Miss Debby catechised her family in a vigorous and determined manner. We children went and stood up with the row of men and maid servants, and Harry proved to have a very good knowledge of the catechism, but Tina and I only compassed our answers by repeating them after Miss Debby; and she applied herself to teaching us as if this were the only opportunity of getting the truth we were ever to have in our lives.

In fact, Miss Debby made a current of electricity that, for the time being, carried me completely away, and I exerted myself to the utmost to appear well before her, especially as had gathered from Aunt Lois and Aunt Keziah's conversations, that whatever went on in this mansion belonged strictly to upper circles of society, dimly known and revered. American democracy had not in those days become a practical thing, so as to outgrow the result of generations of reverence for the upper classes. And the man-servant and the maid-servants seemed so humble, and Miss Debby so victorious and dominant, that I couldn't help feeling what a grand thing the true Church must be, and find growing in myself the desires of a submissive catechumen.

As to the catechism itself, I don't recollect that I thought one moment what a word of it meant, I was so absorbed and busy in the mere effort of repeating it after Miss Debby's rapid dictation.

The only comparison I remember to have made with that which I had been accustomed to recite in school every Saturday respected the superior ease of answering the first question; which required me, instead of relating in metaphysical terms what "man's chief end" was in time and eternity, to give a plain statement of what my own name was on this mortal earth.

This first question, as being easiest, was put to Tina, who dimpled and coloured and flashed out of her eyes, as she usually did when addressed, looked shyly across at Ellery Davenport, who sat with an air of negligent amusement contemplating the scene, and then answered with sufficient precision and distinctness, "Eglantine Percival."

He gave a little start, as if some sudden train of recollection had been awakened, and looked at her with intense attention; and when Ellery Davenport fixed his attention upon anybody, there was so much fire and electricity in his eyes that they seemed to be felt, even at a distance; and I saw that Tina constantly coloured and giggled, and seemed so excited that she scarcely knew what she was saying, till at last Miss Debby, perceiving this, turned sharp round upon him, and said, "Ellery Davenport, if you haven't any

ligion yourself, I wish you wouldn't interrupt my in-
·uctions."

"Bless my soul, cousin! what was I doing? I have been
ting here still as a mouse; but I'll turn my back, and read
good book;"—and round he turned accordingly till the
techising was finished.

When it was all over, and the servants had gone out, we
ouped ourselves around the fire, and Ellery Davenport be-
n: "Cousin Debby, I'm going to come down handsomely
you. I admit that your catechism is much better for chil-
:n than the one I was brought up on. I was well drilled
the formulas of the celebrated Assembly of *dryvines* of
estminster, and dry enough I found it. Now it's a true
verb, 'Call a man a thief, and he'll steal;' 'give a dog a
l name, and he'll bite you;' tell a child that he is 'a mem-
· of Christ, a child of God, and an inheritor of the king-
n of heaven,' and he feels, to say the least, civilly disposed
vards religion; tell him 'he is under God's wrath and
se, and so made liable to all the miseries of this life, to
ith itself, and the pains of hell for ever, because somebody
 an apple five thousand years ago, and his religious as-
iations are not so agreeable,—especially if he has the
;wers whipped into him, or has to go to bed without his
per for not learning them."

"You poor dear!" said the old lady; "did they send you
bed without your supper? They ought to have been
ipped themselves, every one of them."

"Well, you see, I was a little fellow when my parents
d, and brought up under brother Jonathan, who was the
est kind of blue; and he was so afraid that I should mis-
e my naturally sweet temper for religion, that he instructed
daily that I was a child of wrath, and couldn't and didn't,
; never should do one right thing till I was regenerated,

and when that would happen no mortal knew; so I thought, as my account was going to be scored off at that time, it was no matter if I did run up a pretty long one; so I lied and stole whenever it came handy."

"O Ellery, I hope not!" said the old lady; "certainly you never stole anything!"

"Have, though, my blessed aunt,—robbed orchards and water-melon patches; but then St. Augustine did that very thing himself, and he didn't turn about till he was thirty years old, and I'm a good deal short of that yet; so you see there is a great chance for me."

"Ellery, why don't you come into the true Church?" said Miss Debby. "That's what you need."

"Well," said Ellery, "I must confess that I like the idea of a nice old motherly Church, that sings to us, and talks to us, and prays with us, and takes us in her lap and coddles us when we are sick and says,—

"'Hush, my dear, lie still and slumber.'

Nothing would suit me better, if I could get my reason to sleep; but the mischief of a Calvinistic education is, it wakes up your reason, and it never will go to sleep again, and you can't take a pleasant humbug if you would. Now, in this life, where nobody knows anything about anything, a capacity for humbugs would be a splendid thing to have. I wish to my heart I'd been brought up a Roman Catholic! but I have not,—I've been brought up a Calvinist, and so here I am."

"But if you'd try to come into the Church, and believe," said Miss Debby, energetically, "grace would be given you. You've been baptized, and the Church admits your baptism. Now just assume your position."

Miss Debby spoke with such zeal and earnestness, that I, whom she was holding in her lap, looked straight across with

e expectation of hearing Ellery Davenport declare his im-
ediate conversion then and there. I shall never forget the
:pression of his face. There was first a flash of amusement
 he looked at Miss Debby's strong, sincere face, and then
faded into something between admiration and pity; and
en he said to himself in a musing tone: "I a 'member of
 irist, a child of God, and an inheritor of the kingdom of
aven.'" And then a strange, sarcastic expression broke
 er his face, as he added: "Couldn't do it, cousin; not
actly my style. Besides, I shouldn't be much of a credit
 any Church, and whichever catches me would be apt to
 .d a shark in the net. You see," he added, jumping up and
 ilking about rapidly, "I have the misfortune to have an
 tremely exacting nature, and, if I set out to be religious at
 , it would oblige me to carry the thing to as great lengths
 did my grandfather Jonathan Edwards. I should have to
 ιe up the cross and all that, and I don't want to, and don't
 ιan to; and as to all these pleasant, comfortable Churches,
 ιcre a fellow can get to heaven without it, I have the mis-
 tune of not being able to believe in them; so there you
 ι precisely my situation."
 "These horrid old Calvinistic doctrines," said Miss Debby,
 ιe the ruin of children."
 "My dear, they are all in the Thirty-nine Articles as strong
 in the Cambridge platform, and all the other platforms,
 · the good reason that John Calvin himself had the over-
 ιking of them. And, what is worse, there is an abomin-
 le sight of truth in them. Nature herself is a high Calvinist,
 l jade; and there never was a man of energy enough
 feel the force of the world he deals with that wasn't a pre-
 stinarian, from the time of the Greek Tragedians down to
 ι time of Oliver Cromwell, and ever since. The hardest
 ctrines are the things that a fellow sees with his own eyes

going on in the world around him. If you had been in England, as I have, where the true Church prevails, you'd see that pretty much the whole of the lower classes there are predestinated to be conceived and born in sin, and shapen in iniquity; and come into the world in such circumstances that to expect even decent morality of them is expecting what is contrary to all reason. This is your Christian country, after eighteen hundred years' experiment of Christianity. The elect, by whom I mean the bishops and clergy and upper classes, have attained to a position in which a decent and religious life is practicable, and where there is leisure from the claims of the body to attend to those of the soul. These, however, to a large extent are smothering in their own fat, or, as your service to-day had it, 'Their heart is fat as brawn;' and so they don't, to any great extent, make their calling and election sure. Then, as for heathen countries, they are a peg below those of Christianity. Taking the mass of human beings in the world at this hour, they are in such circumstances, that, so far from its being reasonable to expect the morals of Christianity of them, they are not within sight of ordinary human decencies. Talk of purity of heart to a Malay or Hottentot! Why, the doctrine of a clean shirt is an uncomprehended mystery to more than half the human race at this moment. That's what I call visible election and reprobation, get rid of it as we may or can."

"Positively, Ellery, I am not going to have you talk so before these children," said Miss Debby, getting up and ringing the bell energetically. "This all comes of the vile democratic idea that people are to have opinions on all subjects, instead of believing what the Church tells them; and, as you say, it's Calvinism that starts people out to be always reasoning and discussing, and having opinions. I hate folks who are always speculating and thinking, and having new doctrines; all I want to know is *my duty*, and to do it. I want to know what *my* part is, and it's none of my business whether the bishop and the kings and the nobility do theirs or not, if I only do mine. 'To do my duty in that state of life in which it has pleased God to call me,' is all I want, and I think it is all anybody need want."

"*Amen!*" said Ellery Davenport, "*and so be it.*"

Here Mrs. Margery appeared with the candles to take us to bed.

In bidding our adieus for the night, it was customary for good children to kiss all round; but Tina, in performing this ceremony both this night and the night before, resolutely ignored Ellery Davenport, notwithstanding his earnest petitions; and, while she would kiss with ostentatious affection those on each side of him, she hung her head and drew back whenever he attempted the familiarity, yet, by way of reparation, turned back at the door as she was going out, and made him a parting salutation with the air of a princess; and I heard him say, "Upon my word, how she does it!"

After we left the room (this being a particular which, like tellers of stories in general, I learned from other sources) he turned to Lady Lothrop and said: "Did I understand that she said her name was Eglantine Percival, and that she is a sort of foundling?"

"Certainly," said Lady Lothrop; "both these children are orphans, left on the parish by a poor woman who died in a neighbouring town. They appear to be of good blood and breeding, but we have no means of knowing who they are."

"Well," said Ellery Davenport, "I knew a young English officer by the name of Percival, who was rather a graceless fellow. He once visited me at my country-seat, with several others. When he went away, being, as he often was, not very fit to take care of himself, he dropped and left a pocket-book, so some of the servants told me, which was thrown into one of the drawers, and for aught I know may be there now: it's just barely possible that it may be, and that there may be some papers in it which will shed light on these children's parentage. If I recollect rightly, he was said to be connected with a good English family, and it might be possible, if we were properly informed, to shame him, or frighten him into doing something for these children. I will look into the matter myself, when I am in England next winter, where I shall have some business; that is to say, if we can get any clue. The probability is that the children are illegitimate."

"Oh, I hope not," said Lady Lothrop; "they appear to have been so beautifully educated."

"Well," said Ellery Davenport, "he may have seduced his curate's daughter; that's a very simple supposition. At any rate, he never produced her in society, never spoke of her, kept her in cheap, poor lodgings in the country, and the general supposition was that she was his mistress, not his wife."

"No," said a little voice near his elbow, which startled every one in the room,—"no, Mr. Davenport, my mother was my father's wife."

The fire had burnt low, and the candles had not been brought in, and Harry, who had been sent back by Mrs. Margery to give a message as to the night arrangements, had entered the room softly, and stood waiting to get a chance to deliver it. He now came forward, and stood trembling with agitation, pale yet bold. Of course all were very much shocked as he went on: "They took my mother's wedding-ring, and sold it to pay for her coffin; but she always wore it, and often told me when it was put on. But," he added, "she told me, the night she died, that I had no father but God."

"And he is Father enough!" said the old lady, who, entirely broken down and overcome, clasped the little boy in her arms. "Never you mind it, dear; God certainly will take care of you."

"I know He will," said the boy, with solemn simplicity; "but I want you all to believe the truth about my mother."

It was characteristic of that intense inwardness and delicacy which were so peculiar in Harry's character, that, when he came back from this agitating scene, he did not tell me a word of what had occurred, nor did I learn it till years afterwards. I was very much in the habit of lying awake nights, long after he had sunk into untroubled slumbers, and this night I remember that he lay long but silently awake, so very still and quiet, that it was some time before I discovered that he was not sleeping.

The next day Ellery Davenport left us, but we remained to see the wonders of Boston. I remembered my grandmother's orders, and went on to Copps Hill, and to the old Granary burying-ground, to see the graves of the saints, and read the inscriptions. I had a curious passion for this sort of mortuary literature, even as a child,—a sort of nameless, weird strange delight,—so that I accomplished this part of my grandmother's wishes *con amore*.

Boston in those days had not even arrived at being a city, but, as the reader may learn from contemporary magazines, was known as the Town of Boston. In some respects, however, it was even more attractive in those days for private residences than it is at present. As is the case now in some of our large rural towns, it had many stately old houses, which stood surrounded by gardens and grounds, where fruits and flowers were tended with scrupulous care. It was sometimes called "the garden town." The house of Madam Kittery stood on a high eminence overlooking the sea, and had connected with it a stately garden, which, just at the time of year I speak of, was gay with the first crocuses and snow-drops.

In the eyes of the New England people, it was always a sort of mother-town,—a sacred city, the shrine of that religious enthusiasm which founded the States of New England. There were the graves of her prophets and her martyrs,—those who had given their lives through the hardships of that enterprise in so ungenial a climate.

On Easter Monday Lady Lothrop proposed to take us all to see the shops and sights of Boston, with the bountiful intention of purchasing some few additions to the children's wardrobes. I was invited to accompany the expedition, and all parties appeared not a little surprised, and somewhat amused, that I preferred, instead of this lively tour among the living, to spend my time in a lonely ramble in the Copps Hill burying-ground.

I returned home after an hour or two spent in this way, and found the parlour deserted by all except dear old Madam Kittery. I remember, even now, the aspect of that sunny room, and the perfect picture of peace and love that she seemed to me, as she sat on the sofa, with a table full of books drawn up to her, placidly reading.

She called me to her as soon as I came in, and would have me get on the sofa by her. She stroked my head, and looked lovingly at me, and called me "Sonny," till my whole heart opened toward her as a flower opens toward the sunshine.

Among all the loves that man has to women, there is none so sacred and saint-like as that toward these dear, white-haired angels, who seem to form the connecting link between heaven and earth, who have lived to get the victory over every sin and every sorrow, and live perpetually on the banks of the dark river, in that bright, calm land of Beulah, where angels daily walk to and fro, and sounds of celestial music are heard across the water.

Such have no longer personal cares, or griefs, or sorrows. The tears of life have all been shed, and therefore they have hearts at leisure to attend to every one else. Even the sweet, guileless childishness that comes on in this period has a sacred dignity; it is a seal of fitness for that heavenly kingdom which whosoever shall not receive as a little child, shall not enter therein.

Madam Kittery, with all her apparent simplicity, had a sort of simple shrewdness. She delighted in reading, and some of the best classical literature was always lying on her table. She began questioning me about my reading, and asking me to read to her, and seemed quite surprised at the intelligence and expression with which I did it.

I remember, in the course of the reading, coming across a very simple Latin quotation, at which she stopped me. "There," said she, "is one of those Latin streaks that always trouble me in books, because I can't tell what they mean. When George was alive, he used to read them to me."

Now, as this was very simple, I felt myself quite adequate to its interpretation, and gave it with a readiness which pleased her.

"Why! how came you to know Latin?" she said.

Then my heart opened, and I told her all my story, and how my poor father had always longed to go to college, "and died without the sight," and how he had begun to teach me Latin; but how he was dead, and my mother was poor, and grandpapa could only afford to keep Uncle Bill in college, and there was no way for me to go, and Aunt Lois wanted to bind me out to a shoemaker. And then I began to cry, as I always did when I thought of this.

I shall never forget the overflowing, motherly sympathy

which had made it easy for me to tell all this to one who, but a few hours before, had been a stranger; nor how she comforted me, and cheered me, and insisted upon it that I should immediately eat a piece of cake, and begged me not to trouble myself about it, and she would talk to Debby, and something should be done.

Now I had not the slightest idea of what Madam Kittery could do in the situation, but I was exceedingly strengthened and consoled, and felt sure that there had come a favourable turn in my fortunes; and the dear old lady and myself forthwith entered into a league of friendship.

I was thus emboldened, now that we were all alone, and Miss Debby far away, to propound to her indulgent ear certain political doubts, raised by the conflict of my past education with the things I had been hearing for the last day or two.

"If King George was such a good man, what made him oppress the Colonies so?" said I.

"Why, dear, he didn't," she said, earnestly. "That's all a great mistake. Our King is a dear, pious, good man, and wished us all well, and was doing just the best for us he knew how."

"Then was it because he didn't know how to govern us?" said I.

"My dear, you know the King can do no wrong; it was his ministers, if anybody. I don't know exactly how it was, but they got into a brangle, and everything went wrong; then there was so much evil feeling and fighting and killing, and 'there was confusion and every evil work.' There's my poor boy," she said, pointing to the picture with a trembling hand, and to the sword hanging in its crape loop,—"he died for his King, doing his duty in that state of life to which it pleased God to call him. I mustn't be sorry for that; but oh,

I wish there hadn't been any war, and we could have had it all peaceful, and George could have stayed with us. I don't see, either, the use of all these new-fangled notions; but then I try to love everybody, and hope for the best."

So spoke my dear old friend; and has there ever been a step in human progress that has not been taken against the prayers of some good soul, and been washed by tears, sincerely and despondingly shed? But, for all this, is there not a true unity of the faith in all good hearts? and when they have risen a little above the mists of earth, may not both sides— the conqueror and the conquered—agree that God hath given them the victory in advancing the cause of truth and goodness?

Only one other conversation that I heard during this memorable visit fixed itself very strongly in my mind. On the evening of this same day, we three children were stationed at a table to look at a volume of engravings of beautiful birds, while Miss Debby, Lady Widgery, and Madam Kittery sat by the fire. I heard them talking of Ellery Davenport, and, though I had been instructed that it was not proper for children to listen when their elders were talking among themselves, yet it really was not possible to avoid hearing what Miss Debby said, because all her words were delivered with such a sharp and determinate emphasis.

As it appeared, Lady Widgery had been relating to them some of the trials and sorrows of Ellery Davenport's domestic life. And then there followed a buzz of some kind of a story which Lady Widgery seemed relating with great minuteness. At last I heard Miss Deborah exclaim earnestly, "If I had a daughter, catch me letting her be intimate with Ellery Davenport! I tell you that man hasn't read French for nothing."

"I do assure you, his conduct has been marked with perfect decorum," said Lady Widgery.

"So are your French novels," said Miss Deborah; "they

are always talking about decorum; they are full of decorum
and piety! why, the kingdom of heaven is nothing to them!
but somehow they all end in adultery."

"Debby," said the old lady, "I can't bear to hear you
talk so. I think your cousin's heart is in the right place, after
all; and he's a good, kind boy as ever was."

"But, mother, he's a liar! that's just what he is."

"Debby, Debby! how can you talk so?"   -

"Well, mother, people have different names for different
things. I hear a great deal about Ellery Davenport's tact
and knowledge of the world, and all that; but he does a
great deal of what *I* call lying,--so there! Now there are
some folks who lie blunderingly, and unskilfully; but I'll
say for Ellery Davenport, that he can lie as innocently and
sweetly and prettily as a Frenchwoman, and I can't say any
more. And if a woman doesn't want to believe him, she just
mustn't listen to him, that's all. I always believe him when
he is around; but when he's away, and I think him over, I
know just what he is, and see just what an old fool he has
made of me."

These words dropped into my childish mind as if you
should accidentally drop a ring into a deep well. I did not
think of them much at the time; but there came a day in my
life when the ring was fished up out of the well, good as new.

CHAPTER II.

What "Our Folks" said at Oldtown.

We children returned to Oldtown, crowned with victory,
as it were. Then, as now, even in the simple and severe
Puritanical village, there was much incense burnt upon the
altar of gentility—a deity somewhat corresponding to the
unknown god whose altar Paul found at Athens, and pro-

bably more universally worshipped in all the circles of this lower world than any other idol on record.

Now we had been taken notice of, put forward, and patronised, in undeniably genteel society. We had been to Boston and come back in a coach; and what well-regulated mind does not see that that was something to inspire respect?

Aunt Lois was evidently dying to ask us all manner of questions, but was restrained by a sort of decent pride. To exhibit any undue eagerness would be to concede that she was ignorant of good society, and that the ways and doings of upper classes were not perfectly familiar to her. That, my dear reader, is what no good democratic American woman can for a moment concede. Aunt Lois, therefore, for once in her life, looked complacently on Sam Lawson, who continued to occupy his usual roost in the chimney-corner, and who, embarrassed with no similar delicate scruples, put us through our catechism with the usual Yankee thoroughness.

"Well, chillen, I suppose them Kitterys has everythin' in real grander, don't they? I've heerd tell that they hes Turkey carpets on th' floors. You know Josh Kittery, he was in the Injy trade. Turkey carpets is that kind, you know, that lies all up thick like a mat. They had that kind, didn't they?"

We eagerly assured him that they did.

"Want to know, now," said Sam, who always moralised as he went along. "Wal, wal, some folks does seem to receive their good thin's in this life, don't they? S'pose the tea-things all on 'em was solid silver, wan't they? Yeh didn't ask them, did yeh?"

"Oh no," said I; "you know we were told we mustn't ask questions."

"Jes so; very right,—little boys shouldn't ask questions. But I've heerd a good 'eal about the Kittery silver. Jake Marshall, he knew a fellah that had talked with one o' their

servants, that helped bury it in the cellar in war-times, an'
he said thch was porringers an' spoons an' tankards, say nothing of table-spoons, an' silver forks, an' sich. That 'ere
would ha' been a haul for Congress, if they could ha'got hold
on't in war-time, wouldn't it? S'pose ych was sot up all so
grand, and hed servants to wait on ych, behind yer chairs,
didn't ych?"

"Yes," we assured him, "we did."

"Wal, wal; ych mustn't be carried away by these 'ere
glories; they's transitory, arter all; ye must jest come right
daown to plain livin'. How many servants d' ych say they
kep'?"

"Why, there were two men and two women, besides Lady
Widgery's maid and Mrs. Margery."

"And all used to come in to prayers every night," said
Harry.

"Hes prayers reg'lar, does they?" said Sam. "Well, now,
that 'ere beats all! Didn't know as these gran' families wus
so pious as that comes to. Who prayed?"

"Old Madam Kittery," said I. "She used to read prayers
out of a large book."

"Oh yis; these 'ere gran' Tory families is 'Piscopal, pretty
much all on 'em. But now readin' prayers out of a book,
that 'ere don' strike me as just the right kind o' thing. For
my part, I like prayers that come right out o' the heart better.
But then, lordy massy, folks hes thch different ways; an' I
ain't so set as Polly is. Why, I b'lieve, if that 'ere woman
had her way, they wouldn't nobody be 'lowed to do nothin',
except just to suit her. Ych didn't notice, did ych, what the
Kittery coat-of-arms was?"

Yes, we had noticed it; and Harry gave a full description
of an embroidered set of armorial bearings which had been
one of the ornaments of the parlour.

"So you say," said Sam, "'twas a lion upon his hind legs, —that 'ere is what they call 'the lion rampant,'—an' then there was a key an' a scroll. Wal! coats of arms is curus, an' I don't wonder folks kind o' hangs onter um; but then, the Kittery's bein' Tories, they nat'ally has more interest in sech thin's. Do you know where Mis' Kittery keeps her silver nights?"

"No, really," said I; "we were sent to bed early, and didn't see."

Now this inquiry, from anybody less innocent than Sam Lawson, might have been thought a dangerous exhibition of burglarious proclivities; but from him it was received only as an indication of that everlasting thirst for general information which was his leading characteristic.

When the rigour of his cross-examination had somewhat abated, he stooped over the fire to meditate further inquiries. I seized the opportunity to propound to my grandmother a query which had been the result of my singular experiences for a day or two past. So, after an interval in which all had sat silently looking into the great coals of the fire, I suddenly broke out with the inquiry, "Grandmother, what is *The True Church?*"

I remember the expression on my grandfather's calm benign face as I uttered this query. It was an expression of shrewd amusement, such as befits the face of an elder when a younger has propounded a well-worn problem; but my grandmother had her answer at the tip of her tongue, and replied, "It is the whole number of the elect, my son."

I had in my head a confused remembrance of Ellery Davenport's tirade on election, and of the elect who did or did not have clean shirts; so I pursued my inquiry by asking, "Who are the elect?"

"All good people," replied my grandfather. "In every

nation he that feareth God and worketh righteousness is accepted of Him."

"Well, how came you to ask that question?" said my grandmother, turning on me.

"Why," said I, "because Miss Deborah Kittery said that the war destroyed the true Church in this country."

"Oh, pshaw!" said my grandmother; "that's some of her Episcopal nonsense. I really should like to ask her, now, if she thinks there ain't any one going to heaven but Episcopalians."

"Oh no, she doesn't think so," said I, rather eagerly. "She said a great many good people would be saved out of the Church, but they would be saved by uncovenanted mercies."

"*Uncovenanted fiddlesticks!*" said my grandmother, her very cap-border bristling with contempt and defiance. "Now, Lois, you just see what comes of sending children into Tory Episcopal families—coming home and talking nonsense like that!"

"Mercy, mother! what odds does it make?" said Aunt Lois. "The children have got to learn to hear all sorts of things said—may as well hear them at one time as another. Besides, it all goes into one ear, and out at the other."

My grandmother was better pleased with the account that I hastened to give her of my visit to the graves of the saints and martyrs in my recent pilgrimage. Her broad face glowed with delight, as she told over again to our listening ears the stories of the faith and self-denial of those who had fled from an oppressive king and church, that they might plant a new region where life should be simpler, easier, and more natural. And she got out her "Cotton Mather," and, notwithstanding Aunt Lois's reminder that she had often read it before, read to us again, in a trembling yet audible voice, that wonderful document in which the reasons for the first planting of New

England are set forth. Some of these reasons I remember from often hearing them in my childhood. They speak thus quaintly of the old countries of Europe:—

"*Thirdly*, The land grows weary of her inhabitants, insomuch that *man*, which is the most precious of all creatures, is here more vile than the earth he treads upon—children, neighbours, and friends, especially the *poor*, which, if things were right, would be the greatest earthly blessings.

"*Fourthly*, We are grown to that intemperance in all *excess of riot* as no mean estate will suffice a man to keep sail with his *equals*, and he that fails in it must live in scorn and contempt: hence it comes to pass that all *arts* and *trades* are carried in that deceitful manner and unrighteous course, as it is almost impossible for a good, upright man to maintain his constant charge, and live comfortably in them.

"*Fifthly*, The schools of learning and religion are so corrupted as (besides the unsupportable charge of education) most children of the best, wittiest, and of the fairest hopes are perverted, corrupted, and utterly overthrown by the multitude of evil examples and licentious behaviours in these *seminaries*.

"*Sixthly*, The *whole earth* is the Lord's *garden*, and He hath given it to the sons of Adam to be tilled and improved by them. Why then should we stand starving here for places of habitation, and in the meantime suffer whole countries as profitable for the use of man to lie waste without any improvement?"

Language like this, often repeated, was not lost upon us. The idea of self-sacrifice which it constantly inculcated—the reverence for self-denial—the conception of a life which should look, not mainly to selfish interests, but to the good of the whole human race, prevented the hardness and roughness of those early New England days from becoming mere stolid,

material toil.   It was toil and manual labour ennobled by a
new motive.

Even in those very early times there was some dawning
sense of what the great American nation was yet to be. And
every man, woman, and child was constantly taught, by every
fireside, to feel that he or she was part and parcel of a great
new movement in human progress. The old aristocratic ideas,
though still lingering in involuntary manners and customs,
only served to give a sort of quaintness and grace of Old-
World culture to the roughness of new-fledged democracy.

Our visit to Boston was productive of good to us such as
we little dreamed of. In the course of a day or two Lady
Lothrop called, and had a long private interview with the
female portion of the family; after which, to my great delight,
it was announced to us that Harry and I might begin to
study Latin, if we pleased, and if we proved bright, good
boys, means would be provided for the finishing of our education in college.

I was stunned and overwhelmed by the great intelligence,
and Harry and I ran over to tell it to Tina, who jumped about
and hugged and kissed us both with an impartiality which
some years later she quite forgot to practise.

"I'm glad, because you like it," she said; "but I should
think it would be horrid to study Latin."

I afterwards learned that I was indebted to my dear old
friend Madam Kittery for the good fortune which had be-
fallen me. She had been interested in my story, as it appears, to some purpose, and, being wealthy and without a son,
had resolved to console herself by appropriating to the education of a poor boy a portion of the wealth which should
have gone to her own child.

The searching out of poor boys, and assisting them to a
liberal education had ever been held to be one of the appro-

priate works of the minister in a New England town. The schoolmaster who taught the district school did not teach Latin; but Lady Lothrop was graciously pleased to say that, for the present, Dr. Lothrop would hear our lessons at a certain hour every afternoon; and the reader may be assured that we studied faithfully in view of an ordeal like this.

I remember one of our favourite places for study. The brown, sparkling stream on which my grandfather's mill was placed had, just below the mill-dam, a little island which a boy could easily reach by wading through the shallow waters over a bed of many-coloured pebbles. The island was overshadowed by thick bushes, which were all wreathed and matted together by a wild grape-vine; but within I had hollowed out for myself a green little arbour, and constructed a rude wigwam of poles and bark, after the manner of those I had seen among the Indians. It was one of the charms of this place that nobody knew of it—it was utterly secluded; and being cut off from land by the broad belt of shallow water, and presenting nothing to tempt or attract anybody to its shores, it was mine, and mine alone. There I studied, and there I read; there I dreamed and saw visions.

Never did I find it in my heart to tell to any other boy the secret of this woodland shelter, this fairy land, so near to the real outer world; but Harry, with his refinement, his quietude, his sympathetic silence, seemed to me as unobjectionable an associate as the mute spiritual companions whose presence had cheered my lonely, childish sleeping-room.

We moved my father's Latin books into a rough little closet that we constructed in our wigwam; and there, with the water dashing behind us, and the afternoon sun shining down through the green grape-leaves, with bluebirds and bobolinks singing to us, we studied our lessons. More than that, we spent many pleasant hours in reading; and I have now a *résumé*, in our boyish handwriting, of the greater part of Plutarch's Lives, which we wrote out during this summer.

As to Tina, of course she insisted upon it that we should occasionally carry her in a lady-chair over to this island, that she might inspect our operations and our housekeeping, and we read some of these sketches to her for her critical approbation; and if any of them pleased her fancy, she would immediately insist that we should come over to Miss Mehitable's and have a dramatic representation of them up in the garret.

Saturday afternoon, in New England, was considered, from time immemorial, as the children's perquisite; and hard-hearted must be that parent or that teacher who would wish to take away from them its golden hours. Certainly it was not Miss Mehitable, nor my grandmother, that could be capable of any such cruelty.

Our Saturday afternoons were generally spent as Tina dictated; and, as she had a decided taste for the drama, one of our most common employments was the improvising of plays, with Miss Tina for stage-manager. The pleasure we took in these exercises was inconceivable; they had for us a vividness and reality past all expression.

I remember our acting, at one time, the Book of Esther, with Tina, very much be-trinketed and dressed out in an old flowered brocade that she had rummaged from a trunk in the garret, as Queen Esther. Harry was Mordecai, and I was Ahasuerus.

The great trouble was to find a Haman; but, as the hanging of Haman was indispensable to any proper moral effect of the tragedy, Tina petted and cajoled and coaxed old Bose, the yellow dog of our establishment, to undertake the part, instructing him volubly that he must sulk and look cross

when Mordecai went by—a thing which Bose, who was one
of the best-natured of dogs, found difficulty in learning.
Bose would always insist upon sitting on his haunches, in
his free-and-easy, jolly manner, and lolling out his red tongue
in a style so decidedly jocular as utterly to spoil the effect,
till Tina, reduced to desperation, ensconced herself under an
old quilted petticoat behind him, and brought out the proper
expression at the right moment by a vigorous pull at his tail.
Bose was a dog of great constitutional equanimity, but there
were some things that transcended even his powers of endurance, and the snarl that he gave to Mordecai was held to be
a triumphant success; but the thing was, to get him to snarl
when Tina was in front of him, where she could see it; and
now, will it be believed that the all-conquering little mis-
chief-maker actually kissed and flattered and bejuggled old
Polly into taking this part behind the scenes?

No words can more fitly describe the abject state to
which that vehemently moral old soul was reduced.

When it came to the hanging of Haman, the difficulties
thickened. Polly warned us that we must by no means at-
tempt to hang Bose by the neck, as "the crittur was heavy,
and 't was sartin to be the death of him." So we compromised
by passing the rope under his fore paws, or, as Tina called
it, "under his arms." But Bose was rheumatic, and it took
all Tina's petting and caressing, and obliged Polly to go
down and hunt out two or three slices of meat from her
larder, to induce him fairly to submit to the operation; but
hang him we did, and he ki-hied with a vigour that strikingly
increased the moral effect. So we soon let him down again,
and plentifully rewarded him with cold meat.

In a similar manner, we performed a patriotic drama, en-
titled, "The Battle of Bunker Hill," in which a couple of old
guns that we found in the garret produced splendid effects,

and salvos of artillery were created by the rolling across the garret of two old cannon balls; but this was suppressed by order of the authorities, on account of the vigour of the cannonade. Tina, by the by, figured in this as the "Genius of Liberty," with some stars on her head cut out of gilt paper, and wearing an old flag which we had pulled out of one of the trunks.

We also acted the history of "Romulus and Remus," with Bose for the she-wolf. The difference in age was remedied by a vigorous effort of the imagination. Of course, operations of this nature made us pretty familiar with the topography of the old garret. There was, however, one quarter, fenced off by some barrels filled with pamphlets, where Polly strictly forbade us to go.

What was the result of such a prohibition, O reader? Can you imagine it to be any other than that that part of the garret became at once the only one that we really cared about investigating? How we hung about it, and considered it, and peeped over and around and between the barrels at a pile of pictures, that stood with their faces to the wall! What were those pictures, we wondered. When we asked Polly this, she drew on a mysterious face and said, "*Them* was things we mustn't ask about."

We talked it over among ourselves, and Tina assured us that she dreamed about it nights; but Polly had strictly forbidden us even to mention that corner of the garret to Miss Mehitable, or to ask her leave to look at it, alleging as a reason that "'twould bring on her hypos."

We didn't know what "hypos" were, but we supposed of course they must be something dreadful; but the very fearfulness of the consequences that might ensue from our getting behind those fatal barrels only made them still more attractive. Finally, one rainy Saturday afternoon, when we were tired of acting plays, and the rain pattered on the roof, and the wind howled and shook the casings, and there was a generally wild and disorganised state of affairs out of doors, a sympathetic spirit of insubordination appeared to awaken in Tina's bosom. "I declare, I am going inside of those barrels!" she said. "I don't care if Polly does scold us; I know I can bring her all round again fast enough. I can do about what I like with Polly. Now you boys just move this barrel a little bit, and I'll go in and see!"

Just at this moment there was one of those chance lulls in the storm that sometimes occur, and as Tina went in behind the barrels, and boldly turned the first picture, a ray of sunshine streamed through the dusky window and lit it up with a watery light.

Harry and Tina both gave an exclamation of astonishment.

"O Tina! it's the lady in the closet!"

The discovery seemed really to frighten the child. She retreated quickly to the outside of the barrels again, and stood with us, looking at the picture.

It was a pastel of a young girl in a plain, low-necked white dress, with a haughty, beautiful head, and jet-black curls flowing down her neck, and deep, melancholy black eyes, that seemed to fix themselves reproachfully on us.

"Oh, dear me, Harry, what shall we do?" said Tina. "How she looks at us! This certainly is the very same one that we saw in the old house."

"You ought not to have done it, Tina," said Harry, in a rather low and frightened voice; "but I'll go in and turn it back again."

Just at this moment we heard, what was still more appalling,—the footsteps of Polly on the garret stair.

"Well! now I should like to know if there's any mischief

you wouldn't be up to, Tina Percival," she said, coming forward, reproachfully. "When I give you the run of the whole garret, and wear my life out a pickin' up and puttin' up after you, I sh'd think you might let this 'ere corner alone!"

"Oh! but, Polly, you've no idea how I wanted to see it, and *do* pray tell me who it is, and how came it here? Is it anybody that's dead?" said Tiny, hanging upon Polly caressingly.

"Somebody that's dead to us, I'm afraid," said Polly, solemnly.

"Do tell us, Polly, *do!* who was she?"

"Well, child, you mustn't *never* tell nobody, nor let a word about it come out of your lips; but it's Parson Rossiter's daughter Emily, and where she's gone to, the Lord only knows. I took that 'ere pictur' down myself, and put it up here with Mr. Theodore's, so't Miss Mehitable needn't see 'em, 'cause they always give her the hypos."

"And don't anybody know where she is?" said Tina, "or if she's alive or dead?"

"Nobody," said Polly, shaking her head solemnly. "All I hope is, she may never come back here again. You see, children, what comes o' follerin' the natoral heart; it's deceitful above all things, and desperately wicked. She followed her natoral heart, and nobody knows where she's gone to."

Polly spoke with such sepulchral earnestness that, what with gloomy weather and the consciousness of having been accessory to an unlawful action, we all felt, to say the least, extremely sober.

"Do you think I have got such a heart as that?" said Tina, after a deep-drawn sigh.

"Sartain, you have," said the old woman. "We all on us has. Why, if the Lord should give any on us a sight o' our own heart just as it is, it would strike us down dead right on the spot."

"Mercy on us, Polly! I hope He won't, then," said Tina. "But, Polly," she added, getting her arms round her neck and playing with her gold beads, "*you* havn't got such a very bad heart now; I don't believe a word of it. I'm sure you are just as *good* as can be."

"Law, Miss Tina, you don't see into me," said Polly, who, after all, felt a sort of ameliorating gleam stealing over her. "You mustn't try to wheedle me into thinking better of myself than I be; that would just lead to carnal security."

"Well, Polly, don't tell Miss Mehitable, and I'll try and not get you into carnal security."

Polly went behind the barrels, gently wiped the dust from the picture, and turned the melancholy, beseeching face to the wall again; but we pondered and talked many days as to what it might be.

CHAPTER III.
How we kept thanksgiving at Oldtown.

On the whole, about this time in our life we were a reasonably happy set of children. The Thanksgiving festival of that year is particularly impressed on my mind as a white day.

Are there any of my readers who do not know what Thanksgiving-day is to a child? Then let them go back with me, and recall the image of it as we kept it in Oldtown.

People have often supposed, because the Puritans founded a society where there were no professed public amusements, that therefore there was no fun going on in the ancient land of Israel, and that there were no cakes and ale, because they were virtuous. They were never more mistaken in their lives. There was an abundance of sober, well-considered merriment; and the hinges of life were well oiled with that sort of secret humour which to this day gives the raciness to real Yankee wit. Besides this, we must remember that life itself is the greatest possible amusement to people who really believe they can do much with it,—who have that intense sense of what can be brought to pass by human effort, that was characteristic of the New England Colonies. To such it is not exactly proper to say that life is an amusement, but it certainly is an engrossing interest that takes the place of all amusements.

Looking over the world on a broad scale, do we not find that public entertainments have very generally been the sops thrown out by engrossing upper classes to keep lower classes from inquiring too particularly into their rights, and to make them satisfied with a stone, when it was not quite convenient to give them bread? Wherever there is a class that is to be made content to be plundered of its rights, there is an abundance of fiddling and dancing, and amusements, public and private, are in great requisition. It may also be set down, I think, as a general axiom, that people feel the need of amusements less and less, precisely in proportion as they have solid reasons for being happy.

Our good Puritan fathers intended to form a state of society of such equality of conditions, and to make the means of securing the goods of life so free to all, that everybody should find abundant employment for his faculties in a prosperous seeking of his fortunes. Hence, while they forbade theatres, operas, and dances, they made a state of unparalleled peace and prosperity, where one could go to sleep at all hours of day or night with the house-door wide open, without bolt or bar, yet without apprehension of any to molest or make afraid.

There were, however, some few national fêtes:—Election-day, when the Governor took his seat with pomp and rejoicing, and all the housewives outdid themselves in election-cake, and one or two training-days, when all the children were refreshed, and our military ardour quickened, by the roll of drums, and the flash of steel bayonets, and marchings and evolutions,—sometimes ending in that sublimest of military operations, a sham fight, in which nobody was killed. The Fourth of July took high rank, after the Declaration of Independence; but the king and high priest of all festivals, was the autumn Thanksgiving.

When the apples were all gathered, and the cider was all made, and the yellow pumpkins were rolled in from many a hill in billows of gold, and the corn was husked, and the labours of the season were done, and the warm, late days of Indian summer came in, dreamy, and calm, and still, with just frost enough to crisp the ground of a morning, but with warm trances of benignant, sunny hours at noon, there came over the community a sort of genial repose of spirit,—a sense of something accomplished, and of a new golden mark made in advance on the calendar of life,—and the deacon began to say to the minister, of a Sunday, "I suppose it's about time for the Thanksgiving proclamation."

Rural dressmakers about this time were extremely busy in making up festival garments, for everybody's new dress, if she was to have one at all, must appear on Thanksgiving-day.

Aunt Keziah, and Aunt Lois, and my mother, talked over their bonnets, and turned them round and round on their hands, and discoursed sagely of ribbons and linings, and of all the kindred bonnets that there were in the parish, and how they would probably appear after Thanksgiving. My grandmother, whose mind had long ceased to wander on such worldly vanities, was at this time officiously reminded by her daughters, that her bonnet wasn't respectable, or it was announced to her that she *must* have a new gown. Such were the distant horizon gleams of the Thanksgiving festival.

We also felt its approach in all departments of the household,—the conversation at this time beginning to turn on high and solemn culinary mysteries and receipts of wondrous power and virtue. New modes of elaborating squash pies and quince tarts were now ofttimes carefully discussed at the evening fireside by Aunt Lois and Aunt Keziah, and notes seriously compared with the experiences of certain other aunties of high repute in such matters. I noticed that on these occasions their voices often fell into mysterious whispers, and that receipts of especial power and sanctity were communicated in tones so low as entirely to escape the vulgar ear. I still remember the solemn shake of the head with which my Aunt Lois conveyed to Miss Mehitable Rossiter the critical properties of *mace*, in relation to its powers of producing in corn fritters a suggestive resemblance to oysters. As ours was an oyster-getting district, and as that charming bivalve was perfectly easy to come at, the interest of such an imitation can be accounted for only by the fondness of the human mind for works of art.

For as much as a week beforehand, "we children" were employed in chopping mince for pies to a most wearisome fineness, and in pounding cinnamon, allspice, and cloves in a great lignum-vitæ mortar; and the sound of this pounding and chopping re-echoed through all the rafters of the old house with a hearty and vigorous cheer, most refreshing to our spirits.

In those days there were none of the thousand ameliorations of the labours of housekeeping which have since arisen, —no ground and prepared spices and sweet herbs; everything came into our hands in the rough, and in bulk, and the reducing of it into a state for use was deemed one of the appropriate labours of childhood. Even the very salt that we used in cooking was rock-salt, which we were required to wash and dry and pound and sift, before it became fit for use.

At other times of the year we sometimes murmured at these labours, but those that were supposed to usher in the great Thanksgiving festival were always entered into with enthusiasm. There were signs of richness all around us,—stoning of raisins, cutting of citron, slicing of candied orange-peel. Yet all these were only dawnings and intimations of what was coming during the week of real preparation, after the Governor's proclamation had been read.

The glories of that proclamation! We knew beforehand the Sunday it was to be read, and walked to church with alacrity, filled with gorgeous and vague expectations.

The cheering anticipation sustained us through what seemed to us the long waste of the sermon and prayers; and when at last the auspicious moment approached,—when the last quaver of the last hymn had died out,—the whole house rippled with a general movement of complacency, and a satisfied smile of pleased expectation might be seen gleaming on the faces of all the young people, like a ray of sunshine through a garden of flowers.

Thanksgiving now was dawning! We children poked one another, and fairly giggled with unreproved delight as we listened to the crackle of the slowly unfolding document. That great sheet of paper impressed us as something supernatural, by reason of its mighty size, and by the broad seal of the State affixed thereto; and when the minister read therefrom, "By his Excellency, the Governor of the Commonwealth of Massachusetts, a Proclamation," our mirth was with difficulty repressed by admonitory glances from our sympathetic elders. Then, after a solemn enumeration of the benefits which the Commonwealth had that year received at the hands of Divine Providence, came at last the naming of the eventful day, and, at the end of all, the imposing heraldic words, "God save the Commonwealth of Massachusetts." And then, as the congregation broke up and dispersed, all went their several ways with schemes of mirth and feasting in their heads.

And now came on the week in earnest. In the very watches of the night preceding Monday morning, a preternatural stir below-stairs, and the thunder of the pounding-barrel, announced that the washing was to be got out of the way before daylight, so as to give "ample scope and room enough" for the more pleasing duties of the season.

The making of *pies* at this period assumed vast proportions that verged upon the sublime. Pies were made by forties and fifties and hundreds, and made of everything on the earth and under the earth.

The pie is an English institution, which, planted on American soil, forthwith ran rampant, and burst forth into an untold variety of genera and species. Not merely the old traditional mince pie, but a thousand strictly American seedlings from that main stock, evinced the power of American housewives to adapt old institutions to new uses. Pumpkin pies, cranberry pies, huckleberry pies, cherry pies, green-currant pies, peach, pear, and plum pies, custard pies, apple pies, Marlborough-pudding pies,—pies with top crusts, and pies without,—pies adorned with all sorts of fanciful flutings and architectural strips laid across and around, and otherwise varied, attested the boundless fertility of the feminine mind, when once let loose in a given direction.

Fancy the heat and vigour of the great pan-formation,

when Aunt Lois and Aunt Keziah, and my mother and
grandmother, all in ecstasies of creative inspiration, ran,
bustled, and hurried,—mixing, rolling, tasting, consulting,—
alternately setting us children to work when anything could
be made of us, and then chasing us all out of the kitchen
when our misinformed childhood ventured to take too many
liberties with sacred mysteries. Then out we would all fly
at the kitchen door, like sparks from a blacksmith's window.

On these occasions, as there was a great looseness in the
police department over us children, we usually found a ready
refuge at Miss Mehitable's with Tina, who, confident of the
strength of her position with Polly, invited us into the kitchen,
and with the air of a mistress led us around to view the proceedings there.

A genius for entertaining was one of Tina's principal
characteristics; and she did not fail to make free with raisins,
or citron, or whatever came to hand, in a spirit of hospitality
at which Polly seriously demurred. That worthy woman occasionally felt the inconvenience of the state of subjugation
to which the little elf had somehow or other reduced her, and
sometimes rattled her chains fiercely, scolding with a vigour
which rather alarmed us, but which Tina minded not a whit.
Confident of her own powers, she would, in the very midst of
her wrath, mimic her to her face with such irresistible drollery
as to cause the torrent of reproof to end in a dissonant laugh,
accompanied by a submissive cry for quarter.

"I declare, Tina Percival," she said to her one day,
"you're saucy enough to physic a horn-bug! I never did see
the beater of you! If Miss Mehitable don't keep you in
better order, I don't see what's to become of any of us!"

"Why, what did become of you before I came?" was the
undismayed reply. "You know, Polly, you and Aunty both
were just as lonesome as you could be till I came here, and

you never had such pleasant times in your life as you've had since I've been here. You're a couple of old beauties, both of you, and know just how to get along with me. But come, boys, let's take our raisins and go up in the garret and play 'Thanksgiving."

In the corner of the great kitchen, during all these days, the jolly old oven roared and crackled in great volcanic billows of flame, snapping and gurgling as if the old fellow entered with joyful sympathy into the frolic of the hour; and then, his great heart being once warmed up, he brooded over successive generations of pies and cakes, which went in raw and came out cooked, till butteries and dressers and shelves and pantries were literally crowded with a jostling abundance.

A great cold northern chamber, where the sun never shone, and where in winter the snow sifted in at the window-cracks, and ice and frost reigned with undisputed sway, was fitted up to be the storehouse of these surplus treasures. There, frozen solid, and thus well preserved in their icy fetters, they formed a great repository for all the winter months; and the pies baked at Thanksgiving often came out fresh and good with the violets of April.

During this eventful preparation week, all the female part of my grandmother's household, as I have before remarked, were at a height above any ordinary state of mind,—they moved about the house rapt in a species of prophetic frenzy. It seemed to be considered a necessary feature of such festivals that everybody should be in a hurry, and everything in the house should be turned bottom upwards with enthusiasm, —so at least we children understood it, and we certainly did our part to keep the ball rolling.

At this period the constitutional activity of Uncle Fliakim increased to a degree that might fairly be called preternatural. Thanksgiving time was the time for errands of mercy and beneficence through the country; and Uncle Fliakim's immortal old rubber horse and rattling waggon were on the full jump, in tours of investigation into everybody's affairs in the region around. On returning, he would fly through our kitchen like the wind, leaving open the doors, upsetting whatever came in his way,—now a pan of milk, and now a basin of mince,—talking rapidly, and forgetting only the point in every case that gave it significance, or enabled any one to put it to any sort of use. When Aunt Lois checked his benevolent effusions by putting the test questions of practical efficiency, Uncle Fliakim always remembered that he'd "forgotten to inquire about that," and skipping through the kitchen, and springing into his old waggon, would rattle off again on a full tilt to correct and amend his investigations.

Moreover, my grandmother's kitchen at this time began to be haunted by those occasional hangers-on and retainers, of uncertain fortunes, whom a full experience of her bountiful habits led to expect something at her hand at this time of the year. All the poor, loafing tribes, Indian and half-Indian, who at other times wandered selling baskets and other light wares, were sure to come back to Oldtown a little before Thanksgiving-time, and report themselves in my grandmother's kitchen.

The great hogshead of cider in the cellar, which my grandfather called the Indian Hogshead, was on tap at all hours of the day; and many a mugful did I draw and dispense to the tribes that basked in the sunshine at our door.

Aunt Lois never had a hearty conviction of the propriety of these arrangements; but my grandmother, who had a prodigious verbal memory, bore down upon her with such strings of quotations from the Old Testament that she was utterly routed.

4 *

"Now," says my Aunt Lois, "I s'pose we've got to have Betty Poganut and Sally Wonsamug, and old Obscue and his wife, and the whole tribe down, roosting around our doors, till we give 'em something. That's just mother's way; she always keeps a whole generation at her heels."

"How many times must I tell you, Lois, to read your Bible?" was my grandmother's rejoinder; and loud over the sound of pounding and chopping in the kitchen could be heard the voice of her quotations: "If there be among you a poor man in any of the gates of the land which the Lord thy God giveth thee, thou shalt not harden thy heart, nor shut thy hand, from thy poor brother. Thou shalt surely give him; and thy heart shall not be grieved when thou givest to him, because that for this thing the Lord thy God shall bless thee in all thy works; for the poor shall never cease from out of the land."

These words seemed to resound like a sort of heraldic proclamation to call around us all that softly shiftless class, who, for some reason or other, are never to be found with anything in hand at the moment that it is wanted.

"There, to be sure," said Aunt Lois, one day when our preparations were in full blast,—"there comes Sam Lawson down the hill, limpsy as ever; now he'll have his doleful story to tell, and mother'll give him one of the turkeys."

And so, of course, it fell out.

Sam came in with his usual air of plaintive assurance, and seated himself a contemplative spectator in the chimney-corner, regardless of the looks and signs of unwelcome on the part of Aunt Lois.

"Lordy massy, how prosperous everything does seem here!" he said, in musing tones, over his inevitable mug of cider; "so different from what 'tis t' our house. There's Hepsy, she's all in a stew, an' I've just been an' got her thirty-seven cents' wuth o' nutmegs, yet she says she's sure she don't see how she's to keep Thanksgiving, an' she's down on me about it, just as ef't was my fault. Ych see, last winter our old gobbler got froze. You know, Mis' Badger, that 'ere cold night we hed last winter. Wal, I was off with Jake Marshall that night; ye see, Jake, he hed to take old General Dearborn's corpse into Boston, to the family vault, and Jake, he kind o' hated to go alone; 'twas a drefful cold time, and he sees to me, 'Sam, you jes' go 'long with me;' so I was sort o' sorry for him, and I kind o' thought I'd go 'long. Wal, come 'long to Josh Bissel's tahvern, there at the Half-way House, you know, 'twas so swinging cold we stopped to take a little suthin' warmin', an' we sort o' sot an' sot over the fire, till, fust we knew, we kind o' got asleep; and when we woke up we found we'd left the old General hitched up t' th' post pretty much all night. Wal, didn't hurt him none, poor man; 'twas allers a favourite spot o' his'n. But, takin' one thing with another, I didn't get home till about noon next day, an', I tell you, Hepsy she was right down on me. She said the baby was sick, and there hadn't been no wood split, nor the barn fastened up, nor nothin'. Lordy massy, I didn't mean no harm; I thought there was wood enough, and I thought likely Hepsy'd get out an' fasten up the barn. But Hepsy, she was in one o' her contrary streaks, an' she wouldn't do a thing; an', when I went out to look, why, sure 'nuff, there was our old tom turkey froze as stiff as a stake,—his claws jist a stickin' right straight up like this." Here Sam struck an expressive attitude, and looked so much like a frozen turkey as to give a pathetic reality to the picture.

"Well now, Sam, why need you be off on things that's none of your business?" said my grandmother. "I've alked to you plainly about that a great many times, Sam," she continued, in tones of severe admonition. "Hepsy is a hard-working woman, but she can't be expected to see to everything, and you oughter 'ave been at home that night to fasten up your own barn and look after your own creeturs."

Sam took the rebuke all the more meekly as he perceived the stiff black legs of a turkey poking out from under my grandmother's apron while she was delivering it. To be exhorted and told of his shortcomings, and then furnished with a turkey at Thanksgiving, was a yearly part of his family programme. In time he departed, not only with the turkey, but with us boys in procession after him, bearing a mince and a pumpkin pie for Hepsy's children.

"Poor things!" my grandmother remarked; "they ought to have something good to eat Thanksgiving-day; 'taint their fault that they've got a shiftless father."

Sam, in his turn, moralised to us children, as we walked beside him: "A body'd think that Hepsy'd learn to trust in Providence," he said, "but she don't. She allers has a Thanksgiving-dinner pervided; but that 'ere woman ain't grateful for it, by no manner o' means. Now she'll be jest as cross as she can be, 'cause this 'ere ain't *our* turkey, and these 'ere ain't our pies. Folks doos lose so much, that hes sech dispositions."

A multitude of similar dispensations during the course of the week materially reduced the great pile of chickens and turkeys which black Cæsar's efforts in slaughtering, picking, and dressing kept daily supplied.

Besides these offerings to the poor, the handsomest turkey of the flock was sent, dressed in first-rate style, with Deacon Badger's dutiful compliments, to the minister; and we children, who were happy to accompany black Cæsar on this errand, generally received a seed-cake and a word of acknowledgment from the minister's lady.

Well, at last, when all the chopping and pounding and baking and brewing, preparatory to the festival, were gone through with, the eventful day dawned. All the tribes of the Badger family were to come back home to the old house, with all the relations of every degree, to eat the Thanksgiving-dinner. And it was understood that in the evening the minister and his lady would look in upon us, together with some of the select aristocracy of Oldtown.

Great as the preparations were for the dinner, everything was so contrived that not a soul in the house should be kept from the morning service of Thanksgiving in the church, and from listening to the Thanksgiving sermon, in which the minister was expected to express his views freely concerning the politics of the country, and the state of things in society generally, in a somewhat more secular vein of thought than was deemed exactly appropriate to the Lord's day. But it is to be confessed, that, when the good man got carried away by the enthusiasm of his subject to extend these exercises beyond a certain length, anxious glances, exchanged between good wives, sometimes indicated a weakness of the flesh, having a tender reference to the turkeys and chickens and chicken pies, which might possibly be overdoing in the ovens at home. But your old brick oven was a true Puritan institution, and backed up the devotional habits of good house-wives, by the capital care which he took of whatever was committed to his capacious bosom. A truly well-bred oven would have been ashamed of himself all his days, and blushed redder than his own fires, if a God-fearing house-matron away at the temple of the Lord, should come home and find her pie-crust either burned or underdone by his over or under zeal; so the old fellow generally managed to bring things out exactly right.

When sermons and prayers were all over, we children rushed home to see the great feast of the year spread.

What chitterings and chatterings there were all over the house, as all the aunties and uncles and cousins came pouring in, taking off their things, looking at one another's bonnets and dresses, and mingling their comments on the morning sermon with various opinions on the new millinery outfits, and with bits of home news, and kindly neighbourhood gossip.

Uncle Bill, whom the Cambridge College authorities released, as they did all the other youngsters of the land, for Thanksgiving-day, made a breezy stir among them all, especially with the young cousins of the feminine gender.

The best room on this occasion was thrown wide open, and its habitual coldness had been warmed by the burning down of a great stack of hickory logs, which had been heaped up unsparingly since morning. It takes some hours to get a room warm, where a family never sits, and which therefore has not in its walls one particle of the genial vitality which comes from the indwelling of human beings. But on Thanksgiving-day, at least, every year, this marvel was effected in our best room.

Although all servile labour and vain recreation on this day were by law forbidden, according to the terms of the proclamation, it was not held to be a violation of the precept, that all the nice old aunties should bring their knitting-work and sit gently trotting their needles around the fire; nor that Uncle Bill should start a full-fledged romp among the girls and children, while the dinner was being set on the long table in the neighbouring kitchen. Certain of the good elderly female relatives, of serious and discret demeanour, assisted at this operation.

But who shall do justice to the dinner, and describe the

turkey, and chickens, and chicken pies, with all that endless variety of vegetables which the American soil and climate have contributed to the table, and which, without regard to the French doctrine of courses, were all piled together in jovial abundance upon the smoking-board? There was much carving and laughing, and talking and eating, and all showed that cheerful ability to despatch the provisions which was the ruling spirit of the hour. After the meat came the plum-puddings, and then the endless array of pies, till human nature was actually bewildered and overpowered by the tempting variety; and even we children turned from the profusion offered to us, and wondered what was the matter that we could eat no more.

When all was over, my grandfather rose at the head of the table, and a fine venerable picture he made as he stood there, his silver hair flowing in curls down each side of his clear, calm face, while, in conformity to the old Puritan custom, he called their attention to a recital of the mercies of God in his dealings with their family.

It was a sort of family history, going over and touching upon the various events which had happened. He spoke of my father's death, and gave a tribute to his memory; and closed all with the application of a time-honoured text, expressing the hope that as years passed by we might "so number our days as to apply our hearts unto wisdom;" and then he gave out that psalm which in those days might be called the National Hymn of the Puritans:—

> "Let children hear the mighty deeds
> Which God performed of old,
> Which in our younger years we saw,
> And which our fathers told.
>
> "He bids us make His glories known,
> His works of power and grace;
> And we'll convey His wonders down
> Through every rising race.'

> "Our lips shall tell them to our sons,
>   And they again to theirs;
> That generations yet unborn
>   May teach them to their heirs.
>
> "Thus shall they learn in God alone
>   Their hope securely stands;
> That they may ne'er forget His works,
>   But practise His commands."

This we all united in singing to the venerable tune of St.
Martin's, an air which, the reader will perceive, by its multi-
plicity of quavers and inflections, gave the greatest possible
scope to the cracked and trembling voices of the ancients,
who united in it with even more zeal than the younger part
of the community.

Uncle Fliakim Sherril, furbished up in a new crisp black
suit, and with his spindle-shanks trimly incased in the
smoothest of black silk stockings, looking for all the world
just like an alert and spirited black cricket, outdid himself
on this occasion in singing *counter*, in that high weird voice
that he must have learned from the wintry winds that usually
piped around the corners of the old house. But any one who
looked at him, as he sat with his eyes closed, beating time
with head and hand, and, in short, with every limb of his
body, must have perceived the exquisite satisfaction which
he derived from this mode of expressing himself. I much
regret to be obliged to state that my graceless Uncle Bill,
taking advantage of the fact that the eyes of all his elders
were devotionally closed, stationing himself a little in the
rear of my Uncle Fliakim, performed an exact imitation of
his *counter*, with such a killing facility, that all the younger
part of the audience were nearly dead with suppressed
laughter. Aunt Lois, who never shut her eyes a moment on
any occasion, discerned this from a distant part of the room,
and in vain endeavoured to stop it by vigorously shaking
her head at the offender. She might as well have shaken it

at a bobolink tilting on a clover-top. In fact, Uncle Bill was Aunt Lois's weak point, and the corners of her own mouth were observed to twitch in such a suspicious manner that the whole moral force of her admonition was destroyed.

And now, the dinner being cleared away, we youngsters, already excited to a tumult of laughter, tumbled into the best room, under the supervision of Uncle Bill, to relieve ourselves with a game of "blind-man's-buff," while the elderly women washed up the dishes and got the house in order, and the men-folks went out to the barn to look at the cattle, and walked over the farm and talked of the crops.

In the evening the house was all open and lighted with the best of tallow candles, which Aunt Lois herself had made with especial care for this illumination. It was understood that we were to have a dance, and black Cæsar, full of turkey and pumpkin pie, and giggling in the very jollity of his heart, had that afternoon rosined his bow, and tuned his fiddle, and practised jigs and Virginia reels, in a way that made us children think him a perfect Orpheus.

As soon as the candles were lighted came in Miss Mehitable with her brother Jonathan, and Tina, like a gay little tassel, hanging on her withered arm.

Mr. Jonathan Rossiter was a tall, well-made man, with a cleart-cut, aquiline profile, and high round forehead, from which his powdered hair was brushed smoothly back, and hung down behind in a long cue. His eyes were of a piercing dark gray, with that peculiar expression of depth and intensity which marks a melancholy temperament. He had a large mouth, which he kept shut with an air of firmness that suggested something even hard and dictatorial in his nature. He was quick and alert in all his movements, and his eyes had a searching quickness of observation which seemed to lose nothing of what took place around him. There was an air of breeding and self-command about him; and in all his involuntary ways he bore the appearance of a man more interested to make up a judgment of others than concerned as to what their judgment might be about himself.

Miss Mehitable hung upon his arm with an evident admiration and pride, which showed that when he came he made summer at least for her.

After them soon arrived the minister and his lady,—she in a grand brocade satin dress, open in front to display a petticoat brocaded with silver flowers. With her well-formed hands shining out of a shimmer of costly lace, and her feet propped on high-heeled shoes, Lady Lothrop justified the prestige of good society which always hung about her. Her lord and master, in the spotless whiteness of his ruffles on wrist and bosom, and in the immaculate keeping and neatness of all his clerical black, and the perfect *pose* of his grand full-bottomed clerical wig, did honour to her conjugal cares. They moved through the room like a royal prince and princess, with an appropriate, gracious, well-considered word for each and every one. They even returned, with punctilious civility, the awe-struck obeisance of black Cæsar, who giggled over straightway with joy and exultation at the honour.

But conceive of my Aunt Lois's pride of heart, when, following in the train of these august persons, actually came Ellery Davenport, bringing upon his arm Miss Deborah Kittery. Here was a situation! Had the whole island of Great Britain waded across the Atlantic Ocean to call on Bunker Hill, the circumstance could scarcely have seemed to her more critical.

"Mercy on us!" she thought to herself, "all these Episcopalians coming! I do hope mother'll be careful; I hope she won't feel it necessary to give them a piece of her mind, as she's always doing."

Miss Deborah Kittery, however, knew her soundings, and was too genuine an Englishwoman not to know that "every man's house is his castle," and that one must respect one's neighbour's opinions on his own ground.

As to my grandmother, her broad and buxom heart on this evening was so full of motherliness that she could have patted the very King of England on the head if he had been there, and comforted his soul with the assurance that she supposed he meant well, though he didn't exactly know how to manage; so, although she had a full consciousness that Miss Deborah Kittery had turned all America over to un-covenanted mercies, she nevertheless shook her warmly by the hand, and told her she hoped she'd make herself at home. And I think she would have done exactly the same by the Pope of Rome himself, if that poor heathen sinner had presented himself on Thanksgiving-evening. So vast and billowy was the ocean of her loving-kindness, and so firmly were her feet planted on the rock of the Cambridge Platform, that on it she could stand breathing prayers for all Jews, Turks, Infidels, Tories, Episcopalians, and even Roman Catholics. The very man that burnt Mr. John Rogers might have had a mug of cider in the kitchen on this evening, with an exhortation to go and sin no more.

You may imagine the astounding wassail among the young people, when two such spirits as Ellery Davenport and my Uncle Bill were pushing each other on, in one house. My Uncle Bill related the story of "The Wry-mouth Family," with such twists and contortions and killing extremes of the ludicrous as perfectly overcame even the minister; and he was to be seen, at one period of the evening, with a face purple with laughter, and the tears actually rolling down over his well-formed cheeks, while some of the more excit-able young people almost fell in trances, and rolled on the floor in the extreme of their merriment. In fact, the assemblage was becoming so tumultuous, that the scrape of Cæsar's violin, and the forming of sets for a dance, seemed necessary to restore the peace.

Whenever or wherever it was that the idea of the sinfulness of dancing arose in New England, I know not; it is a certain fact that at Oldtown, at this time, the presence of the minister and his lady was held not to be in the slightest degree incompatible with this amusement. I appeal to many of my readers, if they or their parents could not recall a time in New England when in all the large towns dancing assemblies used to be statedly held, at which the minister and his lady, though never uniting in the dance, always gave an approving attendance, and where all the decorous, respectable old church members brought their children, and stayed to watch an amusement in which they no longer actively partook. No one looked on with a more placid and patronising smile than Dr. Lothrop and his lady, as one after another began joining the exercise, which, commencing first with the children and young people, crept gradually upwards among the elders.

Uncle Bill would insist on leading out Aunt Lois, and the bright colour rising to her thin cheeks brought back a fluttering image of what might have been beauty in some fresh early day. Ellery Davenport insisted upon leading - forth Miss Deborah Kittery, notwithstanding her oft-repeated refusals and earnest protestations to the contrary. As to Uncle Fliakim, he jumped and frisked and gyrated among the single sisters and maiden aunts, whirling them into the dance as if he had been the little black gentleman himself. With that true spirit of Christian charity which marked all his actions, he invariably chose out the homeliest and most neglected, and thus worthy Aunt Keziah, dear old soul, was for a time made quite prominent by his attentions.

Of course the dances in those days were of a strictly moral nature. The very thought of one of the round dances of modern times would have sent Lady Lothrop behind her big fan in helpless confusion, and exploded my grandmother like a full-charged arsenal of indignation. As it was, she stood, her broad, pleased face radiant with satisfaction, as the wave of joyousness crept up higher and higher round her, till the elders, who stood keeping time with their heads and feet, began to tell one another how they had danced with their sweethearts in good old days gone by, and the elder women began to blush and bridle, and boast of steps that they could take in their youth, till the music finally subdued them, and into the dance they went.

"Well, well!" quoth my grandmother; "they're all at it so hearty, I don't see why I shouldn't try it myself." And into the Virginia reel she went, amid screams of laughter from all the younger members of the company.

But I assure you my grandmother was not a woman to be laughed at; for whatever she once set on foot, she "put through" with a sturdy energy befitting a daughter of the Puritans.

"Why shouldn't I dance?" she said, when she arrived, red and resplendent, at the bottom of the set. "Didn't Mr. Despondency and Miss Muchafraid and Mr. Readytohalt all dance together in the Pilgrim's Progress?"—and the minister in his ample flowing wig, and my lady in her stiff brocade, gave to my grandmother a solemn twinkle of approbation.

As nine o'clock struck, the whole scene dissolved and melted; for what well-regulated village would think of carrying festivities beyond that hour?

And so ended our Thanksgiving at Oldtown.

CHAPTER IV.

The Raid on Oldtown, and Uncle Fliakim's Bravery.

THE next morning after Thanksgiving, life resumed its usual hard, laborious course, with a sharp and imperative re-action, such as ensues when a strong spring, which has been for some time held back, is suddenly let fly again.

Certainly Aunt Lois appeared to be astir fully an hour earlier than usual, and dispelled all our golden visions of chicken pies and dancings and merry-makings, by the flat, hard summons of every-day life. We had no time to become demoralised and softened.

Breakfast this next morning was half an hour in advance of the usual time, because Aunt Lois was under some vague impression of infinite disturbances in the house, owing to the latitude of the last two weeks, and of great furbishings and repairs to be done in the best room, before it could be again shut up and condemned to silence.

While we were eating our breakfast Sam Lawson came in, with an air of great trepidation.

"Lordy massy, Mis' Badger! what *do* you s'pose has happened?" he exclaimed, holding up his hands. "Wal! if I ever—no, I never did!"—and, before an explanation could be drawn out of him, in fluttered Uncle Fliakim, and began dancing an indignant rigadoon round the kitchen.

"Perfectly abominable! the selectmen ought to take it up!" he exclaimed,—"ought to make a state affair of it, and send to the Governor."

"Do, for mercy's sake, Fliakim, sit down, and tell us what the matter is," said my grandmother.

"I can't! I can't!! I cant!!! I've just got to hitch right up and go on after 'em; and mebbe I'll catch 'em before they get over the State line. I just wanted to borrow your breech-band, 'cause ours is broke. Where is it? Is it out in the barn, or where?"

By this time we had all risen from table, and stood looking at one another, while Uncle Fliakim had shot out of the back-door toward the barn. Of course our information must now be got out of Sam Lawson.

"Wal, you see, Deacon, who ever would ha' thought of it? They've took every child on 'em, every one!"

"Who's taken? what children?" said my grandmother. "Do pray begin at the right end of your story, and not come in here scaring a body to death."

"Wal, it's Aunt Nancy Prime's children. Last night the kidnappers come to her house an' took her an' every single one of the child'en, an' goin' to carry 'em off to York State for slaves. Jake Marshall, he was round to our house this mornin', an' told me 'bout it. Jake, he'd ben over to keep Thanksgivin', over t' Aunt Sally Proddy's; au' way over by the ten-mile tahvern he met the waggin, an' Aunt Nancy, she called out to him, an' he heerd one of the fellers swear at her. . The' was two fellers in the waggin, an' they was a drivin' like mad, an' I jest come runnin' down to Mr. Sheril's, 'cause I know his horse never gits out of a canter, an' 's pretty much used to bein' twitched up sudden. But, Lordy massy, s'posin' he could ketch up with 'em, what could he do? He couldn't much more 'n fly at 'em like an old hen; so I don't see what's to be done."

"Well," said my grandfather, rising up, "if that's the case, it's time we should all be on the move; and I'll go right over to Israel Scran's, and he and his two sons and I'll go over, and I guess there'll be enough of us to teach them reason. These kidnappers always make for the New York State line. Boys, you go out and tackle the old mare, and have our waggon round to the house; and, if Fliakim's waggon will hold together, the two will just carry the party."

"Lordy massy! I should like to go 'long too," said Sam Lawson. "I hain't got no special business to-day but what could be put off as well as not."

"You never do have," said Aunt Lois. "That's the trouble with you."

"Wal, I was a thinkin'," said Sam, "that Jake and me hes been over them roads so often, and we kind o' know all the ups an' downs an' cross-roads. Then we's pretty intimate with some o' them Injun fellers, an' ye git them sot out on a trail arter a body, they's like a huntin' dog."

"Well, father," said Aunt Lois, "I think it's quite likely that Sam may be right here. He certainly knows more about such things than any decent, industrious man ought to, and it's a pity you shouldn't put him to some use when you can."

"Jes' so!" said Sam. "Now, there's reason in that 'ere; an' I'll jes' go over to Israel's store with the Deacon. Yeh see ye can't take both the boys, 'cause one on 'em 'll have to stay and tend the store; but I tell you what 'tis, I ain't no bad of a hand a hittin' a lick at kidnappers. I could pound on 'em as willingly as ever I pounded a horseshoe; an' a woman's a woman, and childr'n's childr'n, ef they be black; that's jes' my 'pinion."

"Sam, you're a good fellow," said my grandmother, approvingly. "But come, go right along."

Here, now, was something to prevent the wave of yesterday's excitement from flatting down into entire insipidity.

Harry and I ran over instantly to tell Tina; and Tina with all her eloquence set it forth to Miss Mehitable and Polly, and we gave vent to our emotions by an immediate rush to the garret and a dramatic representation of the whole scene of the rescue, conducted with four or five of Tina's rag-dolls and a little old box waggon, with which we cantered and re-cantered across the garret floor in a way that would have been intolerable to a less patient and indulgent person than Miss Mehitable.

The fact is, however, that she shared in the universal excitement to such a degree, that she put on her bonnet immediately, and rushed over to the minister's to give vent to her feelings, while Polly, coming up garret, shouldered one of the guns lovingly, and declared she'd "like nothing better than to fire it off at one o' them fellers;" and then she told us how, in her young days, where she was brought up in Maine, the paintors (panthers) used to come round their log cabin at night, and howl and growl; and how they always had to keep the guns loaded; and how once her mother, during her father's absence, had treed a painter, and kept him up in his perch for hours by threatening him whenever he offered to come down, until her husband came home and shot him.

Pretty stanch, reliant blood, about those times, flowed in the bosoms of the women of New England, and Polly relieved the excitement of her mind this morning by relating to us story after story of the wild forest life of her early days.

While Polly was thus giving vent to her emotions at home, Miss Mehitable had produced a corresponding excitement in the minister's family. Ellery Davenport declared his prompt intention of going up and joining the pursuing party, as he was young and strong, with all his wits about him; and, with the prestige of rank in the late revolutionary war, such an accession to the party was of the greatest possible importance. As to Miss Deborah Kittery, she gave it as her opinion that such uprisings against law and order were just what was to be expected in a democracy. "The lower classes, my dear, you know, need to be kept down with a strong hand," she said, with an instructive nod of the head; "and I think we shall find that there's no security in the way things are going on now."

Miss Mehitable and the minister listened with grave amusement while the worthy lady thus delivered herself; and, as they did not reply, she had the comfort of feeling that she had given them something to think of.

All the village that day was in a ferment of expectation; for Aunt Nancy was a general favourite in all the families round, and was sent for in case of elections, or weddings, or other high merry-makings; so that meddling with her was in fact taking away part of the vested property of Oldtown. The loafers who tilted, with their heels uppermost, on the railings of the tavern veranda, talked stringently of State rights, and some were of opinion that President Washington ought to be apprised of the fact without loss of time. My grandmother went about house in a state of indignation all day, declaring it was a pretty state of things, to be sure, and that next they should know they should wake up some morning and find that Cæsar had been gobbled up in the night and run off with. But Harry and I calmed the fears which this seemed to excite in his breast, by a vivid description of the two guns over in Miss Mehitable's garret, and of the use that we should certainly make of them in case of an attack on Cæsar.

The chase, however, was conducted with such fire and ardour, that before moonrise on the same night the captives were brought back in triumph to Oldtown village, and lodged for safe-keeping in my grandmother's house, who spared nothing in their entertainment.

A happy man was Sam Lawson that evening, as he sat in the chimney-corner and sipped his mug of cider, and recounted his adventures.

"Lordy massy! well, 'twas providential we took Colonel

Davenport 'long with us, I tell you; he talked to them fellers
in a way that made 'em shake in their shoes. Why, Lordy
massy, when we fust came in sight on 'em, Mr. Sheril an' me,
we wus in the foremost waggin, an' we saw 'em before us just
as we got to the top of a long, windin' hill, an' I tell you if
they didn't whip up an' go lickity-split down that 'ere hill,—
I tell you, they rattled them child'en as ef they'd ben so many
punkins, an' I tell you one of 'em darned old young-uns flew
right over the side of the waggin, an' jest picked itself up as
lively as a cricket, an' never cried. We didn't stop to take it
up, but jes' kep' right along arter; an' Mr. Sheril, he hollers
out, 'Whoa! whoa! stop! stop thief!' as loud as he could
yell; but they jes' laughed at him; but Colonel Davenport,
he come ridin' by on horseback, like thunder, an' driv' right
by 'em, an' then turned round an' charged down on their
horses, so it driv' 'em right out the road, an' the waggin was
upsot, an' the fellers, they were pitched out, an' in a minute
Colonel Davenport had one on 'em by the collar an' his pistol
right out to the head o' t' other. 'Now,' ses he, 'if you stir
you're a dead man!'

"Wal, Mr. Sheril, he made arter the other one,—he always
means mighty well, Mr. Sheril does,—he gin a long jump, he
did, an' he lit right in the middle of a tuft of blackberry-
bushes, an' tore his breeches as ef the heavens an' 'arth was
agoin' asunder. Yeh see, they never'd a got 'em ef't hadn't
ben for Colonel Davenport. He kep' the other feller under
range of his pistol, an' told him he'd shoot him ef he stirred;
an' the feller, he was scart to death, an' he roared an' begged
for mercy in a way 'twould ha' done your heart good to
hear.

"Wal, wal! the upshot on't all was, when Israel Scran come
down with his boy (they was in the back waggin), they got
out the ropes an' tied 'em up snug, an' have ben a fetchin' on

'em along to jail, where, I guess, they'll have one spell o' considerin' their ways. But, Lordy massy, yeh never see such a sight as your uncle's breeches wus. Mis' Sheril, she says she never see the beater of him for allus goin' off in his best clothes, 'cause, you see, he heard the news early, an' he jes' whips on his Thanksgivin' clothes, an' went off in 'em just as he was. His intentions is allus so good. It's a pity, though, he don't take more time to consider. Now, I think folks ought to take things more moderate. Yeh see, these folks that hurries allus, they gits into scrapes, is just what I'm allus a tellin' Hepsy."

"Who were the fellows, do you know?" said my grandmother.

"Wal, one on 'em was one of them Hessians that come over in the war times,—he is a stupid crittur; but the other is Widdah Huldy Miller's son, down to Black Brook there."

"Do tell," said my grandmother, with the liveliest concern; "has Eph Miller come to that?"

"Yes, yes!" said Sam, "it's Eph, sure enough. He was exalted to heaven in p'int o' privilege, but he took to drink and onstiddy ways in the army, and now here he is in jail. I tell you, I tried to set it home to Eph, when I was a bringin' on him home in the waggin, but, Lordy massy, we don't none of us like to have our sins set in order afore us. There was David, now, he was crank as could be when he thought Nathan was a talkin' about other people's sins. Says David, 'The man that did that shall surely die;' but come to set it home, and say, 'Thou art the man,' David caved right in. 'Lordy massy, bless your soul and body, Nathan,' says he, 'I don't want to die.'"

It will be seen by these edifying moralisings how eminently scriptural was the course of Sam's mind. In fact, his turn

for long-winded, pious reflection was not the least among his
miscellaneous accomplishments.

As to my grandmother, she busied herself in comforting
the hearts of Aunt Nancy and the children with more than
they could eat of the relics of the Thanksgiving-feast, and
bidding them not to be down-hearted nor afeard of anything,
for the neighbours would all stand up for them, confirming
her words with well-known quotations from the Old Testament, to the effect that "the triumphing of the wicked is
short," and that "evil-doers shall soon be cut off from the
earth."

This incident gave Ellery Davenport a wide-spread popu-
larity in the circles of Oldtown.   My grandmother was predisposed to look on him with complacency as a grandson of
President Edwards, although he took, apparently, a freakish
delight in shocking the respectable prejudices, and disap-
pointing the reasonable expectations, of people in this regard,
by assuming in every conversation precisely the sentiments
that could have been least expected of him in view of such a
paternity.

In fact, Ellery Davenport was one of those talkers who
delight to maintain the contrary of every proposition started,
and who enjoy the bustle and confusion which they thus make
in every circle.

In good, earnest, intense New England, where every idea
was taken up and sifted with serious solemnity, and investi-
gated with a view to an immediate practical action upon it
as true or false, this glittering, fanciful system of fencing
which he kept up on all subjects, maintaining with equal
brilliancy and ingenuity this to-day and that to-morrow,
might possibly have drawn down upon a man a certain
horror, as a professed scoffer and a bitter enemy of all that
is good; but Ellery Davenport, with all his apparent care-

lessness, understood himself and the world he moved in perfectly. He never lost sight of the effect he was producing
on any mind, and had an intuitive judgment, in every situation, of exactly how far he might go without going too
far.

The position of such young men as Ellery Davenport, in
the theocratic state of society in New England at this time,
can be understood only by considering the theologic movements of their period.

The first colonists who founded Massachusetts were men
whose doctrine of a Christian Church in regard to the position of its children was essentially the same as that of the
Church of England. Thus we find in Dr. Cotton Mather this
statement :—

"They did all agree with their brethren in Plymouth in
this point: that the children of the faithful were church-
members with their parents; and that their baptism was a
seal of their being so; only, before their admission to fellow-
ship in any particular church, it was judged necessary that,
being free from scandal in life, they should be examined by
the elders of the church, upon whose approbation of their
fitness they should publicly and personally own the covenant,
and so be received unto the table of the Lord. And accordingly the eldest son of Mr. Higginson, being about fifteen
years of age, and laudably answering all the characters expected in a communicant, was then so received."

The colony under Governor Winthrop and Thomas Dudley
was, in fact, composed of men in all but political opinion
warmly attached to the Church of England; and they published, on their departure, a tract called "The Humble Re-
quest of His Majesty's Loyal Subjects, the Governor and
Company lately gone for New England, for the Obtaining of
their Prayers and the Removal of Suspicions and Miscon-

struction of their Intentions;" and in this address they called the Church of England their dear mother, acknowledging that such hope and part as they had attained in the common salvation they had sucked from her breasts; and entreating their many reverend fathers and brethren to recommend them unto the mercies of God, in their constant prayers, as a church now springing out of their own bowels. Originally, therefore, the first young people who grew up in New England were taught in their earliest childhood to regard themselves as already members of the Church, as under obligations to comport themselves accordingly, and at a very early age it was expected of them that they would come forward by their own act and confirm the action of their parents in their baptism, in a manner much the same in general effect as confirmation in England. The immediate result of this was much sympathy on the part of the children and young people with the religious views of their parents, and a sort of growing up into them from generation to generation. But, as the world is always tending to become unspiritual and mechanical in its views and sentiments, the defect of the species of religion thus engendered was a want of that vitality and warmth of emotion which attend the convert whose mind has come out of darkness into marvellous light,—who has passed through interior conflicts which have agitated his soul to the very depths. So there was always a party in New England who maintained that only those who could relate a change so marked as to be characterised as supernatural should hope that they were the true elect of God, or be received in churches and acknowledged as true Christians.

Many pages of Cotton Mather record the earnest attention which not only the ministers, but the governors and magistrates, of New England, in her early days, gave to the question, "What is the true position of the baptized children of the Church?" and Cotton Mather, who was warmly in favour of the Church of England platform in this respect, says: "It was the study of those prudent men who might be called our seers, that the children of the faithful should be kept, as far as may be', under a church watch, in expectation that they might be in a fairer way to receive the grace of God; so that the prosperous condition of religion in our churches might not be a matter of one age alone."

Old Cotton waxes warm in arguing this subject, as follows:—

"The Scriptures tell us that men's denying the children of the Church to have any part in the Lord hath a strong tendency in it to make them cease from fearing the Lord, and harden their hearts from His fear. But the awful obligations of covenant interest have a great tendency to soften the heart and break it, and draw it home to God. Hence, when the Lord would powerfully win men to obedience, He often begins with this: that He *is* their God. The way of the Anabaptists, to admit none unto membership and baptism but adult professors, is the straightest way. One would think it should be a way of great purity; but experience hath shown that it has been an inlet unto great corruption, and a troublesome, dangerous underminer of reformation."

And then old Cotton adds these words, certainly as explicit as even the modern Puseyite could desire:—

"If we do not keep in the way of a converting, grace-giving *covenant*, and keep persons *under those church dispensations wherein grace is given*, the Church will die of a lingering, though not a violent death. The Lord hath not set up churches, only that a few old Christians may keep one another warm while they live, and then carry away the Church into the cold grave with them when they die. No; but that they might with all care and with all the obligations and advantages to that care that may be, nurse up another generation of subjects to our Lord, that may stand up in His kingdom when they are gone."

It was for some time doubtful whether the New England Church would organise itself and seek its own perpetuation on the educational basis which has been the foundation of the majority of the Christian Church elsewhere; and the question was decided, as such society questions often are, by the vigour and power of one man. Jonathan Edwards, a man who united in himself the natures of both a poet and a metaphysician, all whose experiences and feelings were as much more intense than those of common men as Dante's or Milton's, fell into the error of making his own constitutional religious experience the measure and standard of all others, and revolutionising by it the institutions of the Pilgrim Fathers.

Regeneration, as he taught it in his "Treatise on the Affections," was the implantation by Divine Power, of a new spiritual sense in the soul, as diverse from all the other senses as seeing is from hearing, or tasting from smelling. No one that had not received this new, divine, supernatural sense, could properly belong to the Church of Christ, and all men, until they did receive it, were naturally and constitutionally enemies of God to such a degree, that, as he says in a sermon to that effect, "If they had God in their power, they would kill Him."

It was his power and his influence which succeeded in completely upsetting New England from the basis on which the Reformers and the Puritan Fathers had placed her, and casting out of the Church the children of the very saints and martyrs who had come to this country for no other reason than to found a Church.

It is remarkable that, in all the discussions of depravity

inherited from Adam, it never seemed to occur to any theologian that there might also be a counter-working of the great law of descent, by which the feelings and habits of thought wrought in the human mind by Jesus Christ might descend through generations of Christians, so that, in course of time, many might be born predisposed to good, rather than to evil. Cotton Mather fearlessly says, that "*The seed of the Church are born holy,*"—not, of course, meaning it in a strictly theological sense, but certainly indicating that, in his day, a mild and genial spirit of hope breathed over the cradle of infancy and childhood.

Those very persons whom President Edwards addresses in such merciless terms of denunciation in his sermons, telling them that it is a wonder the sun does not refuse to shine upon them,—that the earth daily groans to open under them,—and that the wind, and the sun, and the waters, are all weary of them, and longing to break forth and execute the wrath of God upon them,—were the children for uncounted generations back of fathers and mothers nursed in the bosom of the Church, trained in habits of daily prayer, brought up to patience, and self-sacrifice, and self-denial, as the very bread of their daily being, and lacking only this supernatural sixth sense, the want of which brought upon them a guilt so tremendous. The consequence was, that, immediately after the time of President Edwards, there grew up in the very bosom of the New England Church, a set of young people who were not merely indifferent to religion, but who hated it with the whole energy of their being.

Ellery Davenport's feeling toward the Church and religion, had all the bitterness of the disinherited son, who likes nothing better than to point out the faults in those favoured children who enjoy the privileges of which he is deprived.

All the consequences that good, motherly Cotton Mather had foreseen as likely to result from the proposed system of arranging the Church, were strikingly verified in his case. He had not been able entirely to rid himself of a belief in what he hated. The danger of all such violent recoils from the religion of one's childhood consists in this fact,—that the person is always secretly unsatisfied that he may not be opposing truth and virtue itself; he struggles confusedly with the faith of his mother, the prayers of his father, with whatever there may be holy and noble in the profession of that faith from which he has broken away; and few escape a very serious shock to conscience and their moral nature in doing it.

Ellery Davenport was at war with himself, at war with the traditions of his ancestry, and had the feeling that he was regarded in the Puritan community as an apostate; but he took a perverse pleasure in making his position good by a brilliancy of wit and grace of manner which few could resist; and, truth to say, his success, even with the more rigid, justified his self-confidence. As during these days there were very few young persons who made any profession of religion at all, the latitude of expression which he allowed himself on these subjects, was looked upon as a sort of spiritual sowing of wild oats. Heads would be gravely shaken over him. One and another would say, "Ah! that Edwards blood is smart; it runs pretty wild in youth, but the Lord's time may come by and by;" and I doubt not that my grandmother that very night, before she slept, wrestled with God in prayer for his soul with all the enthusiasm of a Monica for a St. Augustine.

Meantime, with that easy facility which enabled him to please everybody, he became, during the course of a somewhat extended visit which he made at the minister's, rather

a hero in Oldtown.   What Colonel Davenport said, and
what Colonel Davenport did, were spoken of from mouth to
mouth.   Even his wicked wit was repeated by the gravest
and most pious,—of course with some expressions of dis-
claimer, but, after all, with that genuine pleasure which a
Yankee never fails to feel in anything smartly and neatly hit
off in language.

He cultivated a great friendship with Miss Mehitable,—
talking with her of books and literature and foreign countries,
and advising her in regard to the education of Tina, with
great unction and gravity.   With that little princess there
was always a sort of half whimsical flirtation, as she de-
murely insisted on being treated by him as a woman, rather
than as a child,—a caprice which amused him greatly.

Miss Mehitable felt herself irresistibly drawn, in his society,
as almost everybody else was, to make a confidant of him.
He was so winning, so obliging, so gentle, and knew so well
just where and how to turn the conversation to avoid anything that he didn't like to hear, and to hear anything that
he did.   So gently did his fingers run over the gamut of
everybody's nature, that nobody dreamed of being played on.

Such men are not, of course, villains; but, if they ever
should happen to wish to become so, their nature gives them
every facility.

Before she knew what she was about, Miss Mehitable
found herself talking with Ellery Davenport on the strange,
mysterious sorrow which embittered her life, and she found a
most sympathetic and respectful listener.

Ellery Davenport was already versed in diplomatic life,
and had held for a year or two a situation of importance at
the court of France; was soon to return thither, and also to
be employed on diplomatic service in England.   Could he,
would he, find any traces of the lost one there?   On this

subject there were long, and, on the part of Miss Mehitable, agitating interviews, which much excited Miss Tina's curiosity.

CHAPTER V.

My Grandmother's Blue Book.

Reader, this is to be a serious chapter, and I advise all those people who want to go through the world without giving five minutes' consecutive thought to any subject to skip it. They will not find it entertaining, and it may perhaps lead them to think on puzzling subjects, even for so long a time as half an hour; and who knows what may happen to their brains, from so unusual an exercise?

My grandmother, as I have shown, was a character in her way, full of contradictions and inconsistencies, brave, generous, energetic, large-hearted, and impulsive. Theoretically she was an ardent disciple of the sharpest and severest Calvinism, and used to repeat Michael Wigglesworth's "Day of Doom" to us in the chimney-corner, of an evening, with a reverent acquiescence in all its hard sayings, while practically she was the most pitiful, easy-to-be-entreated old mortal on earth, and was ever falling a prey to any lazy vagabond who chose to make an appeal to her astounding charity. She could not refuse a beggar that asked in a piteous tone; she could not send a child to bed that wanted to sit up; she could not eat a meal in peace when there were hungry eyes watching her. She could not, in cool, deliberate moments, even inflict transient and necessary pain for the greater good of a child, and resolutely shut her eyes to the necessity of such infliction. But there lay at the bottom of all this apparent inconsistency a deep cause that made it consistent, and that cause was the theologic stratum on which her mind, and the mind of all New England, was embedded.

Never, in the most intensely religious ages of the world, did the insoluble problem of the WHENCE, the WHY, and the WHITHER of mankind receive such earnest attention. New England was founded by a colony who turned their backs on the civilisation of the Old World, on purpose that they might have nothing else to think of. Their object was to form a community that should think of nothing else.

Working on a hard soil, battling with a harsh, ungenial climate, everywhere being treated by Nature with the most rigorous severity, they asked no indulgence, they got none, and they gave none. They shut out from their religious worship every poetic drapery, every physical accessory that they feared would interfere with the abstract contemplation of hard, naked truth, and set themselves grimly and determinately to study the severest problems of the unknowable and the insoluble. Just as resolutely as they made their farms by blasting rocks and clearing land of ledges of stone, and founded thrifty cities and thriving money-getting communities in places which one would have thought might more properly have been left to the white bears, so resolutely they pursued their investigations amid the grim mysteries of human existence, determined to see and touch and handle everything for themselves, and to get at the absolute truth if absolute truth could be got at.

They never expected to find truth agreeable. Nothing in their experience of life had ever prepared them to think it would be so. Their investigations were made with the courage of the man who hopes little, but determines to know the worst of his affairs. They wanted no smoke of incense to blind them, and no soft opiates of pictures and music to lull them; for what they were after was *truth*, and not happiness, and they valued *duty* far higher than enjoyment.

The underlying foundation of life, therefore, in New Eng-

land, was one of profound, unutterable, and therefore un-
uttered, melancholy, which regarded human existence itself
as a ghastly risk, and, in the case of the vast majority of
human beings, an inconceivable misfortune.

My grandmother believed in statements which made the
fortunate number who escaped the great catastrophe of
mortal life as few and far between as the shivering, half-
drowned mariners, who crawl up on to the shores of some
desert island, when all else on board have perished. In this
view she regarded the birth of an infant with a suppressed
groan, and the death of one with almost satisfaction. That
more than half the human race die in infancy,—that infanti-
cide is the general custom in so many heathen lands,—was
to her a comforting consideration, for so many were held to
escape at once the awful ordeal, and to be gathered into the
numbers of the elect.

As I have said, she was a great reader. On the round
table that stood in her bedroom, next to the kitchen, there
was an ample supply of books. "Rollins' Ancient History,"
"Hume's History of England," and President Edwards' Sermons, were among these.

She was not one of those systematic, skilful housewives
who contrive with few steps and great method to do much
in little time; she took everything the hardest end first, and
attacked difficulties by sheer inconsiderate strength. For
example, instead of putting on the great family pot, filling it
with water, and afterwards putting therein the beef, pork,
and vegetables of our daily meal, she would load up the re-
ceptacle at the sink in the back room, and then, with strong
arm and cap-border erect, would fly across the kitchen with
it and swing it over the fire by main strength. Thus incon-
siderately she rushed at the daily battle of existence. But
there was one point of system in which she never failed.

There was every day a period, sacred and inviolable, which she gave to reading. The noon meal came exactly at twelve o'clock; and immediately after, when the plates and dishes were washed and wiped, and the kitchen reduced to order, my grandmother changed her gown, and retired to the sanctuary of her bedroom to read. In this way she accomplished an amount which a modern housekeeper, with four servants, would pronounce to be wholly incredible.

The books on her table came in time to be my reading as well as hers; for, as I have said, reading was with me a passion, a hunger, and I read all that came in my way.

Her favourite books had different-coloured covers, thriftily put on to preserve them from the wear of handling; and it was by these covers they were generally designated in the family. "Hume's History of England" was known as "The Brown Book;" "Rollins' History" was "The Green Book;" but there was one volume which she pondered oftener and with more intense earnestness than any other, which received the designation of "The Blue Book." This was a volume by the Rev. Dr. Bellamy of Connecticut, called "True Religion Delineated, and Distinguished from all Counterfeits." It was originally published by subscription, and sent out into New England with a letter of introduction and recommendation from the Rev. Jonathan Edwards, who earnestly set it forth as being a condensed summary, in popular language, of what it is vital and important for human beings to know for their spiritual progress. It was written in a strong, nervous, condensed, popular style, such as is fallen into by a practical man speaking to a practical people, by a man thoroughly in earnest to men as deeply in earnest, and lastly, by a man who believed without the shadow of a doubt, and without even the comprehension of the possibility of a doubt.

I cannot give a better idea of the unflinching manner in

which the deepest mysteries of religion were propounded to the common people than by giving a specimen of some of the headings of this book.

Page 248 considers, "Were we by the Fall brought into a state of being worse than not to be?"

The answer to this comprehensive question is sufficiently explicit:—

"Mankind were by their fall brought into a state of being worse than not to be. The damned in hell, no doubt, are in such a state, else their punishment would not be infinite, as justice requires it should be. But mankind, by the Fall, were brought into a state, *for substance*, as bad as that which the damned are in."

The next inquiry to this is, "How could God, consistent with His perfections, put us into a state of being worse than not to be? And how can we ever thank God for such a being?"

The answer to this, as it was read by thousands of reflecting minds like mine, certainly shows that these hardy and courageous investigators often raised spirits that they could not lay. As, for instance, this solution of the question, which never struck me as satisfactory:—

"Inasmuch as God did virtually give being to all mankind, when He blessed our first parents and said, 'Be fruitful and multiply;' and inasmuch as *being*, under the circumstances that man was *then* put in by God, was very desirable: we ought, therefore, to thank God for our being, considered in this light, and justify God for all the evil that has come upon us by apostacy."

On this subject the author goes on to moralise thus:—

"Mankind, by the Fall, were brought into a state of being infinitely worse than not to be; and were they but so far awake as to be sensible of it, they would, no doubt, all over the earth, murmur and blaspheme the God of Heaven. But what then? there would be no just ground for such conduct. We have no reason to think hard of God,—to blame him or esteem Him e'er the less. What He has done was fit and right. His conduct was beautiful, and He is worthy to be esteemed for it. For that constitution was holy, just, and good, as has been proved. And, therefore, a fallen world ought to ascribe to themselves all the evil, and to justify God and say, 'God gave us being under a constitution holy, just, and good, and it was a mercy. We should have accounted it a great mercy in case Adam had never fallen; but God is not to blame for this, nor, therefore, is He the less worthy of thanks.'"

After this comes another and quite practical inquiry, which is stated as follows:—

"But if mankind are thus by nature children of wrath, in a state of being worse than not to be, how can men have the heart to propagate their kind?"

The answer to this inquiry it is not necessary to give at length. I merely state it to show how unblinking was the gaze which men in those days fixed upon the problems of life.

The objector is still further represented as saying:—

"It cannot be thought a blessing to have children, if most of them are thought to be likely to perish."

The answer to this is as follows:—

"The most of Abraham's posterity for these three thousand years, no doubt, have been wicked and perished. And God knew beforehand how it would be, and yet He promised such a numerous posterity under the notion of a great blessing. For, considering children as to this life, they may be a great blessing and comfort to their parents; and we are certain that God will do them no wrong in the life to come. All men's murmuring thoughts about this matter arise from their not liking God's way of governing the world."

The speculative and metaphysical inquiries of this treatise are equally hardy and far reaching; for example:—

"Are all things right or wrong merely because God wills them so to be?"

To this inquiry the following answer is made:—

"If we should suppose, as some do, that there is nothing right or wrong antecedent to a consideration of the general good of the whole system of intelligent created beings, and that right and wrong result originally and entirely from the natural tendency of things to promote or hinder the general good of the whole, then these manifest absurdities would unavoidably follow: First, that the moral perfections of God entirely consist in, or result from, a disposition to love His creatures supremely, and seek their happiness as His only end. Just as if it became the Most High to make a god of His creatures, and Himself a servant. Secondly, That God loves virtue, and rewards it, merely because it tends to make His creatures happy; and hates vice, and punishes it, merely because it tends to make His creatures miserable. Just as if He had no regard to the rights of the Godhead."

I will quote but one more passage, as showing the hardy vigour of assertion on the darkest of subjects,—the origin of evil. The author says:—

"When God first designed the world, and laid out His scheme of government, it was easy for Him to have determined that neither angels nor men should ever sin, and that misery should never be heard of in all His dominions; for He could easily have prevented both sin and misery. Why did not He? Surely not for want of goodness in His nature, for that is infinite; not from anything like cruelty, for there is no such thing in Him; not for want of a suitable regard to the happiness of His creatures, for that He always has: but because in His infinite wisdom He did not think it best on the whole.

"But why was it not best? What could He have in view preferable to the happiness of His creatures? And, if their happiness was to Him above all things most dear, how could He bear the thoughts of their ever any of them being miserable?

"It is certain that He had in view something else merely than the happiness of His creatures. It was something of greater importance. But what was that thing that was of greater worth and importance, and to which He had the greatest regard, making all other things give way to this? What was His great end in creating and governing the world? Why, look what end He is at last likely to obtain, when the whole scheme is finished, and the Day of Judgment passed, and heaven and hell filled with all their proper inhabitants. What will be the final result? What will He get by all? Why, this: that He will exert and display every one of His perfections to the life, and so by all will exhibit a most perfect and exact image of Himself.

"Now it is evident that the fall of angels and of man, together with all those things which have and will come to pass in consequence thereof, from the beginning of the world to the Day of Judgment and throughout eternity, will serve to give a much more lively and perfect representation of God than could possibly have been given had there been no sin or misery."

This book also led the inquirer through all the mazes of mental philosophy, and discussed all the problems of mystical religion, such as—

"Can a man, merely from self-love, love God more than himself?"

"Is our impotency only moral?"

"What is the most fundamental difference between Arminians and Calvinists?"

"How the love to our neighbour, which is commanded by God, is a thing different from natural compassion, from natural affection, from party-spirited love, from any love whatever that arises merely from self-love, and from the love which enthusiasts and heretics have for one another."

I give these specimens, that the reader may reflect what kind of population there was likely to be where such were the daily studies of a plain country farmer's wife, and such the common topics discussed at every kitchen fireside.

My grandmother's blue book was published and recommended to the attention of New England, August, 4, 1750, just twenty-six years before the Declaration of Independence. How popular it was, and how widely read in New England, appears from the list of subscribers which stands at the end of the old copy which my grandmother actually used. Almost every good old Massachusetts or Connecticut family name is there represented. We have the Emersons, the Adams, the Brattles of Brattle Street, the Bromfields of Bromfield Street, the Brinsmades of Connecticut, the Butlers, the Campbells, the Chapmans, the Cottons, the Daggetts, the Hawleys, the Hookers, with many names more of families yet continuing to hold influence in New England. How they regarded this book may be inferred from the fact that some subscribed for six books, some for twelve, some for thirty-six, and some for fifty. Its extension was deemed an act of religious ministry, and there is not the slightest doubt that it was heedfully and earnestly read in every good family of New England; and its propositions were discussed everywhere and by everybody. This is one undoubted fact; the other is, that it was this generation who fought through the

Revolutionary war. They were a set of men and women brought up to *think*,—to think not merely on agreeable subjects, but to wrestle and tug at the very severest problems. Utter self-renunciation, a sort of grand contempt of personal happiness when weighed with things greater and more valuable, was the fundamental principle of life in those days. They who could calmly look in the face, and settle themselves down to, the idea of being resigned and thankful for an existence which was not so good as non-existence,—who were willing to be loyal subjects of a splendid and powerful government which was conducted on quite other issues than a regard for their own private happiness,—were possessed of a courage and a fortitude which no mere earthly mischance could shake. They who had faced eternal ruin with an unflinching gaze were not likely to shrink before the comparatively trivial losses and gains of any mere earthly conflict. Being accustomed to combats with the devil, it was rather a recreation to fight only British officers.

If any should ever be so curious as to read this old treatise, as well as most of the writings of Jonathan Edwards, they will perceive with singular plainness how inevitably monarchical and aristocratic institutions influence theology.

That "the king can do no wrong,"—that the subject owes everything to the king, and the king nothing to the subject,— that it is the king's first duty to take care of himself, and keep up state, splendour, majesty, and royalty; and that it is the people's duty to give themselves up, body and soul, without a murmuring thought, to keep up this state, splendour, and royalty,—was an idea for generations so wrought into the human mind, and transmitted by ordinary generation,—it so reflected itself in literature and poetry and art, and all the great customs of society,—that it was inevitable that systematic theology should be permeated by it.

The idea of God in which theologians delighted, and which the popular mind accepted, was not that of the Good Shepherd that giveth His life for the sheep,—of Him that made Himself of no reputation, and took unto Himself the form of a servant,—of Him who on His knees washed the feet of His disciples, and said that in the kingdom of heaven the greatest was he who served most humbly,—this aspect of a Divine Being had never yet been wrought into systematic theology; because, while the Bible comes from God, theology is the outgrowth of the human mind, and therefore must spring from the movement of society.

When the Puritans arrived at a perception of the political rights of men to each other in the state, and began to enunciate and act upon the doctrine that a king's right to reign was founded upon his power to promote the greatest happiness of his subjects; and when, in pursuance of this theory, they tried, condemned, and executed, a king who had been false to the people, they took a long step forward in human progress. Why did not immediate anarchy follow, as when the French took such a step in regard to their king? It was because the Puritans transferred to God all those rights and immunities, and that unquestioning homage, and worship, and loyalty which hitherto they had given to an earthly king.

The human mind cannot bear to relinquish more than a certain portion of its cherished past ideas in one century. Society falls into anarchy in too entire a change of base.

The Puritans had still a king. The French Revolutionists had nothing; therefore, the Puritan Revolution went on stronger and stronger. The French passed through anarchy back into despotism.

The doctrine of Divine sovereignty was the great rest to the human mind in those days, when the foundations of many generations were broken up. It is always painful to honest and loyal minds to break away from that which they have reverenced,—to put down that which they have respected. And the Puritans were by nature the most reverential, and most loyal portion of the community. Their passionate attachment to the doctrine of Divine sovereignty, at this period, was the pleading and yearning within them of a faculty robbed of its appropriate object, and longing for support and expression.

There is something most affecting in the submissive devotion of these old Puritans to their God. Nothing shows more completely the indestructible nature of the filial tie which binds man to God, of the filial yearning which throbs in the heart of a great child of so great a Father, than the manner in which these men loved and worshipped, and trusted God as the ALL LOVELY, even in the face of monstrous assertions of theology ascribing to him deeds which no father could imitate without being cast out of human society, and no governor without being handed down to all ages as a monster.

These theologies were not formed by the Puritans; they were their legacy from past monarchical and mediæval ages; and the principles of true Christian democracy upon which they founded their new state began, from the time of the American Revolution, to act upon them with a constantly ameliorating power; so that whosoever should read my grandmother's blue book now would be astonished to find how completely New England theology has changed its base.

The artist, in reproducing pictures of New England life during this period, is often obliged to hold his hand. He could not faithfully report the familiar conversations of the common people, because they often allude to and discuss the most awful and tremendous subjects. This, however, was the inevitable result of the honest, fearless manner in which the

New England ministry of this second era discussed the Divine administration. They argued for it with the common people in very much the tone, and with much the language in which they defended the Continental Congress and the ruling President; and every human being was addressed as a competent judge.

The result of such a mode of proceeding, in the long run, changed the theology of New England from what it was when Jonathan Edwards recommended my grandmother's blue book, into what it is at this present writing. But, during the process of this investigation, every child born in New England found himself beaten backwards and forwards, like a shuttlecock, between the battledoors of discussion. Our kitchen used to be shaken constantly by what my grandfather significantly called "the battle of the Infinites," especially when my Uncle Bill came home from Cambridge on his vacations, fully charged with syllogisms which he hurled like catapults back on the syllogisms which my grandmother had drawn from the armoury of her blue book.

My grandmother would say, for example: "Whatever sin is committed against an infinite being is an infinite evil. Every infinite evil deserves infinite punishment; therefore, every sin of man deserves an infinite punishment."

Then Uncle Bill, on the other side, would say: "No sin of a finite being can be infinite. Man is a finite being; therefore no sin of man can be infinite. No finite evil deserves infinite punishment. Man's sins are finite evils; therefore man's sins do not deserve infinite punishment." When the combatants had got thus far, they generally looked at each other in silence.

As a result, my grandmother being earnest and prayerful, and my uncle careless and worldly, the thing generally ended in her believing that he was wrong, though she could not

answer him; and in his believing that she, after all, might
be right, though he could answer her; for it is inevitable, in
every battle of opinion, that honest, sincere, moral earnestness has a certain advantage over mere intellectual cleverness.

It was inevitable that a people who had just carried
through a national revolution, and declared national independence on the principle that "governments owe their just
power to the consent of the governed," and who recognised
it as an axiom that the greatest good to the greatest number
was the object to be held in view in all just governments,
should very soon come into painful collision with forms of
theological statement, in regard to God's government, which
appeared to contravene all these principles, and which could
be supported only by referring to the old notion of the divine
right and prerogative of the King Eternal.

President Edwards had constructed a marvellous piece of
logic to show that, while true virtue in man consisted in
supreme devotion to the general good of all, true virtue in
God consisted in supreme regard for Himself. This "Treatise
on True Virtue" was one of the strongest attempts to back
up by reasoning the old monarchial and aristocratic ideas of
the supreme right of the king and upper classes. The whole
of it falls to dust before the one simple declaration of Jesus
Christ, that, in the eyes of heaven, one lost sheep is worth
more than all the ninety and nine that went not astray, and
before the parable in which the father runs, forgetful of
parental prerogative and dignity, to cast himself on the neck
of the far-off prodigal.

Theology being human, and a reflection of human infirmities, nothing is more common than for it to come up point-
blank in opposition to the simplest declarations of Christ.

I must beg my readers' pardon for all this, but it is a fact
that the true tragedy of New England life, its deep, un-

utterable pathos, its endurances and its sufferings, all depended upon, and were woven into, this constant wrestling of thought with infinite problems which could not be avoided, and which saddened the days of almost every one who grew up under it.

Was this entire freedom of thoughts and discussion a bad thing, then? Do we not see that strength of mind and strength of will, and the courage and fortitude and endurance which founded this great American Government, grew up out of characters formed thus to think, and struggle, and suffer? It seems to be the law of this present existence, that all the changes by which the world is made better are brought about by the struggle and suffering, and sometimes the utter shipwreck, of individual human beings.

In regard to our own family, the deepest tragedy in it, and the one which for a time brought the most suffering and sorrow on us all, cannot be explained, unless we take into consideration this peculiar state of society.

In the neighbouring town of Adams there lived one of the most remarkable clergymen that New England has ever produced. His career influenced the thinking of Massachusetts, both in regard to those who adopted his opinions, and in the violent reaction from those opinions which was the result of his extreme manner of pushing them.

Dr. Moses Sterne is a figure well remembered by me in my boyhood. Everybody knew him, and when he appeared in the pulpit everybody trembled before him. He moved among men, but seemed not of men. An austere, inflexible, grand indifference to all things earthly seemed to give him the prestige and awe of a supernatural being. His Calvinism was of so severe and ultra a type, and his statements were so little qualified, either by pity of human infirmity, or fear of human censure, or desire of human approbation, that he re-

minded one of some ancient prophet, freighted with a mission
of woe and wrath, which he must always speak, whether
people would hear, or whether they would forbear.

The revolutionary war had introduced into the country a
great deal of scepticism, of a type of which Paine's "Age of
Reason" was an exponent; and to meet this movement of the
human mind, the ministry of New England was not slow or
unskilful.

Dr. Sterne's mode of meeting this attitude of the popular
mind was by an unflinching, authoritative, vehement reitera-
tion of all the most unpopular and unpleasant points of Calvinism. Now as nature is, in many of her obvious aspects,
notoriously uncompromising, harsh, and severe, the Calvinist
who begins to talk to common-sense people has this advantage on his side,—that the things which ho represents the
Author of nature as doing, and being ready to do, are not
very different from what the common-sense man sees that
the Author of nature is already in the habit of doing.

The farmer who struggles with the hard soil, and with
drouth, and frost, and caterpillars, and fifty other insect
plagues,—who finds his most persistent and well-calculated
efforts constantly thwarted by laws whose workings he never
can fully anticipate, and which never manifest either care for
his good intentions, or sympathy for his losses, is very apt to
believe that the God who created nature may be a generally
benevolent, but a severe and unsympathetic Being, governing
the world for some great, unknown purpose of His own, of
which His private improvement and happiness may or may
not form a part.

Dr. Sterne, with characteristic independence and fearlessness, on his own simple authority, cut loose from and repu-
diated the whole traditional idea of the fall of Adam as having anything to do with the existence of human depravity;

and made up his own theory of the universe, and began preaching it to the farmers of North Adams. It was simply this: that the Divine Being is the efficient cause of all things, not only in matter, but in mind,—that every good and every evil volition of any being in the universe is immediately caused by Him, and tends equally well in its way to carry on His great designs. But, in order that this might not interfere with the doctrines of human responsibility, he taught that all was accomplished by omniscient skill and knowledge in such a way as not in the slightest degree to interfere with human free agency; so that the whole responsibility of every human being's actions must rest upon himself.

Thus was this system devised, like a skilful engine of torture, to produce all the mental anguish of the most perfect sense of helplessness with the most torturing sense of responsibility. Alternately he worked these two great levers with an almost supernatural power,—on one Sunday demonstrating with the most logical clearness, and by appeals to human consciousness, the perfect freedom of man; and, on the next, demonstrating with no less precision and logic the perfect power which an Omniscient Being possessed and exercised of controlling all His thoughts and volitions and actions.

Individually, Dr. Sterne, like many other teachers of severe, uncompromising theories, was an artless, simple-hearted, gentle-mannered man. He was a close student and wore two holes in the floor opposite his table in the spot where year after year his feet were placed in study. He refused to have the smallest thing to do with any temporal affair of this life. Like the other clergymen, he lived on a small salary, and the support of his family depended largely on the proceeds of a farm. But it is recorded of him, that once, when his whole summer's crop of hay was threatened

with the bursting of a thunder-shower, and, farm-hands
being short, he was importuned to lend a hand to save it, he
resolutely declined, saying, that if he once began to allow
himself to be called on in any emergency for temporal affairs,
he should become forgetful of his great mission.

The same inflexible, unbending perseverance he showed
in preaching, on the basis of his own terrible theory, the
most fearful doctrines of Calvinism. His sermons on Judas,
on Jeroboam, and on Pharaoh, were pieces of literature so
startling and astounding, that, even in those days of interrupted travel, when there were neither railroads nor good
roads of any kind, and almost none of our modern com-
municative system of magazines and newspapers, they were
heard of all over New England. So great was the revulsion
which his doctrines excited, that, when he exchanged with
his brother ministers, his appearance in the pulpit was the
signal for many of the most independent of the congregation
to get up and leave the meeting-house. But, as it was one
of his maxims that the minister who does not excite the
opposition of the natural heart fails to do his work, he regarded such demonstrations as evident signs of a faithful
ministry.

The science of Biblical criticism in his day was in its infancy; the Bible was mostly read by ministers, and proof-
texts quoted from it as if it had been a treatise written in the
English language by New-Englanders, and in which every
word must bear the exact sense of a metaphysical treatise.
And thus interpreting the whole wide labyrinth of poetry
and history, and Oriental allegory and hyperbole, by literal
rules. Dr. Sterne found no difficulty in making it clear to
those who heard him that there was no choice between believing his hard doctrines and giving up the Bible altogether.
And it shows the deep and rooted attachment which the

human heart has for that motherly book, that even in this dreadful dilemma the majority of his hearers did not revolt from the Bible.

As it was, in the town where he lived his preaching formed the strongest, most controlling of all forces. No human being could hear his sermons unmoved. He would not preach to an inattentive audience, and on one occasion, observing a large number of his congregation asleep, he abruptly descended from the pulpit and calmly walked off home, leaving the astonished congregation to their own reflections; nor would he resume public services until messages of contrition and assurances of better conduct had been sent him.

Dr. Sterne was in his position irresistible, simply because he cared nothing at all for the things which men ordinarily care for, and which therefore could be used as motives to restrain the declarations and actions of a clergyman. He cared nothing about worldly prosperity, so called; he was totally indifferent to money; he utterly despised fame and reputation; and therefore from none of these sources could he be in the slightest degree influenced. Such a man is generally the king of his neighbourhood,—the one whom all look up to, and all fear, and whose word in time becomes law.

Dr. Sterne never sought to put himself forward otherwise than by the steady preaching of his system to the farming population of Adams. And yet, so great was his influence and his fame, that in time it became customary for young theological students to come and settle themselves down there as his students. This was done at first without his desire, and contrary to his remonstrance.

"I can't engage to teach you," he said; but still, when scholars came and continued to come, he found himself, without seeking it, actually at the head of a school of theology.

Let justice be done to all; it is due to truth to state that the theological scholars of Dr. Sterne, wherever they went in the United States, were always marked men,—marked for an unflinching adherence to principle, and especially for a great power in supporting unpopular truths.

The Doctor himself lived to an extreme old age, always retaining and reiterating with unflinching constancy his opinions. He was the last of the New England ministers who retained the old clerical dress of the theocracy. Long after the cocked hat and small-clothes, silk stockings and shoe-buckles, had ceased to appear in modern life, his venerable figure, thus apparelled, walked the ways of modern men, seeming like one of the primitive Puritans risen from the dead.

He was the last, also, of the New England ministers that claimed for himself that peculiar position, as God's ambassador, which was such a reality in the minds of the whole early Puritan community. To extreme old age, his word was law in his parish, and he calmly and positively felt that it should be so. In time, his gray hairs, his fine, antique figure and quaint costume came to be regarded with the sort of appreciative veneration that every one gives to the monuments of the past. When he was near his ninetieth year, he was invited to New York to give the prestige of his venerable figure and presence to the religious anniversaries which then were in the flush of newly-organised enthusiasm, and which gladly laid hold of this striking accessory to the religious picturesque.

Dr. Sterne was invited and fêted in the most select halls of the upper circles of the Celestial City, and treated with attentions which would have been flattering had he not been too entirely simple-minded and careless of such matters even to perceive what they meant.

But at this same time the Abolitionists, who were regarded as most improper people to be recognised in the religious circles of good society, came to New York, resolving to have their anniversary also; and knowing that Dr. Sterne had always professed to be an antislavery man, they invited him to sit on the stage with them; and Dr. Sterne went. Shocking to relate, and dreadful to behold, this very cocked hat and these picturesque gray hairs, that they had brought to New York on purpose to ornament religious anniversaries, which were all agreed in excluding and ignoring the Abolitionists, had gone right over into the camp of the enemy! and he was so entirely ignorant and uninstructible on the subject, and came back among them, after having committed this abomination, with a face of such innocent and serene gravity, that nobody dared to say a word to him on the subject.

He was at this time the accepted guest in a family whose very religion consisted in a gracious carefulness and tenderness lest they should wake up the feelings of their Southern brethren on the delicate subject of slavery. But then Dr. Sterne was a man that it did no good to talk to, since it was well known that, wherever there was an unpopular truth to be defended, his cocked hat was sure to be in the front ranks.

Let us do one more justice to Dr. Sterne, and say that his utter inflexibility toward human infirmity and human feeling spared himself as little as it spared any other. In his early life he records, in a most affecting autobiography, the stroke which deprived him, within a very short space, of a beloved wife and two charming children. In the struggle of that hour, he says, with affecting simplicity, "I felt that I should die if I did not submit; and I did submit then, once for all." Thenceforward the beginning and middle and end of his whole preaching was *submission*,—utter, absolute, and uncon-ditional.

In extreme old age, trembling on the verge of the grave, and looking back over sixty years of intense labour, he said, "After all, it is quite possible that I may not be saved;" but he considered himself as but one drop in the ocean, and his personal salvation as of but secondary account. His devotion to the King Eternal had no reference to a matter so slight. In all this, if there is something terrible and painful, there is something also which is grand, and in which we can take pride, as the fruit of our human nature. Peace to his ashes! he has learned better things ere now.

If my readers would properly understand the real depth of sorrowful perplexity in which our friend Miss Mehitable Ros-siter was struggling, they must go back with us some years before, to the time when little Emily Rossiter was given up to the guardianship and entire control of her Aunt Farns-worth.

Zedekiah Farnsworth was one of those men who embody qualities which the world could not afford to be without, and which yet are far from being the most agreeable. Uncom-promising firmness, intense self-reliance, with great vigour in that part of the animal nature which fits man to resist and to subdue and to hold in subjection the forces of nature, were his prominent characteristics. His was a bold and granite formation,—most necessary for the stability of the earth, but without a flower.

His wife was a woman who had once been gay and beauti-ful, but who, coming under the dominion of a stronger nature, was perfectly magnetised by it, so as to assimilate and be-come a modified reproduction of the same traits. A calm, intense, severe conscientiousness, which judged alike herself

and others with unflinching severity, was her leading characteristic.

Let us now imagine a child inheriting from the mother a
sensitive, nervous organisation, and from the father a predis-
position to morbid action, with a mind as sensitive to external
influence as a daguerreotype-plate, brought suddenly from the
warmth of a too-indulgent household to the arctic regularity
and frozen stillness of the Farnsworth mansion. It will be
seen that the consequences must have been many conflicts,
and many struggles of nature with nature, and that a character
growing up thus must of course grow up into unnatural and
unhealthy development.

The problem of education is seriously complicated by the
peculiarities of womanhood. If we suppose two souls, exactly
alike, sent into bodies, the one of man, the other of woman,
that mere fact alone alters the whole mental and moral history
of the two.

In addition to all the other sources of peril which beset the
little Emily, she early developed a beauty so remarkable as
to draw upon her constant attention, and, as she grew older,
brought to her all the trials and the dangers which extraordinary beauty brings to woman. It was a part of her Aunt
Farnsworth's system to pretend to be ignorant of this great
fact, with a view, as she supposed, of checking any disposition
to pride or vanity which might naturally arise therefrom.
The consequence was that the child, hearing this agreeable
news from every one else who surrounded her, soon learned
the transparent nature of the hoax, and with it acquired a
certain doubt of her Aunt's sincerity.

Emily had a warm, social nature, and had always on hand
during her school-days a list of enthusiastic friends, whose
admiration of her supplied the light and warmth which were
entirely wanting from every other source.

Mrs. Farnsworth was not insensible to the charms of her niece. She was, in fact, quite proud of them, but was pursuing conscientiously the course in regard to them which she felt that duty required of her. She loved the child, too, devotedly, but her own nature had been so thoroughly frozen by maxims of self-restraint that this love seldom or never came into outward forms of expression.

It is sad to be compelled to trace the ill effects produced by the overaction and misapplication of the very noblest faculties of the human mind.

The Farnsworth family was one in which there was the fullest sympathy with the severest preaching of Dr. Sterne. As Emily grew older, it was exacted of her, as one of her Sabbath duties, to take notes of his discourses at church, which were afterwards to be read over on Sunday evening by her aunt and uncle, and preserved in an extract-book.

The effect of such kinds of religious teaching on most of the children and young people in the town of Adams was to make them consider religion, and everything connected with it, as the most disagreeable of all subjects, and to seek practically to have as little to do with it as possible; so that there was among the young people a great deal of youthful gaiety and of young enjoyment in life, notwithstanding the preaching from Sunday to Sunday of assertions enough to freeze every heart with fear. Many formed the habit of thinking of something else during the sermon-time, and many heard without really attaching any very definite meaning to what they heard.

The severest utterances, if constantly reiterated, lose their power, and come to be considered as nothing. But Emily Rossiter had been gifted with a mind of far more than ordinary vigour, and with even a Greek passion for ideas, and with capabilities for logical thought which rendered it impossible for her to listen to discourses so intellectual without taking in their drift and responding to their stimulus by a corresponding activity of intellectual action.

Dr. Sterne set the example of a perfectly bold and independent manner of differing from the popular theology of his day in certain important respects; and where he did differ, it was with a hardihood of self-assertion, and an utter disregard of popular opinion, and a perfect reliance on his own powers of discovering truth, which were very apt to magnetise these same qualities in other minds. People who thus set the example of free and independent thinking in one or two respects, and yet hope to constrain their disciples to think exactly as they do on all other subjects, generally reckon without their host; and there is no other region in Massachusetts where all sorts of hardy free-thinking are so rife at the present day, as in the region formerly controlled by Dr. Sterne.

Before Emily was fourteen years old she had passed through two or three of those seasons of convulsed and agonised feeling which are caused by the revolt of a strong sense of justice and humanity against teachings which seem to accuse the great Father of all of the most frightful cruelty and injustice. The teachings were backed up by literal quotations from the Bible, which in those days no common person possessed the means, or the habits of thought, for understanding, and thus were accepted by her at first as divine declarations.

When these agonised conflicts occurred, they were treated by her aunt and uncle only as active developments of the natural opposition of the human heart to God. Some such period of active contest with the divine nature was on record in the lives of some of the most eminent New England saints. President Edwards recorded the same; and therefore they looked upon them hopefully, just as the medical faculty of those same uninstructed times looked upon the writhings and agonies which their administration of poison produced in the human body.

The last and most fearful of these mental struggles came after the death of her favourite brother Theodore, who, being supposed to die in an unregenerate state, was forthwith judged and sentenced, and his final condition spoken of with a grim and solemn certainty by her aunt and uncle.

How far the preaching of Dr. Sterne did violence to the most cherished feelings of human nature on this subject, will appear by an extract from a sermon preached about this time.

The text was from Rev. xix. 3, "And again they said Alleluia.　And her smoke rose up for ever and ever."

The subject is thus announced:—

"The heavenly hosts will praise God for punishing the finally impenitent for ever."

In the *improvement* or practical application of this text, is the following passage:—

"Will the heavenly hosts praise God for all the displays of His vindictive justice in the punishment of the damned? then we may learn that there is an essential difference between saints and sinners.　Sinners often disbelieve and deny this distinction; and it is very difficult to make them see and believe it. . . . They sometimes freely say that they do not think that heaven is such a place as has been described; or that the inhabitants of it say, 'Amen, Alleluia,' while they see the smoke of the torments of the damned ascend up for ever and ever. They desire and hope to go to heaven, without ever being willing to speak such a language, or to express such feelings in the view of the damned.　And is not this saying that their hearts are essentially different from those who feel such a spirit, and are willing to adopt the language of heaven?

Good men do adopt the language of heaven before they arrive there. And all who are conscious that they cannot say 'Amen, Alleluia,' may know that they are yet sinners, and essentially different from saints, and altogether unprepared to go with them to heaven and join with them in praising God for the vindictive justice He displays in dooming all unholy creatures to a never-ending torment.

"2d, If any sinners desire to go to heaven, it is a clear evidence that they are ignorant of heaven and their own hearts.

"Though they should be admitted to heaven, their hearts would rise against God, and all the heavenly hosts who praise Him, for dooming the impenitent to regions of darkness and despair. Instead of saying 'Amen, Alleluia' they would be speechless, and inwardly curse God and die. If God would give them the best place in heaven, and offer them the whole universe to fall down and cordially join the heavenly host in praising Him for punishing any creature eternally, they would reject the offer. They would wish to exchange heaven for any other place.

"It would appear, from what has been said, that it is as easy for any to comply with the terms of salvation as it is to be in heaven and cordially unite with the heavenly hosts in their enjoyments and employments. Do some say that a love to a damning God is a term of salvation? But does not a sincere desire to be in heaven necessarily imply a desire to see and adore God in casting the wicked into hell? All the heavenly hosts see, admire, and praise God for doing this. Do some say that a willingness to be damned is a term of salvation? But is it any more difficult for any one to be cast off himself than to be willing to see others cast off for ever, though he has been nearly and tenderly connected with them?

The holy angels have been willing to see the apostate angels cast off forever; the spirits of just men have been willing to see those with whom they have been intimately connected cast off for ever; the eleven apostles have been willing to see Judas cast off forever, and no doubt but David has been willing to see Absalom, his darling son, cast off forever. The truth is, there is nothing which God requires men to do in this life, in order to go to heaven, that is harder to be done than to be willing to be in heaven. The difficulty lies not in *going*, but in *being*. Let heaven be properly described, and let natural men really understand wherein its enjoyments and employments consist, they would not be willing to comply with any terms in order to gain admission into it."

It was this sermon that finally broke those cords which years of pious descent had made so near and tender between the heart of Emily and her father's Bible.

No young person ever takes a deliberate and final leave of the faith of their fathers without a pang; and Emily suffered so much in the struggle, that her aunt became alarmed for her health. She was sent to Boston to spend a winter under the care of another sister of her mother's, who was simply a good-natured woman of the world, who was proud of her niece's beauty and talents, and resolved to make the most of them in a purely worldly way.

At this time she formed the acquaintance of a very interesting French family of high rank, who, for certain family reasons, were just then exiled to America. She became fascinated with their society, and plunged into the study of the French language and literature, with all the enthusiasm of a voyager who finds himself among enchanted islands. And French literature at this time, was full of the life of a new era,—the era which produced both the American and the French Revolution.

The writings of Voltaire were too cold and cynical for her enthusiastic nature; but Rousseau was to her like a sudden translation from the ice and snow of Massachusetts, to the tropical flowers of a February in Florida. In "La Nouvelle Héloïse," she found not merely a passionate love story, but the consideration, on the author's side, of just such problems as had been raised by her theological education.

When she returned from this visit, she was apparently quiet and at peace. Her peace was the peace of a river, which has found an underground passage, and therefore chafes and frets no more. Her philosophy was the philosophy of Émile, her faith the faith of the Savoyard vicar, and she imitated Dr. Sterne only in utter self-reliance and fearlessness of consequences in pursuit of what she believed true.

Had her aunt and uncle been able to read the French language, they would have found her note-book of sermons sometimes interspersed by quotations from her favourite author, which certainly were quite in point; as, for instance, at the foot of a severe sermon on the doctrine of reprobation, was written:—

"Quand cette dure et décourageante doctrine se déduit de l'Écriture elle-même, mon premier devoir n'est-il pas d'honorer Dieu? Quelque respect que je doive au texte sacré, j'en dois plus encore à son Auteur; et *j'aimerais mieux croire la Bible falsifiée ou inintelligible, que Dieu injuste ou malfaisant.* St. Paul ne veut pas que le vase dise au potier, Pourquoi m'as-tu fait ainsi? Cela est fort bien si le potier n'exige du vase que des services qu'il l'a mis en état de lui rendre; mais s'il s'en prenait au vase de n'être pas propre à un usage pour lequel il ne l'aurait pas fait, le vase aurait-il tort de lui dire, Pourquoi m'as-tu fait ainsi?" *

* "When this harsh, discouraging doctrine is deduced from the Scriptures themselves, is not my first duty to honour God? Whatever respect I

After a period of deceitful quiet and calm, in which Emily read, and wrote, and studied alone in her room, and moved about in her daily circle like one whose heart is afar off, she suddenly disappeared from them all. She left ostensibly to go on a visit to Boston to her aunt, and all that was ever heard from her after that, was a letter of final farewell to Miss Mehitable, in which she told her briefly, that, unable any longer to endure the life she had been leading, and to seem to believe what she could not believe, and being importuned to practise what she never intended to do, she had chosen her lot for herself, and requested her neither to seek her out nor inquire after her, as all such inquiries would be absolutely vain.

All that could be ascertained on the subject was, that about this time the Marquis de Conté and his lady were found to have sailed for France.

This was the sad story which Miss Mehitable poured into the sympathetic ear of Ellery Davenport.

CHAPTER VI.

We begin to be grown-up People.

We begin to be grown-up people. We cannot always remain in the pleasant valley of childhood. I myself, good reader, have dwelt on its scenes longer, because, looking back on it from the extreme end of life, it seems to my weary eyes so fresh and beautiful; the dew of the morning land lies on it,—that dew which no coming day will restore.

owe to the sacred text, I owe still more to its Author, *and I should prefer to believe the Bible falsified or unintelligible to believing God unjust or cruel.* St. Paul would not that the vase should say to the potter, Why hast thou made me thus? That is all very well if the potter exacts of the vase only such services as he has fitted it to render; but if he should require of it a usage for which he has not fitted it, would the vase be in the wrong for saying, Why hast thou made me thus?"

Our childhood, as the reader has seen, must be confessed to have been reasonably enjoyable. Its influences were all homely, innocent, and pure. There was no seductive vice, no open or covert immorality. Our worst form of roaring dissipation consisted in being too fond of huckleberry parties, or in the immoderate pursuit of chestnuts and walnuts. Even the vagrant associates of uncertain social standing who abounded in Oldtown were characterised by a kind of woodland innocence, and were not much more harmful than woodchucks and squirrels.

Sam Lawson, for instance, though he dearly loved lazy lounging, and was devoted to idle tramps, was yet a most edifying vagrant. A profane word was an abomination in his sight; his speculations on doctrines were all orthodox, and his expositions of Scripture as original and abundant as those of some of the dreamy old fathers. As a general thing he was a devout Sunday keeper and a pillar of the sanctuary, playing his bass-viol to the most mournful tunes with evident relish.

I remember being once left at home alone on Sunday, with an incipient sore-throat, when Sam volunteered himself as my nurse. In the course of the forenoon stillness, a wandering Indian came in, who, by the joint influence of a large mug of cider and the weariness of his tramp, fell into a heavy sleep on our kitchen floor, and somehow Sam was beguiled to amuse himself by tickling his nose with a broom-straw, and laughing, until the tears rolled down his cheeks, at the sleepy snorts and struggles and odd contortions of visage which were the results. Yet so tender was Sam's conscience, that he had frequent searchings of heart, afterward, on account of this profanation of sacred hours, and indulged in floods of long-winded penitence.

Though Sam abhorred all profanity, yet for seasons of

extreme provocation he was well provided with that gentler Yankee litany which affords to the irritated mind the comfort of swearing, without the commission of the sin. Under great pressure of provocation Sam Lawson freely said, "Darn it!" The word "darn," in fact, was to the conscientious New England mind a comfortable resting-place, a refreshment to the exacerbated spirit that shrunk from that too similar word with an *m* in it.

In my boyhood I sometimes pondered that other hard word, and vaguely decided to speak it, with that awful curiosity which gives to an unknown sin a hold upon the imagination. What would happen if I should say "damn?" I dwelt on that subject with a restless curiosity which my grandmother certainly would have told me was a temptation of the devil. The horrible desire so grew on me, that once, in the sanctity of my own private apartment, with all the doors shut and locked, I thought I would boldly try the experiment of saying "damn" out loud, and seeing what would happen. I did it, and looked up apprehensively to see if the walls were going to fall on me, but they didn't, and I covered up my head in the bedclothes and felt degraded. I had committed the sin, and got not even the excitement of a catastrophe. The Lord apparently did not think me worth His notice.

In regard to the awful questions of my grandmother's blue book, our triad grew up with varying influences. Harry, as I have said, was one of those quiet human beings, of great force in native individuality, who silently draw from all scenes and things just those elements which their own being craves, and resolutely and calmly think their own thoughts, and live their own life, amid the most discordant influences; just as the fluid, sparkling waters of a mountain brook dart this way and that amid stones and rubbish, and hum to themselves their own quiet, hidden tune.

A saintly woman, whose heart was burning itself away in the torturing fires of a slow martyrdom, had been for the first ten years of his life his only companion and teacher, and, dying, had sealed him with a seal given from a visibly opened heaven; and thenceforward no theologies, and no human authority, had the power and weight with him that had the remembrance of those dying eyes, and the sanctity of those last counsels.

By native descent Harry was a gentleman of the peculiarly English stock. He had the shy reserve, the silent, self-respecting pride and delicacy, which led him to keep his own soul as a castle, and that interested, because it left a sense of something veiled and unexpressed.

We were now eighteen years old, and yet, during all these years that he had lived side by side with me in closest intimacy, he had never spoken to me freely and frankly of that which I afterwards learned was always the intensest and bitterest mortification of his life, namely, his father's desertion of his mother and himself. Once only do I remember ever to have seen him carried away by anger, and that was when a coarse and cruel bully among the school-boys applied to him a name which reflected on his mother's honour. The anger of such quiet people is often a perfect convulsion, and it was so in this case. He seemed to blaze with it,—to flame up and redden with a delirious passion, and he knocked down and stamped upon the boy with a blind fury which it was really frightful to see, and which was in singular contrast with his usual unprovokable good-humour.

Ellery Davenport had made good his promise of looking for the pocket-book which Harry's father had left in his country-seat, and the marriage certificate of his mother had been found in it, and carefully lodged in the hands of Lady Lothrop; but nothing had been said to us children about it; it was merely held quietly, as a document that might be of use in time in bringing some property to the children. And even at the time of this fight with the school-boy, Harry said so little afterward, that the real depth of his feeling on this subject was not suspected.

I have reason to believe, also, that Ellery Davenport did succeed in making the father of Harry and Tina aware of the existence of two such promising children, and of the respectability of the families into which they had been adopted. Captain Percival, now Sir Harry Percival, had married again in England, so Ellery Davenport had informed Miss Mehitable in a letter, and had a son by this marriage, and so had no desire to bring to view his former connexion. It was understood, I believe, that a sum of money was to be transmitted yearly to the hands of the guardians of the children, for their benefit, and that they were to be left undisturbed in the possession of those who had adopted them.

Miss Mehitable had suffered so extremely herself by the conflict of her own earnest, melancholy nature with the theologic ideas of her time, that she shrunk with dread from imposing them on the gay and joyous little being whose education she had undertaken. Yet she was impressed by that awful sense of responsibility which is one of the most imperative characteristics of the New England mind; and she applied to her brother earnestly to know what she should teach Tina, with regard to her own spiritual position. The reply of her brother was characteristic, and we shall give it here:—

"MY DEAR SISTER,—I am a Puritan,—the son, the grandson, the great-grandson of Puritans,—and I say to you, Plant the footsteps of your child on the ground of the old Cambridge Platform, and teach her as Winthrop and Dudley and the Mathers taught their children,—that she 'is already a member in the Church of Christ,—that she is in covenant with God, and hath the seal thereof upon her, to wit, baptism; and so, if not regenerate, is yet in a more hopeful way of attaining regeneration and all spiritual blessings, both of the covenant and seal.'* By teaching the child this, you will place her mind in natural and healthful relations with God and religion. She will feel in her Father's house, and under her Father's care, and the long and weary years of a sense of disinheritance with which you struggled will be spared to her.

"I hold Jonathan Edwards to have been the greatest man, since St. Augustine, that Christianity has turned out. But when a great man, instead of making himself a great ladder for feeble folks to climb on, strikes away the ladder, and bids them come to where he stands at a step, his greatness and his goodness both may prove unfortunate for those who come after him. I go for the good old Puritan platform.—Your affectionate brother,   JONATHAN ROSSITER."

The consequence of all this was, that Tina adopted, in her glad and joyous nature, the simple, helpful faith of her brother,—the faith in an ever good, ever present, ever kind Father, whose child she was, and in whose household she had grown up. She had a most unbounded faith in prayer, and in the indulgence and tenderness of the Heavenly Power. All things to her eyes were seen through the halo of a cheerful, sanguine, confiding nature. Life had for her no cloud, or darkness, or mystery.

As to myself, I had been taught in the contrary doctrines,

* Cambridge Platform. Mather's "Magnalia," p. 227, Art. 7.

—that I was a disinherited child of wrath. It is true that this doctrine was contradicted by the whole influence of the minister, who, as I have said before, belonged to the Arminian wing of the Church, and bore very mildly on all these great topics. My grandmother sometimes endeavoured to stir him up to more decisive orthodoxy,, and especially to a more vigorous presentation of the doctrine of native human depravity. I remember once, in her zeal, her quoting to him as a proof-text the quatrain of Dr. Watts:—

> "Conceived in sin, oh woeful state!
> Before we draw our breath;
> The first young pulse begins to beat
> Iniquity and death."

"'That, madam," said Dr. Lothrop, who never forgot to be the grand gentleman under any circumstances,—"that, madam, is not the New Testament, but Dr. Isaac Watts, allow me to remind you."

"Well," said my grandmother, "Dr. Watts got it from the Bible."

"Yes, madam, a *very long way* from the Bible, allow me to say."

And yet, after all, though I did not like my grandmother's Calvinistic doctrines, I must confess that she, and all such as thought like her, always impressed me as being more earnestly religious than those that held the milder and more moderate doctrines.

Once in a while old Dr. Sterne would preach in our neighbourhood, and I used to go to hear him. Everybody went to hear him. A sermon on reprobation from Dr. Sterne would stir up a whole community in those days, just as a presidential election stirs one up now. And I remember that he used to impress me as being more like a messenger from the other world than any other minister. Dr. Lothrop's sermons, by his side, were like Pope's Pastorals beside the Tragedies of Æschylus. Dr. Lothrop's discourses were smooth, they were sensible, they were well worded, and everybody went to sleep under them; but Dr. Sterne shook and swayed his audience like a field of grain under a high wind. There was no possibility of not listening to him, or of hearing him with indifference, for he dealt in assertions that would have made the very dead turn in their graves. One of his sermons was talked of for months afterward, with a sort of suppressed breath of supernatural awe, such as men would use in discussing the reappearance of a soul from the other world.

But meanwhile I believed neither my grandmother, nor Dr. Sterne, nor the minister. The eternal questions seethed and boiled and burned in my mind without answer. It was not my own personal destiny that lay with weight on my mind; it was the incessant, restless desire to know the real truth from some unanswerable authority. I longed for a visible, tangible communion with God; I longed to see the eternal beauty, to hear a friendly voice from the eternal silence. Among all the differences with regard to doctrinal opinion, I could see clearly that there were two classes of people in the world,—those who had found God, and felt Him as a living power upon their spirits, and those who had not; and that unknown experience was what I sought.

Such, then, were we three children when Harry and I were in our nineteenth year, and Tina in her fifteenth. And just at this moment there was among the high consulting powers that regulated our destiny a movement as to what further was to be done with the two that had hitherto grown up together.

Now, if the reader has attentively read ancient and modern history, he will observe that there is a class of women to be found in this lower world, who, wherever they are, are sure to be in some way the first and last cause of everything that is going on. Everybody knows, for instance, that Helen was the great instigator of the Trojan war, and if it had not been for her we should have had no Homer. In France, Madame Récamier was, for the time being, reason enough for almost anything that any man in France did; and yet one cannot find out that Madame Récamier had any uncommon genius of her own, except the sovereign one of charming every human being that came in her way, so that all became her humble and subservient subjects. The instance is a marked one, because it operated in a wide sphere, on very celebrated men, in an interesting historic period. But it individualises a kind of faculty which, generally speaking, is peculiar to women, though it is in some instances exercised by men,—a faculty of charming and controlling every person with whom one has to do.

Tina was now verging toward maturity; she was in just that delicious period in which the girl has all the privileges and graces of childhood, its freedom of movement and action, brightened with a sort of mysterious aurora by the coming dawn of womanhood; and everything indicated that she was one of this powerful class of womankind. Can one analyse the charm which such women possess? I have a theory that, in all cases, there is a certain amount of genius with it,— genius which does not declare itself in literature, but in social life, and which devotes itself to pleasing, as other artists devote themselves to painting or to poetry.

Tina had no inconsiderable share of self-will; she was very pronounced in her tastes, and fond of her own way; but she had received from nature this passion for entertaining, and been endowed with varied talents in this line which made her always, from early childhood, the coveted and desired

person in every circle. Not a visage in Oldtown was so set
in grimmest of care that it did not relax its lines when it saw
Tina coming down the street; for Tina could mimic and sing
and dance, and fling back joke for joke in a perfect meteoric
shower. So long as she entertained, she was perfectly indifferent who the party was. She would display her accomplishments to a set of strolling Indians, or for Sam Lawson and
Jake Marshall, as readily as for anyone else. She would run
up and catch the minister by the elbow as he solemnly and
decorously moved down street, and his face always broke
into a laugh at the sight of her.

The minister's lady, and Aunt Lois, and Miss Deborah
Kittery, while they used to mourn in secret places over her
want of decorum in thus displaying her talents before the
lower classes, would afterward laugh till the tears rolled
down their cheeks and their ancient whalebone stays creaked,
when she would do the same thing over in a select circle for
them.

We have seen how completely she had conquered Polly,
and what difficulty Miss Mehitable found in applying the
precepts of Mrs. Chapone and Miss Hannah More to her case.
The pattern young lady of the period, in the eyes of all respectable females, was expressed by Lucilla Stanley, in
"Cœlebs in Search of a Wife." But when Miss Mehitable,
after delighting herself with the Johnsonian balance of the
rhythmical sentences which described this paragon as "not
so much perfectly beautiful as perfectly elegant,"—this model
of consistency, who always blushed at the right moment,
spoke at the right moment, and stopped at the right moment,
and was, in short, a woman made to order, precisely to suit
a bachelor who had traversed the whole earth, "not expecting perfection, but looking for consistency,"—she was perfectly dismayed at contemplating her scholar. She felt the

power by which Tina continually charmed and beguiled her, and the empire which she exercised over her; and, with wonderful good sense, she formally laid down the weapons of authority when she found she had no heart to use them.

"My child," she said to Tina one day, when that young lady was about eleven years of age, "you are a great deal stronger than I. I am weak because I love you, and because I have been broken by sorrow, and because, being a poor old woman, I don't trust myself. And you are young and strong and fearless; but remember, dear, the life you have to live is yours and not mine. I have not the heart to force you to take my way instead of your own, but I shall warn you that it will be better you should do so, and then leave you free. If you don't take my way, I shall do the very best for you that I can in your way, and you must take the responsibility in the end."

This was the only kind of system which Miss Mehitable was capable of carrying out. She was wise, shrewd, and loving, and she gradually controlled her little charge more and more by simple influence, but she had to meet in her education the opposition force of that universal petting and spoiling which everybody in society gives to an entertaining child.

Life is such a monotonous, dull affair, that anybody that has the gift of making it pass off gaily is in great demand. Tina was sent for to the parsonage, and the minister took her on his knee and encouraged her to chatter all sorts of egregious nonsense to him. And Miss Deborah Kittery insisted on having her sent for to visit them in Boston, and old Madam Kittery overwhelmed her with indulgence and caresses. Now Tina loved praises and caresses; incense was the very breath of her nostrils; and she enjoyed being fêted and petted as much as a cat enjoys being stroked.

It will not be surprising to one who considers the career of this kind of girl to hear that she was not much of a student. What she learned was by impulses and fits and starts, and all of it immediately used for some specific purpose of entertainment, so that among simple people she had the reputation of being a prodigy of information, on a very small capital of actual knowledge. Miss Mehitable sighed after thorough knowledge and discipline of mind for her charge, but she invariably found all Tina's teachers becoming accomplices in her superficial practices by praising and caressing her when she had been least faithful, always apologising for her deficiencies, and speaking in the most flattering terms of her talents. During the last year the schoolmaster had been observed always to walk home with her and bring her books, with a humble, trembling subserviency and prostrate humility which she rewarded with great apparent contempt; and finally she announced to Miss Mehitable that she didn't intend to go to school any more, because the master acted so silly.

Now Miss Mehitable, during all her experience of life, had always associated with the men of her acquaintance without ever being reminded in any particular manner of the difference of sex, and it was a subject which, therefore, was about the last to enter into her calculations with regard to her little charge. So she said, "My dear, you shouldn't speak in that way about your teacher; he knows a great deal more than you do."

"He may know more than I do about arithmetic, but he does not know how to behave. What right has he to put his old hand under my chin? and I won't have him putting his arm round me when he sets my copies! and I told him to-day he shouldn't carry my books home any more,—so there!"

Miss Mehitable was struck dumb. She went that afternoon and visited the minister's lady.

"Depend upon it, my dear," said Lady Lothrop, "it's time to try a course of home-reading."

A bright idea now struck Miss Mehitable. Her cousin, Mr. Mordecai Rossiter, had recently been appointed a colleague with the venerable Dr. Lothrop. He was a young man, finely read, and of great solidity and piety, and Miss Mehitable resolved to invite him to take up his abode with them for the purpose of assisting her educational efforts. Mr. Mordecai Rossiter accordingly took up his abode in the family, used to conduct family-worship, and was expected now and then to drop words of good advice and wholesome counsel to form the mind of Miss Tina. A daily hour was appointed, when he was to superintend her progress in arithmetic.

Mr. Mordecai Rossiter was one of the most simple-minded, honest, sincere human beings that ever wore a black coat. He accepted his charge in sacred simplicity, and took a prayerful view of his young catechumen, whom he was in hopes to make realise, by degrees, the native depravity of her own heart, and to lead through a gradual process to the best of all results.

Miss Tina also took a view of her instructor, and without any evil intentions, simply following her strongest instinct, which was to entertain and please, she very soon made herself an exceedingly delightful pupil. Since religion was evidently the engrossing subject in his mind, Tina also turned her attention to it, and instructed and edified him with flights of devout eloquence which were to him perfectly astonishing. Tina would discourse on the goodness of God, and ornament her remarks with so many flowers, and stars, and poetical fireworks, and be so rapt and carried away with her

subject, that he would sit and listen to her as if she was
an inspired being, and wholly forget the analysis which he
meant to propose to her, as to whether her emotions of love
to God proceeded from self-love, or from disinterested benevolence.

As I have said, Tina had a genius for poetry, and had
employed the dull hours which children of her age usually
spend in church, in reading the psalm-book and committing
to memory all the most vividly emotional psalms and hymns.
And these she was fond of repeating with great fervour and
enthusiasm to her admiring listener.

Miss Mehitable considered that the schoolmaster had been
an ill-taught, presumptuous man, who had ventured to take
improper liberties with a mere child; but, when she established
this connection between this same child and a solemn young
minister, it never occurred to her to imagine that there would
be any embarrassing consequences from the relation. She
considered Tina as a mere infant,—as not yet having approached the age when the idea of anything like love or marriage could possibly be suggested to her.

In course of time, however, she could not help remarking
that her cousin was in some respects quite an altered man.
He reformed many little negligences in regard to his toilet
which Miss Tina had pointed out to him with the nonchalant
freedom of a young empress. And he would run and spring
and fetch and carry in her service with a zeal and alertness
quite wonderful to behold. He expressed privately to Miss
Mehitable the utmost astonishment at her mental powers, and
spoke of the wonderful work of divine grace which appeared
to have made such progress in her heart. Never had he been
so instructed and delighted before by the exercises of any
young person. And he went so far as to assure Miss Mehitable

that in many things he should be only too happy to sit at her feet and learn of her.

"Good gracious me!" said Miss Mehitable to herself, with a sort of half start of awakening, though not yet fully come to consciousness; "what does ail everybody that gets hold of Tina?"

What got hold of her cousin in this case she had an opportunity of learning, not long after, by overhearing him tell her young charge that she was an angel, and that he asked nothing more of Heaven than to be allowed to follow her lead through life. Now Miss Tina accepted this, as she did all other incense, with great satisfaction. Not that she had the slightest idea of taking this clumsy-footed theological follower round the world with her; but having the highest possible respect for him, knowing that Miss Mehitable and the minister and his wife thought him a person of consideration, she had felt it her duty to *please* him,—had taxed her powers of pleasing to the utmost, in his own line, and had met with this gratifying evidence of success.

Miss Mehitable was for once really angry. She sent for her cousin to a private interview, and thus addressed him :—

"Cousin Mordecai, I thought you were a man of sense when I put this child under your care! My great trouble in bringing her up is, that everybody flatters her and defers to her; but I thought that in you I had got a man that could be depended on!"

"I do *not* flatter her, cousin," replied the young minister, earnestly.

"You pretend you don't flatter her? didn't I hear you calling her an angel?"

"Well, I don't care if I did; she *is* an angel," said Mr. Mordecai Rossiter, with tears in his eyes; she is the most perfectly heavenly being I ever saw."

"Ah! bah!" said Miss Mehitable, with intense disgust; "what fools you men are!"

Miss Mehitable now, much as she disliked it, felt bound to have some cautionary conversation with Miss Tina.

"My dear," she said, "you must be very careful in your treatment of Cousin Mordecai. I overheard some things he said to you this morning which I do not approve of."

"Oh yes, Aunty, he does talk in a silly way sometimes. Men always begin to talk silly to me. Why, you've no idea the things they will say. Well, of course, I don't believe them; it's only a foolish way they have; but they all talk just alike."

"But I thought my cousin would have had his mind on better things," said Miss Mehitable. "The idea of his making love to you!"

"I know it; only think of it, Aunty! how very funny it is! and there, I haven't done a single thing to make him. I've been just as religious as I could be, and said hymns to him, and everything, and given him good advice,—ever so much, —because, you see, he didn't know about a great many things till I told him."

"But, my dear, all this is going to make him too fond of you; you know you ought not to be thinking of such things now."

"What things, Aunty?" said the catechumen, innocently.

"Why, love and marriage; that's what such feelings will come to, if you encourage them."

"Marriage! oh dear me, what nonsense!" and Tina laughed till the room rang again. "Why, dear Aunty, what absurd ideas have got into your head! Of course, you can't think that he's thinking of any such thing; he's only getting very fond of me, and I'm trying to make him have a good time,—that's all."

But Miss Tina found that was not all, and was provoked beyond endurance at the question proposed to her in plain terms, whether she would not look upon her teacher as one destined in a year or two to become her husband. Thereupon at once the whole gay fabric dissolved like a dream. Tina was as vexed at the proposition as a young unbroken colt is at the sight of a halter. She cried, and said she didn't like him, she couldn't bear him, and she never wanted to see him again,—that he was silly and ridiculous to talk so to a little girl. And Miss Mehitable sat down to write a long letter to her brother, to inquire what she should do next.

CHAPTER VII.

What shall we do with Tina?

"My dear brother,—I am in a complete *embarrass* what to do with Tina. She is the very light of my eyes,—the sweetest, gayest, brightest, and best-meaning little mortal that ever was made; but somehow or other I fear I am not the one that ought to have undertaken to bring her up.

"She has a good deal of self-will; so much that I have long felt it would be quite impossible for me to control her merely by authority. In fact I laid down my sceptre long ago, such as it was. I never did have much of a gift in that way. But Tina's self-will runs in the channel of a most charming persuasiveness. She has all sorts of pretty phrases, and would talk a bird off from a bush, or a trout out of a brook, by dint of sheer persistent eloquence; and she is always so delightfully certain that her way is the right one, and the best for me and all concerned. Then she has no end of those peculiar gifts of entertainment which are rather dangerous things for a young woman. She is a born mimic, she is a natural actress, and she has always a repartee or a smart saying quite *apropos* at the tip of her tongue. All this makes her an immense favourite with people who have no responsibility about her,—who merely want to be amused with her drolleries, and then shake their heads wisely when she is gone, and say that Miss Mehitable Rossiter ought to keep a close hand on that girl.

"It seems to be the common understanding that everybody but me is to spoil her; for there isn't anybody, not even Dr. Lothrop and his wife, that won't connive at her mimicking and fripperies, and then talk gravely with me afterward about the danger of these things, as if I were the only person to say anything disagreeable to her. But then, I can see very plainly that the little chit is in danger on all sides of becoming trivial and superficial,—of mistaking wit for wisdom, and thinking she has answered an argument when she has said a smart thing and raised a laugh.

"Of late, trouble of another kind has been added. Tina is a little turned of fifteen; she is going to be very beautiful; she is very pretty now; and, in addition to all my other perplexities, the men are beginning to talk that atrocious kind of nonsense to her which they seem to think they must talk to young girls. I have had to take her away from the school on account of the schoolmaster, and when I put her under the care of Cousin Mordecai Rossiter, whom I thought old enough, and discreet enough, to make a useful teacher to her, he has acted like a natural fool. I have no kind of patience with him. I would not have believed a man could be so devoid of common-sense. I shall have to send Tina somewhere,— though I can't bear to part with her, and it seems like taking the very sunshine out of the house; so I remember what you told me about sending her up to you.

"Lady Lothrop and Aunt Lois and I have been talking together, and we think the boys might as well go up too to your academy, as our present schoolmaster is not very competent, and you will give them a thorough fitting for college."

To this came the following reply:—

"Sister Mehitable,—The thing has happened that I have foreseen. Send her up here; she shall board in the minister's family; and his daughter Esther, who is wisest, virtuousest, discreetest, best, shall help keep her in order.

"Send the boys along, too; they are bright fellows, as I remember, and I would like to have a hand at them. One of them might live with us and do the out-door chores and help hoe in the garden, and the other might do the same for the minister. So send them along.—Your affectionate brother,

"Jonathan Rossiter."

This was an era in our lives. Harry and I from this time felt ourselves to be *men*, and adopted the habit of speaking of ourselves hereafter familiarly as "a man of my character," "a man of my age," and "a man in my circumstances." The comfort and dignity which this imparted to us were wonderful. We also discussed Tina in a very paternal way, and gravely considered what was best for her. We were, of course, properly shocked at the behaviour of the schoolmaster, and greatly applauded her spirit in defending herself against his presumption.

Then Tina had told Harry and me all about her trouble with the minister, and I remember at this time how extremely aged and venerable I felt, and what quantities of good advice I gave to Tina, which was all based on the supposition of her dangerously powerful charms and attractions. This is the edifying kind of counsel with which young gentlemen of my age instruct their lady friends, and it will be seen at once

that advice and admonition which rest on the theory of super-
human excellence and attractions in the advised party are
far more agreeable than mere rough, common admonition,
unseasoned by any such pleasing hallucination.

In my own mind I had formed my plan of life. I was to
go to college, and therefrom soar to an unmeasured height of
literary distinction, and when I had won trophies and laurels
and renown, I was to come back and lay all at Tina's feet.
This was what Harry and I agreed on, in many a conversation, as the destined result of our friendship.

Harry and I had sworn friendship by all the solemn oaths
and forms known in ancient or modern history. We changed
names with each other, and in our private notes and letters
addressed each by the name of the other, and felt as if this
was some sacred and wonderful peculiarity. Tina called us
both brothers, and this we agreed was the best means of preserving her artless mind unalarmed and undisturbed until the
future hour of the great declaration. As for Tina, she absolutely could not keep anything to herself if she tried. Whatever agitated her mind or interested it had to be told to us.
She did not seem able to rest satisfied with herself till she had
proved to us that she was exactly right, or made as share
her triumphs in her achievements, or her perplexity in her
failures.

At this crisis Miss Mehitable talked very seriously and
sensibly with her little charge. She pointed out to her the
danger of living a trivial and superficial life,—of becoming
vain, and living merely for admiration. She showed her how
deficient she had been in those attainments which require
perseverance and steadiness of mind, and earnestly recommended her now to devote herself to serious studies.

Nobody was a better subject to preach such a sermon to
than Tina. She would even take up the discourse and en-

large upon it, and suggest new and fanciful illustrations; she
entered into the project of Miss Mehitable with enthusiasm;
she confessed all her faults, and resolved hereafter to become
a pattern of the contrary virtues. And then she came and related the whole conversation to us, and entered into the project of devoting herself to study with such a glow of enthusiasm, that we formed at once the most brilliant expectations.

The town of Cloudland, whither we were going, was a two
days' journey up into the mountains; and, as travelling faci-
lities then were, it was viewed as such an undertaking to
send us there, that the whole family conclave talked gravely
of it, and discussed it in every point of view for a fortnight
before we started. Our Uncle Jacob, the good, meek, quiet
farmer of whom I have spoken, had a little business in regard
to some property that had been left by a relative of his wife
in that place, and suggested the possibility of going up with
us himself. So weighty a move was at first thrown out as a
mere proposal to be talked of in the family circle. Grandmother, and Aunt Lois, and Aunt Keziah, and my mother
picked over and discussed this proposition for days, as a lot
of hens will pick over an ear of corn, turning it from side to
side, and looking at it from every possible point of view.
Uncle Fliakim had serious thoughts of offering his establishment, but it was universally admitted that his constant charities had kept it in such a condition of frailty that the mountain roads would finish it, and thus deprive multitudes of the
female population of Oldtown of an establishment which was
about as much their own as if they had the care and keeping
of it.

I don't know anybody who could have been taken from
Oldtown whose loss would have been more universally felt
and deplored than little Miss Tina's. In the first place,

Oldtown had come into the way of regarding her as a sort of Child of the Regiment: and then Tina was one of those sociable, acquaintance-making bodies that have visited everybody, penetrated everybody's affairs, and given a friendly lift now and then in almost everybody's troubles.

"Why, lordy massy!" said Sam Lawson, "I don't know nothin' what we're any on us goin' to do when Tiny's gone. Why, there ain't a dog goes into the meetin'-house but wags his tail when he sees her a-coming. I expect she knows about every yellow-bird's nest an' blue jay's an' bobolink's an' meadow-lark's that there's ben round here these five years; and how they's going to set and hatch without her's best known to 'emselves, I s'pose. Lordy massy! that child can sing so like a skunk blackbird that you can't tell which is which. Wal, I'll say one thing for her; she draws the fire out o' Hepsy, an' she's 'bout the only livin' critter that can; but some nights when she's ben inter our house a-playin' checkers or fox an' geese with the child'en, she'd railly git Hepsy slicked down so that 't was kind o' comfortable bein' with her. I'm sorry she's goin', for my part, an' all the child'en 'll be sorry."

As for Polly, she worked night and day on Tina's outfit, and scolded and hectored herself for certain tears that now and then dropped on the white aprons that she was ironing. On the night before Tina was to depart, Polly came into her room and insisted upon endowing her with her string of gold beads, the only relic of earthly vanity in which that severe female had ever been known to indulge. Tina was quite melted, and fell upon her neck.

"Why, Polly! No, no; you dear old creature, you, you've been a thousand times too good for me, and I've nearly plagued the life out of you, and you shan't give me your poor, dear, old gold beads, but keep them yourself; for you're as good as gold any day, and so it's a great deal better that you should wear them."

"O Tina, child, you don't know my heart," said Polly, shaking her head solemnly; "if you could see the depths of depravity that there are there!"

"I don't believe a word of it, Polly."

"Ah! but, you see, the Lord seeth not as man sees, Tina."

"I know He don't," said Tina; "He's a thousand times kinder, and makes a thousand more excuses for us than we ever do for ourselves or each other. You know the Bible says, 'He knoweth our frame; He remembereth that we are dust.' "

"O Tina, Tina, you always was a wonderful child to talk," said Polly, shaking her head doubtfully; "but then you know the heart is so deceitful, and then you see there's the danger that we should mistake natural emotions for grace."

"Oh, I dare say there are all sorts of dangers," said Tina; "of course there are. I know I'm nothing but just a poor little silly bird; but He knows it too, and He's taken care of ever so many such little silly people as I am, so that I'm not afraid. He won't let me deceive myself. You know, when that bird got shut in the house the other day, how much time you and I and Miss Mehitable all spent in trying to keep it from breaking its foolish head against the glass, and flying into the fire, and all that, and how glad we were when we got it safe out into the air. I'm sure we are not half as good as God is, and, if we take so much care about a poor little bird that we didn't make, and had nothing to do with, He must care a good deal more about us when we are His children. And God is all the Father I have or ever knew."

This certainly looked to Polly like very specious reasoning, but, after all, the faithful creature groaned in spirit. Might not this all be mere natural religion, and not the supernatural grace? So she said, trembling, "O Tina, did you always feel so towards God? Wan't there a time when your heart rose in opposition to Him?"

"Oh, certainly," said Tina; "when Miss Asphyxia used to talk to me about it, I thought I never wanted to hear of Him, and I never said my prayers; but as soon as I came to Aunty, she was so loving and kind that I began to see what God must be like,—because I know He is kinder than she can be, or you, or anybody can be. That's so, isn't it? You know the Bible says His loving kindness is infinite."

The thing in this speech which gave Polly such peculiar satisfaction was the admission that there had been a definite point of time in which the feelings of her little friend had undergone a distinct change. Henceforth she was better satisfied,—never reflecting how much she was trusting to a mere state of mind in the child, instead of resting her faith on the Almighty Friend who so evidently had held her in charge during the whole of her short history.

As for me, the eve of my departure was to me one of triumph. When I had seen all my father's Latin books fairly stowed away in my trunk, with the very simple wardrobe which belonged to Harry and me, and the trunk had been shut and locked and corded, and we were to start at sunrise the next morning, I felt as if my father's unfulfilled life-desire was at last going to be accomplished in me.

It was a bright, clear, starlight night in June, and we were warned to go to bed early, that we might be ready in season the next morning. As usual, Harry fell fast asleep, and I was too nervous and excited to close my eyes. I began to think of the old phantasmagoria of my childish days, which now so seldom appeared to me. I felt stealing over me that peculiar

thrill and vibration of the great central nerves which used to
indicate the approach of those phenomena, and, looking up,
I saw distinctly my father, exactly as I used to see him, standing between the door and the bed. It seemed to me that he
entered by passing through the door, but there he was, every
line and lineament of his face, every curl of his hair, exactly
as I remembered it. His eyes were fixed on mine with a
tender human radiance. There was something soft and compassionate about the look he gave me, and I felt it vibrating
on my nerves with that peculiar electric thrill of which I have
spoken. I learned by such interviews as these how spirits
can communicate with one another without human language.

The appearance of my father was vivid and real even to
the clothing that he used to wear, which was earthly and
home-like, precisely as I remembered it. Yet I felt no disposition to address him, and no need of words. Gradually
the image faded; it grew thinner and fainter, and I saw the
door through it as if it had been a veil, and then it passed
away entirely.

What are these apparitions? I know that this will be read
by many who have seen them quite as plainly as I have, who,
like me, have hushed back the memory of them into the most
secret and silent chamber of their hearts.

I know, with regard to myself, that the sight of my father
was accompanied by such a vivid conviction of the reality of
his presence, such an assurance radiated from his serene eyes
that he had at last found the secret of eternal peace, such an
intense conviction of continued watchful affection and of
sympathy in the course that I was now beginning, that I
could not have doubted if I would. And when we remember
that, from the beginning of the world, some such possible
communication between departed love and the beloved on
earth has been among the most cherished legends of

humanity, why must we always meet such phenomena with a resolute determination to account for them by every or any supposition but that which the human heart most craves? Is not the great mystery of life and death made more cruel and inexorable by this rigid incredulity? One would fancy, to hear some moderns talk, that there was no possibility that the departed, even when most tender and most earnest, could, if they would, recall themselves to their earthly friends.

For my part, it was through some such experiences as these that I learned that there are truths of the spiritual life which are intuitive, and above logic, which a man must believe because he cannot help it,—just as he believes the facts of his daily experience in the world of matter, though most ingenious and unanswerable treatises, have been written to show that there is no proof of its existence.

CHAPTER VIII.

The Journey to Cloudland.

THE next morning Aunt Lois rapped at our door, when there was the very faintest red streak in the east, and the birds were just in the midst of that vociferous singing which nobody knows anything about who isn't awake at this precise hour. We were forward enough to be up and dressed, and before our breakfast was through, Uncle Jacob came to the door.

The agricultural population of Massachusetts at this time were a far more steady set, as regards locomotion, than they are in these days of railroads. At this time, a journey from Boston to New York took a fortnight,—a longer time than it now takes to go to Europe,—and my Uncle Jacob had never been even to Boston. In fact, the seven-mile tavern in the neighbourhood had been the extent of his wanderings, and it

was evident that he regarded the two days' journey as quite
a solemn event in his life. He had given a fortnight's
thought to it; he had arranged all his worldly affairs, and
given charges and messages to his wife and children, in case,
as he said, "anything should happen to him." And he
informed Aunt Lois that he had been awake the biggest part
of the night thinking it over. But when he had taken Tina
and her little trunk on board, and we had finished all our
hand-shakings, and Polly had told us over for the fourth or
fifth time exactly where she had put the cold chicken and
the biscuits and the cakes and pie, and Miss Mehitable had
cautioned Tina again and again to put on her shawl in case
a shower should come up, and my grandmother and Aunt
Lois had put in their share of parting admonitions, we at last
trolled off as cheery and merry a set of youngsters as the sun
ever looked upon in a dewy June morning.

Our road lay first along the beautiful brown river, with its
sweeping bends, and its prattling curves of water dashing
and chattering over mossy rocks. Towards noon we began
to find ourselves winding up and up amid hemlock forests,
whose solemn shadows were all radiant and aglow with clouds
of blossoming laurel. We had long hills to wind up, when we
got out and walked, and gathered flowers, and scampered and
chased the brook up stream from one little dashing waterfall
to another, and then, suddenly darting out upon the road
again, we would meet the waggon at the top of the hill.

Can there be anything on earth so beautiful as these mountain rides in New England? At any rate, we were full in the
faith that there could not. When we were riding in the
waggon, Tina's powers of entertainment were brought into
full play. The great success of the morning was her exact
imitation of a squirrel eating a nut, which she was requested
to perform many times, and which she did, with variations,

until at last Uncle Jacob remarked, with a grin, that "if he should meet her and a squirrel sitting on a stone fence together, he believed he shouldn't know which was which."

Besides this, we acted various impromptu plays, assuming characters and supporting them as we had been accustomed to do in our theatrical rehearsals in the garret, till Uncle Jacob declared that he never did see such a musical set as we were. About nightfall we came to Uncle Sim Geary's tavern, which had been fixed upon for our stopping-place. This was neither more nor less than a mountain farm-house, where the few travellers who ever passed that way could find accommodation.

Uncle Jacob, after seeing to his horses, and partaking of a plentiful supper, went immediately to bed. as was his innocent custom every evening, as speedily as possible. To bed, but not to sleep, for when, an hour or two afterward, I had occasion to go into his room, I found him lying on his bed with his clothes on, his shoes merely slipped off, and his hat held securely over the pit of his stomach.

"Why, Uncle Jacob," said I, "ain't you going to bed?"

"Well, I guess I'll just lie down as I be; no knowin' what may happen when you're travelling. It's a very nice house, and a very respectable family, but it's best always to be prepared for anything that may happen. So I think you children had better all go to bed and keep quiet."

What roars of laughter there were among us when I described this scene and communicated the message of Uncle Jacob! It seemed as if Tina could not be got to sleep that night, and we could hear giggling, through the board partition that separated our room from hers, every hour of the night.

Happy are the days when one can go to sleep and wake up laughing. The next morning, however, Uncle Jacob reaped the reward of his vigilance by finding himself ready dressed at six o'clock, when I came in and found him sleeping profoundly. The fact was, that, having kept awake till near morning, he was sounder asleep at this point of time than any of us, and was snoring away like a grist-mill. He remarked that he shouldn't wonder if he had dropped asleep, and added, in a solemn tone, "We've got through the night wonderfully, all things considered."

The next day's ride was the same thing over, only the hills were longer; and by and by we came into great vistas of mountains, whose cloudy purple heads seemed to stretch and veer around our path like the phantasmagoria of a dream. Sometimes the road seemed to come straight up against an impenetrable wall, and we would wonder what we were to do with it; but lo! as we approached, the old mountain seemed gracefully to slide aside, and open to us a passage round it. Tina found ever so many moralities and poetical images in these mountains. It was like life, she said. Your way would seem all shut up before you, but, if you only had faith and went on, the mountains would move aside for you and let you through.

Towards night we began to pull in earnest up a series of ascents towards the little village of Cloudland. Hill after hill, hill after hill, how long they seemed! but how beautiful it was when the sun went down over the distant valleys! and there was such a pomp and glory of golden clouds and rosy vapours wreathing around the old mountain-tops as one must go to Cloudland to know anything about.

At last we came to a little terrace of land, where were a white meeting-house, and a store, and two or three houses, and to the door of one of these our waggon drove. There stood Mr. Jonathan Rossiter and the minister and Esther. You do not know Esther, do you? neither at this minute did we. We saw a tall, straight, graceful girl, who looked at us out of a pair of keen, clear, hazel eyes, with a sort of inquisitive yet not unkindly glance, but as if she meant to make up her mind about us; and when she looked at Tina I could see that her mind was made up in a moment.

LETTER FROM TINA TO MISS MEHITABLE.

"CLOUDLAND, *June 6.*

"Here we are, dear Aunty, up in the skies, in the most beautiful place that you can possibly conceive of. We had such a good time coming! you've no idea of the fun we had. You know I am going to be very sober, but I didn't think it was necessary to begin while we were travelling, and we kept Uncle Jacob laughing so that I really think he must have been tired.

"Do you know, Aunty, I have got so that I can look exactly like a squirrel? We saw ever so many on the way, and I got a great many new hints on the subject, and now I can do squirrel in four or five different attitudes, and the boys almost killed themselves laughing.

"Harry is an old sly-boots. Do you know, he is just as much of a mimic as I am, for all he looks so sober; but when we get him a-going he is perfectly killing. He and I and Horace acted all sorts of plays on the way. We agreed with each other that we'd give a set of Oldtown representations, and see if Uncle Jacob would know who they were, and so Harry was Sam Lawson and I was Hepsy, and I made an unexceptionable baby out of our two shawls, and Horace was Uncle Fliakim come in to give us moral exhortations. I do wish you could hear how we did it. Uncle Jacob isn't the brightest of all mortals, and not very easily roused, but we made him laugh till he said his sides were sore; and to pay for it he made us laugh when we got to the tavern where we stopped all night. Do you believe, Aunty, Uncle Jacob really was frightened, or care-worn, or something, so that he hardly slept any all night? It was just the quietest place that ever you saw, and there was a good motherly woman, who got us the nicest kind of supper, and a peaceable, slow, dull old man, just like Uncle Jacob. There wasn't the least thing that looked as if we had fallen into a cave of banditti, or a castle in the Apennines, such as Mrs. Radcliffe tells about in the "Mysteries of Udolpho;" but, for all that, Uncle Jacob's mind was so oppressed with care that he went to bed with all his clothes on, and lay broad awake with his hat in his hand all night. I didn't think before that Uncle Jacob had such a brilliant imagination. Poor man! I should have thought he would have lain down and slept as peaceably as one of his own oxen.

"We got up into Cloudland about half-past six o'clock in the afternoon, the second day; and such a sunset! I thought of a good subject for a little poem, and wrote two or three verses, which I'll send you some time; but I must tell you now about the people here.

"I don't doubt I shall become very good, for just think what a place I am in,—living at the minister's! and then I room with Esther! You ought to see Esther. She's a beautiful girl; she's tall, and straight, and graceful, with smooth black hair, and piercing dark eyes that look as if they could read your very soul. Her face has the features of a statue, at least such as I think some of the beautiful statues that I've read about might have; and what makes it more statuesque is, that she's so very pale; she is perfectly healthy, but there doesn't seem to be any red blood in her cheeks; and, dear Aunty, she is alarmingly good. She knows so much, and does so much, that it is really discouraging to me to think of it. Why, do you know, she has read through Virgil, and is reading a Greek tragedy now with Mr. Rossiter; and she teaches a class in mathematics in school, besides being her father's only housekeeper, and taking care of her younger brothers.

"I should be frightened to death at so much goodness, if it were not that she seems to have taken the greatest possible fancy to me. As I told you, we room together; and such a nice room as it is! everything is just like wax; and she gave me half of everything,—half the drawers and half the closet, and put all my things so nicely in their places, and then in the morning she gets up at unheard-of hours, and she was beginning to pet me and tell me that I needn't get up. Now you know, Aunty, that's just the way people are always doing with me, and the way poor dear old Polly would spoil me; but I told Esther all about my new resolutions, and exactly how good I intended to be, and that I thought I couldn't do better than to do everything that she did, and so when she gets up I get up; and really, Aunty, you've no idea what a sight the sunrise is here in the mountains; it really is worth getting up for.

"We have breakfast at six o'clock, and then there are about three hours before school, and I help Esther wash up the breakfast-things, and we make our bed and sweep our room, and put everything up nice, and then I have ever so long to study, while Esther is seeing to all her family cares and directing black Dinah about the dinner, and settling any little cases that may arise among her three younger brothers. They are great, strong, nice boys, with bright red cheeks, and a good capacity for making a noise, but she manages them nicely. Dear Aunty, I hope some of her virtues will rub off on to me by contact; don't you?

"I don't think your brother likes me much. He hardly noticed me at all when I was first presented to him, and

seemed to have forgotten that he had ever seen me. I tried
to talk to him, but he cut me quite short, and turned round
and went to talking to Mr. Avery, the minister, you know. I
think that these people that know so much, might be civil to
us little folks, but then I dare say it's all right enough; but
sometimes it does seem as if he wanted to snub me. Well,
perhaps it's good for me to be snubbed; I have such good
times generally, that I ought to have something that isn't
quite so pleasant.

"Life is to me such a beautiful story! and every morning
when I open my eyes and see things looking so charming as
they do here, I thank God that I am alive.

"Mr. Rossiter has been examining the boys in their
studies. He isn't a man that ever praises anybody, I suppose, but I can see that he is pretty well pleased with them.
We have a lady-principal, Miss Titcomb. She is about forty
years old, I should think, and very pleasant and affable. I
shall tell you more about these things by and by.

"Give my love to dear old Polly, and to Grandma and
Aunt Lois, and all the nice folks in Oldtown.

"Dear Aunty, sometimes I used to think that you were de-
pressed, and had troubles that you did not tell me; and something you said once about your life being so wintry, made
me quite sad. Do let me be your little Spring, and think
always how dearly I love you, and how good I am going to
try to be for your sake.—Your own affectionate little

TINA."

CHAPTER IX.

School-life in Cloudland.

THE academy in Cloudland was one of those pure wells
from which the hidden strength of New England is drawn, as
her broad rivers are made from hidden mountain brooks. The

first object of every colony in New England, after building the Church, was to establish a school-house; and a class of the most superior men of New England, in those days of simple living, were perfectly satisfied to make it the business of their lives to teach in the small country academies with which the nooks and hollows of New England were filled.

Could materials be got as profuse as Boswell's "Life of Johnson," to illustrate the daily life and table-talk of some of the academy schoolmasters of this period, it would be an acquisition for the world.

For that simple, pastoral germ-state of society, is a thing forever gone. Never again shall we see that union of perfect repose in regard to outward surroundings and outward life, with that intense activity of the inward and intellectual world, that made New England, at this time, the vigorous, germinating seed-bed for all that has since been developed of politics, laws, letters, and theology, through New England to America, and through America to the world. The hurry of railroads, and the rush and roar of business, that now fill it, would have prevented that germinating process. It was necessary that there should be a period like that we describe, when villages were each a separate little democracy, shut off by rough roads and forests from the rest of the world, organised round the church and school as a common centre, and formed by the minister and the schoolmaster.

The academy of Cloudland had become celebrated in the neighbourhood, for the skill and ability with which it was conducted, and pupils had been drawn, even from as far as Boston, to come and sojourn in our mountain town to partake of these advantages. They were mostly young girls, who were boarded at very simple rates in the various families of the place. In all, the pupils of the academy numbered about a hundred, equally divided between the two sexes. There was a class of about fifteen young men who were preparing for college, and a greater number of boys who were studying with the same ultimate hope.

As a general rule, the country academies of Massachusetts have been equally open to both sexes. Andover and Exeter, so far as I know, formed the only exceptions to this rule, being by their charters confined rigorously to the use of the dominant sex. But, in the generality of country academies, the girls and boys studied side by side, without any other restriction as to the character of their studies than personal preference. As a general thing, the classics and the higher mathematics were more pursued by the boys than the girls. But if there were a daughter of Eve who wished, like her mother, to put forth her hand to the tree of knowledge, there was neither cherubim nor flaming sword to drive her away.

Mr. Rossiter was always stimulating the female part of his subjects to such undertakings, and the consequence was, that in his school an unusual number devoted themselves to these pursuits, and the leading scholar in Greek and the higher mathematics was our new acquaintance, Esther Avery.

The female principal, Miss Titcomb, was a thorough-bred, old-fashioned lady, whose views of education were formed by Miss Hannah More, and whose style, like Miss Hannah More's, was profoundly Johnsonian. This lady had composed a set of rules for the conduct of the school, in the most ornate and resounding periods. These rules, briefly epitomised, required of us *only* absolute moral perfection, but they were run into details which caused the reading of them to take up about a quarter of an hour every Saturday morning. I would that I could remember some of the sentences. It was required of us all, for one thing, that we should be perfectly polite. "Persons truly polite," it was added, "invariably treat their superiors with reverence, their equals with exact consideration, and their inferiors with condescension." Again, under the head of manners, we were warned "not to consider romping as indicative of sprightliness, or loud laughter a mark of wit."

The scene every Saturday morning, when these rules were read to a set of young people, on whom the mountain air acted like champagne, and among whom both romping and loud laughter were fearfully prevalent, was sufficiently edifying.

There was also a system of marks, quite complicated, by which our departure from any of these virtuous proprieties was indicated. After a while, however, the reading of these rules, like the reading of the Ten Commandments in churches, and a great deal of other good substantial reading, came to be looked upon only as a Saturday-morning decorum, and the Johnsonian periods, which we all knew by heart, were principally useful in pointing a joke. Nevertheless, we were not a badly-behaved set of young people.

Miss Titcomb exercised a general supervision of the manners, morals, and health of the young ladies connected with the institution, taught history and geography, and also gave especial attention to female accomplishments. These, so far as I could observe, consisted largely in embroidering mourning pieces, with a family monument in the centre, a green ground worked in chenille and floss silk, with an exuberant willow-tree, and a number of weeping mourners, whose faces were often concealed by flowing pocket-handkerchiefs.

Pastoral pieces were also in great favour, representing fair young shepherdesses sitting on green chenille banks, with crooks in their hands, and tending some animals of au

uncertain description, which were to be received by faith as
sheep. The sweet, confiding innocence which regarded the
making of objects like these as more suited to the tender
female character than the pursuit of Latin and mathematics,
was characteristic of the ancient *régime.* Did not Penelope
embroider, and all sorts of princesses, ancient and modern?
and was not embroidery a true feminine grace? Even Esther
Avery, though she found no time for works of this kind,
looked upon it with respect, as an accomplishment for which
nature unfortunately had not given her a taste.

Mr. Rossiter, although he of course would not infringe on
the kingdom of his female associate, treated these accomplishments with a scarce concealed contempt. It was, perhaps, the frosty atmosphere of scepticism which he breathed
about him touching those works of art, that prevented his
favourite scholars from going far in the direction of such
accomplishments. The fact is, that Mr. Rossiter, during the
sailor period of his life, had been to the Mediterranean, had
seen the churches of Spain and Italy, and knew what
Murillos and Titians were like, which may account somewhat for the glances of civil amusement which he sometimes
cast over into Miss Titcomb's department, when the adjuncts
and accessories of a family tombstone were being eagerly
discussed.

Mr. Jonathan Rossiter held us all by the sheer force of his
personal character and will, just as the ancient mariner held
the wedding guest with his glittering eye. He so utterly
scorned and contemned a lazy scholar, that trifling and in-
efficiency in study were scorched and withered by the very
breath of his nostrils. We were so awfully afraid of his
opinion, we so hoped for his good word and so dreaded his
contempt, and we so verily believed that no such man ever
before walked this earth, that he had only to shake his

ambrosial locks and give the nod to settle us all as to any matter whatever.

In an age when in England schools were managed by the grossest and most brutal exercise of corporeal punishments, the schoolmasters of New England, to a great extent, had entirely dropped all resort to such barbarous measures, and carried on their schools as republics, by the sheer force of moral and intellectual influences. Mr. Jonathan Rossiter would have been ashamed of himself at even the suggestion of caning a boy,—as if he were incapable of any higher style of government. And yet never was a man more feared and his will had in more awful regard. Mr. Rossiter was sparing of praise, but his praise bore a value in proportion to its scarcity. It was like diamonds and rubies,—few could have it, but the whole of his little commonwealth were working for it.

He scorned all conventional rules in teaching, and he would not tolerate a mechanical lesson, and took delight in puzzling his pupils and breaking up all routine business by startling and unexpected questions and assertions. He compelled every one to think, and to think for himself. "Your heads may not be the best in the world," was one of his sharp, off-hand sayings; "but they are the best God has given you, and you must use them for yourselves."

To tell the truth, he used his teaching somewhat as a mental gratification for himself. If there was a subject he wanted to investigate, or an old Greek or Latin author that he wanted to dig out, he would put a class on it, without the least regard to whether it was in the course of college preparation or not, and if a word was said by any poor mechanical body, he would blast out upon us with a sort of despotic scorn.

"Learn to read Greek perfectly," he said, "and it's no

matter what you read;" or, "Learn to use your own heads, and you can learn anything."

There was little idling and no shirking in his school, but a slow, dull, industrious fellow, if he showed a disposition to work steadily, got more notice from him than even a bright one.

Mr. Rossiter kept house by himself in a small cottage adjoining that of the minister. His housekeeper, Miss Minerva Randall, generally known to the village as "Miss Nervy Randall," was one of those preternaturally well-informed old mermaids who, so. far as I know, are a peculiar product of the State of Maine. Study and work had been the two passions of her life, and in neither could she be excelled by man or woman. Single-handed, and without a servant, she performed all the labours of Mr. Jonathan Rossiter's little establishment. She washed for him, ironed for him, plaited his ruffled shirts in neatest folds, brushed his clothes, cooked his food, occasionally hoed in the garden, trained flowers around the house, and found, also, time to read Greek and Latin authors, and to work out problems in mathematics and surveying and navigation, and to take charge of boys in reading Virgil.

Miss Minerva Randall was one of those female persons who are of Sojourner Truth's opinion,—that if women want any rights, they had better take them, and say nothing about it. Her *sex* had never occurred to her as a reason for doing or not doing anything which her hand found to do. In the earlier part of her life, for the mere love of roving and improving her mind by seeing foreign countries, she had gone on a Mediterranean voyage with her brother Zachariah Randall, who was wont to say of her that she was a better mate than any man he could find. And true enough, when he was confined to his berth with a fever, Miss Minerva not only nursed him, but navigated the ship home in the most matter-of-fact way in the world. She had no fol-de-rol about woman's rights, but she was always wide-awake to perceive when a thing was to be done, and to do it. Nor did she ever after in her life talk of this exploit as a thing to be boasted of, seeming to regard it as a matter too simple, and entirely in the natural course of things, to be mentioned. Miss Minerva, however, had not enough of the external illusive charms of her sex, to suggest to a casual spectator any doubt on that score of the propriety of her doing or not doing anything. Although she had not precisely the air of a man, she had very little of what usually suggests the associations of femininity. There was a sort of fishy quaintness about her that awakened grim ideas of some unknown ocean product, —a wild and withered appearance, like a wind-blown juniper on a sea promontory,—unsightly and stunted, yet not, after all, commonplace and vulgar. She was short, square, and broad, and the circumference of her waist was, if anything, greater where that of other females decreases. What the colour of her hair might have been in days of youthful bloom was not apparent; but she had, when we knew her, thin tresses of a pepper-and-salt mixture of tint, combed tightly, and twisted in a very small nut on the back of her head, and fastened with a reddish-yellowish horn comb. Her small black eyes were overhung by a grizzled thicket of the same mixed colour as her hair. For the graces of the toilet Miss Nervy had no particular esteem. Her clothing and her person, as well as her housekeeping and belongings, were of a scrupulous and wholesome neatness; but the idea of any other beauty than that of utility had never suggested itself to her mind. She wore always a stuff petticoat of her own spinning, with a striped linen short-gown, and probably in all her life never expended twenty dollars a-year for clothing;

10*

and yet Miss Nervy was about the happiest female person
whose acquaintance it has ever been my fortune to make.
She had just as much as she wanted of exactly the two
things she liked best in the world,—books and work; and
when her work was done, there were the books, and life could
give no more.   Miss Nervy had no sentiment,—not a particle
of romance,—she was the most perfectly contented mortal
that could possibly be imagined.   As to station and position,
she was as well known and highly respected in Cloudland as
the schoolmaster himself: she was one of the fixed facts of
the town, as much as the meeting-house.   Days came and
went, and spring flowers and autumn leaves succeeded each
other, and boys and girls, like the spring flowers and autumn
leaves, came and went in Cloudland Academy, but there was
always Miss Nervy Randall, not a bit older, not a bit changed,
doing her spinning and her herb-drying, working over her
butter and plaiting Mr. Jonathan's ruffled shirts, and teaching
her Virgil class.   What gave a piquancy to Miss Nervy's
discourse was, that she always clung persistently to the racy
Yankee dialect of her childhood; and when she was dis-
coursing of Latin and the classics, the idioms made a droll
mixture.   She was the most invariably good-natured of
mortals, and helpful to a degree; and she would always stop
her kitchen work, take her hands out of the bread, or turn
away from her yeast in a critical moment, to show a puzzled
boy the way through a hard Latin sentence.

  "Why, don't you know what that 'ere is?" she would say.
"That 'ere is part of the gerund in *dum;* you've got to decline
it, and then you'll find it.   Look here!" she'd say, "run that
'ere through the moods an' tenses, and ye'll get it in the sub-
junctive;" or, "Massy, child! that 'ere is one o' the deponent
verbs.   'Tain't got any active form; them deponent verbs
allus does trouble boys till they git used to 'em."

Now these provincialisms might have excited the risibles of a set of grammarians so keen 'as we were, only that Miss Randall was a dead shot in any case of difficulty presented by the learned languages. No matter how her English phrased it, she had taught so many boys that she knew every hard rub and difficult stepping-stone and tight place in the Latin grammar by heart, and had relief at her tongue's end for any distressed beginner.

In the cottage over which Miss Randall presided, Harry and I had our room, and we were boarded at the master's table; and so far we were fortunate. Our apartment, which was a roof-room of a gambrel-roofed cottage, was, to be sure, unplastered and carpetless; but it looked out through the boughs of a great apple-tree, up a most bewildering blue vista of mountains, whence the sight of a sunset was something forever to be remembered. All our physical appointments, though rustically plain, were kept by Miss Nervy in the utmost perfection of neatness. She had as great a passion for soap and sand as she had for Greek roots, and probably for the same reason. These wild sea-coast countries seemed to produce a sort of superfluity of energy which longed to wreak itself on something, and delighted in digging and delving mentally as well as physically.

Our table had a pastoral perfection in the articles of bread and butter, with honey furnished by Miss Minerva's bees, game and fish brought in by the united woodcraft of the minister and Mr. Rossiter.

Mr. Rossiter pursued all the natural sciences with an industry and enthusiasm only possible to a man who lives in so lonely and retired a place as Cloudland, and who has, therefore, none of the thousand dissipations of time which come from our modern system of intercommunication, which is fast producing a state of shallow and superficial knowledge. He had a ponderous herbarium, of some forty or fifty folios, of his own collection and arrangement, over which he glouted with affectionate pride. He had a fine mineralogical cabinet; and there was scarcely a ledge of rocks within a circuit of twelve miles that had not resounded to the tap of his stone hammer and furnished specimens for his collection; and he had an entomologic collection, where luckless bugs impaled on steel pins stuck in thin sheets of cork struggled away a melancholy existence, martyrs to the taste for science. The tender-hearted among us sometimes ventured a remonstrance in favour of these hapless beetles, but were silenced by the authoritative dictum of Mr. Rossiter. "Insects," he declared, "are unsusceptible of pain, the structure of their nervous organisation forbidding the idea, and their spasmodic action being simply nervous contraction." As nobody has ever been inside of a beetle to certify to the contrary, and as the race have no mode of communication, we all found it comfortable to put implicit faith in Mr. Rossiter's statements till better advised.

It was among the awe-inspiring legends that were current of Mr. Rossiter in the school, that he corresponded with learned men in Norway and Sweden, Switzerland and France, to whom he sent specimens of American plants and minerals and insects, receiving in return those of other countries. Even in that remote day, little New England had her eyes and her thoughts and her hands everywhere where ship could sail.

Mr. Rossiter dearly loved to talk and to teach, and out of school-hours it was his delight to sit surrounded by his disciples, to answer their questions, and show them his herbarium and his cabinet, to organise woodland tramps, and to start us on researches similar to his own. It was fashionable in his school to have private herbariums and cabinets, and before a month was passed our garret-room began to look quite like a grotto. In short, Mr. Rossiter's system resembled that of those gardeners who, instead of bending all their energies toward making a handsome head to a young tree, encourage it to burst out in suckers clear down to the root, bringing every part of it into vigorous life and circulation.

I still remember the blessed old fellow, as he used to sit among us on the steps of his house, in some of those resplendent moonlight nights which used to light up Cloudland like a fairy dream. There he still sits, in memory, with his court around him,—Esther, with the thoughtful shadows in her eyes and the pensive Psyche profile, and Tina, ever restless, changing, enthusiastic; Harry with his sly, reticent humour and silent enjoyment; and he, our master, talking of everything under the sun, past, present, and to come,—of the cathedrals and pictures of Europe, describing those he had not seen apparently with as minute a knowledge as those he had,—of plants and animals,—of the ancients and the moderns,—of theology, metaphysics, grammar, or rhetoric, or whatever came uppermost, always full and suggestive, startling us with paradoxes, provoking us to arguments, setting us out to run eager tilts of discussion with him, yet in all holding us in a state of unmeasured admiration. Was he conscious, our great man and master, of that weakness of his nature which made an audience, and an admiring one, always a necessity to him? Of a soul naturally self-distrustful and melancholy, he needed to be constantly reinforced and built up in his own esteem by the suffrage of others. What seemed the most trenchant self-assertion in him was, after all, only the desperate struggles of a drowning man to keep his head above water; and, though he seemed at times to despise us all, our good opinion, our worship and reverence, were the raft that kept him from sinking in despair.

The first few weeks that Tina was in school, it was evident

that Mr. Rossiter considered her as a spoiled child of fortune, whom the world had conspired to injure by over-much petting. He appeared resolved at once to change the atmosphere and the diet. For some time in school it seemed as if she could do nothing to please him. He seemed determined to put her through a sort of Spartan drill, with hard work and small praise.

[Tina had received from nature and womanhood that inspiration in dress and toilet attraction which led her always and instinctively to some little form of personal adornment. Every wild spray or fluttering vine in our woodland rambles seemed to suggest to her some caprice of ornamentation. Each day she had some new thing in her hair,—now a feathery fern-leaf, and anon some wild red berry, whose presence just where she placed it was as picturesque as a French lithograph; and we boys were in the habit of looking each day to see what she would wear next. One morning she came into school, fair as Ariadne, with her viny golden curls rippling over and around a crown of laurel-blossoms. She seemed to us like a little woodland poem. We all looked at her, and complimented her, and she received our compliments, as she always did coin of that sort, with the most undisguised and radiant satisfaction. Mr. Rossiter was in one of his most savage humours this morning, and eyed the pretty toilet grimly. "If you had only an equal talent for ornamenting the *inside* of your head," he said to her, "there might be some hopes of you."

Tears of mortification came into Tina's eyes, as she dashed the offending laurel-blossoms out of the window, and bent resolutely over her book. At recess-time she strolled out with me into the pine woods back of the school-house, and we sat down on a mossy log together, and I comforted her and took her part.

"I don't care, Horace," she said,—"I don't care!" and
she dashed the tears out of her eyes. "I'll *make* that man
like me yet,—you see if I don't. He shall like me before
I'm done with him, so there! I don't care how much he
scolds. I'll give in to him, and do exactly as he tells me,
but I'll conquer him,—you see if I don't."

And true enough Miss Tina from this time brushed her
curly hair straight as such rebellious curls possibly could be
brushed, and dressed herself as plainly as Esther, and went
at study as if her life depended on it. She took all Mr.
Rossiter's snubs and despiteful sayings with the most prostrate humility, and now we began to learn, to our astonishment, what a mind the little creature had. In all my experience of human beings, I never saw one who learned so easily
as she. It was but a week or two after she began the Latin
grammar before, jumping over all the intermediate books,
she alighted in a class in Virgil among scholars who had
been studying for a year, and kept up with them, and in some
respects stood clearly as the first scholar. The *vim* with
which the little puss went at it, the zeal with which she turned
over the big dictionary and whirled the leaves of the grammar,
the almost inspiration which she showed in seizing the
poetical shading of words over which her more prosaic companions blundered, were matters of never-ending astonishment and admiration to Harry and myself. At the end of the
first week she announced to us gravely that she intended to
render Virgil into English verse; and we had not the smallest
doubt that she would do it, and were so immensely wrought
up about it that we talked of it after we went to bed that
night. Tina, in fact, had produced quite a clever translation
of the first ten lines of "Arma virumque," and we wondered
what Mr. Rossiter would say to it. One of us stepped in and
laid it on his writing-desk.

"Which of you boys did this?" he said the next morning, in not a disapproving tone.

There was a pause, and he slowly read the lines aloud.

"Pretty fair!" he said,—"pretty fair! I shouldn't be surprised if that boy should be able to write English one of these days."

"If you please, sir," said I, "it's Miss Tina Percival that wrote that."

Tina's cheeks were red enough as he handed her back her poetry.

"Not bad," he said,—"not bad; keep on as you've began, and you may come to something yet."

This scanty measure of approbation was interpreted as high praise, and we complimented Tina on her success. The project of making a poetical translation of Virgil, however, was not carried out, though every now and then she gave us little jets and spurts, which kept up our courage.

Bless me, how we did study everything in that school! English grammar, for instance. The whole school was divided into a certain number of classes, each under a leader, and at the close of every term came on a great examination, which was like a tournament and passage at arms in matters of the English language. To beat in this great contest of knowledge was what held all our energies waiting. Mr. Rossiter searched out the most difficult specimens of English literature for us to parse, and we were given to understand that he was laying up all the most abstruse problems of grammar to propound to us. All that might be raked out from the coarse print and the fine print of grammar was to be brought to bear on us; and the division that knew the most,—the division that could not be puzzled by any subtlety, that had anticipated every possible question, and was prepared with an answer,—would be the victorious division and would be crowned with laurels as glorious in our eyes as those of the old Olympic games. For a week we talked, spoke, and dreamed of nothing but English grammar. Each division sat in solemn, mysterious conclave, afraid lest one of its mighty secrets of wisdom should possibly take wing and be plundered by some of the outlying scouts of another division.

We had for a subject Satan's address to the sun, in Milton, which in our private conclaves we tore limb from limb with as little remorse as the anatomist dissects a once lovely human body.

The town doctor was a noted linguist and grammarian, and his son was contended for by all the divisions, as supposed to have access to the fountain of his father's wisdom on these subjects; and we were so happy in the balloting as to secure him for our side. Esther was our leader, and we were all in the same division, and our excitement was indescribable. We had also to manage a quotation from Otway, which I remember contained the clause, "Were the world on fire." To parse "on fire" was a problem which kept the eyes of the whole school waking. Each division had its theory, of which it spoke mysteriously in the presence of outsiders; but we had George Norton, and George had been in solemn conclave with Dr. Norton. Never shall I forget the excitement as he came rushing up to our house at nine o'clock at night with the last results of his father's analysis. We shut the doors and shut the windows,—for who knew what of the enemy might be listening?—and gathered breathlessly around him, while, in a low, mysterious voice he unfolded to us how to parse "on fire." At that moment George Norton enjoyed the full pleasure of being a distinguished individual, if he never did before or after.

Mr. Rossiter all this while was like the Egyptian Sphinx, perfectly unfathomable, and severely resolved to sift and test us to the utmost.

Ah,' well! to think of the glories of the day when our division beat!—for we did beat. We ran along neck and neck with Ben Baldwin's division, for Ben was an accomplished grammarian, and had picked up one or two recondite pieces of information wherewith he threatened for a time to turn our flank, but the fortunes of the field turned when it came to the phrase "on fire," when our success was complete and glorious. It was well to have this conflict over, for I don't believe that Tina slept one night that week without dreams of particles and prepositions, Tina, who was as full of the enthusiasm of everything that was going on as a flossy evening cloud is of light, and to whose health I really do believe a defeat might have caused a serious injury.

Never shall I forget Esther, radiant, grave, and resolved, as she sat in the midst of her division through all the fluctuations of the contest. A little bright spot had come in each of her usually pale cheeks, and her eyes glowed with a fervour which showed that she had it in her to have defended a fortress, or served a cannon, like the Maid of Saragossa. We could not have felt more if our division had been our country, and she had led us in triumph through a battle.

Besides grammar, we gave great attention to rhetoric. We studied Dr. Blair with the same kind of thoroughness with which we studied the English grammar. Every week a division of the school was appointed to write compositions; but there was, besides, a call for volunteers, and Mr. Rossiter had a smile of approbation for those who volunteered to write every week; and so we were always among that number.

It was remarkable, that the very best writers, as a general thing, were among the female part of the school. There were several young men, of nineteen and twenty years of age, whose education had been retarded by the necessity of earning for themselves the money which was to support them while preparing for college. They were not boys, they were men, and, generally speaking, men of fine minds and fine characters. Some of them have since risen to distinction, and acted leading parts at Washington. But, for all that, the best writers of the school, as I have before said, were the girls. Nor was the standard of writing low: Mr. Rossiter had the most withering scorn for ordinary sentimental nonsense and school-girl platitudes. If a bit of weakly poetry got running among the scholars, he was sure to come down upon it with such an absurd parody that nobody could ever recall it again without a laugh.

We wrote on such subjects as "The Difference between the Natural and Moral Sublime," "The Comparative Merits of Milton and Shakespeare," "The Comparative Merits of the Athenian and Lacedæmonian Systems of Education." Sometimes, also, we wrote criticisms. If, perchance, the master picked up some verbose Fourth of July oration, or some sophomorical newspaper declamation, he delivered it over to our tender mercies with as little remorse as a huntsman feels in throwing a dead fox to the dogs. Hard was the fate of any such composition thrown out to us. With what infinite zeal we attacked it! how we riddled and shook it! how we scoffed, and sneered, and jeered at it; how we exposed its limping metaphors, and hung up in triumph its deficient grammar! Such a sharp set of critics we became, that our compositions read to each other, went through something of an ordeal.

Tina, Harry, Esther, and I, were a private composition

club. Many an hour have we sat in the old school-room long after all the other scholars had gone, talking to one another of our literary schemes and plans. We planned poems and tragedies; we planned romances that would have taken many volumes to write out; we planned arguments and discussions; we gravely criticised each other's style, and read morsels of projected compositions to one another.

It was characteristic of the simple, earnest fearlessness of those times in regard to all matters of opinion, that the hardest theological problems were sometimes given out as composition subjects, and we four children not unfrequently sat perched on the old high benches of the school-room during the fading twilight hours, and like Milton's fallen angels,—

> " Reasoned high
> Of providence, foreknowledge, will, and fate;
> Fixed fate, free will, foreknowledge absolute, . . .
> Of happiness and final misery."

Esther, Harry, and I, were reading the "Prometheus Bound" with Mr. Rossiter. It was one of his literary diversions, into which he carried us; and the Calvinism of the old Greek tragedian, mingling with the Calvinism of the pulpit and of modern New England life, formed a curious admixture in our thoughts.

Tina insisted on reading this with us, just as of old she insisted on being carried in lady-chair over to our woodland study in the island. She had begun Greek with great zeal under Mr. Rossiter, but of course was in no situation to venture upon any such heights; but she insisted upon always being with us when we were digging out our lesson, and in fact, when we were talking over doubtfully the meaning of a passage, would irradiate it with such a flood of happy conjecture as ought to have softened the stern facts of moods and tenses, and *made* itself the meaning. She rendered some parts of it into verse much better than any of us could have done it, and her versifications, laid on Mr. Rossiter's desk, called out a commendation that was no small triumph to her.

"My *forté* lies in picking knowledge out of other folks and using it," said Tina, joyously. "Out of the least bit of ore that you dig up, I can make no end of gold-leaf!" O Tina, Tina, you never spoke a truer word, and while you were with us you made everything glitter with your "no end of gold-leaf."

It may seem to some impossible that, at so early an age as ours, our minds should have striven with subjects such as have been indicated here; but let it be remembered that these problems are to every human individual a part of an unknown tragedy in which he is to play the rôle either of the conqueror or the victim. A ritualistic Church, which places all souls under the guardianship of a priesthood, of course shuts all these doors of discussion so far as the individual is concerned. "The Church" is a great ship, where you have only to buy your ticket and pay for it, and the rest is none of your concern. But the New England system, as taught at this time, put on every human being the necessity of crossing the shoreless ocean alone on his own raft; and many a New England child of ten or twelve years of age, or even younger, has trembled at the possibilities of final election or reprobation.

I remember well that at one time the composition subject given out at school was, "Can the Benevolence of the Deity be Proved by the Light of Nature?" Mr. Rossiter generally gave out the subject, and discussed it with the school in an animated conversation, stirring up all the thinking matter that there was among us by vigorous questions, and by arguing before us first on one side and then on the other, until our minds were strongly excited about it; and when he had wrought up the whole school to an intense interest, he called for volunteers to write on either side. Many of these compositions were full of vigour and thought; two of those on the above-mentioned subject were very striking. Harry took the affirmative ground, and gave a statement of the argument, so lucid, and in language so beautiful, that it has remained fixed in my mind like a gem ever since. It was the statement of a nature harmonious and confiding, naturally prone to faith in goodness, harmonising and presenting all those evidences of tenderness, mercy, and thoughtful care which are furnished in the workings of natural laws. The other composition was by Esther; it was on the other and darker side of the subject, and as perfect a match for it as the "Penseroso" to the "Allegro." It was condensed and logical, fearfully vigorous in conception and expression, and altogether a very melancholy piece of literature to have been conceived and written by a girl of her age. It spoke of that fearful law of existence by which the sins of parents who often themselves escape punishment are visited on the heads of innocent children, as a law which seems made specifically to protect and continue the existence of vice and disorder from generation to generation. It spoke of the apparent injustice of an arrangement by which human beings, in the very outset of their career in life, often inherit almost uncontrollable propensities to evil. The sorrows, the perplexities, the unregarded wants and aspirations, over which the unsympathetic laws of nature cut their way regardless of quivering nerve or muscle, were all bitterly dwelt upon. The sufferings of dumb animals, and of helpless infant children, apparently so useless and so needless, and certainly so undeserved, were also energetically mentioned. There was a bitter intensity in the style that was most painful. In short, the two compositions were two perfect pictures of the world and life as they appear to two classes of minds. I remember looking at Esther while her composition was reading, and being struck with the expression of her face,—so pale, so calm, so almost hopeless,—its expression was very like despair. I remember that Harry noticed it as well as I, and when school was over he took a long and lonely ramble with her, and from that time a nearer intimacy arose between them.

Esther was one of those intense, silent, repressed women that have been a frequent outgrowth of New England society. Moral traits, like physical ones, often intensify themselves in course of descent, so that the child of a long line of pious ancestry may sometimes suffer from too fine a moral fibre, and become a victim to a species of morbid *spiritual ideality*.

Esther looked to me, from the first, less like a warm, breathing, impulsive woman, less like ordinary flesh and blood, than some half-spiritual organisation, every particle of which was a thought.

Old Dr. Donne says of such a woman, "One might almost say her body thought:" and it often came in my mind when I watched the movements of intense yet repressed intellect and emotion in Esther's face.

With many New England women at this particular period, when life was so retired and so cut off from outward sources of excitement, *thinking* grew to be a disease. The great subject of thought was, of course, theology; and woman's nature has never been consulted in theology. Theologic systems, as to the expression of their great body of ideas, have as yet been the work of man alone. They have had their origin, as in St. Augustine, with men who were utterly ignorant of moral and intellectual companionship with woman, looking on her only in her animal nature as a temptation and a snare. Consequently, when, as in this period of New England, the theology of Augustine began to be freely discussed by every

individual in society, it was the women who found it hardest
to tolerate or to assimilate it, and many a delicate and sensitive nature was utterly wrecked in the struggle.

Plato says somewhere that the only perfect human thinker
and philosopher who will ever arise will be the MAN-WOMAN,
or a human being who unites perfectly the nature of the two
sexes. It was Esther's misfortune to have, to a certain degree,
this very conformation. From a long line of reasoning, thinking, intellectual ancestry she had inherited all the strong
logical faculties, and the tastes and inclinations for purely
intellectual modes of viewing things, which are supposed to
be more particularly the characteristic of man. From a line
of saintly and tender women, half refined to angel in their
nature, she had inherited exquisite moral perceptions, and
all that flattering host of tremulous, half-spiritual, half-
sensuous intuitions that lie in the border-land between the
pure intellect and the animal nature. The consequence of
all this was the internal strife of a divided nature. Her heart
was always rebelling against the conclusions of her head.
She was constantly being forced by one half of her nature to
movements, inquiries, and reasonings which brought only
torture to the other half.

Esther had no capacity for illusions; and in this respect
her constitution was an unfortunate one.

Tina, for example, was one of those happily organised
human beings in whom an intellectual proposition, fully as-
sented to, might lie all her life dormant as the wheat-seed
which remained thousands of years ungerminate in the wrap-
pings of a mummy. She thought only of what she liked to
think of; and a disagreeable or painful truth in her mind
dropped at once out of sight,—it sank into the ground and
roses grew over it.

Esther never could have made one of those clinging, submissive, parasitical wives who form the delight of song and story, and are supposed to be the peculiar gems of womanhood. It was her nature always to be obliged to see her friends clearly through the understanding, and to judge them by a refined and exquisite conscientiousness. A spot or stain on the honour of the most beloved could never have become invisible to her. She had none of that soft, blinding, social aura,—that blending, blue haze, such as softens the sharp outlines of an Italian landscape, and in life changes the hardness of reality into illusive and charming possibilities. Her clear, piercing hazel eyes seemed to pass over everything with a determination to know only and exactly the truth, hard and cold and unwelcome though it might be.

Yet there is no doubt that the warm, sunny, showery, rainbow nature of Tina acted as a constant and favourable alterative upon her. It was a daily living poem acting on the unused poetical and imaginative part of her own nature; for Esther had a suppressed vigour of imagination, and a passionate capability of emotion, stronger and more intense than that of Tina herself.

I remarked this to Harry, as we were talking about them one day. "Both have poetical natures," I said; "both are intense; but how different they are!"

"Yes," said Harry, "Tina's is electricity, and that snaps and sparkles and flashes; Esther is galvanism, that comes in long, intense waves, and shakes and convulses; she both thinks and feels too much on all subjects."

"That was a very strange composition," I said.

"It is an unwholesome course of thought," said Harry, after thinking for a few moments, with his head on his hands; "none but bitter berries grow on those bushes."

"But the reasoning was very striking," said I.

"Reasoning!" said Harry, impatiently; "we must trust

the intuition of our hearts above reason. That is what I am trying to persuade Esther to do. To me it is an absolute demonstration that God never could make a creature who would be *better* than Himself. We must look at the noblest, best human beings. We must see what generosity, what tenderness, what magnanimity can be in man and woman, and believe all that and more in God. All that there is in the best fathers and best mothers *must* be in Him."

"But the world's history does not look like this, as Mr. Rossiter was saying."

"We have not seen the world's history yet," said Harry. "What does this green aphide, crawling over this leaf, know of the universe?"

CHAPTER X.

Our Minister in Cloudland.

THE picture of our life in Cloudland, and of the developing forces which were there brought to bear upon us, would be incomplete without the portrait of the minister.

Even during the course of my youth, the principles of democratic equality introduced and maintained in the American Revolution were greatly changing the social position and standing of the clergy. Ministers like Dr. Lothrop, noble men of the theocracy, men of the cocked hat, were beginning to pass away, or to appear among men only as venerable antiquities, and the present order of American citizen clergy was coming in.

Mr. Avery was a cheerful, busy, manly man, who posed himself among men as a companion and fellow-citizen, whose word on any subject was to go only so far as its own weight and momentum should carry it. His preaching was a striking contrast to the elegant Addisonian essays of Parson

Lothrop. It was a vehement address to our intelligent and reasoning powers—an address made telling by a back force of burning enthusiasm. Mr. Avery preached a vigorous system of mental philosophy in theology, which made our Sundays, on the whole, about as intense an intellectual drill as any of our week-days. If I could describe its character by any one word, I should call it *manly* preaching.

Every person has a key-note to his mind which determines all its various harmonies. The key-note of Mr. Avery's mind was "the free agency of man." Free agency was with him the universal solvent, the philosopher's stone in theology; every line of his sermons said to every human being, "You are free, and you are able." And the great object was to intensify to its highest point, in every human being, the sense of individual, personal responsibility.

Of course, as a Calvinist, he found food for abundant discourse in reconciling this absolute freedom of man with those declarations in the standards of the Church, which assert the absolute government of God over all His creatures and all their actions. But the cheerfulness and vigour with which he drove and interpreted and hammered in the most contradictory statements, when they came in the way of his favourite ideas, was really quite inspiring.

During the year we had a whole course of systematic theology, beginning with the history of the introduction of moral evil, the fall of the angels, and the consequent fall of man, and the work of redemption resulting therefrom. In the treatment of all these subjects, the theology and imagery of Milton figured so largely that one might receive the impression that Paradise Lost was part of the sacred canon. '

Mr. Avery not only preached these things in the pulpit, but talked them out in his daily life. His system of theology was to him the vital breath of his being. His mind was always running upon it, and all nature was, in his sight, giving daily tributary illustrations to it. In his farming, gardening, hunting, or fishing, he was constantly finding new and graphic forms of presenting his favourite truths. The most abstract subject ceased to be abstract in his treatment of it, but became clothed upon with the homely, every-day similes of common life.

I have the image of the dear good man now, as I have seen him, seated on a hay-cart, mending a hoe-handle, and at the same moment vehemently explaining to an inquiring brother minister the exact way that Satan first came to fall, as illustrating how a perfectly holy mind can be tempted to sin. The familiarity that he showed with the celestial arcana —the zeal with which he vindicated his Maker—the perfect knowledge that he seemed to have of the strategic plans of the evil powers in the first great insurrection—are traits strongly impressed on my memory. They seemed as vivid and as much a matter of course to his mind as if be had read them out of a weekly newspaper.

Mr. Avery indulged the fond supposition that he had solved the great problem of the origin of evil in a perfectly satisfactory manner. He was fond of the Socratic method, and would clench his reasoning in a series of questions, thus—

"Has not God power to make any kind of thing He pleases?"

"Yes."

"Then He can make a kind of being incapable of being governed except by motive?"

"Yes."

"Then, when He has made that kind of being, He cannot govern them except by motive, can He?"

"No."

"Now, if there is no motive in existence strong enough to govern them by, He cannot keep them from falling, can He?"

"No."

"You see, then, the necessity of moral evil: there must be experience of evil to work out motive."

The Calvinism of Mr. Avery, though sharp and well defined, was not dull, as abstractions often are, nor gloomy and fateful like that of Dr. Sterne. It was permeated through and through by cheerfulness and hope.

Mr. Avery was one of the kind of men who have a passion for saving souls. If there is such a thing as apostolic succession, this passion is what it ought to consist in. It is what ought to come with the laying on of hands, if the laying on of hands is what it is sometimes claimed to be.

Mr. Avery was a firm believer in hell, but he believed also that nobody need go there, and he was determined, so far as he was concerned, that nobody should go there if he could help it. Such a tragedy as the loss of any one soul in his parish he could not and would not contemplate for a moment; and he had such a firm belief in the truths he preached, that he verily expected with them to save anybody that would listen to him.

Goethe says, "Blessed is the man who believes that he has an idea by which he may help his fellow-creatures." Mr. Avery was exactly that man. He had such faith in what he preached that he would have gone with it to Satan himself, could he have secured a dispassionate and unemployed hour, with a hope of bringing him round.

Generous and ardent in his social sympathies, Mr. Avery never could be brought to believe that any particular human being had finally perished. At every funeral he attended he contrived to see a ground for hope that the departed had found mercy. Even the slightest hints of repentance were magnified in his warm and hopeful mode of presentation. He has been known to suggest to a distracted mother, whose thoughtless boy had been suddenly killed by a fall from a horse, the possibilities of the merciful old couplet:—

> "Between the saddle and the ground,
> Mercy was sought, and mercy found."

Like most of the New England ministers, Mr. Avery was a warm believer in the millennium. This millennium was the favourite recreation-ground, solace, and pasture-land, where the New England ministry fed their hopes and courage. Men of large hearts and warm benevolence, their theology would have filled them with gloom, were it not for this overplus of joy and peace to which human society on earth was in their view tending. Thousands of years, when the poor old earth should produce only a saintly race of perfected human beings, were to them some compensation for the darkness and losses of the great struggle.

Mr. Avery believed, not only that the millennium was coming, but that it was coming fast, and, in fact, was at the door. Every political and social change announced it. Our Revolution was a long step towards it, and the French Revolution, now in progress, was a part of that distress of nations which heralded it; and every month, when the *Columbia Magazine* brought in the news from Europe, Mr. Avery rushed over to Mr. Rossiter, and called him to come and hear how the thing was going.

Mr. Rossiter took upon himself that right which every freeborn Yankee holds sacred,—the right of contravening his minister. Though, if he caught one of his boys swelling or ruffling with any opposing doctrine, he would scath and scorch the youngster with contemptuous irony, and teach him to comport himself modestly in talking of his betters, yet it was the employment of a great many of his leisure hours to run argumentative tilts against Mr. Avery. Sometimes, when we were sitting in our little garret-window digging out the Greek lessons, such a war of voices and clangour of assertion and contradiction would come up from among the tassels of the corn, where the two were hoeing together in the garden, as would have alarmed people less accustomed to the vigorous manners of both the friends.

"Now, Rossiter, that will never do. Your system would upset moral government entirely. Not an angel could be kept in his place upon your supposition."

"It is not my supposition. I haven't got any supposition, and I don't want any; but I was telling you that, if you must have a theory of the universe, Origen's was a better one than yours."

"And I say that Origen's system would upset everything, and you ought to let it alone."

"I shan't let it alone!"

"Why, Rossiter, you will destroy responsibility, and annihilate all the motives of God's government."

"That's just what you theologians always say. You think the universe will go to pieces if we upset your pine-shingle theology."

"Rossiter, you must be careful how you spread your ideas."

"I don't want to spread my ideas; I don't want to interfere with your system. It's the best thing you can make your people take; but you ought to know that no system is anything more than human theory."

"It's eternal truth."

"There's truth in it, but it isn't eternal truth."

"It's Bible."

"Part, and part Milton and Edwards, and part Mr. Avery."

Harry and I were like adopted sons in both families, and the two expressed their minds about each other freely before us. Mr. Avery would say, "The root of the matter is in Rossiter. I don't doubt that he's a really regenerate man, but he has a head that works strangely. We must wait for him; he'll come along by and by."

And Mr. Rossiter would say of Mr. Avery, "That's a growing man, boys; he hasn't made his terminal buds yet. Some men make them quick, like lilac-bushes. They only grow a little way and stop. And some grow all the season through, like locust-trees. Avery is one of that sort; he'll never be done thinking and growing, particularly if he has me to fight him on all hands. He'll grow into different opinions on a good many subjects before he dies."

It was this implied liberty of growth—the liberty to think and to judge freely upon all subjects—that formed the great distinctive educational force of New England life, particularly in this period of my youth. Monarchy, aristocracy, and theocracy, with their peculiar trains of ideas, were passing away, and we were coming within the sweep of pure republican influences, in which the *individual* is *everything*. Mr. Avery's enthusiastic preaching of free agency and personal responsibility was more than an *individual impulse*. It was the voice of a man whose ideas were the reflection of a period in American history. While New England theology was made by loyal monarchists, it reflected monarchial ideas. The rights and immunities of divine sovereignty were its favourite topics. When, as now, the government was becoming settled in the hands of the common people, the freedom of the individual, his absolute power of choice, and the consequent reasonableness of the duties he owed to the Great Sovereign Authority, began to be the favourite subjects of the pulpit.

Mr. Avery's preaching was immensely popular. There were in Cloudland only about half a dozen families of any prestige as to ancestral standing or previous wealth and cultivation. The old aristocratic idea was represented only in the one street that went over Cloudland Hill, where was a series of wide, cool, roomy, elm-shadowed houses, set back in deep door-yards, and flanked with stately, well-tended gardens. The doctor, the lawyer, the sheriff of the county, the schoolmaster, and the minister, formed here a sort of nucleus; but outlying in all the hills and valleys round were the mountain and valley farmers. Their houses sat on high hills or sunk in deep valleys, and their flaming windows at morning and evening looked through the encircling belts of forest solitudes as if to say, "We are here, and we are a power." These hard-working farmers formed the body of Mr. Avery's congregation. Sunday morning, when the little bell pealed out its note of invitation loud and long over the forest-feathered hills, it seemed to evoke a caravan of thrifty, well-filled farm waggons, which, punctual as the village clock itself, came streaming from the east and west, the north and south. Past the parsonage they streamed, with the bright cheeks and fluttering ribbons of the girls, and the cheery, rubicund faces of children, and with the inevitable yellow dog of the family faithfully pattering in the rear. The audience that filled the rude old meeting-house every Sunday would have astonished the men who only rode through the village of a week-day. For this set of shrewd, toil-hardened, vigorous, full-blooded republicans I can think of no preaching more admirably adapted than Mr. Avery's. It was preaching that was on the move, as their minds were, and which was slowly shaping out and elaborating those new forms of doctrinal statement that inevitably grow out of new forms of society. Living, as these men did, a lonely, thoughtful, secluded life, without any of the thousand stimulants which railroads and magazines and newspaper literature cast into our existence, their two Sunday sermons were the great intellectual stimulus which kept their minds bright, and they were listened to with an intense interest, of which the scattered and diversified state of modern society gives few examples. They felt the compliment of being talked to as if they were capable of understanding the very highest of subjects, and they liked it. Each hard, heroic nature flashed like a flint at the grand thought of a free agency with which not even their Maker would interfere. Their God himself asked to reign over them, not by force, but by the free, voluntary choice of their own hearts. "*Choose* you this day whom ye will serve. If the Lord be God, serve him, and if Baal be God, serve him," was a grand appeal, fit for freemen.

The reasoning on moral government, on the history of man, —the theories of the universe, past, present, and to come,— opened to these men a grand Miltonic poem, in which their own otherwise commonplace lives shone with a solemn splendour. Without churches or cathedrals or physical accessories to quicken their poetic nature, their lives were redeemed only by this poetry of ideas.

Calvinism is much be-rated in our days; but let us look at the political, social, and materialistic progress of Calvinistic countries, and ask if the world is yet far enough along to dispense with it altogether? Look at Spain at this hour, and look back at New England at the time of which I write,—both having just finished a revolution, both feeling their way along the path of national independence,—and compare the Spanish peasantry with the yeomen of New England, such as made up Mr. Avery's congregation;—the one set made by reasoning, active-minded Calvinism, the other by pictures, statues, incense, architecture, and all the sentimental paraphernalia of ritualism.

If Spain had had not a single cathedral, if her Murillos had been all sunk in the sea, and if she had had, for a hundred years past, a set of schoolmasters and ministers working together as I have described Mr. Avery and Mr. Rossiter as working, would not Spain be infinitely better off for this life at least, whether there is any life to come or not? This is a point that I humbly present to the consideration of society.

Harry and I were often taken by Mr. Avery on his preaching tours to the distant farm parishes. There was a brown school-house in this valley, and a red school-house in that, and another on the hill, and so on for miles around, and Mr. Avery kept a constant stream of preaching going on in one or other of these every evening. We liked these expeditions with him, because they were often excursions amid the wildest and most romantic of the mountain scenery, and we liked them furthermore because Mr. Avery was a man that made himself, for the time being, companionable to every creature of human shape that was with him.

With boys he was a boy,—a boy in the vigour of his animal life, his keen delight in riding, hunting, fishing. With farmers he was a farmer. Brought up on a farm, familiar during all his early days with its wholesome toils, he still had a farmer's eye and a farmer's estimates, and the working-people felt him bone of their bone, and flesh of their flesh. It used to be a saying among them, that, when Mr. Avery hoed more than usual in his potato-field, the Sunday-sermon was sure to be better.

But the best sport of all was when some of Mr. Avery's preaching tours would lead up the course of a fine mountain trout-brook in the vicinity. Then sometimes Mr. Rossiter,

Mr. Avery, Harry, and I would put our supper in our pockets, and start with the sun an hour or two high, designing to bring up at the red school-house, as the weekly notice phrased it, at "early candle-lighting."

A person who should accidentally meet Mr. Avery on one of these tours, never having seen him before, might imagine him to be a man who had never thought or dreamed of anything but catching trout all his days, he went into it with such *abandon*. Eye, voice, hand, thought, feeling, all were concentrated on trout. He seemed to have the quick perception, the rapid hand, and the noiseless foot of an Indian, and the fish came to his hook as if drawn there by magic. So perfectly absorbed was he that we would be obliged to jog his memory, and, in fact, often to drag him away by main force, when the hour for the evening lecture arrived. Then our spoils would be hid away among the bushes, and with wet feet he would hurry in; but, once in, he was as completely absorbed in his work of saving sinners as he had before been in his temporal fishery. He argued, illustrated, stated, guarded, answered objections, looking the while from one hard, keen, shrewd face to another, to see if he was being understood. The phase of Calvinism shown in my grandmother's blue-book had naturally enough sowed through the minds of a thoughtful community hosts of doubts and queries. A great part of Mr. Avery's work was to remove these doubts by substituting more rational statements. It was essential that he should feel that he had made a hit somewhere, said something that answered a purpose in the minds of his hearers, and helped them at least a step or two on their way.

After services were over, I think of him and Mr. Rossiter cheerily arguing with and contradicting each other a little beyond us in the road, while Harry and I compared our own

notes behind. Arrived at the parsonage, there would be Tina
and Esther coming along the street to meet us. Tina full of
careless, open, gay enthusiasm, Esther with a shy and wistful
welcome, that said far less, and perhaps meant more. Then
our treasures were displayed and exulted over; the sup-
per-table was laid, and Mr. Avery, Mr. Rossiter, and we boys
applied ourselves to dressing our fish; and then Mr. Avery,
disdaining Dinah, and, in fact, all female supervision, presided himself over the frying-pan, and brought our woodland
captives on the table in a state worthy of a trout-brook. It
should have comforted the very soul of a trout taken in our
snares to think how much was made of him, and how perfectly Mr. Avery respected his dignity, and did him justice in
his cookery.

We two boys were in fact domesticated as sons in the
family. Although our boarding-place was with the master,
we were almost as much with the minister as if we had been
of his household. We worked in his garden, we came over
and sat with Esther and Tina. Our windows faced their
windows, so that in study hours we could call to one another
backward and forward, and tell where the lesson began, and
what the root of the verb was, or any other message that
came into our heads. Sometimes, of a still summer morning,
while we were gravely digging at our lessons, we would hear
Esther in tones of expostulation at some madcap impulse of
Tina, and looking across, would see her bursting out in some
freak of droll pantomimic performance, and then an immediate whirlwind of gaiety would seize us all. We would drop
our dictionaries and grammars, rush together, and have a
general outbreak of jollity.

In general, Tina was a most praiseworthy and zealous
student, and these wild, sudden whisks of gaiety seemed only
the escape-valves by which her suppressed spirits vented

themselves; but, when they came, they were perfectly irresistible. She devoted herself to Esther with that sympathetic adaptation which seemed to give her power over every nature. She was interested in her housekeeping, in all its departments, as if it had been her own glory and pride; and Tina was one that took glory and pride in everything of her friends, as if it had been her own. Esther had been left by the death of her mother only the year before the mistress of the parsonage. The great unspoken sorrow of this loss lay like a dark chasm between her and her father, each striving to hide from the other its depth and coldness by a brave cheerfulness.

Esther, strong as was her intellectual life, had that intense sense of the worth of a well-ordered household, and of the dignity of house-economics, which is characteristic of New England women. Her conscientiousness pervaded every nook and corner of her domestic duties with a beautiful perfection; nor did she ever feel tempted to think that her fine mental powers were a reason why these homely details should be considered a slavery. Household cares are a drudgery only when unpervaded by sentiment. When they are an offering of love, a ministry of care and devotion to the beloved, every detail has its interest.

There were certain grand festivals of a minister's family which fill a housekeeper's heart and hands, and in which all of us made common interest with her. The Association was a reunion when all the ministers of the county met together and spent a social day with the minister, dining together, and passing their time in brotherly converse, such as reading essays, comparing sermons, taking counsel with each other in all the varied ups and downs of their pastoral life. The Consociation was another meeting of the clergy, but embracing also with each minister a lay delegate, and thus uniting, not only the ministry, but the laymen of the county, in a general fraternal religious conference.

The first Association that Esther had to manage quite alone, as sole mistress of the parsonage, occurred while we were with her. Like most solemn festivals of New England, these seasons were announced under the domestic roof by great preparatory poundings and choppings, by manufacture, on a large scale, of cakes, pies, and provisions for the outer man; and at this time Harry, Tina, and I devoted all our energies, and made ourselves everywhere serviceable. We ran to the store on errands, we chopped mince for pies with a most virtuous pertinacity, we cut citron and stoned raisins, we helped put up curtains and set up bedsteads. We were all of us as resolved as Esther that the housekeeping of the little parsonage should be found without speck or flaw, and should reflect glory upon her youthful sovereignty.

Some power or other gilded and glorified these happy days,—for happy enough they were. What was it that made everything that we four did together so harmonious and so charming? "Friendship, only friendship," sang Tina, with silver tongue. "Such a *perfect* friendship," she remarked, "was *never* known except just in our particular case;" it exceeded all the classical records, all the annals, ancient and modern.

But what instinct or affinity in friendship made it a fact that when we four sat at table together, with our lessons before us, Harry somehow was always found on Esther's side? I used to notice it, because his golden-brown mat of curls was such a contrast to the smooth, shining black satin-bands of her hair as they bent together over the dictionary, and looked up innocently into each other's eyes, talking of verbs and adjectives and terminations, innocently conjugating "amo, amare" to each other. Was it friendship that made Esther's dark, clear eyes, instinctively look towards Harry for his opinion, when we were reading our compositions to one another? Was it friendship, that starry brightness that began to come in Harry's eyes, and made them seem darker and bluer and deeper, with a sort of mysterious meaning when he looked at Esther? Was it friendship that seemed to make him feel taller, stronger, more manly, when he thought of her, and that always placed him at her hand when there was some household task that required a manly height or handiness? It was Harry and Esther together who put up the white curtains all through the parsonage that spring, that made it look so trim and comely for the ministers' meeting. Last year, Esther said, innocently, she had no one to help her, and the work tired her so. How happy, how busy, how bright they were as they measured and altered, and Harry, in boundless complacency, went up and down at her orders, and changed and altered and arranged, till her fastidious eye was satisfied, and every fold hung aright! It was Harry who took down and cleansed the family portraits, and hung them again, and balanced them so nicely; it was Harry who papered over a room where the walls had been disfigured by an accident, and it was Esther by him who cut the paper and trimmed the bordering, and executed all her little sovereignties of taste and disposal by his obedient hands. And Tina and I at this time gathered green boughs and ground-pine for the vases, and made floral decorations without end, till the bare little parsonage looked like a woodland bower.

I have pleasant recollections of those ministers' meetings. Calvinistic doctrines, in their dry, abstract form, are, I confess, rather hard; but Calvinistic ministers, so far as I have ever had an opportunity to observe, are invariably a jolly set of fellows. In those early days the ministry had not yet felt the need of that generous decision which led them afterwards to forego all dangerous stimulants, as an example to their flock. A long green wooden case, full of tobacco-pipes and a quantity of papers of tobacco, used to be part of the hospitable stock prepared for the reception of the brethren. No less was there a quantity of spirituous liquor laid in. In those days its dispensation was regarded as one of the inevitable duties of hospitality. The New England ministry of this period were men full of interest. Each one was the intellectual centre of his own district, and supplied around him the stimulus which is now brought to bear through a thousand other sources. It was the minister who overlooked the school, who put parents upon the idea of giving their sons liberal educations. In poor districts the minister often practised medicine, and drew wills and deeds, thus supplying the place of both lawyer and doctor. Apart from their doctrinal theology, which was a constant source of intellectual activity to them, their secluded life led them to many forms of literary labour.

As a specimen of these, it is recorded of the Rev. Mr. Taylor of Westfield, that he took such delight in the writings of Origen, that, being unable to purchase them, he copied them in four quarto volumes, that he might have them for his own study. These are still in the possession of his descendants. Other instances of literary perseverance and devotion, equally curious, might be cited.

The lives that these men led were simple and tranquil. Almost all of them were practical farmers, preserving about them the fresh sympathies and interests of the soil, and labouring enough with their hands to keep their muscles in good order, and prevent indigestion. Mingling very little with the world, each one a sort of autocrat in his way, in his own district, and with an idea of stability and perpetuity in his office, which, in these days, does not belong to the position of a minister anywhere, these men developed many originalities and peculiarities of character, to which the simple state of society then allowed full scope. They were humorists,—like the mossy old apple-trees which each of them had in his orchard, bending this way and turning that, and throwing out their limbs with quaint twists and jerks, yet none the less acceptable, so long as the fruit they bore was sound and wholesome.

We have read of "Handkerchief Moody," who for some years persisted in always appearing among men with his face covered with a handkerchief,—an incident which Hawthorne has worked up in his weird manner into the story of "The Minister with the Black Veil."

Father Mills, of Torringford, was a gigantic man who used to appear in the pulpit in a full-bottomed white horse-hair wig. On the loss of a beloved wife, he laid aside his wig for a year, and appeared in the pulpit with his head tied up in a black handkerchief, representing to the good house-wives of his parish that, as he always dressed in black, he could in no other way testify to his respect for his dear wife's memory; and this tribute was accepted by his parish with the same innocent simplicity with which it was rendered.

On the whole, the days which brought all the brother ministers to the parsonage were days of enlivenment to all us young people. They seemed to have such a hearty joy in their meeting, and to deliver themselves up to mirth and good-fellowship with such a free and hearty *abandon*, and the jokes and stories which they brought with them were chorused by such roars of merriment, as made us think a ministers' meeting the most joyous thing on earth.

I know that some say this jocund mirthfulness indicated

a want of faith in the doctrines they taught. But do not you and I, honest friends, often profess our belief in things which it would take away our appetite and wither our strength to realise, but notwithstanding which we eat and drink and sleep joyously? You read in your morning paper that the city of so-and-so has been half submerged by an earthquake, and that after the earthquake came a fire and burnt the crushed inhabitants alive in the ruins of their dwellings. Nay, if you are an American, you may believe some such catastrophe to have happened on the Erie Railroad a day or two before, and that men, women, and children have been cooped up and burnt, in lingering agonies, in your own vicinity. And yet, though you believe these things, you laugh and talk and are gay, and plan for a party in the evening and a ride on the same road the next week.

No; man was mercifully made with the power of ignoring what he believes. It is all that makes existence in a life like this tolerable. And our ministers, conscious of doing the very best they can to keep the world straight, must be allowed their laugh and joke, sin and Satan to the contrary notwithstanding.

There was only one brother, in the whole confraternity, that used to meet at Mr. Avery's who was not a married man; and he, in spite of all the snares and temptations which must beset a minister who guides a female flock of parishioners, had come to the afternoon of life in the state of bachelorhood. But oh, the jokes and witticisms which always set the room in a roar at his expense! It was a subject that never wearied or grew old. To clap Brother Boardman on the back and inquire for Mrs. Boardman,—to joke him about some suitable widow, or bright-eyed young lamb of his flock, at each ministers' meeting,—was a provocative of mirth ever fresh and ever young. But the undaunted old bachelor was always a

match for these attacks, and had his rejoinder ready to fling
back into the camp of the married men. He was a model of
gallant devotion to womanhood in the abstract, and seemed
loath to give up to one what was meant for womankind. So,
the last that I ever heard of him, he was still unmarried,—
a most unheard-of thing for a New England parson.

Mr. Avery was a leader among the clergy of his State.
His zeal, enthusiasm, eloquence, and doctrinal vigour, added
to a capacity for forming an indefinite number of personal
friendships, made him a sort of chief among them.

What joyous hours they spent together in the ins and the
outs, the highways and by-ways, of metaphysics and theology! Harry and Esther and Tina and I learned them all. We
knew all about the Arminians and Pelagians and the Tasters
and the Exercisers, and made a deal of fun with each other
over it in our private hours. We knew precisely every shade
of difference between tweedle-dum and tweedle-dee which
the different metaphysicians had invented, and tossed our
knowledge joyously back and forward at one another in our
gayer hours, just as the old ministers did when they smoked
and argued in the great parsonage dining-room. Everything is joyful that is learned by two young men in company
with two young women with whom they are secretly in love.
Mathematics, metaphysics, or no matter what of dry and
desolate, buds and blossoms as the rose under such circumstances.

Did you ever go out in the misty gray of morning dawn,
when the stars had not yet shut their eyes, and still there
were rosy bands lying across the east? And then have you
watched a trellis of morning-glories, with all the buds asleep,
but ready in one hour to waken? The first kiss of sunlight,
and they will be open! That was just where we were.

CHAPTER XI.
The Revival of Religion.

No New England boy or girl comes to maturity without a full understanding of what is meant by the term at the head of this chapter.

Religion was, perhaps, never so much the governing idea in any commonwealth before. Nowhere has there been a people, the mass of whom acted more uniformly on considerations drawn from the unseen and future life; yet nowhere a people who paid a more earnest attention to the life that is seen and temporal.

The New England colonies were, in the first instance, the outgrowth of a religious enthusiasm. Right alongside of them, at the same period of time, other colonies were founded from a religious enthusiasm quite as intense and sincere. The French missionary settlers in Canada had a grandeur of self-sacrifice, an intensity of religious devotion, which would almost throw in the shade that of the Pilgrim Fathers; and the sole reason why one set of colonists proved the seed of a great nation, and the other attained so very limited success, is the difference between the religions taught by the two.

The one was the religion of asceticism, in view of which contempt of the body and of material good was taught as a virtue, and its teachers were men and women to whom marriage and its earthly relations were forbidden. The other was the spirit of the Old Testament, in which material prosperity is always spoken of as the lawful reward of piety, in which marriage is an honour, and a numerous posterity a thing to be desired. Our forefathers were, in many essential respects, Jews in their thoughts and feelings with regard to this life, but they superadded to this broad physical basis the intense spiritualism of the New Testament. Hence came a peculiar race of men, uniting the utmost extremes of the material and the spiritual.

Dr. Franklin represents that outgrowth of the New England mind which moves in the material alone, and scarcely ever rises to the spiritual. President Edwards represents the mind so risen to the spiritual as scarcely to touch the material. Put these two together, and you have the average New England character,—that land in which every *ism* of social or religious life has had its origin,—that land whose hills and valleys are one blaze and buzz of material and manufacturing production.

A revival of religion in New England meant a time when that deep spiritual undercurrent of thought and emotion with regard to the future life, which was always flowing quietly under its intense material industries, exhaled and steamed up into an atmosphere which pervaded all things, and made itself for a few weeks the only thought of every person in some town, or village, or city. It was the always-existing spiritual becoming visible and tangible.

Such periods would come in the labours of ministers like Mr. Avery. When a man of powerful mind, and shrewd tact, and great natural eloquence lives among a people already thoughtfully predisposed, for no other purpose than to stir them up to the care of their souls, it is evident that there will come times when the results of all his care and seeking, his public ministrations, his private conversations with individuals, will come out in some marked social form; and such a period in New England is called a revival of religion.

There were three or four weeks in the autumn of the first year that we spent in Cloudland, in which there was pervading the town a sort of subdued hush of emotions,—a quiet sense of something like a spiritual presence brooding through the mild autumn air. This was accompanied by a general inclination to attend religious services, and to converse on religious subjects. It pervaded the school; it was to be heard at the store. Every kind of individual talked on and about religion in his own characteristic way, and in a small mountain town like Cloudland everybody's characteristic way is known to every one else.

Ezekiel Scranton, the atheist of the parish, haunted the store where the farmers tied up their waggons when they brought their produce, and held, after his way, excited theological arguments with Deacon Phineas Simons, who kept the store,—arguments to which the academy boys sometimes listened, and of which they brought astounding reports to the school-room.

Tina, who was so intensely sympathetic with all social influences that she scarcely seemed to have an individuality of her own, was now glowing like a luminous cloud with religious zeal.

"I could convert that man," she said; "I know I could! I wonder Mr. Avery hasn't converted him long ago!"

At this time Mr. Avery, who had always kept a watchful eye upon us, had a special conversation with Harry and myself, the object of which was to place us right in our great foundation relations. Mr. Avery stood upon the basis that most good New England men, since Jonathan Edwards, have adopted, and regarded all young people, as a matter of course, out of the fold of the Church, and devoid of anything truly acceptable to God, until they had passed through a mental process designated, in well-known language, as conviction and conversion.

He began to address Harry, therefore, upon this supposition. I well remember the conversation.

"My son," he said, "is it not time for you to think seriously of giving your heart to God?"

"I have given my heart to God," replied Harry, calmly.

"Indeed!" said Mr. Avery, with surprise; "when did that take place?"

"I have always done it."

Mr. Avery looked at him with a gentle surprise.

"Do you mean to say, my son, that you have always loved God?"

"Yes, sir," said Harry, quietly.

Mr. Avery felt entirely incredulous, and supposed that this must be one of those specious forms of natural piety spoken of depreciatingly by Jonathan Edwards, who relates in his own memoirs similar exercises of early devotion as the mere fruits of the ungrafted natural heart. Mr. Avery, therefore, proceeded to put many theological questions to Harry on the nature of sin and holiness, on the difference between manly, natural affections, and emotions, and those excited by the supernatural movement of a divine power on the soul,—the good man begging him to remember the danger of self-deception, saying that nothing was more common than for young people to mistake the transient movements of mere natural emotions for real religion.

I observed that Harry, after a few moments, became violently agitated. Two large blue veins upon his forehead swelled out, his eyes had that peculiar flash and fire that they had at rare intervals, when some thought penetrated through the usual gentle quietude of his surface life to its deepest internal recesses. He rose and walked up and down the room, and finally spoke in a thick, husky voice, as one who pants with emotion. He was one of the most reserved human beings I have ever known. There was a region of emotion deep within him, which it was almost like death to him to express. There is something piteous and even fearful in the convulsions by which such natures disclose what is nearest to their hearts.

"Mr. Avery," he said, "I have heard your preaching ever since I have been here, and thought of it all. It has done me good, because it has made me think deeply. It is right and proper that our minds should be forced to think on all these subjects; but I have not thought, and cannot think, exactly like you, nor exactly like any one that I know of. I must make up my opinions for myself. I suppose I am peculiar, but I have been brought up peculiarly. My lot in life has been very different from that of ordinary boys. The first ten years of my life, all that I can remember is the constant fear and pain and distress and mortification and want through which my mother and I passed together—she a stranger in this strange land—her husband and my father worse than nothing to us, oftentimes our greatest terror. We should both of us have died, if it had not been for one thing: she believed that her Saviour loved her, and loved us all. She told me that these sorrows were from Him—that He permitted them because He loved us—that they would be for good in the end. She died at last alone and utterly forsaken by everybody but her Saviour, and yet her death was blessed. I saw it in her eyes, and she left it as her last message to me, whatever happened to me, *never to doubt God's love*—in all my life to trust Him, to seek His counsel in all things, and to believe that all that happened to me was ordered by Him. This was and is my religion; and, after all that I have heard, I can have no other. I do love God because He is good, and because He has been good to me. I believe that Jesus Christ is God, and I worship God always through Him, and I leave everything for myself, for life and death are in His hands. I know that I am not very good. I know, as you say, I am liable to make mistakes, and to deceive myself in a thousand ways; but *He* knows all things, and He can and will teach me; He will not let me lose myself, I feel sure."

"My son," said Mr. Avery, "you are blessed. I thank God with all my heart for you. Go on, and God be with you!"

It is to be seen that Mr. Avery was a man who always corrected theory by common-sense. When he perceived that a child could be trained up a Christian, and grow into the love of a heavenly Father as he grows into the love of an earthly one, by a daily and hourly experience of goodness, he yielded to the perceptions of his mind in that particular case.

Of course our little circle of four had, at this time, deep communings. Tina was buoyant and joyous, full of poetic images, delighted with the news of every conversion, and taking such an interest in Mr. Avery's preaching that she several times suggested to him capital subjects for sermons. She walked up to Ezekiel Scranton's, one afternoon, for no other object than to convert him from his atheism, and succeeded so far as to exact a promise from him that he would attend all Mr. Avery's meetings for a fortnight. Ezekiel was one of the converts of that revival, and Harry and I, of course, ascribed it largely to Tina's influence.

A rough old New England farmer, living on the windy side of a high hill, subsisting largely on codfish and hard cider, does not often win the flattering attention of any little specimen of humanity like Tina; and therefore it was not to be wondered at that the results of her missionary zeal appeared to his mind something like that recorded in the New Testament, where "an angel went down at a certain season, and troubled the waters."

But while Tina was thus buoyant and joyous, Esther seemed to sink into the very depths of despondency. Hers, as I have already intimated, was one of those delicate and sensitive natures, on which the moral excitements of New England acted all the while with too much power. The work and care of a faithful pastor are always complicated by the fact that those truths, and modes of presenting truths, which are only just sufficient to arouse the attention of certain classes of hearers, and to prevent their sinking into apathetic materialism, are altogether too stimulating and exciting for others of a more delicate structure.

Esther Avery was one of those persons for whom the peculiar theory of religious training which prevailed in New England at this period, however invigorating to the intellect of the masses, might be considered as a personal misfortune. Had she been educated in the tender and paternal manner recommended by the Cambridge Platform, and practised among the earlier Puritans, recognised from infancy as a member of Christ's Church, and in tender covenant relations with Him, her whole being would have responded to such an appeal; her strongest leading faculties would have engaged her to fulfil, in the most perfect manner, the sacred duties growing out of that relation, and her course into the full communion of the Church would have been gentle and insensible as a flowing river.

"'Tis a tyranny," says old Dr. Cotton Mather, "to impose upon every man a record of the precise time and way of their conversion to God. Few that have been restrained by a religious education can give such an one."

Esther, however, had been trained to expect a marked and decided period of conversion,—a change that could be described in the same language in which Paul described the conversion of the heathen at dissolute Corinth and Ephesus.

She was told, as early as she was capable of understanding language, that she was by nature in a state of alienation from God, in which every thought of her heart and action of her life was evil, and evil only; and continually that she was entirely destitute of holiness, and exposed momently to the wrath of God; and that it was her immediate duty to escape from this state by an act of penitence for sin and supreme love to God.

The effort to bring about in her heart that state of emotion was during all her youth a failure. She was by constitution delicately, intensely self-analytic, and her analysis was guided by the most exacting moral ideality. Every hopeful emotion of her higher nature, as it rose, was dissolved in this keen analysis, as diamond and pearls disappeared in the smelting furnaces of the old alchemists. We all know that self-scrutiny is the death of emotion, and that the analytic, self-inspective habit is its sure preventive. Had Esther applied to her feelings for her own beloved father the same tests by which she tried every rising emotion of love to the Divine Being, the result would have been precisely the same.

Esther was now nineteen years of age; she was the idol of her father's heart; she was the staff and stay of her family; she was, in all the duties of life, inspired by a most faultless conscientiousness. Her love of the absolute right was almost painful in its excess of minuteness, and yet, in her own view, in the view of the Church, in the view even of her admiring and loving father, she was no Christian. Perfectly faultless in every relation so far as human beings could observe, reverent to God, submissive to His will, careful in all outward religious observances, yet wanting in a certain emotional experience, she judged herself to be, and was judged to be by the theology which her father taught, utterly devoid of virtue or moral excellence of any kind in the sight of God. The theology of the times also taught her that the act of grace which should put an end to this state, and place her in the relation of a forgiven child with her Heavenly Father, was a voluntary one, momently in her power, and that nothing but her own persistent refusal prevented her performing it; yet taught at the same time that, so desperate was the obstinacy of the human heart, no child of Adam ever would, or ever could, perform it without a special interposition of God,—an interposition which might or might not come. Thus all the responsibility and the guilt rested upon her. Now, when a nature intensely conscientious is constantly oppressed by a sense of unperformed duty, that sense becomes a gnawing worm at the very root of life. Esther had in vain striven to bring herself into the required state of emotion. Often for weeks and months she offered daily, and many times a day, prayers which brought no brightness and no relief, and read conscientiously that Bible, all whose tender words and comforting promises were like the distant vision of Eden to the fallen exiles, guarded by a flaming sword which turned every way. Mute and mournful she looked into the paradise of peace, possessed by the favoured ones whom God had chosen to help through the mysterious passage, and asked herself, would that helping hand ever open the gate to her?

Esther had passed through two or three periods of revival of religion, and seen others far less consistent gathered into the fold of the Church, while she only sunk at each period into a state of hopeless gloom and despondency which threatened her health. Latterly her mind, wounded and bruised, had begun to turn in bitter reactions. From such experiences as hers come floods of distracting intellectual questions. Scepticism and doubt are the direct children of unhappiness. If she had been, as her standards stated, born "utterly indisposed, disabled, and made opposite to all good,

and wholly inclined to all evil," was not this an excuse for
sin? Was it *her* fault that she was born so? and, if her
Creator had brought her into being in this state, was it not
an act of simple justice to restore her mind to a normal condition?

When she addressed these questions to her father, he was
alarmed, and warned her against speculation. Mr. Avery did
not consider that the Assembly's Catechism and the Cambridge Platform and a great part of his own preaching were,
after all, but human speculation,—the uninspired *inferences*
of men from the Bible, and not the Bible itself,—and that
minds once set going in this direction often cannot help a
third question after a second, any more than they can help
breathing; and that third question may be one for which
neither God nor nature has an answer. Such inquiries as
Esther's never arose from reading the parables of Christ, the
Sermon on the Mount: they are the legitimate children of
mere human attempts at systematic theology.

How to deliver a soul that has come from excessive harass-
ments, introspections, self-analysis, into that morbid state of
half-sceptical despondency, was a problem over which Mr.
Avery sighed in vain. His cheerful hopefulness, his sympathetic vitality, had drawn many others through darkness
into light, and settled them in cheerful hope. But with his
own daughter he felt no power,—his heart trembled,—his
hand was weak as the surgeon's who cannot operate when it
is the life of his best beloved that lies under his hands.

Esther's deliverance came through that greatest and holiest
of all the natural sacraments and means of grace,—Love.

An ancient gem has upon it a figure of a Psyche sitting
with bound wings, and blindfolded and weeping, whose bonds
are being sundered by Love. It is an emblem of what often
occurs in woman's life.

It has sometimes been thrown out as a sneer on periods of religious excitement, that they kindle the enthusiasm of man and woman towards each other into earthly attachments; but the sneer should wither as something satanic before the purity of love as it comes to noble natures. The man who has learned to think meanly of *that*, to associate it with vulgar thoughts and low desires,—the man who has not been lifted by love to aspire after unworldly excellence, to sigh for unworldly purity, to reverence unworldly good,—has lost his one great chance of regeneration.

Harry and Esther had moved side by side for months, drawn daily to each other,—showing each other their compositions, studying out of the same book, arguing together in constant friendly differences,—and yet neither of them exactly conscious whither they were tending. A great social, religious excitement has often this result, that it throws open between friends the doors of the inner nature. How long, how long we may live in the same house, sit at the same table, hold daily converse with friends to whom and by whom these inner doors are closed! We cannot even tell whether we should love them more or less if they were open,—they are a mystery. But a great, pure, pervading, social excitement breaks like some early spring day around us; the sun shines, the birds sing; and forthwith open fly all the doors and windows, and let in the sunshine, and the breeze, and the bird-song!

In such an hour Esther saw that she was beloved!—beloved by a poet soul,—one of that rare order to whom the love of woman is a religion!—a baptism!—a consecration!

Her life, hitherto so chill and colourless, so imprisoned and bound in the chains of mere and cold intellect, awoke with a sudden thrill of consciousness to a new and passionate life. She was as changed as the poor and silent Jungfrau of the Swiss mountains, when the gray and ghostly cold of the night bursts into rosy light, as the morning sunbeams rise upon it. The most auspicious and beautiful of all phenomena that ever diversify this weary life is that wonderful moment in which two souls, who hitherto have not known each other, suddenly, by the lifting of a veil or the falling of a barrier, become in one moment and for ever after one.   Henceforth each soul has in itself the double riches of the other.   Each weakness is made strong by some corresponding strength in the other; for the truest union is where each soul has precisely the faculty which the other needs.

Harry was by nature and habit exactly the reverse of Esther. His conclusions were all intuitions.   His religion was an emanation from the heart, a child of personal experience, and not a formula of the head.   In him was seen the beginning of that great *reaction* which took place largely in the young mind of New England against the tyranny of mere logical methods as applied to the ascertaining of moral truths.

The hour of full heart union that made them one placed her mind under the control of his.   His simple faith in God's love was an antidote to her despondent fears.   His mind bore hers along on its current.   His imagination awakened hers.   She was like one carried away by a winged spirit, lifted up and borne heavenward by his faith and love.   She was a transfigured being.   An atmosphere of joy brightened and breathed around her; her eyes had a mysterious depth, her cheeks a fluttering colour.   The winter was over and past for her, and the time of the singing of birds had come.

Mr. Avery was in raptures. The long agony was past. He had gained a daughter and a son, and he was too joyful, too willing to believe, to be analytic or critical.   Long had he secretly hoped that such faultless consistency, such strict attention to duty, might perhaps indicate a secret work of divine grace, which would spring into joy if only recognised and believed in. But now, when the dove that had long wandered actually bent her white wings at the window of the ark, he stretched forth his hand and drew her in with a trembling eagerness.

CHAPTER XII.

After the Revival.

But the revival could not always last. The briefness of these periods, and the inevitable gravitation of everybody back to the things of earth, has sometimes been mentioned with a sneer.

"Where's your revival now?"

The deacon whose face was so radiant as he talked of the love of Christ, now sits with the same face drawn into knots and puckers over his account-book; and he thinks the money for the mortgage is due, and the avails for the little country store are small; and somehow a great family of boys and girls eat up and wear out; and the love of Christ seems a great way off, and the trouble about the mortgage very close at hand; and so the deacon is cross, and the world has its ready sneer for the poor man. "He can talk about the love of Christ, but he's a terrible screw at a bargain," they say. Ah, brother, have mercy! the world screws us, and then we are tempted to screw the world. The soil is hard, the climate cold, labour incessant, little to come of it, and can you sneer that a poor soul has, for a brief season, forgotten all this, and risen out of his body and above his cares, and been for a little while a glorified deacon, instead of a poor, haggling, country store-keeper?

Plato says that we all once had wings, and that they still tend to grow out in us, and that our burnings and aspirations for higher things are like the teething pangs of children.

We are trying to cut our wings. Let us not despise these teething seasons. Though the wings do not become apparent, they may be starting under many a rough coat, and on many a clumsy pair of shoulders.

But in our little town of Cloudland, after the heavenly breeze had blown over, there were to be found here and there immortal flowers and leaves from the tree of life, which had blown into many a dwelling.

Poor old drunken Culver, who lived under the hill, and was said to beat his wife, had become a changed man, and used to come out to weekly prayer-meetings. Some tough old family quarrels, such as follow the settlement of wills in a poor country, had at last been brought to an end, and brother had shaken hands with brother: the long root of bitterness had been pulled up and burned on the altar of love. It is true that nobody had become an angel. Poor sharp-tongued Miss Krissy Pike, still went on reporting the wasteful excesses she had seen in the minister's swill-barrel. And some that were crabbed and cross-grained before, were so still, and some, perhaps, were a little more snarly than usual, on account of the late over-excitement.

A revival of religion merely makes manifest for a time what religion there is in a community, but it does not exalt men above their nature or above their times. It is neither revelation nor inspiration; it is impulse. It gives no new faculties, and it goes at last into that general average of influences, which go to make up the progress of a generation.

One terrestrial result of the revival in our academy was, that about half a dozen of the boys fell desperately in love with Tina. I have always fancied Tina to be one of that species of woman-kind that used to be sought out for priestesses to the Delphic oracle. She had a flame-like, impulsive, ethereal temperament, a capacity for sudden inspirations, in which she was carried out of herself, and spoke winged words that made one wonder whence they came. Her religious zeal had impelled her to be the adviser of every one who came near her, and her sayings were quoted, and some of our shaggy, rough-coated mountain boys, thought that they had never had an idea of the beauty of holiness before. Poor boys! they were so sacredly simple about it. And Tina came to me with wide brown eyes, that sparkled like a cairngorm-stone, and told me that she believed she had found what her peculiar calling was: it was to influence young men in religion! She cited, with enthusiasm, the wonderful results she had been able to produce, the sceptical doubts she had removed, the conceptions of heavenly things that she had been able to pour into their souls.

The divine priestess and I had a grand quarrel one day, because I insisted upon it that these religious ministrations on the part of a beautiful young girl to those of the opposite sex would assuredly end in declarations of love and hopes of marriage.

Girls like Tina are often censured as flirts,—most unjustly so, too. Their unawakened nature gives them no power of perceiving what must be the full extent of their influence over the opposite sex. Tina was warmly social; she was enthusiastic and self-confident, and had precisely that spirit which should fit a woman to be priestess or prophetess, to inspire and to lead. She had a magnetic fervour of nature, an attractive force that warmed in her cheeks and sparkled in her eyes, and seemed to make summer around her. She excited the higher faculties,—poetry, ideality, blissful dreams seemed to be her atmosphere,—and she had a power of quick sympathy, of genuine spontaneous outburst, that gave to her looks and words almost the value of a caress, so that she was an unconscious deceiver, and seemed always to say more for the individual than she really meant. All men are lovers of sunshine and spring gales, but they are no one's in particular; and he who seeks to hold them to one heart finds his mistake. Like all others who have a given faculty, Tina loved its exercise,—she loved to influence, loved to feel her power, alike, over man and woman. But who does not know that the power of the sibyl is doubled by the opposition of sex? That which is only acquiescence in a woman friend becomes devotion in a man. That which is admiration from a woman becomes adoration in a man. And of all kinds of power which can be possessed by man or woman, there is none which I think so absolutely intoxicating as this of personal fascination. You may as well blame a bird for wanting to soar and sing as blame such women for the instinctive pleasure they feel in their peculiar kind of empire. Yet, in simple good faith, Tina did not want her friends of the other sex to become lovers. She was willing enough that they should devote themselves, under all sorts of illusive names of brother and friend and what-not, but when they proceeded to ask her for herself there was an instant revulsion, as when some person has unguardedly touched a strong electric circle. The first breath of passion repelled her; the friend that had been so agreeable the hour before was unendurable. Over and over again have I seen her go the same illusive round, always sure that in this instance it was understood that it was to be friendship, and only friendship, or brotherly or Christian love, till the hour came for the electric revulsion, and the friend was lost.

Tina had not learned the modern ways of girls, who count their lovers and offers as an Indian does his scalps, and parade the number of their victims before their acquaintances. Every incident of this kind struck her as a catastrophe; and as Esther, Harry, and I were always warning her, she would come to us like a guilty child, and seek to extenuate her offence. I think the girl was sincere in the wish she often uttered, that she could be a boy, and be loved as a comrade and friend only. "Why must, why would, they always persist in falling into this tiresome result?" "O Horace!" she would say to me, "if I were only Tom Percival, I should be perfectly happy! but it is so stupid to be a girl!"

In my own secret soul I had no kind of wish that she should be Tom Percival, but I did not tell her so. No, I was too wise for that. I knew that my only chance of keeping my position as father-confessor to this elastic young penitent consisted in a judicious suppression of all peculiar claims or hopes on my part, and I was often praised and encouraged for this exemplary conduct, and the question pathetically put to me, "Why couldn't the others do as I did?" O Tina, Tina! did your brown eyes see, and your quick senses divine, that there was something in me which you dreaded to awaken, and feared to meet?

There are some men who have a faculty of making themselves the confidants of women. Perhaps because they have a certain amount of the feminine element in their own composition. They seem to be able to sympathise with them on their feminine side, and are capable of running far in a friendship without running fatally into love.

I think I had this power, and on it I founded my hopes in this regard. I enjoyed, in my way, almost as much celebrity in our little circle for advising and guiding my friends of the other sex as Tina did, and I took care to have on hand such a list of intimates as would prevent my name from being coupled with hers in the school gossip.

In these modern times, when man's fair sister is asking

admission at the doors of classic halls, where man has hitherto reigned in monastic solitude, the query is often raised by our modern sociologists, Can man and woman, with propriety, pursue their studies together? Does the great mystery of sex, with its wide laws of attraction, and its strange, blinding, dazzling influences, furnish a sufficient reason why the two halves of creation, made for each other, should be kept during the whole course of education rigorously apart? This question, like a great many others, was solved without discussion by the good sense of our Puritan ancestors, in throwing the country academies, where young men were fitted for college, open alike to both sexes, and in making the work of education of such dignity in the eyes of the community, that first-rate men were willing to adopt it for life. The consequences were, that, in some lonely mountain town, under some brilliant schoolmaster, young men and women actually were studying together the branches usually pursued in college.

"But," says the modern objector, "bring young men and young women together in these relations, and there will be flirtations and love affairs."

Even so, my friend, there will be. But flirtations and love affairs among a nice set of girls and boys, in a pure and simple state of community, where love is never thought of, except as leading to lawful marriage, are certainly not the worst things that can be thought of,—not half so bad as the grossness and coarseness and roughness and rudeness of those wholly male schools in which boys fight their way on alone, with no humanising influences from the other sex.

There was, to be sure, a great crop of love affairs, always green and vigorous, in our academy, and vows of eternal constancy interchanged between boys and girls who afterwards forgot and outgrew them, without breaking their hearts on either side; but, for my own part, I think love-making over one's Latin and Greek much better than the fisting and cuffing and fagging of English schools, or than many another thing to which poor, blindly fermenting boyhood runs when separated from home, mother, and sister, and confined to an atmosphere and surroundings sharply and purely male. It is certain that the companionship of the girl improves the boy, but more doubt has been expressed whether the delicacy of womanhood is not impaired by an early experience of the flatteries and gallantries of the other sex. But, after all, it is no worse for a girl to coquette and flirt in her Latin and mathematical class than to do it in the German or the polka. The studies and drill of the school have a certain repressive influence, wholly wanting in the ball-room and under the gas-light of fashionable parties. In a good school, the standard of attraction is, to some extent, intellectual. The girl is valued for something besides her person; her disposition and character are thoroughly tested, the powers of her mind go for something, and, what is more, she is known in her every-day clothes. On the whole, I do not think a better way can be found to bring the two sexes together, without that false glamour which obscures their knowledge of each other, than to put them side by side in the daily drill of a good literary institution.

Certainly, of all the days that I look back upon, this academy life in Cloudland was the most perfectly happy. It was happier than college life, because of the constant interwining and companionship with woman, which gave a domestic and family charm to it. It was happy because we were in the first flush of belief in ourselves and in life.

O that first belief! those incredible first visions! when all things look possible, and one believes in the pot of gold at the end of the rainbow, and sees enchanted palaces in the sunset clouds.

What faith we had in one another, and how wonderful we were in one another's eyes! Our little clique of four was a sort of holy of holies in our view. We believed that we had secrets of happiness and progress known only to ourselves. We had full faith in one another's destiny; we were all remarkable people, and destined to do great things.

At the close of the revival, we four, with many others, joined Mr. Avery's church,—a step which in New England, at this time, meant a conviction of some spiritual experience gained, of some familiar communion with the Great Invisible. Had I found it then? Had I laid hold of that invisible hand, and felt its warmth and reality? Had I heard the beatings of a warm heart under the cold exterior of the regular laws of nature, and found a living God? I thought so. That hand and heart were the hand and heart of Jesus,—the brother, the friend, and the interpreting God for poor, blind, and helpless man.

As we stood together before the pulpit, with about fifty others, on that Sunday most joyful to Mr. Avery's heart, we made our religious profession with ardent sincerity. The dear man found in that day the reward of all his sorrows, and the fruit of all his labours. He rejoiced in us as first-fruits of the millennium, which having already dawned in his good, honest heart, he thought could not be far off from the earth.

Ah! those days of young religion were vaguely and ignorantly beautiful, like all the rest of our outlook on life. We were sincere, and meant to be very good and true and pure, and we knew so little of the world we were living in! The village of Cloudland, without a pauper, with scarcely an ignorant person in it, with no temptation, no dissipation, no vice,—what could we know there of the appalling questions of real life? We were hid there together, as in the hollow of God's hand; and a very sweet and lovely hiding-place it was.

Harry had already chosen his profession; he was to be a clergyman, and study with Mr. Avery when his college course was finished. In those days the young aspirants for the pulpit were not gathered into seminaries, but distributed through the country, studying, writing, and learning the pastoral work by sharing the labours of older pastors. Life looked, therefore, very bright to Harry, for life was, at that age, to live with Esther. Worldly care there was none. Mr. Avery was rich on two hundred and fifty dollars, and there were other places in the mountains where birds sung and flowers grew, where Esther could manage another parsonage, as now her father's. She lived in the world of taste and intellect and thought. Her love of the beautiful was fed by the cheap delights of nature, and there was no onerous burden of care in looking forward to marriage, such as now besets a young man when he meditates taking to himself some costly piece of modern luxury,—some exotic bird, who must be fed on incense and odours, and for whom any number of gilded cages and costly surroundings may be necessary. Marriage, in the days of which I speak, was a very simple and natural affair, and Harry and Esther enjoyed the full pleasure of talking over and arranging what their future home should be; and Tina, quite as interested as they, drew wonderful pictures of it, and tinted them with every hue of the rainbow.

Mr. Avery talked with me many times to induce me to choose the same profession. He was an enthusiast for it; it was to him a calling that eclipsed all others, and he could wish the man he loved no greater blessedness than to make him a minister.

But I felt within myself a shrinking doubt of my own ability to be the moral guide of others, and my life-long habit of half-sceptical contemplation made it so impossible to believe the New England theology with the perfect, undoubting faith that Mr. Avery had, that I dared not undertake. I did not disbelieve. I would not for the world controvert; but I could not believe with his undoubting enthusiasm. His sword and spear, so effective in his hands, would tremble in mine. I knew that Harry would do something. He had a natural call, a divine impulse, that led him from childhood to sacred ministries; and though he did not more than accept the system of new-school theology as complete truth, yet I could see that it would furnish to his own devotional nature a stock from which vigorous grafts would shoot forth.

Shall I say, also, that my future was swayed unconsciously by a sort of instinctive perception of what yet might be desired by Tina? Something a little more of this world I seemed to want to lay at her feet. I felt, somehow, that there was in her an aptitude for the perfume and brightness and gaieties of this lower world. And as there must be, not only clergymen, but lawyers, and as men will pay more for getting their own will than for saving their souls, I dreamed of myself, in the future, as a lawyer,—of course a rising one; of course I should win laurels at the bar, and win them by honourable means. I *would* do it; and Tina should be mistress of a fine, antique house in Boston, like the Kitterys', with fair, large gardens and pleasant prospects, and she should glitter and burn and twinkle like a gem, in the very front ranks of society. Yes, I was ambitious, but it was for her.

One thing troubled me: every once in a while, in the letters from Miss Mehitable, came one from Ellery Davenport,

written in a free, gay, dashing, cavalier style, and addressing
Tina with a kind of patronising freedom that made me in-
effably angry. I wanted to shoot him. Such are the risings
of the ancient Adam in us, even after we have joined the
Church. Tina always laughed at me because I scolded and
frowned at these letters, and, I thought, seemed to take
rather a perverse pleasure in them. I have often speculated
on that trait wherein lovely woman slightly resembles a cat;
she cannot, for the life of her, resist the temptation to play
with her mouse a gentle, and rouse it with little pats of her
velvet paw, just to see what it will do.

I was, of course, understood to be under solemn bond and
promise to love Tina only as a brother; but was it not a
brother's duty to watch over his sister? With what satisfaction did I remember all Miss Debby Kittery's philippics
against Ellery Davenport! Did I not believe every word of
them heartily? I hated the French language with all my
soul, and Ellery Davenport's proficiency in it; and Tina
could not make me more angry than by speaking with admiration of his graceful fluency in French, and expressing
rather wilful determinations that, when she got away from Mr.
Rossiter's dictation, she would study it. Mr. Davenport had
said that, when he came back to America, he would give her
French lessons. He was always kind and polite, and she
didn't doubt that he'd give *me* lessons too, if I'd take them.
"French is the language of modern civilisation," said Tina,
with the decision of a professor. But she made me promise
that I wouldn't say a word to her about it before Mr.
Rossiter.

"Now, Horace dear, you know," she said, "that French
to him is just like a red rag to a bull; he'd begin to roar and
lash his sides the minute you said the words; and Mr.
Rossiter and I are capital friends now. You've no idea,

Horace, how good he is to me. He takes such an interest in the development of my mind. He writes me a letter or note almost every week about it, and I take his advice, you know, and I wouldn't want to hurt his feelings about French or anything else. What do you suppose he hates the French so for? I should think he was a genuine Englishman, that had been kept awake nights during all the French wars."

"Well, Tina," I said, "you know there is a great deal of corrupt and dangerous literature in the French language."

"What nonsense, Horace! just as if there wasn't in the English language too, and I none the worse for it. And I'm sure there are no ends of bad things in the classical dictionary, and in the mythology. He'd better talk about the French language! No, you may depend upon it, Horace, I shall learn French as soon as I leave school."

It will be inferred from this that my young lady had a considerable share of that quality which Milton represents to have been the ruin of our first mother—namely, a determination to go her own way and see for herself, and have little confidential interviews with the serpent, notwithstanding all that could be urged to the contrary by sober old Adam.

"Of course, Adam," said Eve, "I can take care of myself, and don't want you always lumbering after me with your advice. You think the serpent will injure me, do you? That just shows how little you know about me. The serpent, Adam, is a very agreeable fellow, and helps one to pass away one's time; but he don't take me in. Oh no! there's no danger of his ever getting around *me!* So, my dear Adam, go your own way in the garden, and let me manage for myself."

Whether in the celestial regions there will be saints and angels who develop this particular form of self-will, I know not; but in this world of what Mr. Avery called "imperfect sanctification," religion doesn't prevent the fair angels of the other sex from developing this quality in pretty energetic forms. In fact, I found that, if I was going to guide my Ariadne at all, I must let out my line fast, and let her feel free and unwatched.

CHAPTER XIII.

The Minister's Wood-spell.

It was in the winter of this next year that the minister's "wood-spell" was announced.

"What is a wood-spell?" you say. Well, the pastor was settled on the understanding of receiving two hundred dollars a year and his wood; and there was a certain day set apart in the winter, generally in the time of the best sleighing, when every parishioner brought the minister a sled-load of wood; and thus, in the course of time, built him up a mighty wood-pile.

It was one of the great seasons of preparation in the minister's family, and Tina, Harry, and I had been busy for two or three days beforehand, in helping Esther to create the wood-spell cake, which was to be made in quantities large enough to give ample slices to every parishioner. Two days beforehand the fire was besieged with a row of earthen pots, in which the spicy compound was rising to the necessary lightness, and Harry and I spilt incredible amounts of oven-wood, and in the evening we sat together stoning raisins round the great kitchen fire, with Mr. Avery in the midst of us, telling us stories and arguing with us, and entering into the hilarity of the thing like a boy. He was so happy in Esther, and delighted to draw the shy colour into her cheeks, by some sly joke or allusion, when Harry's head of golden curls came into close proximity with her smooth black satin tresses.

The cake came out victorious, and we all claimed the merit of it; and a mighty cheese was bought, and every shelf of the closet, and all the dressers of the kitchen, were crowded with the abundance.

We had a jewel of a morning,—one of those sharp, clear, sunny winter days, when the sleds squeak over the flinty snow, and the little icicles tingle along on the glittering crust as they fall from the trees, and the breath of the slow-pacing oxen steams up like a rosy cloud in the morning sun, and then fall back condensed in little icicles on every hair.

We were all astir early, full of life and vigour. There was a holiday in the academy. Mr. Rossiter had been invited over to the minister's, to chat and tell stories with the farmers, and give them high entertainment. Miss Nervy Randall, more withered and wild in her attire than usual, but eminently serviceable, stood prepared to cut cake and cheese without end, and dispense it with wholesome nods and messages of comfort. The minister himself heated two little old andirons red-hot in the fire, and therewith from time to time stirred up a mighty bowl of flip, which was to flow in abundance to every corner. Not then had the temperance reformation dawned on America, though ten years later Mr. Avery would as soon have been caught in a gambling-saloon as stirring and dispensing a bowl of flip to his parishioners.

Mr. Avery had recently preached a highly popular sermon on agriculture, in which he set forth the dignity of the farmer's life from the text, "For the king himself is served of the field;" and there had been a rustle of professional enthusiasm in all the mountain farms around, and it was resolved, by a sort of general consent, that the minister's wood-pile this year should be of the best; none of your old make-shifts, —loads made out with crooked sticks and snapping chestnut logs, most noisy and destructive to good wives' aprons. Good straight shagbark-hickory was voted none too good for the minister. Also the axe was lifted up on many a proud oak, and beech, and maple. What destruction of glory and beauty there was in those mountain regions! How ruthlessly man destroys in a few hours that which centuries cannot bring again!

What an idea of riches in those glorious woodland regions! We read legends of millionnaires who fed their fires with cinnamon, and rolled up thousand-dollar bills into lamp-lighters, in the very wantonness of profusion. But what was that compared to the prodigality which fed our great roaring winter fires on the thousand-leafed oaks, whose conception had been ages ago,—who were children of the light and of the day,—every fragment and fibre of them made of most celestial influences, of sunshine and rain-drops, and night-dews and clouds, slowly working for centuries, until they had wrought the wondrous shape into a gigantic miracle of beauty? And then snuffling old Heber Atwood, with his two hard-fisted boys, cut one down in a forenoon, and made logs of it for the minister's wood-pile. If this isn't making light of serious things, we don't know what is. But think of your wealth, oh ye farmers!—think what beauty and glory every year perish to serve your cooking-stoves and chimney-corners.

To tell the truth, very little of such sentiment was in Mr. Avery's mind or in any of ours. We lived in a woodland region, and we were *blasé* with the glory of trees. We did admire the splendid elms that hung their cathedral arches over the one central street of Cloudland Village, and on this particular morning they were all aflame like Aladdin's palace, hanging with emeralds and rubies and crystals, flashing and glittering and dancing in the sunlight. And when the first sled came squeaking up the village street, we did not

look upon it as the funereal hearse bearing the honoured
corpse of a hundred summers, but we boys clapped our hands
and shouted, "Hurrah for old Heber!" as his load of magnificent oak, well-bearded with gray moss, came scrunching
into the yard. Mr. Avery hastened to draw the hot flip-iron
from the fire and stir the foaming bowl. Esther began cutting the first loaf of cake, and Mr. Rossiter walked out and
cracked a joke on Heber's shoulder, whereat all the cast-iron
lineaments of his hard features relaxed. Heber had not the
remotest idea at this moment that he was to be branded as a
tree-murderer. On the contrary, if there was anything for
which he valued himself, and with which his heart was at
this moment swelling with victorious pride, it was his power
of cutting down trees. Man he regarded in a physical point
of view as principally made to cut down trees, and trees as
the natural enemies of man. When he stood under a magnificent oak, and heard the airy rustle of its thousand leaves,
to his ear it was always a rustle of defiance, as if the old oak
had challenged him to single combat; and Heber would feel
of his axe and say, "Next winter, old boy, we'll see,—we'll
see!" And at this moment he and his two tall, slab-sided,
big-handed boys came into the kitchen with an uplifted air,
in which triumph was but just repressed by suitable modesty.
They came prepared to be complimented, and they were
complimented accordingly.

"Well, Mr. Atwood," said the minister, "you must have
had pretty hard work on that load; that's no ordinary oak; it
took strong hands to roll those logs, and yet I don't see but
two of your boys. Where are they all now?"

"Scattered, scattered!" said Heber, as he sat with a great
block of cake in one hand, and sipped his mug of flip, looking, with his grizzly beard and shaggy hair and his iron features, like a cross between a polar bear and a man,—a very

shrewd, thoughtful, reflective polar bear, however, quite up
to any sort of argument with a man.

"Yes, they're scattered," he said. "We're putty lonesome now't our house. Nobody there but Pars, Dass, Dill,
Noah, and 'Liakim. I ses to Noah and 'Liakim this mornin',
'Ef we had all our boys to hum, we sh'd haf to take up two
loads to the minister, sartin, to make it fair on the wood-spell
cake.'"

"Where are your boys now?" said Mr. Avery. "I haven't
seen them at meeting now for a good while."

"Wal, Sol and 'Tim's gone up to Umbagog, lumberin';
and 'Tite, he's sailed to Archangel; and Jeduth, he's gone to
th' West Injies for molasses; and Pete, he's gone to the West.
Folks begins to talk now 'bout that 'ere Western kentry, and
so Pete, he must go to Buffalo, and see the great West. He's
writ back about Niagry Falls. His letters is most amazin'.
The old woman, she can't feel easy 'bout him no way. She
insists 'pon it them Injuns 'll scalp him. The old woman is
just as choice of her boys as if she hadn't got just es many es
she has."

"How many sons have you!" said Harry, with a countenance of innocent wonder.

"Wal," said Heber, "I've seen the time when I had fourteen good straight boys,—all on 'em a turnin' over a log together."

"Dear me?" said Tina. "Hadn't you any daughters?"

"Gals?" said Heber, reflectively. "Bless you, yis. There's
been a gal or two 'long, in between, here an' there—don't jest
remember where they come; but, any way, there's plenty of
women folks 't our house."

"Why!" said Tina, with a toss of her pretty head, "you
don't seem to think much of women."

"Good in their way," said Heber, shaking his head; "but
14*

Adam was fust formed, and then Eve, you know." Looking
more attentively at Tina, as she stood bridling and dimpling
before him, like a bird just ready to fly, Heber conceived an
indistinct idea that he must say something gallant, so he
added, "Give all honour to the women, as weaker vessels, ye
know; that's sound doctrine, I s'pose."

Heber having now warmed and refreshed himself, and endowed his minister with what he conceived to be a tip-top,
irreproachable load of wood, proceeded also to give him the
benefit of a little good advice, prefaced by gracious words of
encouragement. "I wus tellin' my old woman this mornin'
that I didn't grudge a cent of my subscription, 'cause your
preachin' lasts well, and pays well. Ses I, 'Mr. Avery ain't
the kind of man that strikes twelve the fust time. He's a
man that 'll wear.' That's what I said fust, and I've followed
y' up putty close in yer preachin'; but then I've jest got one
word to say to ye. Ain't free agency a gettin' a leetle too
top-heavy in yer preachin'? Ain't it kind o' overgrown sovereignty? Now, ye see, divine sovereignty hes got to be took
care of as well as free agency. That's all, that's all. I
thought I'd jest drop the thought, ye know, and leave you to
think on't. This 'ere last revival you run along considerable
on 'whosoever will may come,' an' all that. Now, p'r'aps, ef
you'd jest tighten up the ropes a leetle t'other side, and give
'em sovereignty, the hull load would sled easier."

"Well," said Mr. Avery, "I'm much obliged to you for
your suggestions."

"Now there's my wife's brother, Josh Baldwin," said
Heber, "he was delegate to the last Consociation, and he
heerd your openin' sermon, and ses he to me, ses he, 'Your
minister sartin does slant a leetle towards th' Arminians; he
don't quite walk the crack,' Josh says, ses he. Ses I, 'Josh,
we ain't none on us perfect; but,' ses I, 'Mr. Avery ain't no

Arminian, I can tell you. Yeh can't judge Mr. Avery by one sermon,' ses I. 'You hear him preach the year round, and ye'll find that all the doctrines gits their place.' Ye see I stood up for ye, Mr. Avery, but I thought 'twouldn't do no harm to kind o' let ye know what folks is sayin'."

Here the theological discussion was abruptly cut short by Deacon Zachary Chipman's load, which entered the yard amid the huzzahs of the boys. Heber and his boys were at the door in a minute. "Wal, railly, ef the deacon hain't come down with his shagbark! Wal, wal, the revival has operated on him some, I guess. Last year the deacon sent a load that I'd ha' been ashamed to had in my back yard, an' I took the liberty o' tellin' on him so. Good, straight-grained shagbark. Wal, wal! I'll go out an' help him unload it. Ef that 'ere holds out to the bottom, the deacon's done putty wal, an' I shall think grace *has* made some progress."

The deacon, a mournful, dry, shivery-looking man, with a little round bald head, looking wistfully out of a great red comforter, all furry and white with the sharp frosts of the morning, and, with his small red eyes weeping tears through the sharpness of the air, looked as if he had come as chief mourner at the hearse of his beloved hickory-trees. He had cut down the very darlings of his soul, and come up with his precious load, impelled by a divine impulse like that which made the lowing kine, in the Old Testament story, come slowly bearing the ark of God, while their brute hearts were turning toward the calves that they had left at home. Certainly, if virtue is in proportion to sacrifice, Deacon Chipman's load of hickory had more of self-sacrifice in it than a dozen loads from old Heber; for Heber was a forest prince in his way of doing things, and, with all his shrewd calculations of money's worth, had an open-handed generosity of nature that made him take a pride in liberal giving.

The little man shrank mournfully into a corner, and sipped his tumbler of flip, and ate his cake and cheese as if he had been at a funeral.

"How are you all at home, deacon?" said Mr. Avery, heartily.

"Just crawlin', thank you,—just crawlin'. My old woman don't git out much; her rheumatiz gits a dreadful strong hold on her; and, Mr. Avery, she hopes you'll be round to visit her 'fore long. Since the revival, she's kind o' fell into darkness, and don't see no cheerin' views. She ses sometimes the universe ain't nothin' but blackness and darkness to her."

"Has she a good appetite?" said Mr. Avery.

"Wal, no. She don't enjoy her vittles much. Some say she's got the jaunders. I try to cosset her up, and git her to take relishin' things. I tell her ef she'd eat a good sassage for breakfast of a cold mornin', with a good hearty bit o' mince-pie, and a cup o' strong coffee, 'twould kind o' set her up for the day; but, somehow, she don't git no nourishment from her food."

"'There, Rossiter,' we heard Mr. Avery whisper aside, "you see what a country minister has to do,—give cheering views to a dyspeptic that breakfasts on sausages and mince-pies."

And now the loads began coming thick and fast. Sometimes two and three, and sometimes four and five, came stringing along, one after another, in unbroken procession. For every one, Mr. Avery had an appreciative word. Its especial points were noticed and commended, and the farmers themselves, shrewdest observers, looked at every load and gave it their verdict. By and by the kitchen was full of a merry, chatting circle, and Mr. Rossiter and Mr. Avery were telling their best stories, and roars of laughter came from the house.

Tina glanced in and out among the old farmers, like a bright tropical bird, carrying the cake and cheese to each one, laughing and telling stories, dispensing smiles to the younger ones,—treacherous smiles, which meant nothing, but made the hearts beat faster under their shaggy coats; and if she saw a red-fisted fellow in a corner, who seemed to be having a bad time, she would go and sit down by him, and be so gracious and warming and winning that his tongue would be loosened, and he would tell her all about his steers and his calves and his last crop of corn, and his load of wood, and then wonder all the way home whether he should ever have, in a house of his own, a pretty little woman like that.

By afternoon, the minister's wood-pile was enormous. It stretched beyond anything before seen in Cloudland; it exceeded all the legends of neighbouring wood-piles and wood-spells related by deacons and lay delegates in the late Consociation. And truly, among things picturesque and graceful among childish remembrances, dear and cheerful, there is nothing that more speaks to my memory than the dear, good old mossy wood-pile. Harry, Tina, Esther, and I ran up and down and in and about the piles of wood that evening with a joyous satisfaction. How fresh and spicy and woodsy it smelt! I can smell now the fragrance of the hickory, whose clear, oily bark in burning cast forth perfume quite equal to cinnamon. Then there was the fragrant black birch, sought and prized by us all for the high-flavoured bark on the smaller limbs, which was a favourite species of confectionery to us. There were also the logs of white birch, gleaming up in their purity, from which we made sheets of woodland parchment.

It is recorded of one man who stands in a high position at Washington, that all his earlier writing lessons were performed upon leaves of the white birch bark, the only paper used in the family.

Then there were massive trunks of oak, veritable worlds of mossy vegetation in themselves, with tufts of green velvet nestled away in their bark, and sheets of greenness carpeting their sides, and little white, hoary trees of moss, with little white, hoary apples upon them, like miniature orchards.

One of our most interesting amusements was forming landscapes in the snow, in which we had mountains and hills and valleys, and represented streams of water by means of glass, and clothed the sides of our hills with orchards of apple-trees made of this gray moss. It was an incipient practice at landscape-gardening, for which we found rich material in the wood-pile. Esther and 'Tina had been filling their aprons with these mossy treasures. for which we had all been searching together, and now we all sat chatting in the evening light. The sun was going down. The sleds had ceased to come, the riches of our woodland treasures were all in, the whole air was full of the trembling rose-coloured light that turned all the snow-covered landscape to brightness. All around us not a fence to be seen,—nothing but waving hollows of spotless snow, glowing with the rosy radiance, and fading away in purple and lilac shadows; and the evening stars began to twinkle, one after another, keen and clear through the frosty air, as we all sat together in triumph on the highest perch of the wood-pile. And Harry said to Esther, "One of these days they'll be bringing in our wood," and Esther's cheeks reflected the pink of the sky.

"Yes, indeed!" said Tina. "And then I am coming to live with you. I'm going to be an old maid, you know, and I shall help Esther as I do now. I never shall want to be married."

Just at this moment the ring of sleigh-bells was heard

coming up the street. Who and what now? A little one-horse sleigh drove swiftly up to the door, the driver sprang out with a lively alacrity, hitched his horse, and came toward the house. In the same moment Tina and I recognised Ellery Davenport!

CHAPTER XIV.

Ellery Davenport.

Tina immediately turned and ran into the house, laughing, and up-stairs into her chamber, leaving Esther to go seriously forward,—Esther, always tranquil and always ready. For myself, I felt such a vindictive hatred at the moment as really alarmed me. What had this good-natured man done, with his frank, merry face, and his easy, high-bred air, that I should hate him so? What sort of Christian was I, to feel in this way? Certainly it was a temptation of the devil, and I would put it down, and act like a reasonable being. So I went forward with Harry, and he shook hands with us.

"Hulloa, fellows!" he said, "you've made the great leap since I saw you, and changed from boys into men."

"Good evening, Miss Avery," he said, as we presented him to her. "May I trench on your hospitality a little? I am a traveller in these arctic regions, and Miss Mehitable charged me to call and see after the health and happiness of our young friends here. I see," he said, looking at us, "that there need be no inquiries after health; your looks speak for themselves."

"Why, Percival!" he said, turning to Harry, "what a pair of shoulders you are getting! Genuine Saxon blood runs in your veins plainly enough, and one of these days, when you get to be Sir Harry Percival, you'll do honour to the name."

The proud, reserved blood, flushed into Harry's face, and his blue eyes, usually so bright and clear, sparkled with displeasure. I was pleased to see that Ellery Davenport had made him angry. "Yes," I said to myself, "What want of tact for him to dare to touch on a subject that Harry's most intimate friends never speak of?"

Esther looked fixedly at him with those clear, piercing hazel eyes, as if she were mentally studying him. I hoped she would not like him; yet why should I hope so?

He saw in a moment that he had made a mistake, and glided off quickly to another subject.

"Where's my fair little enemy, Miss Tina?" he said.

His "fair little enemy" was at this moment attentively studying him through a crack in the window-curtain. Shall I say, too, that the first thing she did, on rushing up to her room, was to look at her hair, and study herself in the glass, wondering how she would look to him now. Well, she had not seen herself for some hours, and self-knowledge is a virtue, we all know. And then our scamper over the wood-pile, in the fresh evening air, must have deranged something, for Tina had one of those rebellious heads of curls that every breeze takes liberties with, and that have to be looked after, and watched, and restrained. Esther's satin bands of hair could pass through a whirlwind, and not lose their gloss. It is curious how character runs even to the minutest thing,— the very hairs of our heads are numbered by it,—Esther, always in everything self-poised, thoughtful, reflective; Tina, the child of every wandering influence, tremulously alive to every new excitement, a wind-harp for every air of heaven to breathe upon.

It would be hard to say what mysterious impulse for good or ill made her turn and run when she saw Ellery Davenport. That turning and running in girls means something: it means

that the electric chain has been struck in some way; but
how?

Mr. Davenport came into the house, and was received
with frank cordiality by Mr. Avery. He was a grandson of
Jonathan Edwards, and the good man regarded him as, in
some sort, a son of the Church, and had, no doubt, instant-
aneous promptings for his conversion. Mr. Avery, though
he believed stringently in the doctrine of total depravity, was
very innocent in his application of it to individuals. That
Ellery Davenport was a sceptic was well known in New
England wherever the reputation of his brilliant talents and
person had circulated, and Mr. Avery had often longed for
an opportunity to convert him. The dear, good man had
no possible idea that anybody could go wrong from anything
but mistaken views, and he was sure, in the case of Ellery
Davenport, that his mind must have been perplexed about
free agency and decrees, and thus he hailed with delight the
Providence which had sent him to his abode. He plunged
into an immediate conversation with him about the state of
France, whence he had just returned.

Esther, meanwhile, went up-stairs to notify Tina of his
arrival.

"Mr. Ellery Davenport is below, and has inquired for
you."

Nobody could be more profoundly indifferent to any piece
of news.

"Was that Mr. Ellery Davenport? How stupid of him to
come here when we are all so tired! I don't think I can go
down; I am too tired."

Esther, straightforward Esther, took the thing as stated.
Tina, to be sure, had exhibited no symptoms of fatigue up to
that moment; but Esther now saw that she had been allowing
her to over-exert herself.

"My darling," she said, "I have been letting you do too much altogether. You are quite right; you should lie down here quietly, and I'll bring you up your tea. Perhaps, by and by, in the evening, you might come down and see Mr. Davenport, when you are rested."

"Oh, nonsense about Mr. Davenport! he doesn't come to see me. He wants to talk to your father, I suppose."

"But he has inquired for you two or three times," said Esther, "and he really seems to be a very entertaining, well-informed man; so by and by, if you feel rested, I should think you had better come down."

Now I, for my part, wondered then and wonder now, and always shall, what all this was for. Tina certainly was not a coquette; she had not learned the art of trading in herself, and using her powers and fascinations as women do who have been in the world, and learned the precise value of everything that they say and do. She was, at least now, a simple child of nature, yet she acted exactly as an artful coquette might have done.

Ellery Davenport constantly glanced at the door as he talked with Mr. Avery, and shifted uneasily on his chair; evidently he expected her to enter, and when Esther returned without her he was secretly vexed and annoyed. I was glad of it too, like a fool as I was. It would have been a thousand times better for my hopes had she walked straight out to meet him, cool and friendly, like Esther. There was one comfort; he was a married man; but then that crazy wife of his might die, or might be dead now. Who knew? To be sure, Ellery Davenport never had the air of a married man, —that steady, collected, sensible, restrained air which belongs to the male individual, conscious, wherever he moves, of a home tribunal, to which he is responsible. He had gone loose in society, pitied and petted and caressed by ladies, and everybody said, if his wife should die, Ellery Davenport might marry whom he pleased. Esther knew nothing about him, except a faint general outline of his history. She had no prepossessions for or against, and he laid himself out to please her in conversation, with that easy grace and quick perception of character which were habitual to him. Ellery Davenport had been a thriving young Jacobin, and Mr. Avery and Mr. Rossiter were fierce Federalists.

Mr. Rossiter came in to tea, and both of them bore down exultingly on Ellery Davenport in regard to the disturbances in France.

"Just what I always said!" said Mr. Rossiter. "French democracy is straight from the devil. It's the child of misrule, and leads to anarchy. See what their revolution is coming to. Well, I may not be orthodox entirely on the question of total depravity, but I always admitted the total depravity of the whole French nation."

"O the French are men of like passions with us!" said Ellery Davenport. "They have been ground down and debased and imbruted till human nature can bear no longer, and now there is a sudden outbreak of the lower classes,— the turning of the worm."

"Not a worm," said Mr. Rossiter; "a serpent, and a strong one."

"Davenport," said Mr. Avery, "don't you see that all this is because this revolution is in the hands of atheists?"

"Certainly I do, sir. These fellows have destroyed the faith of the common people, and given them nothing in its place."

"I am glad to see you recognise that," said Mr. Avery.

"Recognise, my dear sir! Nobody knows the worth of religion as a political force better than I do. Those French people are just like children,—full of sentiment, full of feel-

ing, full of fire, but without the cold, judging, logical power
that is frozen into men here by your New England theology.
If I have got to manage a republic, give me Calvinists."

"You admit, then," said Mr. Avery, delightedly, "the
worth of Calvinism."

"As a political agent, certainly I do," said Ellery Davenport. "Men must have strong, positive religious beliefs to
give them vigorous self-government; and republics are founded
on the self-governing power of the individual."

"Davenport," said Mr. Avery, affectionately laying his
hand on his shoulder, "I should like to have said that thing
myself, I couldn't have put it better."

"But do you suppose," said Esther, trembling with eagerness, "that they will behead the Queen?"

"Certainly I do," said Ellery Davenport, with that air of
cheerful composure with which the retailer of the last horror
delights to shock a listener. "Oh, certainly! I wouldn't
give a pin for her chance. You read the account of the trial,
I suppose; you saw that it was a foregone conclusion?"

"I did, indeed," said Esther. "But, O Mr. Davenport!
can nothing be doné? There is Lafayette; can he do nothing?"

"Lafayette may think himself happy if he keeps his own
head on his shoulders," said Davenport. "The fact is, that
there is a wild beast in every human being. In our race it
is the lion. In the French race it is the tiger,—hotter, more
tropical, more blindly intense in rage and wrath. Religion,
government, education, are principally useful in keeping the
human dominant over the beast; but when the beast gets
above the human in the community, woe be to it."

"Davenport, you talk like an apostle," said Mr. Avery.

"You know the devils believe and tremble," said Ellery.

"Well, I take it," said Mr. Rossiter, "you've come home from France disposed to be a good Federalist."

"Yes, I have," said Ellery Davenport. "We must all live and learn, you know."

And so in one evening Ellery witched himself into the good graces of every one in the simple parsonage; and when Tina at last appeared she found him reigning king of the circle. Mr. Rossiter, having drawn from him the avowal that he was a Federalist, now looked complacently upon him as a hopeful young neophyte. Mr. Avery saw evident marks of grace in his declarations in favour of Calvinism, while yet there was a spicy flavour of the prodigal son about him,— enough to engage him for his conversion. Your wild, wicked, witty prodigal son is to a spiritual huntsman an attractive mark, like some rare kind of eagle, whose ways must be studied, and whose nest must be marked, and in whose free, savage gambols in the blue air and on the mountain-tops he has a kind of hidden sympathy.

When Tina entered, it was with an air unusually shy and quiet. She took all his compliments on her growth and change of appearance with a negligent, matter-of-course air, seated herself in the most distant part of the room, and remained obstinately still and silent. Nevertheless, it was to be observed that she lost not a word that he said or a motion that he made. Was she in that stage of attraction which begins with repulsion? or did she feel stirring within her that intense antagonism which woman sometimes feels toward man, when she instinctively divines that he may be the one who shall one day send a herald and call on her to surrender. Women are so intense, they have such prophetic, fore-reaching, nervous systems, that sometimes they appear to be endowed with a gift of prophecy. Tina certainly was an innocent child at this time, uncalculating, and acting by inetinct alone, and she looked upon Ellery Davenport as a married man, who was and ought to be and would be nothing to her; and yet, for the life of her, she could not treat him as she treated other men.

If there was in him something which powerfully attracted, there was also something of the reverse pole of the magnet, that repelled, and inspired a feeling not amounting to fear, but having an undefined savour of dread, as if some invisible spirit about him gave mysterious warning. There was a sense of such hidden, subtle power under his suavities; the grasp of the iron hand was so plain through the velvet glove, that delicate and impressible natures felt it. Ellery Davenport was prompt and energetic and heroic; he had a great deal of impulsive good-nature, as his history in all our affairs shows. He was always willing to reach out the helping hand, and helped to some purpose when he did so; and yet I felt, rather than could prove, in his presence, that he could be very remorseless and persistently cruel.

Ellery Davenport inherited the whole Edwards nature, without its religious discipline,—a nature strong both in intellect and passion. He was an unbelieving Jonathan Edwards. It was this whole nature that I felt in him, and I looked upon the gradual interest which I saw growing in Tina toward him, in the turning of her thoughts on him, in her flights from him and attractions to him, as one looks on the struggles of a fascinated bird, who flees and returns, and flees and returns, each time drawn nearer and nearer to the diamond eyes.

These impressions which come to certain kinds of natures are so dim and cloudy, it is so much the habit of the counter-current of life to disregard them, and to feel that an impression of which you have no physical external proof is of necessity an absurdity and a weakness, that they are seldom acted

on,—seldom, at least, in New England, where the habit of
logic is so formed from childhood in the mind, and the believing of nothing which you cannot prove is so constant a
portion of the life education. Yet with regard to myself, as I
have stated before, there was always a sphere of impression
surrounding individuals, for which often I could give no
reasonable account. It was as if there had been an emanation from the mind like that from the body. From some it
was an emanation of moral health and purity and soundness;
from others, the sickly effluvium of moral decay, sometimes
penetrating through all sorts of outward graces and accomplishments, like the smell of death through the tube-roses and
lilies on the coffin.

I could not prove that Ellery Davenport was a wicked
man; but I had an instinctive abhorrence of him, for which
I reproached myself constantly, deeming it only the madness
of an unreasonable jealousy.

His stay with us at this time was only for a few hours.
The next morning, he took Harry alone and communicated
to him some intelligence quite important to his future.

"I have been to visit your father," he said, "and have
made him aware what treasures he possesses in his children."

"His children have no desire that he should be made
aware of it," said Harry, coldly. "He has broken all ties
between them and him."

"Well, well!" said Ellery Davenport, "the fact is, Sir
Harry has gone into the virtuous stage of an Englishman's
life, where a man is busy taking care of his gouty feet, looking after his tenants, and repenting at his leisure of the sins
of his youth. But you will find, when you come to enter
college next year, that there will be a handsome allowance at
your disposal; and, between you and me, I'll just say to you
that young Sir Harry is about as puny and feeble a little bit

of mortality as I ever saw. To my thinking, they'll never
raise him; and his life is all that stands between you and the
estate. You know that I got your mother's marriage certificate, and it is safe in Parson Lothrop's hands. So you see
there may be a brilliant future before you and your sister. It
is well enough for you to know it early, a keep yourself and
her free from entanglements. School friendships and flirtations, and all that sort of thing, are pretty little spring flowers,
—very charming in their way and time; but it isn't advisable
to let them lead us into compromising ourselves for life. If
your future home is to be England, of course you will want
your marriage to strengthen your position there."

"My future home will never be England," said Harry,
briefly. "America has nursed me and educated me, and I
shall always be, heart and soul, an American. My life must
be acted in this country."

The other suggestion contained in Ellery Davenport's advice was passed over without a word. Harry was not one
that could discuss his private relations with a stranger. He
could not but feel obliged to Ellery Davenport for the interest
that he had manifested in him, and yet there was something
about this easy, patronising manner of giving advice that
galled him. He was not yet old enough not to feel vexed at
being reminded that he was young.

It seemed but a few hours, and Ellery Davenport was
gone again; and yet how he had changed everything! The
hour that he drove up, how perfectly innocently happy and
united we all were! Our thoughts needed not to go beyond
the present moment: the moss that we had gathered from the
wood-pile, and the landscapes that we were going to make
with it, were greater treasures than all those of that unknown
world of brightness and cleverness, and wealth and station,

out of which Ellery Davenport had shot like a comet, to astonish us, and then go back and leave us in obscurity.

Harry communicated the intelligence given him by Ellery Davenport, first to me, then to Tina and Esther and Mr. Avery, but begged that it might not be spoken of beyond our little circle. It could and it should make no change, he said. But can expectations of such magnitude be awakened in young minds without a change?

On the whole, Ellery Davenport left a trail of brightness behind him, notwithstanding my sinister suspicions. "How open-handed and friendly it was of him," said Esther, "to come up here, when he has so much on his hands! He told father that he should have to be in Washington next week, to talk with them there about French affairs."

"And I hope he may do Tom Jefferson some good!" said Mr. Avery, indignantly,—"teach him what he is doing in encouraging this hideous, atheistical French Revolution! Why, it will bring discredit on republics, and put back the cause of liberty in Europe a century! Davenport sees into that as plainly as I do."

"He's a shrewd fellow," said Mr. Rossiter. "I heard him talk three or four years ago, when he was over here, and he was about as glib-tongued a Jacobin as you'd wish to see; but now my young man has come round handsomely. I told him he ought to tell Jefferson just how the thing is working. I go for government by the respectable classes of society."

"Davenport evidently is not a regenerated man," said Mr. Avery, thoughtfully; "but as far as speculative knowledge goes, he is as good a theologian as his grandfather. I had a pretty thorough talk with him, before we went to bed last night, and he laid down the distinctions with a clearness and a precision that were astonishing. He sees right through .

that point of the difference between natural and moral inability, and he put it into a sentence that was as neat and compact and clear as a quartz crystal. I think there was a little rub in his mind on the consistency of the freedom of the will with the divine decrees, and I just touched him off with an illustration or two there, and I could see, by the flash of his eye, how quickly he took it. 'Davenport,' said I to him, 'you are made for the pulpit; you ought to be in it.'"

" 'I know it,' he said, 'Mr. Avery; but the trouble is, I am not good enough. I think,' he said, 'sometimes I should like to have been as good a man as my grandfather; but then, you see, there's the world, the flesh, and the devil, who all have something to say to that.'

" 'Well,' says I, 'Davenport, the world and the flesh last only a little while'——

" 'But the devil and I last for ever, I suppose you mean to say,' said he, getting up with a sort of careless swing; and then he said he must go to bed; but before he went he reached out his hand, and smiled on me, and said, 'Good night, and thank you, Mr. Avery.' That man has a beautiful smile. It's like a spirit in his face."

Had Ellery Davenport been acting the hypocrite with Mr. Avery? Supposing a man is made like an organ, with two or three banks of keys, and ever so many stops so that he can play all sorts of tunes on himself; is it being a hypocrite with each person to play precisely the tune, and draw out exactly the stop, which he knows will make himself agreeable and further his purposes? Ellery Davenport did understand the New England theology as thoroughly as Mr. Avery. He knew it from turret to foundation-stone. He knew all the evidences of natural and revealed religion, and, when he chose to do so, could make most conclusive arguments upon them. He had a perfect appreciation of devotional religion,

and knew precisely what it would do for individuals. He saw
into politics with unerring precision, and knew what was in
men, and whither things were tending. His unbelief was
purely and simply what has been called in New England the
natural opposition of the heart to God. He loved his own
will, and he hated control, and he determined, *per fas aut
nefas*, to carry his own plans in this world, and attend to the
other when he got into it. To have his own way, and to
carry his own points, and to do as he pleased, were the ruling
purposes of his life.

CHAPTER XV.
Last Days in Cloudland.

THE day was coming now that the idyl of Cloudland must
end, and our last term wound up with a grand dramatic entertainment.

It was a time-honoured custom in New England academies
to act a play once a year as the closing exercise, and we
resolved that our performance should surpass all others in
scenic effect.

The theme of the play was to be the story of Jephthah's
daughter, from the Old Testament. It had been suggested
at first to take Miss Hannah More's sacred drama upon this
subject; but Tina insisted upon it that it would be a great
deal better to write an original drama ourselves, each one
taking a character, and composing one's own part.

Tina was to be Jephthah's daughter, and Esther her
mother; and a long opening scene between them was gotten
up by the two in a private session at their desks in the school-
room one night, and, when perfected, was read to Harry and
me for our critical judgment. The conversation was conducted in blank verse, with the usual appropriate trimmings
and flourishes of that species of literature, and, on the whole,

even at this time, I do not see but that it was quite as good
as Miss Hannah More's.

There was some skirmishing between Harry and myself
about our parts, Harry being, as I thought, rather too golden-
haired and blue-eyed for the grim resolve and fierce agonies
of Jephthah. Moreover, the other part was to be that of
Tina's lover, and he was to act very desperate verses indeed,
and I represented to Harry privately that here, for obvious
reasons, I was calculated to succeed. But Tina overruled
me with that easy fluency of good reasons which the young
lady always had at command. "Harry would make altogether the best lover," she said; "he was just cut out for a
lover. Then, besides, what does Horace know about it?
Harry has been practising for six months, and Horace hasn't
even begun to think of such things yet."

This was one of those stringent declarations that my
young lady was always making with regard to me, giving me
to understand that her whole confidence in me was built entirely on my discretion. Well, I was happy enough to let it
go so; for Ellery Davenport had gone like an evening meteor,
and we had ceased talking and thinking about him. He was
out of our horizon entirely. So we spouted blank verse at
each other, morning, noon, and night, with the most cheerful
courage. Tina and Harry had, both of them, a considerable
share of artistic talent, and made themselves very busy in
drawing and painting scenery,—a work in which the lady
principal, Miss Titcomb, gave every assistance; although, as
Tina said, her views of scenery were mostly confined to what
was proper for tombstones. "But then," she added, "let her
have the whole planning of my grave, with a great weeping-
willow over it,—that 'll be superb! I believe the weeping-
willows will be out by that time, and we can have real
branches. Won't that be splendid!"

Then there was the necessity of making our drama popular, by getting in the greatest possible number of our intimate friends and acquaintances. . So Jephthah had to marshal an army on the stage; and there was no end of paper helmets to be made. In fact, every girl in school who could turn her hand to anything was making a paper helmet.

There was to be a procession of Judæan maidens across the stage, bearing the body of Jephthah's daughter on a bier, after the sacrifice. This took in every leading girl in the school; and as they were all to be dressed in white, with blue ribbons, one may fancy the preparation going on in all the houses far and near. There was also to be a procession of youths, bearing the body of the faithful lover, who, of course, was to die, to keep the departed company in the shades.

We had rehearsals every night for a fortnight, and Harry, Tina, and I officiated as stage-managers. It is incredible the trouble we had. Esther acted the part of Judæan matron to perfection,—her long black hair being let down and dressed after a picture in the Biblical Dictionary, which Tina insisted upon must be authentic. Esther, however, rebelled at the nose-jewels. There was no making her understand the Oriental taste of the thing; she absolutely declined the embellishment, and finally it was agreed among us that the nose-jewels should be left to the imagination.

Harry looked magnificent, with the help of a dark moustache, which Tina very adroitly compounded of black ravelled yarn, arranging it with such delicacy that it had quite the effect of hair. The difficulty was that in impassioned moments the moustache was apt to get awry; and once or twice, while on his knees before Tina in tragical attitudes, this occurrence set her off into hysterical giggles, which spoiled the effect of the rehearsal. But at last we contrived a plaster which the most desperate plunges of agony could not possibly disarrange.

As my eyes and hair were black, when I had mounted a towering helmet, overshadowed by a crest of bear-skin, fresh from an authentic bear that Heber Atwood had killed only two weeks before, I made a most fateful and portentous Jephthah, and flattered myself secretly on the tragical and gloomy emotions excited in the breasts of divers of my female friends.

I composed for myself a most towering and lofty entrance-scene, when I came in glory at the head of my troops. I could not help plagiarising Miss Hannah More's first line:—

"On Jordan's banks proud Ammon's banners wave."

Any writer of poems will pity me, when he remembers his own position, if he has ever tried to make a verse on some subject, and been stuck and pierced through by some line of another poet, which so sticks in his head and his memory that there is no possibility of his saying the thing any other way. I tried beginning,—

"On Salem's plains the summer sun is bright;"

but when I looked at my troop of helmets and the very startling banner which we were to display, and reflected that Josh Billings was to give an inspiring blast on a bugle behind the scenes, I perfectly longed to do the glorious and magnificent, and this resounding line stood right in my way.

"Well, dear me, Horace," said Tina, "take it, and branch off from it,—make a text of it."

And so I did. How martial and Miltonic I was! I really made myself feel quite serious and solemn with the pomp and glory of my own language; but I contrived to introduce into my resounding verses a most touching description of my daughter, in which I exhausted Oriental images and similes on her charms. Esther and I were to have rather a tender scene on parting, as she was to be my wife; but then we minded it not a jot. The adroitness with which both these young girls avoided getting into relations that might savour of reality was an eminent instance of feminine tact. And while Harry was playing the impassioned lover at Tina's feet, Esther looked at him slyly, with just the slightest shade of consciousness,—something as slight as the quivering of an eyelash or the tremulous flush on her fair cheek. There was fire under that rose-coloured snow after all, and that was what gave the subtle charm to the whole thing.

We had an earnest discussion among us four as to what was proper to be done with the lover. Harry insisted upon it, that, after tearing his hair and executing all the other proprieties of despair, he should end by falling on his sword; and he gave us two or three extemporaneous representations of the manner in which he intended to bring out this last scene. How we screamed with laughter over these discussions, as Harry, whose mat of curls was somewhat prodigious, ran up and down the room, howling distractedly, running his fingers through his hair until each separate curl stood on end, and his head was about the size of a half-bushel! We nearly killed ourselves laughing over our tragedy, but still the language thereof was none the less broken-hearted and impassioned.

Tina was vindictive and bloodthirsty in her determination that the tragedy should be of the deepest dye. She exhibited the ferocity of a little pirate in her utter insensibility to the details of blood and murder, and would not hear of any concealment or half-measures to spare anybody's feelings. She insisted upon being stabbed on the stage, and she had rigged up a kitchen carving-knife with a handle of gilt paper, ornamented with various breastpins of the girls, which was celebrated in florid terms in her part of the drama as the Tyrian dagger.

"Why Tyrian," objected Harry, "when it is the Jews that are fighting the Ammonites?"

"Oh nonsense, Harry! Tyrian sounds a great deal better, and the Ammonites, I don't doubt, had Tyrian daggers," said Tina, who displayed a feminine facility in the manufacture of facts. "Tyre, you know," she added, "was the country where all sorts of things were made: Tyrian purple and Tyrian mantles—why, of course they must have made daggers, and the Jews must have got them—of course they must! I'm going to have it, not only a Tyrian dagger, but a sacred dagger, taken away from a heathen temple, and consecrated to the service of the Lord. And only see what a sheath I have made for it! Why, at this distance it couldn't be told from gold! And how do you suppose that embossed work is made? Why, it's different-coloured grains of rice and gilt paper rolled up!"

It must be confessed that nobody enjoyed Tina's successes more heartily than she did herself. I never knew anybody who had a more perfect delight in the work of her own hands.

It was finally concluded, in full concert, that the sacrifice was to be performed at an altar, and here came an opportunity for Miss Titcomb's proficiency in tombstones to exercise itself. Our altar was to be like the lower part of a monument, so we decided, and Miss Titcomb had numerous patterns of this kind, subject to our approval. It was to be made life size, of large sheets of pasteboard, and wreathed with sacrificial garlands.

Tina was to come in at the head of a chorus of wailing maidens, who were to sing a most pathetic lamentation over her. I was to stand grim and resolved, with my eyes rolled up into my helmet, and the sacrificial Tyrian dagger in my hands, when she was to kneel down before the altar, which was to have real flame upon it. The top of the altar was

made to conceal a large bowl of alcohol, and before the entering of the procession the lights were all to be extinguished,
and the last scene was to be witnessed by the lurid glare of
the burning light on the altar.   Any one who has ever tried
the ghostly, spectral, supernatural appearance which his very
dearest friend may be made to have by this simple contriv-
ance, can appreciate how very sanguine our hopes must have
been of the tragical power of this *dénouement*.

All came about quite as we could have hoped.   The academy hall was packed and crammed to the ceiling, and our
acting was immensely helped by the loudly-expressed sympathy of the audience, who entered into the play with the
most undisguised conviction of its reality.   When the lights
were extinguished, and the lurid flame flickered up on the
altar, and Tina entered, dressed in white, with her long hair
streaming around her, and with an inspired look of pathetic
resignation in her large, earnest eyes, a sort of mournful
shudder of reality came over me, and the words I had said
so many times concerning the sacrifice of the victim became
suddenly intensely real; it was a sort of stage illusion, an
overpowering belief in the present.

The effect of the ghastly light on Tina's face, on Esther's
and Harry's, as they grouped themselves around in the pre-
concerted attitudes, was really overwhelming.

It had been arranged that, at the very moment when my
hand was raised, Harry, as the lover, should rush forward
with a shriek, and receive the dagger in his own bosom.
This was the last modification of our play, after many
successive rehearsals, and the success was prodigious.   I
stabbed Harry to the heart, Tina gave a piercing shriek, and
fell dead at his side, and then I plunged the dagger into my
own heart, and the curtain fell, amid real weeping and wailing
from many unsophisticated, soft-hearted old women.

Then came the last scene—the procession of youths and maidens across the stage, bearing the bodies of the two lovers—the whole ending in an admirably-constructed monument, over which a large willow was seen waving. This last gave to Miss Titcomb, as she said, more complete gratification that any scene that had been exhibited. The whole was a most triumphant success.

Heber Atwood's "old woman" declared that she caught her breath, and thought she "should ha' fainted clean away when she see that gal come in." And as there was scarcely a house in which there was not a youth or a maiden who had borne part in the chorus, all Cloudland shared in the triumph.

By way of dissipating the melancholy feelings consequent upon the tragedy, we had a farce called "Our Folks," which was acted extemporaneously by Harry, Tina, and myself, consisting principally in scenes between Harry as Sam Lawson, Tina as Hepsie, and myself as Uncle Fliakim, come in to make a pastoral visit, and exhort them how to get along and manage their affairs more prosperously. There had been just enough strain upon our nerves, enough reality of tragic exultation, to excite that hysterical quickness of humour which comes when the nervous system is well up. I let off my extra steam in Uncle Fliakim with a good will, as I danced in in my black silk tights, knocking down the spinning-wheel, upsetting the cradle, setting the babies to crying, and starting Hepsie's tongue, which lost nothing of force or fluency in Tina's reproduction. How the little elf could have transformed herself in a few moments into such a peaked, sharp, wiry-featured, virulent-tongued virago, was matter of astonishment to us all; while Harry, with a suit of fluttering old clothes, with every joint dissolving in looseness, and with his bushy hair in a sort of dismayed tangle, with his cheeks sucked in and his eyes protruding, gave an inimitable Sam Lawson.

The house was convulsed; the screams and shrieks of laughter quite equalled the moans of distress in our tragedy.

And so the curtain fell on our last exhibition in Cloudland. The next day was all packing of trunks and taking of leave, and last words from Mr. Rossiter and Mr. Avery to the school, and settling of board-bills and school-bills, and sending back all the breastpins from the Tyrian dagger, and a confused kicking about of helmets, together with interchanges between various Johns and Joans of vows of eternal constancy, assurances from some fair ones that, "though they could not *love*, they should always regard as a brother," and from some of our sex to the same purport toward gentle-hearted Aramintas, —very pleasant to look upon, and charming to dwell upon,— who were not, after all, our chosen Aramintas; and there was no end of three and four paged notes written, in which Susan Ann told Susan Jane that "never, never shall we forget the happy hours we've spent together on Cloudland hill, —never shall the hand of friendship grow cold, or the heart of friendship cease to beat with emotion."

Poor dear souls, all of us! We meant every word that we said.

It was only the other day that I called in a house on Beacon Street to see a fair sister, to whom on this occasion I addressed a most pathetic note, and who sent me a very pretty curl of golden-brown hair. Now she is Mrs. Boggs, and the sylph that was is concealed under a most enormous matron; the room trembles when she sets her foot down. But I found her heart in the centre of the ponderous mass, and, as I am somewhat inclining to be a stout old gentleman, we shook the room with our merriment. Such is life!

The next day Tina was terribly out of spirits, and had two

or three hours of long and bitter crying, the cause of which
none of our trio could get out of her.

The morning that we were to leave she went around bidding
good-bye to everybody and everything, for there was not a
creature in Cloudland that did not claim some part in her,
and for whom she had not a parting word. And, finally, I
proposed that we should go in to the schoolmaster together,
and have a last good time with him, and then, with one of her
sudden impulsive starts, she turned her back on me.

"No, no, Horace! I don't want to see him any more!"

I was in blank amazement for a moment, and then I remembered the correspondence on the improvement of her
mind.

"Tina, you don't tell me," said I, "that Mr. Rossiter
has"——

She turned quickly round, and faced on the defensive.

"Now, Horace, you need not talk to me, for it is *not my
fault! Could* I dream of such a thing, now? *Could* I? Mr.
Rossiter, of all the men on earth! Why, Horace, I do love
him dearly. I never had any father—that cared for me, at
least," she said, with a quiver in her voice; "and he was
beginning to seem so like a father to me. I loved him, I
respected him, I reverenced him,—and now was I wrong to
express it?"

"Why, but, Tina," said I, in amazement, "Mr. Rossiter
cannot—he could not mean to marry you!"

"No, no. He says that he would not. He asked nothing.
It all seemed to come out before he thought what he was saying,—that he has been thinking altogether too much of me,
and that when I go, it will seem as if *all* was gone that he
cares for. I can't tell you how he spoke, Horace; there was
something fearful in it, and he trembled. Oh, Horace, he
loves me nobly, disinterestedly, truly; but I felt guilty for

it. I felt that such a power of feeling never ought to rest on such a bit of thistle-down as I am. Oh! why wouldn't he stay on the height where I had put him, and let me reverence and admire him, and have him to love as my father?"

"But, Tina, you cannot, you must not now"——

"I know it, Horace. I have lost him for a friend, and father, and guide, because he will love me too well."

And so ends Mr. Jonathan Rossiter's Spartan training.

My good friends of the American Republic, if ever we come to have mingled among the senators of the United States specimens of womankind like Tina Percival, we men remaining such as we by nature are and must be, will not the general hue of politics take a decidedly new and interesting turn?

Mr. Avery parted from us with some last words of counsel. ·

"You are going into college life, boys, and you must take care of your bodies. Many a boy breaks down because he keeps his country appetite, and loses his country exercise. You must balance study and brain-work by exercise and muscle-work, or you'll be down with dyspepsia, and won't know what ails you. People have wondered where the seat of original sin is; I think it's in the stomach. A man eats too much, and neglects exercise, and the devil has him all his own way, and the little imps, with their long black fingers, play on his nerves like a piano. Never overwork either body or mind, boys. All the work that a man can do that can be *rested by one night's sleep is good for him*, but fatigue that goes into the next day is always bad. Never get discouraged at difficulties. 1 give you both this piece of advice. When you get into a tight place, and everything goes against you, till it seems as if you couldn't hold on a minute longer, *never give up then*, for that's just the place and time that the tide'll turn. Never trust to prayer without using every means in your power, and never use the means without trusting in prayer. Get your evidences of grace by pressing forward to the mark, and not by groping with a lantern after the boundary-lines,—and so, boys, go, and God bless you!"

CHAPTER XVI.
We enter College.

HARRY and I entered Cambridge with honour. It was a matter of pride with Mr. Rossiter that his boys should go more than ready,—that an open and abundant entrance should be administered unto them in the classic halls; and so it was with us. We were fully prepared on the conditions of the sophomore year, and thus, by Mr. Rossiter's drill, had saved the extra expenses of one year of college life.

We had our room in common, and Harry's improved means enabled him to fit it up and embellish it in an attractive manner. Tina came over and presided at the inauguration, and helped us hang our engravings, and fitted up various little trifles of shell and moss work,—memorials of Cloudland.

Tina was now visiting at the Kitterys', in Boston, dispensing smiles and sunbeams, inquired after and run after by every son of Adam who happened to come in her way, all to no purpose, so far as her heart was concerned:—

> "Favours to none, to all she smiles extends;
> Oft she rejects, but never once offends."

Tina's education was now, in the common understanding of society, looked upon as finished. Harry's and mine were commencing; we were sophomores in college. She was a young lady in society; yet she was younger than either of us, and had, I must say, quite as good a mind, and was fully as capable of going through our college course with us as of having walked thus far.

However, with her the next question was, Whom will she marry?—a question that my young lady seemed not in the slightest hurry to answer. I flattered myself on her want of susceptibility that pointed in the direction of marriage. She could feel so much friendship,—such true affection,—and yet was apparently so perfectly devoid of passion.

She was so brilliant and so fitted to adorn society, that one would have thought she would have been *ennuyée* in the old Rossiter house, with only the society of Miss Mehitable and Polly; but Tina was one of those whose own mind and nature 'are sufficient excitement to keep them always burning. She loved her old friend with all her little heart, and gave to her all her charms and graces, and wound round her in a wildrose garland, like the eglantine that she was named after.

She had cultivated her literary tastes and powers. She wrote and sketched and painted for Miss Mehitable, and Miss Mehitable was most appreciative. Her strong, shrewd, well-cultivated mind felt and appreciated the worth and force of everything there was in Tina, and Tina seemed perfectly happy and satisfied with one devoted admirer. However, she had two, for Polly still survived, being of the dry immortal species, and seemed, as Tina told her, quite as good as new. And Tina, once more, had uproarious evenings with Miss Mehitable and Polly, delighting herself with the tumults of laughter which she awakened.

She visited and patronised Sam Lawson's children, gave them candy and told them stories, and now and then brought home Hepsie's baby for a half-day, and would busy herself dressing it up in something new of her own invention and construction. Poor Hepsie was one of those women fated always to have a baby in which she seemed to have no more maternal pleasure than an old fowling-piece. But Tina looked at her on the good-natured and pitiful side, although, to be sure, she did study her with a view to dramatic representation, and made no end of capital of her in this way in the bosom of her own family.

Tina's mimicry and mockery had not the slightest tinge of contempt or ill-feeling in it; it was pure merriment, and seemed to be just as natural to her as the freakish instincts of the mocking-bird, who sits in the blossoming boughs above your head, and sends back every sound that you hear with a wild and airy gladness.

Tina's letters to us were full of this mirthful, effervescent sparkle, to which everything in Oldtown afforded matter of amusement; and the margins of them were scrawled with droll and lifelike caricatures, in which we recognised Sam Lawson, and Hepsie, and Uncle Fliakim, and, in fact, all the Oldtown worthies,—not even excepting Miss Mehitable and Polly, the minister and his lady, my grandmother, Aunt Lois, and Aunt Keziah. What harm was there in all this, when Tina assured us that aunty read the letters before they went, and laughed until she cried over them?

"But, after all," I said to Harry one day, "it's rather a steep thing for girls that have kept step with us in study up to this point, and had their minds braced just as ours have been, with all the drill of regular hours and regular lessons, to be suddenly let down, with nothing in particular to do."

"Except to wait the coming man," said Harry, "who is to teach her what to do."

"Well," said I, "in the interval, while this man is coming,

what has Tina to do but to make a frolic of life?—to live like a bobolink on a cloverhead, to sparkle like a dewdrop in a thorn-bush, to whirl like a bubble on a stream? Why couldn't she as well find the coming man while she is doing something as while she is doing nothing? Esther and you found each other while you were *working* side by side, your minds lively and braced, toiling at the same great ideas, knowing each other in the very noblest part of your natures; and you are true companions; it is a mating of *souls*, and not merely of bodies."

"I know that," said Harry, "I know, too, that in these very things that I set my heart on in the college course Esther is by far my superior. You know, Horace, that she was ahead of us both in Greek and mathematics; and why should she not go through the whole course with us as well as the first part? The fact is, a man never sees a subject thoroughly until he sees a woman will think of it, for there is a woman's view of every subject, which has a different shade from a man's view, and that is what you and I have insensibly been absorbing in all our course hitherto. How splendidly Esther lighted up some of those passages of the Greek tragedy! and what a sparkle and glitter there were in some of Tina's suggestions! All I know, Horace, is that it is confoundedly dull being without them; these fellows are well enough, but they are cloddish and lumpish."

"Well," said I, "that isn't the worst of it. When such a gay creature of the elements as Tina is has nothing earthly to do to steady her mind and task her faculties, and her life becomes a mere glitter, and her only business to amuse the passing hour, it throws her open to all sorts of temptations from that coming man, whoever he may be. Can we wonder that girls love to flirt, and try their power on lovers? And then they are fair game for men who want to try their powers

16*

on them, and some man who has a vacation in his life purpose, and wants something to amuse him, makes an episode by getting up some little romance, which is an amusement to him, but all in all to her.   Is that fair?"

"True," said Harry; "and there's everything about Tina to tempt one; she is so dazzling and bewildering and exciting that a man might intoxicate himself with her for the mere pleasure of the thing, as one takes opium or champagne; and that sort of bewilderment and intoxication girls often mistake for love! I would to Heaven, Horace, that I were as sure that Tina loves you as I am that Esther loves me."

"She does love me with her *heart*," said I, "but not with her imagination. The trouble with Tina, Harry, is this: she is a woman that can really and truly love a man as a sister, or as a friend, or as a daughter, and she is a woman that no man can love in that way long. She feels nothing but affection, and she always creates passion. I have not the slightest doubt that she loves me dearly, but I have a sort of vision that between her and me will come some one who will kindle her imagination; and all the more so, that she has nothing serious to do, nothing to keep her mind braced, and her intellectual and judging faculties in the ascendant, but is fairly set adrift, just like a little flowery boat, without steersman or oars, on a bright, swift-rushing river. Did you ever notice, Harry, what a singular effect Ellery Davenport seems to have on her?"

"No," said Harry, starting and looking surprised. "Why, Horace, Ellery Davenport is a good deal older than she is, and a married man too."

"Well, Harry, didn't you ever hear of married men that liked to try experiments with girls? and in our American society they can do it all the more safely, because here, thank heaven! nobody ever dreams but what marriage is a perfect regulator and safeguard."

"But," said Harry, rubbing his eyes like a person just waking up, "Horace, it must be the mere madness of jealousy that would put such a thing into your head. Why, there hasn't been the slightest foundation for it."

"That is to say, Harry, you've been in love with Esther, and your eyes and ears and senses have all run one way. But I have lived in Tina, and I believe I have a sort of divining power, so that I can almost see into her heart. I *feel in myself* how things affect her, and I *know*, by feeling and sensation, that from her childhood Ellery Davenport has had a peculiar magnetic effect upon her."

"But, Horace, he is a married man," persisted Harry.

"A fascinating married man, victimised by a crazy wife, and ready to throw himself on the sympathies of womanhood in this affliction. The fair sex are such Good Samaritans that some fellows make capital of their wounds and bruises."

"Well, but," said Harry, "there's not the slightest thing that leads me to think that he ever cared particularly about Tina."

"That's because you are Tina's brother, and not her lover," said I. "I remember as long ago as when we were children, spending Easter at Madam Kittery's, how Ellery Davenport's eyes used to follow her,—how she used constantly to seem to excite and interest him; and all this zeal about your affairs, and his coming up to Oldtown, and cultivating Miss Mehitable's acquaintance so zealously, and making himself so necessary to her; and then he has always been writing letters or sending messages to Tina, and then, when he was up in Cloudland, didn't you see how constantly his eyes followed her? He came there for nothing but to see her, —I'm perfectly sure of it."

"Well, Horace, you are about as absurd as a lover need be!" said Harry. "Mr. Davenport is rather a conceited man of the world; I think he patronised me somewhat extensively; but all this about Tina is a romance of your own spinning, you may be sure of it."

This conversation occurred one Saturday morning, while we were dressing and arraying ourselves to go to Boston, where we had engaged to dine at Madam Kittery's.

From the first of our coming to Cambridge, we had remembered our old-time friendship for the Kitterys, and it was an arranged thing that we were to dine with them every Saturday. The old Kittery mansion we had found the same still, charming, quaint, inviting place that it seemed to us in our childhood. The years that had passed over the silvery head of dear old Madam Kittery had passed lightly and reverently, each one leaving only a benediction.

She was still to be found, when we called, seated, as in days long ago, on her little old sofa in the sunny window, and with her table of books before her, reading her Bible and Dr. Johnson, and speaking on "Peace and good-will to men."

As to Miss Debby, she was as up-and-down, as high-stepping and outspoken and pleasantly sub-acid as ever. The French Revolution had put her in a state of good-humour hardly to be conceived of. It was so delightful to have all her theories of the bad effects of republics on lower classes illustrated and confirmed in such a striking manner, that even her indignation at the destruction of such vast numbers of the aristocracy was but a slight feature in comparison with it.

She kept the newspapers and magazines at hand which contained all the accounts of the massacres, mobbings, and outrages, and read them, in a high tone of voice, to her serving-women, butler, and footman after family prayers. She catechised more energetically than ever, and bore more stringently on ordering one's-self lowly and reverently to one's betters, enforcing her remarks by the blood-and-thunder stories of the guillotine in France.

We were hardly seated in the house, and had gone over the usual track of inquiries which fill up the intervals, when she burst forth on us triumphant.

"Well, my English papers have come in. Have you seen the last news from France? They're at it yet, hotter than ever. One would think that murdering the king and queen might have satisfied them, but it don't a bit. Everybody is at it now, cutting everybody's else throat, and there really does seem to be a prospect that the whole French nation will become extinct."

"Indeed," said Harry, with an air of amusement. "Well, Miss Debby, I suppose you think that would be the best way of settling things."

"Don't know but it would," said Miss Debby, putting on her spectacles in a manner which pushed her cap-border up into a bristling, helmet-like outline, and whirling over her file of papers, seemingly with a view to edifying us with the most startling morsels of French history for the six months past.

"Here's the account of how they worshipped 'the Goddess of Reason!'" she cried, eyeing us fiercely, as if we had been part and party in the transaction. "Here's all about how their philosophers and poets, and what not, put up a drab, and worshipped her as their 'Goddess of Reason!' And then they annulled the Sabbath, and proclaimed that 'Death is an eternal sleep!' Now, that is just what Tom Jefferson likes; it's what suits him. I read it to Ellery Davenport yesterday, to show him what his principles come to."

Harry immediately hastened to assure Miss Debby that we were stanch Federalists, and not in the least responsible for any of the acts or policy of Thomas Jefferson.

"Don't know anything about that; you see it's the Democrats that have got the country, and are running as hard as they can after France. Ah, here it is," Miss Debby added, still turning over her files of papers. "Here are the particulars of the execution of the queen. You can see,—they had her on a common cart, hands tied behind her, rattling and jolting, with all the vile fishwomen and dirty drabs of Paris, leering and jeering at her, and they even had the cruelty," she added, coming indignantly at us as if we were responsible for it, "to stop the cart in front of her palace, so that she might be agonised at seeing her former home, and they might taunt her in her agonies! Anybody that can read that, and not say the French are devils, I'd like to know what they are made of!"

"Well," said Harry, undismayed by the denunciations; "the French are an exceedingly sensitive and excitable people, who had been miseducated and mismanaged, and taught brutality and cruelty by the examples of the clergy and nobility."

"Excitable fiddlesticks!" said Miss Debby, who, like my grandmother, had this peculiar way of summing up an argument. "I don't believe in softening sin and iniquity by such sayings as that."

"But you must think," said Harry, "that the French are human beings, and only act as any human beings would, under their circumstances."

"Don't believe a word of it!" said she, shortly. "I agree with the man who said, 'God made two kinds of nature,—human nature and French nature.' Voltaire, wasn't it, himself, that said the French were a compound of the tiger and the monkey. I wonder what Tom Jefferson thinks of his beautiful, darling French Republic now! I presume he likes it. I don't doubt it is just such a state of things as he is trying to bring to pass here in America."

"O," said I, "the Federalists will head him at the next election."

"I don't know anything about your Democrats and your Federalists," said she. "I thank heaven I wash my hands of this government."

"And does King George still reign here?" said Harry.

"Certainly he does, young gentleman! Whatever happens to *this* government, *I* have no part in it."

Miss Debby, upon this, ushered us to the dinner-table, and said grace in a resounding and belligerent voice, and, sitting down, began to administer the soup to us with great determination.

Old Madam Kittery, who had listened with a patient smile to all the preceding conversation, now began in a gentle aside to me.

"I really don't think it is good for Debby to read those blood-bone stories, morning, noon, and night, as she does," she said. "She really almost takes away my appetite some days, and it does seem as if she wouldn't talk about anything else. Now, Horace," she said to me, appealingly, "the Bible says, 'Charity rejoiceth not in iniquity,' and I can't help feeling that Debby talks as if she were really glad to see those poor French making such a mess of things. I can't feel so. If they are French, they're our brothers, you know, and Debby really seems to go against the Bible,—not that she means to, dear," she added, earnestly, laying her hand on mine; "Debby is an excellent woman; but, between you and me, I think she is a little excitable."

"What's that mother's saying?" said Miss Debby, who

kept a strict survey over all the sentiments expressed in her household. "What was mother saying?"

"I was saying, Debby, that I didn't think it did any good for you to keep reading over and over those dreadful things."

"And who does keep reading them over?" said Miss Debby, "I should like to know. I'm sure I don't; except when it is absolutely necessary to instruct the servants, and put them on their guard. I'm sure I am as averse to such details as anybody can be."

Miss Debby said this with that innocent air with which good sort of people very generally maintain that they never do things which most of their acquaintances consider them particular nuisances for doing.

"By the by, Horace," said Miss Debby, by way of changing the subject, "have you seen Ellery Davenport since he came home?"

"No," said I, with a sudden feeling as if my heart was sinking down into my boots. "Has he come home to stay?"

"O yes," said Miss Debby; "his dear, sweet, model republican France grew too hot to hold him. He had to flee to England, and now he has concluded to come home and make what mischief he can here, with his democratic principles and his Rousseau and all the rest of them."

"Debby isn't as set against Ellery as she seems to be," said the old lady, in an explanatory aside to me. "You know, dear, he's her cousin."

"And you really think he intends to live in this country for the future?" said I.

"Well, I suppose so," said Miss Debby. "You know that poor, miserable, crazy wife of his is dead, and my lord is turned loose on society as a widower at large, and all the talk here in good circles is, Who is the blessed woman that shall be Mrs. Ellery Davenport the second? The girls are all pulling caps for him, of course."

It was perfectly ridiculous and absurd, but I suddenly lost all appetite for my dinner, and sat back in my chair playing with my knife and fork, until the old lady said to me compassionately—

"Why, dear, you don't seem to be eating anything! Debby, put an *oyster-pâté* on Horace's plate; he don't seem to relish his chicken."

I had to submit to the *oyster-pâté*, and sit up and eat it like a man, to avoid the affectionate importunity of my dear old friend. In despair, I plunged into the subject least agreeable to me, and remarked—

"Mr. Davenport is a very brilliant man, and, I suppose, in very good circumstances; is he not?"

"Yes, enormously rich," said Miss Debby. "He still passes for young, with that face of his that never will grow old, I believe. And then he has a tongue that could wheedle a bird out of a tree; so I don't know what is to hinder him from having as many wives as Solomon, if he feels so disposed. I don't imagine there is anybody would say 'No' to him."

" Well, I hope he will marry a good girl," said the old lady, "poor, dear boy. I always loved Ellery; and he would make any woman happy, I am sure."

"That depends," said Miss Debby, "on what the woman wants. If she wants laces and cashmere shawls, and horses and carriages, and a fine establishment, Ellery Davenport will give her those. But if she wants a man to love her all her life, that's what Ellery Davenport can't do for any woman. He is a man that never cares for anything he has got. It's always the thing that he hasn't got that he's after. It's the 'pot of money at the end of the rainbow,' or the 'philosopher's

stone,' or any other thing that keeps a man all his life on a
canter, and never getting anywhere. And no woman will ever
be anything to him but a temporary diversion. He can amuse
himself in too many ways to want *her*."

"Yes," said the old lady, "but when a man marries he
promises to cherish her."

"My dear mother, that is in the Church Service, and I
assure you Ellery Davenport has got beyond that. He's
altogether too fine and wise and enlightened to think that a
man should spend his days in cherishing a woman merely
because he went through the form of marriage with her in
church. Much cherishing his crazy wife got of him! but he
used his affliction to get half-a-dozen girls in love with him,
so that he might be cherished himself. I tell you what,—
Ellery Davenport lays out to marry a real angel. He's to
swear and she's to pray! He is to wander where he likes,
and she is always to meet him with a smile and ask no
questions. That is the part for Mrs. Ellery Davenport to
act."

"I don't believe a word of it, Debby," said the old lady.
"You'll see now,—you'll see."

CHAPTER XVII.

Night Talks.

We walked home that night by starlight, over the long
bridge between Boston and Cambridge, and watched the
image of the great round moon just above the horizon, breaking and shimmering in the water into a thousand crystal
fragments, like an orb of golden glass. We stopped midway
in the calm obscurity, with our arms around each other, and
had one of those long talks that friends, even the most confidential, can have only in the darkness. Cheek to cheek

under the soft dim mantle of the starlight, the night flowers of the innermost soul open.

We talked of our loves, our hopes, of the past, the present, and the great hereafter, in which we hoped for ever to mingle. And then Harry spoke to me of his mother, and told in burning words of that life of bitterness and humiliation and sorrow through which he had passed with her.

"O Harry," said I, "did it not try your faith, that God should have left her to suffer all that?"

"No, Horace, no, because in all that suffering she conquered,—she was more than conqueror. O, I have seen such divine peace in her eyes, at the very time when everything earthly was failing her! Can I ever doubt? I who saw into heaven when she entered? No, I have seen her crowned, glorified, in my soul as plainly as if it had been a vision."

At that moment I felt in myself that magnetic vibration of the great central nerves which always prefaced my spiritual visions, and looking up I saw that the beautiful woman I had seen once before was standing by Harry, but now more glowing and phosphorescent than I saw her last; there was a divine, sweet, awful radiance in her eyes, as she raised her hands above her head, he, meanwhile, stooping down and looking intently into the water.

"Harry," said I, after a few moments of silence, "do you believe your mother sees and knows what you do in this world, and watches over you?"

"That has always been one of those things that I have believed without reasoning," said Harry, musingly. "I never could help believing it; and there have been times in my life when I felt so certain that she must be near me, that it seemed as though, if I spoke, she must answer,—if I reached out my hand, it would touch hers. It is one of my instinctive certainties. It is curious," he added, "that the difference between Esther and myself is just the reverse kind of that which generally subsists between man and woman. She has been all her life so drilled in what logicians call reasoning, that, although she has a glorious semi-spiritual nature and splendid moral instincts, she never trusts them. She is like an eagle that should insist upon climbing a mountain by beak and claw instead of using wings. She must always see the syllogism before she will believe."

"For my part," said I, "I have always felt the tyranny of the hard New England logic, and it has kept me from really knowing what to believe about many phenomena of my own mind that are vividly real to me." Here I faltered and hesitated, and the image that seemed to stand by us slowly faded. I could not and did not say to Harry how often I had seen it.

"After all I have heard and thought on this subject," said Harry, "my religious faith is what it always was,—a deep, instinctive certainty, an embrace by the soul of *something* which it could not exist without. My early recollections are stronger than anything else of perfect and utter helplessness, of troubles entirely beyond all human aid. My father"—— He stopped and shuddered. "Horace, he was one of those whom intemperance makes mad. For a great part of his time he was a madman, with all the cunning, all the ingenuity, the devilishness of insanity, and I have had to stand between him and my mother, and to hide Tina out of his way." He seemed to shudder as one convulsed. "One does not get over such a childhood," he said. "It has made all my religious views, my religious faith, rest on two ideas,—man's helplessness and God's helpfulness. We are sent into this world in the midst of a blind, confused jangle of natural laws, which we cannot by any possibility understand, and which cut their way through and over and around us. They tell us nothing; they have no sympathy; they hear no prayer; they spare neither vice nor virtue. And if we have no friend above to guide us through the labyrinth, if there is no Father's heart, no helping hand, of what use is life? I would throw myself into this river, and have it over with at once."

"I always noticed your faith in prayer," said I. "But how can it consist with this known inflexibility of natural laws?"

"And what if natural laws were meant as servants of man's moral life? What if Jesus Christ and his redeeming, consoling work were the *first* thing, and all things made by him for this end? Inflexible physical laws are necessary; their very inflexibility is divine order; but 'what law cannot do, in that it is weak through the flesh, God did by sending His Son in the likeness of sinful flesh.' Christ delivers us from slavery to natural law; he comes to embody and make visible the paternal idea; and if you and I, with our small knowledge of physical laws, can so turn and arrange them that their inflexible course shall help and not hinder, much more can their Maker."

"You always speak of Christ as God."

"I have never thought of God in any other way," he answered. "Christ is the God of sufferers; and those who learn religion by sorrow always turn to him. No other than a suffering God could have helped my mother in her anguish."

"And do you think," said I, "that prayer is a clue strong enough to hold amid the rugged realities of life?"

"I do," said Harry. "At any rate, there is my great venture; that is my life-experiment. My mother left me that as her only legacy."

"It certainly seems to have worked well for you so far, Harry," said I, "and for me too, for God has guided us to

what we scarcely could have hoped for, two poor boys as we
were, and so utterly helpless. But then, Harry, there must
be a great many prayers that are never answered."

"Of course," said Harry, "I do not suppose that God has
put the key of all the universe into the hand of every child;
but it is a comfort to have a Father to ask of, even though
he refuse five times out of six, and it makes all the difference
between having a father and being an orphan. Yes," he
added, after a few moments of thought, "my poor mother's
prayers seemed often to be denied, for she prayed that my
father might reform. She often prayed from day to day that
we might be spared miseries that he still brought upon us.
But I feel sure that she has seen by this time that her Father
heard the prayers that he seemed to deny, and her faith in
him never failed. What is that music?" he said.

At this moment there came softly over the gleaming water,
from the direction of the sea, the faintest possible vibration
of a sound, like the dying of an organ tone. It might be
from some ship, hidden away far off in the mist, but the
effect was soft and dreamy as if it came from some spirit-land.

"I often think," said Harry, listening for a moment, "that
no one can pronounce on what this life has been to him until
he has passed entirely through it, and turns around and sur-
veys it from the other world. I think then we shall see everything in its true proportions; but till then we must walk by
faith and not by sight,—faith that God loves us, faith that
our Saviour is always near us, and that all things are working
together for good."

"Harry," said I, "do you ever think of your father
now?"

"Horace, there is where I wish I could be a more perfect
Christian than I am. I have a bitter feeling toward him,
that I fear is not healthful, and that I pray God to take

away. To-night, since we have been standing here, I have had a strange, remorseful feeling about him, as if some good spirit were interceding for him with me, and trying to draw me to love and forgive him. I shall never see him, probably, until I meet him in the great Hereafter, and then, perhaps, I shall find that her prayers have prevailed for him."

It was past twelve o'clock when we got to our room that night, and Harry found lying on his table a great sealed package from England. He opened it, and found in it, first, a letter from his father, Sir Harry Percival. The letter was as follows:—

"HOLME HOUSE.

"MY SON HARRY,—I have had a dozen minds to write to you before now, having had good accounts of you from Mr. Davenport; but, to say truth, have been ashamed to write. I did not do right by your mother, nor by you and your sister, as I am now free to acknowledge. She was not of a family equal to ours, but she was too good for me. I left her in America, like a brute as I was, and God has judged me for it.

"I married the woman my father picked out for me when I came home, and resolved to pull up and live soberly like a decent man. But nothing went well with me. My children died one after another; my boy lived to be seven years old, but he was feeble, and now he is dead too, and you are the heir. I am thinking that I am an old sinner, and in a bad way. Have had two turns of gout in the stomach that went hard with me, and the doctor don't think I shall stand many such. I have made my will with a provision for the girl, and you will have the estate in course. I do wish you would come over and see a poor old sinner before he dies. It isn't in the least jolly being here, and I am devilish cross, they say. I suppose I am, but if you were minded to come, I'd try and behave myself, and so make amends for what's past beyond recall.—Your father,   HARRY PERCIVAL."

Accompanying this letter was a letter from the family lawyer, stating that on the 18th day of the month past Sir Harry Percival had died of an attack of gout. The letter went on to give various particulars about the state of the property, and the steps which had been taken in relation to it, and expressing the hope that the arrangements made would meet with his approbation.

It may well be imagined that it was almost morning before we closed our eyes, after so very startling a turn in our affairs. We lay long discussing it in every possible light, and now first I found courage to tell Harry of my own peculiar experiences, and of what I had seen that very evening. "It seems to me," said Harry, when I had told him all, "as if I *felt* what you saw. I had a consciousness of a sympathetic presence, something breathing over me like wind upon harp-strings, something particularly predisposing me to think kindly of my father. My feeling towards him has been the weak spot of my inner life always, and I had a morbid horror of him. Now I feel at peace with him. Perhaps her prayers have prevailed to save him from utter ruin."

CHAPTER XVIII.

Spring Vacation at Oldtown.

IT was the spring vacation, and Harry and I were coming again to Oldtown; and ten miles back, where we changed horses, we had left the crawling old Boston stage, and took a footpath through a patch of land known as the Spring Pasture. Our road lay pleasantly along the brown, sparkling river, which was now just waked up, after its winter nap, as fussy and busy and chattering as a housekeeper that has overslept herself. There were downy catkins on the willows, and the water-maples were throwing out their crimson tassels. The sweet-flag was just showing its green blades above the water, and here and there, in nooks, there were yellow cowslips reflecting their bright gold faces in the dark water.

Harry and I had walked this way that we might search under the banks and among the dried leaves for the white waxen buds and flowers of the trailing arbutus. We were down on our knees, scraping the leaves away, when a well-known voice came from behind the bushes.

"Wal, lordy massy, boys! Here ye be! Why, I ben up to Siah's tahvern, an' looked inter the stage, an' didn't see yer. I jest thought I'd like to come an' kind o' meet yer. Lordy massy, they's all a-lookin' out for yer't all the winders; 'n' Aunt Lois, she's ben bilin' up no end o' doughnuts, an' tearin' round 'nough to drive the house out o' the winders to git everything ready for ye. Why, it beats the Prodigal Son all holler, the way they're killin' the fatted calves for yer; an' everybody in Oldtown's a-wantin' to see Sir Harry."

"Oh, nonsense, Sam!" said Harry, colouring. "Hush about that! We don't have titles over here in America."

"Lordy massy, that's just what I wus a tellin' on 'em up to store. It's a pity, ses I, this yere happened arter peace was signed, 'cause we might ha' had a real live Sir Harry round among us. An' I think Lady Lothrop', she kind o' thinks so too."

"Oh, nonsense!" said Harry. "Sam, are the folks all well?"

"Oh, lordy massy, yes! Chirk and chipper as can be. An' there's Tiny, they say she's a goin' to be an heiress nowadays, an' there's no end of her beaux. There's Ellery

Devenport ben down here these two weeks, a-puttin' up at the tahvern, with a landau an' a span o' crack horses, a-takin' on her out to ride every day, and Miss Mehitable, she's so sot up, she's really got a bran-new bonnet, an' left off that 'ere old un o' horn that she's had trimmed over spring an' full goin' on these 'ere ten years. I thought that 'ere bonnet's goin' to last out my time, but I see it hain't. An' she's got a new Injy shawl that Mr. Devenport gin her. Yeh see, he understan's courtin', all round."

This intelligence, of course, was not the most agreeable to me. I hope, my good friends, that you have never known one of those quiet hours of life, when, while you are sitting talking and smiling, and to all appearance quite unmoved, you hear a remark or learn a fact that seems to operate on you as if somebody had quietly turned a faucet that was letting out your very life. Down, down, down, everything seems sinking, the strength passing away from you as the blood passes when an artery is cut. It was with somewhat this sensation that I listened to Sam's chatter, while I still mechanically poked away the leaves and drew out the long waxy garlands that I had been gathering for *her!*

Sam seated himself on the bank, and, drawing his knees up to his chin, and clasping his hands upon them, began moralizing in his usual strain.

"Lordy massy, lordy massy, what a changin' world this 'ere is! It's jest soe-saw, teeter-tawter, up an' down. To-day it's I'm up an' you're down, an' to-morrow it's you're up and I'm down! An' then, by an' by, death comes an' takes us all. I've ben kind o' dwellin' on some varses to-day,—

"Death, like a devourin' deluge,
    Sweeps all away;
  The young, the old, the middle-aged,
    To him become a prey."

That 'ere is what Betty Poganut repeated to me the night we sot up by Statiry's corpse. You 'member Statiry Poganut? Well, she's dead at last. Yeh see, we all gits called in our turn. We hain't here no continuin' city."

"But, Sam," said I, "how does business get along? Havan't you anything to do but tramp the pastures and moralise?"

"Wal," said Sam, "I've hed some pretty consid'able spells of blacksmithin' lately. There's Mr. Devenport, he's sech a pleasant-spoken man, he told me he brought his team all the way up from Bostin a purpose so that I might 'tend to their huffs. I've ben a-shoein' on 'em fresh all round, an' the off horse, he'd kind o' got a crack in his huff, an' I've been a-doctorin' on 't; an' Mr. Devenport, he said he hadn't found nobody that knew how to doctor a horse's huffs ekal to me. Very pleasant-spoken man Mr. Devenport is; he's got a good word for everybody. They say there ain't no end to his fortin', an' he goes a-flingin' on 't round, right an' left, like a prince. Why, when I'd done shoein' his hosses, he jest put his hand inter his pocket an' handed me out ten dollars! ripped it out, he did, jest as easy as water runs! But there was Tiny a-standin' by; I think she kind o' sot him on. O lordy massy, it's plain to be seen that *she* rules him. It's all cap in hand to her, an' 'What you will, madam,' an' 'Will ye have the end o' the rainbow, or a slice out o' the moon, or what is it?' It's all ekal to him, so as Miss Tiny wants it. Lordy massy," he said, lowering his voice confidentially to Harry, "course these 'ere things is all temporal, an' our hearts oughtn't to be too much sot on 'em; still he's got about the most amazin' fortin' there is round Bostin. Why, if you b'lieve me, 'tween you an' me, it's him as owns the Dench Place, where you and Tiny put up when you wus children! Don't ye 'member when I found ye? Ye little guessed whose house ye wus a puttin' up at then; did yer? Lordy massy, lordy massy, who'd ha thought it? The wonderful ways of Providence! 'He setteth the poor on high, an' letteth the runagates continoo in scarceness.' Wal, wal, it's a kind o' instructive world."

"Do you suppose," said Harry to me, in a low voice, "that this creature knows anything of what he is saying?"

"I'm afraid he does," said I. "Sam seems to have but one talent, and that is picking up news; and generally his guesses turn out to be about true."

"Sam," said I, by way of getting him to talk of something else, rather than on what I dreaded to hear, "you haven't said a word about Hepsy and the children. How are they all?"

"Wal, the young uns hés all got the whoopin' cough," said Sam, "an' I'm e'en a'most beat out with 'em. For fust it's one barks, an' then another, an' then altogether. An' then Hepsy, she gets riled, an' she scolds; an', take it all together, a feller's head gits kind o' turned. When ye hes a lot o' young uns, there's allus suthin' a goin' on among 'em; ef 't ain't whoopin' cough, it's measles; an' ef 't ain't measles, it's chicken-pox, or else it's mumps, or scarlet-fever, or suthin'. They's all got to be gone through, fust an' last. It's enough to wean a body from this world. Lordy massy, yest'day arternoon I see yer Aunt Keziah an' yer Aunt Lois out a cuttin' cowslip greens t' other side o' th' river, an' the sun it shone so bright, an' the turtles an' frogs they kind o' peeped so pleasant, an' yer aunts they sot on the bank so kind o' easy an' free, an' I stood there a-lookin' on 'em, an' I couldn't help a-thinkin', 'Lordy massy, I wish t' I wus an old maid.' Folks 'scapes a great deal that don't hev no young uns a-hangin' onter 'em."

"Well, Sam," said Harry, "isn't there any news stirring round in the neighbourhood?"

"S'pose ye hain't heerd about the great church-quarrel over to Needmore?" he said.

"Quarrel? Why, no," said Harry. "What is it about?"

"Wal, ye see, there's a kind o' quarrel ris 'tween Parson Perry and Deacon Bangs. I can't jest git the right on't, but it's got the hull town afire. I b'lieve it cum up in a kind o' dispute how to spell Saviour. The Deacon he's on the school-committee, an' Parson Perry he's on't; an' the Deacon he spells it *iour*, an' Parson Perry he spells it *ior*, an' they wouldn't neither on 'em give up. Wal, ye know Deacon Bangs,—I *s'pose* he's a Christian,—but, lordy massy, he's one o' yer dreadful ugly kind o' Christians, that, when they gits their backs up, will do worse things than sinners will. I reelly think they kind o' take advantage o' their position, an' think, es they're goin' to be saved by grace, grace shell hev enough on't. Now, to my mind, ef either on 'em wus to give way, the Deacon oughter give up to the Parson; but the Deacon he don't think so. Between you and me," said Sam, "it's my opinion that ef Ma'am Perry hedn't died jest when she did, this 'ere thing would never ha' growed to where 'tis. But ye see Ma'am Perry she died, an' that left Parson Perry a widower, an' folks did talk about him an' Mahaley Bangs, an' fact was, 'long about last spring, Deacon Bangs an' Mis' Bangs an' Mahaley wus jest as thick with the Parson as they could be. Why, Granny Watkins told me about their havin' on him to tea two an' three times a week, an' Mahaley'd made two kinds o' cake, an' they'd have preserved vatermelon rinds, an' peaches, an' cranberry sauce, an' then twas all sugar an' all sweet, an' the Deacon he talked 'bout raisin' Parson Perry's salary. Wal, then, ye see, Parson Pery he went over to Oldtown an' married Jerushy Peabody. Now, Jerushy's a nice, pious gal, an' it's a free country, an' parsons hes a right to suit 'emselves as

well's other men. But Jake Marshall, he ses to me, when
he heerd o' that, ses he, 'They'll be findin' fault with Parson
Perry's doctrines now afore two months is up; ye see if they
don't.' Wal, sure enuff, this 'ere quarrel 'bout spellin'
Saviour came on fast, an' Deacon Bangs he fit the Parson
like a bulldog. An' next town-meetin' day he told Parson
Perry right out before everybody thet he was wuss then 'n
Armenian—that he was a rank Pelagian; 'n' he said there
was folks thet hed taken notes o' his sermons for two years
back, 'n' they could show thet he hedn't preached the real
doctrine of total depravity, nor 'riginal sin, an' thet he'd got
the plan o' salvation out o' jint intirely; he was all kind o'
flattin' out onter morality. An' Parson Perry he sed he'd
preached jest's he allers hed. 'Tween you 'n' me, we know
he *must* ha' done that, 'cause these 'ere ministers that hev to
go preachin' round 'n' round like a hoss in a cider-mill,—wal,
course they *must* preach the same sermons over. I s'pose
they kind o' trim 'em up with new collars 'n' wris'bands.
But we used to say thet Parson Lothrop hed a bar'l o' sermons, 'n' when he got through the year he turned his bar'l
t'other side up, and begun at t'other end. Lordy massy,
who's to know it, when half on em's asleep? And I guess
the preaching's full as good as the pay anyhow! Wal, the
upshot on't all is, they got a gret counsel there, an' they're a
tryin' Mr. Perry for heresy an' what not. Wal, I don't b'lieve
there's a yaller dog goes into the Needmore meetin'-house
now that ain't got his mind made up one way or t'other
about it. Yer don't hear nothin' over there now 'xcept about
Armenians, an' Pelagians, an' Unitarians, an' total depravity.
Lordy massy! wal, they lives up to that doctrine any way.
What do ye think of old Sphyxy Smith's bein' called in as
one o' the witnesses in council? She don't know no more
'bout religion than an old heichel, but she's fierce as can be

on Deacon Bang's side, an' Old Crab Smith he hes to hev his
say 'bout it."

"Do tell," said Harry, wonderingly, "if that old creature
is alive yet!"

"'Live? Why, yis, ye may say so," said Sam. "Much
alive as ever he was. Ye see he kind o' pickles himself in
hard cider, an' I dunno but he may live to hector his wife till
he's ninety. But he's gret on the trial now, an' very much
interested 'bout the doctrines. He ses that he hain't heard
a sermon on sovereignty, or 'lection, or reprobation, sence he
can remember. Wal, t'other side, they say they don't see
what business Old Crab an' Miss Sphyxy hev to be meddlin'
so much, when they ain't church-members. Why, I was over
to Needmore town-meetin' day jest to hear 'em fight over it;
they talked a darned sight more 'bout that than 'bout the
turnpikes or town business. Why, I heard Deacon Brown
(he's on the parson's side) tellin' Old Crab he didn't see what
business *he* had to *boss* the doctrines, when he warn't a church-
member, and Old Crab said it *was* his bisness about the
doctrines, 'cause he *paid* to hev 'em. 'Ef I *pay* for good
strong doctrine, why, I want to *hev* good strong doctrine,'
says Old Crab, says he. 'Ef I pays for hell-fire, I want to
hev hell-fire, and hev it hot too. I don't want none o' your
prophesyin' smooth things. Why,' says he, 'look at Dr.
Sterne. His folks hes the very hair took off their heads 'most
every Sunday, and he don't get no more 'n we pay Parson
Perry. I tell yew,' says Old Crab, 'he's a-lettin' on us all go
to sleep, and it's no wonder I ain't in the church.' Ye see,
Old Crab and Sphyxy, they seem to be kind o' settin' it down
to poor old Parson Perry's door that he hain't converted 'em,
an' made saints on 'em long ago, when they've paid up their
part o' the salary reg'lar every year. Jes' so onreasonable
folks will be; they give a man two hundred dollars a-year

an' his wood, an' 'spect him to git all on 'em inter the kingdom o' heaven, whether they will or no, jest as the angels got Lot's wife and daughters out o' Sodom."

"That poor little old woman!" said Harry. "Do tell if she is living yet!"

"Oh yis, she's all right," said Sam; "she's one o' these 'ere little thin, dry old women that keep a good while. But ain't ye heerd? their son Obid 's come home an' bought a farm, an' married a nice gal, and he insists on it his mother shall live with him. An' so Old Crab and Miss Sphyxy, they fight it out together. So the old woman is delivered from him most o' the time. Sometimes he walks over there an' stays a week, an' takes a spell o' aggravatin' on 'er, that kind o' sets him up, but he's so busy now 'bout the quarrel, 't I b'lieve he lets her alone."

By this time we had reached the last rail-fence which separated us from the grassy street of Oldtown, and here Sam took his leave of us.

"I promised Hepsy when I went out," he said, "thet I'd go to the store and git her some corn-meal, but I'll be round agin in th' evening. Look 'ere," he added, "I wus out this mornin', an' I dug some sweet-flag root for yer. I know ye used ter like sweet-flag root. 'T ain't time for young wintergreen yit, but here's a bunch I picked yer, with the berries an' old leaves. Do take 'em, boys, jest for the sake o' old times!"

We thanked him, of course; there was a sort of aroma of boyhood about these things, that spoke of spring days and melting snows, and long Saturday afternoon rambles that we had had with Sam years before. And we saw his lean form go striding off with something of an affectionate complacency.

"Horace," said Harry, the minute we were alone, "you mustn't mind too much about Sam's gossip."

"It is just what I have been expecting," said I; "but in a few moments we shall know the truth."

We went on until the square white front of the old Rossiter house rose upon our view. We stopped before it, and down the walk from the front door to the gate, amid the sweet budding lilacs, came gleaming and glancing the airy form of Tina. So airy she looked, so bright, so full of life and joy, and threw herself into Harry's arms, laughing and crying.

"Oh Harry, Harry! God has been good to us! And you, dear brother Horace," she said, turning to me, and giving me both her hands, with one of those frank, loving looks that said as much as another might say by throwing herself into your arms. "We are all so happy!" she said.

I determined to have it over at once, and I said, "Am I then to congratulate you, Tina, on your engagement?"

She laughed and blushed, and held up her hand, on which glittered a great diamond, and hid her face for a moment on Harry's shoulder.

"I couldn't write to you about it, boys,—I couldn't! But I meant to tell you myself, and tell you the first thing too. I wanted to tell you about him, because I think you none of you know him, or half how noble and good he is! Come, come in," she said, taking us each by the hand and drawing us along with her. "Come in and see Aunty; she'll be so glad to see you!"

If there was any one thing for which I was glad at this moment, it was that I had never really made love to Tina. It was a comfort to me to think that she did not and could not possibly know the pain she was giving me. All I know is that, at the moment, I was seized with a wild, extravagant gaiety, and rattled and talked and laughed with a reckless *abandon* that quite astonished Harry. It seemed to me as if every ludicrous story, and every droll remark that I had ever heard came thronging into my head together. And I believe that Tina really thought that I was sincere in rejoicing with her. Miss Mehitable talked with us gravely about it while Tina was out of the room. It was most sudden and unexpected, she said, to her; she always had supposed that Ellery Davenport had admired Tina, but never that he had thought of her in this way. In a worldly point of view, the match was a more brilliant one than could ever have been expected. He was of the best old families in the country,—of the Edwards and the Davenport stock,—his talents were splendid, and his wealth would furnish everything that wealth could furnish. "There is only one thing," she continued, gravely; "I am not satisfied about his religious principles. But Tina is an enthusiast, and has perfect faith that he will come all right in this respect. He seems to be completely dazzled and under her influence now," said Miss Mehitable, taking a leisurely pinch of snuff; "but then, you see, that's a common phenomenon about this time in a man's life. But," she added, "where there is such a strong attachment on both sides, all we can do is to wish both sides well, and speed them on their way. Mr. Davenport has interested himself in the very kindest manner in regard to both Tina and Harry, and I suppose it is greatly owing to this that affairs have turned out as prosperously as they have. As you know, Sir Harry made a handsome provision for Tina in his will. I confess I am glad of that," she said, with a sort of pride. "I wouldn't want my little Tina to have passed into his arms altogether penniless. When first love is over, men sometimes remember those things."

"If my father had not done justice to Tina in his will,"

said Harry, "I should have done it. My sister should not have gone to any man a beggar."

"I know that, my dear," said Miss Mehitable, "but still it is a pleasure to think that your father did it. It was a justice to your mother's memory that I am glad he rendered."

"And when is this marriage to take place?" said I.

"Mr. Davenport wants to carry her away in June," said Miss Mehitable. "That leaves but little time; but he says he must go to join the English Embassy certainly by midsummer, and as there seems to be a good reason for his haste, I suppose I must not put my feelings in the way. It seems now as if I had had her only a few days, and she has been so very sweet and lovely to me. Well," said she, after a moment, "I suppose the old sweetbrier-bushes feel lonesome when we cut their blossoms and carry them off, but the old thorny things mustn't have blossoms if they don't expect to have them taken. That's all we scraggly old people are good for."

CHAPTER XIX.

What our Folks thought about It.

At home that evening, before the great open fire, still the same subject was discussed. Tina's engagement to Ellery Davenport was spoken of as the next most brilliant stroke of luck to Harry's accession to the English property. Aunt Lois was all smiles and suavity, poor dear old soul! How all the wrinkles and crinkles of her face smoothed out under the influence of prosperity! and how providential everything appeared to her!

"Providence gets some pay-days," said an old divine. Generally speaking, his account is suffered to run on with very lax attention. But when a young couple make a fortunate engagement, or our worldly prospects take a sudden turn to go as we would, the account of Providence is gladly balanced; praise and thanksgiving come in over-measure.

For my part, I couldn't see the Providence at all in it, and found this looking into happiness through other people's eyes a very fatiguing operation.

My grandfather and grandmother, as they sat pictured out by the light of a magnificent hickory fire, seemed scarcely a year older; but their faces this evening were beaming complacently; and my mother, in her very quiet way, could scarcely help triumphing over Aunt Lois. I was a sophomore in Cambridge, and Harry a landed proprietor, and Tina an heiress to property in her own right, instead of our being three poor orphan children without any money, and with the up-hill of life to climb.

In the course of the evening, Miss Mehitable came in with Ellery Davenport and Tina. Now, much as a man will dislike the person who steps between him and the lady of his love, I could not help, this evening, myself feeling the power of that fascination by which Ellery Davenport won the suffrages of all hearts.

Aunt Lois, as usual, was nervous and fidgety with the thought that the call of the splendid Mr. Davenport had surprised them all at the great kitchen fire, when there was the best room cold as Nova Zembla. She looked almost reproachfully at Tina, and said, apologetically, to Mr. Davenport, "We are rough working folks, and you catch us just as we are. If we'd known you were coming, we'd have had a fire in the parlour."

"Then, Miss Badger, you would have been very cruel, and deprived us of a rare enjoyment," said he. "What other land but our own America can give this great, joyous, abundant home-fire? The great kitchen-fire of New England," he added, seating himself admiringly in front of it, "gives you all the freshness and simplicity of forest life, with a sense of shelter and protection. It's like a camp-fire in the woods, only that you have a house over you, and a good bed to sleep in at hand; and there is nothing that draws out the heart like it. People never can talk to each other as they do by these great open fires. For my part," he said, "I am almost a fire-worshipper. I believe in the divine properties of flame. It purifies the heart and warms the affections, and when people sit and look into the coals together, they feel a sort of glow of charity coming over them that they never feel anywhere else."

"Now, I should think," said Aunt Lois, "Mr. Davenport, that you must have seen so much pomp and splendour and luxury abroad, that our rough life here would seem really disagreeable to you."

"Quite the contrary," said Ellery Davenport. "We go abroad to appreciate our home. Nature is our mother, and the life that is lived nearest to nature is, after all, the one that is the pleasantest. I met Brant at court last winter. You know he was a wild Indian to begin with, and he has seen both extremes, for now he is Colonel Brant, and has been moving in fashionable society in London. So I thought he must be a competent person to decide on the great question between savage and civilised life, and he gave his vote for the savage."

"I wonder at him," said my grandmother.

"Well, I remember," said Tina, "we had one day and night of savage life—don't you remember, Harry?—that was very pleasant. It was when we stayed with the old Indian woman,—do you remember? It was all very well, so long as the sun shone; but then when the rain fell, and the wind blew, and the drunken Indian came home, it was not so pleasant."

"That was the time, young lady," said Ellery Davenport, looking at her with a flash in his blue eyes, "that you established yourself as housekeeper on my premises! If I had only known it, I might have picked you up then, as a waif on my grounds."

"It's well you did not," said Tina, laughing; "you would have found me troublesome to keep. I don't believe you would have been as patient as dear old Aunty here," she added, laying her head on Miss Mehitable's shoulder. "I was a perfect brier-rose,—small leaves and a great many prickles."

"By the by," said Harry, "Sam Lawson has been telling us this morning about our old friends Miss Asphyxia Smith and Old Crab."

"Is it possible," said Tina, laughing, "that those creatures are living yet? Why, I look back on them as some awful pre-Adamite monsters."

"Who was Miss Asphyxia?" said Ellery Davenport. "I haven't heard of her."

"Oh, 'twas a great threshing-machine of a woman that caught me between its teeth some years ago," said Tina. "What do you suppose would ever have become of me, Aunty, if she had kept me? Do you think she ever could have made me a great stramming, threshing, scrubbing, floor-cleaning machine, like herself? She warned Miss Mehitable," continued Tina, looking at Ellery and laughing shyly, "that I never should grow up to be good for anything; and she spoke a fatal truth, for, since she gave me up, every mortal creature has tried to pet and spoil me. Dear old Aunty and Mr. Rossiter have made some feeble attempts to make me good for something, but they haven't done much at it."

"Thank heaven!" said Ellery Davenport. "Who would think of training a wild rose? I sometimes look at the way a sweetbrier grows over one of our rough stone walls, and think what a beautiful defiance it is to gardeners."

"That is all very pretty to say," said Tina, "when you happen to be where there are none but wild roses; but when you were among marchionesses and duchesses, how was it then?"

For answer, Ellery Davenport bent over her, and said something which I could not hear. He had the art, without seeming to whisper, of throwing a sentence from him so that it should reach but one ear; and Tina laughed, and blushed, and dimpled, and looked as if a thousand little graces were shaking their wings around her.

It was one of Tina's great charms that she was never for a moment at rest. In this she was like a bird, or a brook, or a young tree, in which there is always a little glancing shimmer of movement. And when anything pleased her, her face sparkled as a river does when something falls into it. I noticed Ellery Davenport's eyes followed all these little motions as if he had been enchanted. Oh, there was no doubt that the great illusion, the delicious magic, was in full development between them. And Tina looked so gladly satisfied, and glanced about the circle and at him with such a quiet triumph of possession, and such satisfaction in her power over him, that it really half reconciled me to see that she was so happy. And, after all, I thought to myself as I looked at the airy and *spiritual* style of her beauty,—a beauty that conveyed the impression of fragility and brilliancy united to the highest point,—such a creature as that is made for luxury, made for perfume, and flowers, and jewelry, and pomp of living, and obsequious tending, for old aristocratic lands and court circles, where she would glitter as a star. And what had I to offer,—I, a poor sophomore in Harvard, owing that position to the loving charity of my dear old

friend? My love to her seemed a madness and a selfishness,
—as if I had wished to take the evening star out of the
heavens, and burn it for a household lamp. "How fortunate,
how fortunate," I thought to myself, "that I have never told
her! For now I shall keep the love of her heart. We are
friends, and she shall be the lady of my heart for ever,—the
lady of my dreams."

I knew, too, that I had a certain hold upon her; and even
at this moment I saw her eye often, as from old habit, looking across to me, a little timidly and anxiously, to see what
I thought of her prize. She was Tina still,—the same old
Tina, that always needed to be approved, and loved, and
sympathised with, and have all her friends go with her,
heart and hand, in all her ways. So I determined to like
him.

At this moment Sam Lawson came in. It was a little
curious to know how he had managed it with his conscience,
to leave his domestic circle under their trying circumstances,
but I was very soon satisfied as to this point.

Sam, who had watched the light flaring out from the
windows, and flattened his nose against the window-pane,
while he announced to Hepsy that "Mr. Devenport, and Miss
Mehitable, and Tiny, were all a-goin' into the Deacon's to
spend th' evenin'," could not resist the inexpressible yearning
to have a peep himself at what was going on there.

He came in with a most prostrate air of dejection. Aunt
Lois frowned with stern annoyance, and looked at my grandmother, as much as to say, "To think *he* should come in
when Mr. Davenport is making a call here!"

Ellery Davenport, however, received him with a patronising cheerfulness,—"Why, hulloa, Sam, how are you?" It
was Ellery Davenport's delight to start Sam's loquacity, and
develop his conversational powers, and he made a welcoming

movement toward the block of wood in the chimney-corner. "Sit down," he said—"sit down, and tell us how Hepsy and the children are."

Tina and he looked at each other with eyes dancing with merriment.

"Wal, wal," said Sam, sinking into the seat and raising his lank hands to the fire, while his elbows rested on his knees, "the children's middlin',—Doctor Merrill sees he thinks they've got past the wust on't,—but Hepsy, she's clean tuckered out, and kind o' discouraged. An' I thought I'd come over an' jest ask Mis' Badger ef she wouldn't kind o' jest mix'er up a little milk punch, to kind o' set 'er up agin."

"What a considerate husband!" said Ellery Davenport, glancing around the circle with infinite amusement.

My grandmother, always prompt at any call on her charity, was already half across the floor toward her buttery, whence she soon returned with a saucepan of milk.

"I'll watch that 'ere Mis' Badger," said Sam. "Jest rake out the coals this way, an' when it begins ter simmer I'll put in the sperits, ef ye'll gin 'em to me. 'Give strong drink ter him as is ready to perish,' the Scriptur' says. Hepsy's got an amazin' sight o' grit in her; but I 'clare for't, she's ben up an' down nights so much lately with them young uns thet she's a'most clean wore out. An' I should be too, ef I didn't take a tramp now 'n' then to kind o' keep me up. Wal, ye see, the head o' the family, he *hes* to take car' o' himself, 'cause ye see, ef *he* goes down, all goes down. 'The man is the head o' the woman,' ye know," said Sam, as he shook his skillet of milk.

I could see Tina's eyes dancing with mirthfulness as Ellery Davenport answered, "I'm glad to see, Sam, that you have a proper care of your health. You are such an important

member of the community, that I don't know what Oldtown
would be without you!"

"Wal, now, Mr. Devenport, ye flatter me; but then everybody don't seem to think so. I don't think folks like me, as
does for this one, an' does for that one, an' kind o' spreads
out permiskus, is appreciated allers. There's Hepsy, she's
allers at me, a-sayin', I don't do nothin' for her, an' yet there
las' night I wus up in my shirt, a-shiverin' an' a-goin' roun',
fust ter one and then ter 'nuther, a-hevin' on 'em up an'
a-thumpin' on their backs, an' clarin' the phlegm out o' their
thruts, till I wus e'en a'most fruz; and Hepsy, she lay there
abed scoldin' 'cause I hedn't sawed no wood that arternoon
to keep up the fire. Lordy massy, I jest went out ter dig a
leetle sweet-flag root ter gin ter the boys,' cause I wus so kind
o' wore out. I don't think these 'ere women ever 'flects on
men's trials. They railly don't keep count o' what we do
for 'em."

"What a picture of conjugal life!" said Ellery Davenport,
glancing at Tina. "Yes, Sam, it is to be confessed that the
female sex are pretty exorbitant creditors. They make us
pay dear for serving them."

"Jes' so! jes' so!" said Sam. "They don't know nothin'
what we undergo. I don't think Hepsy keeps no sort o'
count o' the nights an' nights I've walked the floor with the
baby, whishin' an' shooin' on't, and singin' to't till my thrut
wus sore, an' then hed to git up afore daylight to split oven-
wood, an' then right to my blacksmithin', jest to git a little
money to git the meat an' meal and suthin' comfort'ble fur
dinner! An' then, ye see, there don't nothin' *last*, when
there's so many mouths to eat it up: an' there 'tis, it's jest
roun' an' roun'. Ye get a good piece o' beef Tuesday an' pay
for't, an' by Thursday it's all gone, an' ye hev to go to work
agin! Lordy massy, this 'ere life don't seem hardly wuth

hevin'. I s'pose, Mr. Davenport, you've been among the gret folks o' th' earth, over there in King George's court? Why, they say here that you've ben an' tuk tea with the king, with his crown on 's head! I s'pose they all goes roun' with their crowns on over there; don't they?"

"Well, no, not precisely," said Ellery Davenport. "I think they rather mitigate their splendours when they have to do with us poor republicans, so as not to bear us down altogether."

"Jes' so," said Sam, "like Moses, that put a veil over 's face 'cause th' Israelites couldn't bear the glory."

"Well," said Allery Davenport, "I've not been struck with any particular resemblance between King George and Moses."

"The folks here 'n Oldtown, Mr. Devenport, 's amazin' curus to hear the partic'lars 'bout them grand things 't you must ha' seen; I's a-tellin' on 'em up to store how you'd ben with lords 'n' ladies 'n' dukes 'n' duchesses, 'n' seen all the kingdoms o' the world, an' the glory on 'em. I told 'em I didn't doubt you'd et off 'em plates o' solid gold, an' ben in houses where the walls was all a crust o' gold 'n' diamonds 'n' precious stones, 'n' yit ye didn't seem ter be one bit lifted up nor proud, so 't yer couldn't talk ter common folks. I s'pose them gret fam'lies they hes as much 's fifty or a hunderd servants, don't they?"

"Well, sometimes," said Ellery Davenport.

"Wal, now," said Sam, "I sh'd think a man 'd feel kind o' curus,—sort o' 's ef he was keepin' a hotel, an' boardin' all the lower classes."

"It is something that way, Sam," said Ellery Davenport. "That's one way of providing for the lower classes."

"Jest what th' Lord told th' Israelites when they would hev a king," said Sam. "Ses he, 'He'll take yer daughters to be confectioners 'n' cooks 'n' bakers, an' he'll take the best 'o' yer fields 'n' yer vineyards 'n' olive-yards, an' give 'em to his sarvints, an' he'll take a tenth o' yer seed 'n' give 'em ter his officers, an' he'll take yer men-sarvints 'n' yer maid-sarvints, 'n' yer goodliest young asses, an' put 'em ter his works.'"

"Striking picture of monarchical institutions, Sam," said Ellery Davenport.

"Wal, now, I tell ye what," said Sam, slowly shaking his shimmering skillet of milk, "I shouldn't want ter get inter that 'ere pie, unless I could be some o' the top crust. It's jest like a pile o' sheepskins,—'s only the top un lies light. I guess th' undermost one's queezed putty flat."

"I'll bet it is, Sam," said Ellery Davenport, laughing.

"Wal," said Sam, "I go for republics, but yit it's human natur' ter kind o' like ter hold onter titles. Now over here a man likes ter be a deacon, 'n' a cap'n, 'n' a colonel in the milishy, 'n' a sheriff, 'n' a judge, 'n' all thet. Lordy massy, I don't wonder them grand English folks sticks to their grand titles, an' the people all kind o' bows down to 'em, as they did to Nebuchadnezzar's golden image."

"Why, Sam," said Ellery Davenport, "your speculations on pilitics are really profound."

"Wal," said Sam, "Mr. Devenport, there's one pint I want ter consult ye 'bout, an' thet is, what the king o' England's name is. There's Jake Marshall 'n' me, we's argood that pint these many times. Jake ses his name is George Rix,—R-i-x,—an' thet ef he'd come over here, he'd be called Mr. Rix. I ses to him, 'Why, Jake, 'tain't *Rix*, an' 'tain't his name, it's his litle,' ses I,—'cause the boys told me thet Rex was Latin, 'n' meant king; but Jake 's one o' them fellers thet allers thinks he knows. Now, Mr. Devenport, I'd like to put it down from you ter him,

'cause you've just come from the court o' England, an'
you'd know."

"Well you may tell your friend Jake that you are quite in
the right," said Ellery Davenport. "Give him my regards,
and tell him he's been mistaken."

"But you don't call the king Rex when ye speak to 'im,
do yer?" said Sam.

"Not precisely," said Ellery Davenport.

"Mis' Badger," said Sam, gravely, "this 'ere milk's come
to the bile, 'n' ef you'll be so kind's to hand me the sperits 'n'
the sugar, I'll fix this 'ere. Hepsy likes her milk punch putty
hot."

"Well, Sam," said my grandmother, as she handed him
the bottle, "take an old woman's advice, and don't go stramming off another afternoon. If you'd been steady at your
blacksmithin', you might have earned enough money to buy
all these things yourself, and Hepsy'd like it a great deal
better."

"I suppose it's about the two hundred and forty-ninth
time mother has told him that," said Aunt Lois, with air of
weary endurance.

"Wal, Mis' Badger," said Sam, "'all work an' no play
makes Jack a dull boy,' ye know. I *hes* to recreate, else I
gits quite wore out. Why, lordy massy, even a saw-mill hes
ter stop sometimes ter be greased. 'Tain't everybody that's
like Sphyxy Smith, but she grits and screeches all the time,
jest 'cause she keeps to work without bein' 'iled. Why, she
could work on, day 'n' night, these twenty years, 'n' never
feel it. But, lordy massy, I gits so 'xhausted, an' has sech a
sinking 't my stomach, 'n' then I goes out 'n' kind o' *Injunin'*
round, an' git flag-root, 'n' winter-green, 'n' spruce boughs,
'n' gensing root, 'n' sarsafras, 'n' sich, fur Hepsy to brew up

a beer. I ain't a wastin' my time ef I be enjoyin' myself. I say it's a part o' what we's made for."

"You are a true philosopher, Sam," said Ellery Davenport.

"Wal," said Sam, "I look at it this 'ere way,—ef I keep on a-grindin' and a-grindin' day 'n' night, I never shell hev nothin', but ef I takes now 'n' then an arternoon to lie roun' in the sun, *I gits suthin' 's I go 'long.* Lordy massy, it's jest all the comfort I hes, kind o' watchin' the clouds 'n' the birds, 'n' kind o' forgettin' all 'bout Hepsy 'n' the children 'n' the blacksmithin'."

"Well," said Aunt Lois, smartly, "I think you are forgetting all about Hepsy and the children now, and I advise you to get that milk punch home as quick as you can, if it's going to do her any good. Come, here's a tin pail to put it into. Cover it up, and do let the poor woman have some comfort as well as you!"

Sam received his portion in silence, and, with reluctant glances at the warm circle, went out into the night.

"I don't see how you all can bear to listen to that man's maundering!" said Aunt Lois. "He puts me out of all sort of patience. 'Head of the woman' to be sure! when Hepsy earns the most of what that family uses, except what we give 'em. And I know exactly how she feels; the poor woman is mad with shame and humiliation half the time at the charities he will accept from us."

"Oh come, Miss Lois," said Ellery Davenport, "you must take an æsthetic view of him. Sam's a genuine poet in his nature, and poets are always practically useless. And now Sam's about the only person in Oldtown, that I have seen that has the least idea that life is meant, in any way, for enjoyment. Everybody else seems to be sword in hand, fighting against the possibility of future suffering, toiling and depriving themselves of all present pleasure, so that they may not come to want by and by. Now I've been in countries where the whole peasantry are like Sam Lawson."

"Good gracious!" said Aunt Lois, "what a time they must have of it!"

"Well, to say the truth, there's not much progress in such communities, but there is a great deal of clear, sheer animal enjoyment. And when trouble comes, it comes on them as it does on animals, unfeared and unforeseen, and therefore unprovided for."

"Well," said my grandmother, "you don't think that is the way for rational and immortal creatures to live?"

"Well," said Ellery Davenport, "taking into account the rational and immortal, perhaps not; but I think if we could mix the two races together it would be better. The Yankee lives almost entirely for the future, the Italian enjoys the present."

"Well, but do you think it is *right* to live merely to enjoy the present?" persisted Aunt Lois.

"The eternal question!" said Ellery. "After all, who knows anything about it? What *is* right, and what *is* wrong? Mere geographical accidents! What is right for the Greenlander is wrong for me; what is right for me is wrong for the Hindoo. Take the greatest saint on earth to Greenland, and feed him on train-oil and candles, and you make one thing of him; put him under the equator, with the thermometer at one hundred in the shade, and you make another."

"But right is right, and wrong is wrong," said Aunt Lois, persistently, "after all."

"I sometimes think," said Ellery Davenport, "that right and wrong are just like colour, mere accidental properties. There is no colour where there's no light, and a thing is all sorts of colours according to the position you stand in and the

hour of the day. There's your rocking-chair in the setting
sun becomes a fine crimson, and in the morning comes out
dingy gray. So it is with human actions. There's nothing
so bad that you cannot see a good side to it, nothing so good
that you cannot see a bad side to it. Now we think it's
shocking for our Indian tribes, some of them, to slay their old
people; but I'm not sure, if the Indian could set forth his
side of the case, with all the advantages of our rhetoric, but
that he would have the best of it. He does it as an act of
filial devotion, you see. He loves and honours his father too
much to let him go through all that horrid process of drain-
ing out life drop by drop that we think the thing to protract
in our high civilisation. For my part, if I were an Indian
chief, I should prefer, when I came to be seventy, to be respectfully knocked on the head by my oldest son, rather than
to shiver and drivel and muddle and cough my life out a
dozen years more."

"But God has given his commandments to teach us what
is right," said Aunt Lois. "'Honour thy father and mother.'"

"Precisely," said Ellery; "and my friends the Sioux
would tell you that they *do* honour their fathers and mothers
by respectfully putting them out of the way when there is no
more pleasure in living. They send them to enjoy eternal
youth in the hunting-grounds of the fathers, you know."

"Positively, Ellery," said Tina, "I shan't have this sort
of heathen stuff talked any longer. Why, you put one's head
all in a whirl! and you know you don't believe a word of it
yourself. What's the use of making everybody think you're
worse than you are?"

"My dear," said Ellery, "there's nothing like hearing all
that can be said on both sides of subjects. Now, there's my
good grandfather made an argument on the will, that is, and

for ever will remain, unanswerable, because he proves both
sides of a flat contradiction perfectly; that method makes a
logic-trap out of which no mortal can get his foot."

"Well," said my grandmother, "Mr. Davenport, if you'll
take an old woman's advice, you'll take up with your grandfather's *good resolutions*, and not be wasting your strength in
such talk."

"I believe there were about seventy-five—or eighty, was
it?—of those resolutions," said Ellery.

"And you wouldn't be the worse for this world or the next
if you'd make them yourself," said my grandmother.

"Thank you, madam," said Ellery, bowing, "I'll think
of it."

"Well, come," said Tina, rising, "it's time for us to go;
and," she said, shaking her finger warningly at Ellery Davenport, "I have a private lecture for you."

"I don't doubt it," he said, with a shrug of mock apprehension; "the preaching capacities of the fair sex are something terrific.   I see all that is before me."

They bade adieu, the fire was raked up in the great fireplace, all the members of the family went their several ways
to bed, but Harry and I sat up in the glimmer and gloom of
the old kitchen, lighted, now and then, by a sputtering jet of
flame, which burst from the sticks.   All round the large dark
hearth the crickets were chirping as if life were the very
merriest thing possible.

"Well, Harry," I said, "you see the fates have ordered it
just as I feared."

"It is almost as much of a disappointment to me as it can
be to you," said Harry.   "And it is the more so because I
cannot quite trust this man."

"I never trusted him," said I.   "I always had an instinctive doubt of him."

"My doubts are not instinct," said Harry; "they are founded on things I have heard him say myself. It seems to me that he has formed the habit of trifling with all truth, and that nothing is sacred in his eyes."

"And yet Tina loves him," said I. "I can see that she has gone to him heart and soul, and she believes in him with all her heart, and so we can only pray that he may be true to her. As for me, I can never love another. It only remains to live worthily of my love."

CHAPTER XX.

Marriage Preparations.

AND now for a time there was nothing thought of or talked of but marriage preparations and arrangements. Letters of congratulation came pouring in to Miss Mehitable from her Boston friends and acquaintances.

When Harry and I returned to college, we spent one day with our friends the Kitterys, and found it the one engrossing subject there, as everywhere.

Dear old Madam Kittery was dissolved in tenderness, and whenever the subject was mentioned reiterated all her good opinions of Ellery, and her delight in the engagement, and her sanguine hopes of its good influence on his spiritual prospects.

Miss Debby took the subject up energetically. Ellery Davenport was a near family connexion, and it became the Kitterys to make all suitable and proper advances. She insisted upon addressing Harry by his title, notwithstanding his blushes and disclaimers.

"My dear sir," she said to him, "it appears that you are an Englishman and a subject of his Majesty; and I should not be surprised, at some future day, to hear of you in the

House of Commons; and it becomes you to reflect upon your position, and what is proper in relation to yourself; and, at least under this roof, you must allow me to observe these proprieties, however much they may be disregarded elsewhere. I have already informed the servants that they are always to address you as Sir Harry, and I hope that you will not interfere with my instructions."

"Oh certainly not," said Harry. "It will make very little difference with me."

"Now, in regard to this marriage," said Miss Debby, "as there is no *church* in Oldtown, and no clergyman, I have felt that it would be proper in me, as a near kinswoman to Mr. Davenport, to place the Kittery mansion at Miss Mehitable Rossiter's disposal for the wedding."

"Well, I confess," said Harry, blushing, "I never thought but that the ceremony would be performed at home, by Parson Lothrop."

"My dear Sir Harry!" said Miss Debby, laying her hand on his arm with solemnity, "consider that your excellent parents, Sir Harry and Lady Percival, were both members of the Established Church of England, the only true Apostolic Protestant Church,—and can you imagine that their spirits, looking down from heaven, would be pleased and satisfied that their daughter should consummate the most solemn union of her life out of the Church? and, in fact, at the hands of a man who has never received ordination?"

It was with great difficulty that Harry kept his countenance during this solemn address. His blue eyes actually laughed, though he exercised a rigid control over the muscles of his face.

"I really had not thought about it at all, Miss Debby," he said. "I think you are exceedingly kind."

"And I'm sure," said she, "that you must see the propriety

of it now that it is suggested to you. Of course, a marriage performed by Mr. Lothrop would be a legal one, so far as the civil law is concerned; but I confess I always have regarded marriage as a religious ordinance, and it would be a disagreeable thing to me to have any connexions of mine united merely by a *civil* tie. These Congregational marriages," said Miss Debby, in a contemptuous voice, "I should think would lead to immorality. How can people feel as if they were married that don't utter any vows themselves, and don't have any wedding-ring put on their finger? In my view it's not respectable; and, as Mrs. Ellery Davenport will probably be presented in the first circles of England, I desire that she should appear there with her wedding-ring on, like an honest woman. I have therefore despatched an invitation to Miss Mehitable to bring your sister and spend the month preceding the wedding with us in Boston. It will be desirable for other reasons, as all the shopping and dressmaking and millinery work must be done in Boston. Oldtown is a highly respectable little village, but, of course, affords no advantages for the outfit of a person of quality, such as your sister is and is to be. I have had a letter from Lady Widgery this morning. She is much delighted, and sends congratulations. She always, she said, believed that you had distinguished blood in your veins when she first saw you at our house."

There was something in Miss Debby's satisfied, confiding faith in everything English and aristocratic that was vastly amusing to us. The perfect confidence she seemed to have that Sir Harry Percival, after all the sins of his youth, had entered heaven *ex officio* as a repentant and glorified baronet, a member of the only True Church, was really *naïve* and affecting. What would a church be good for that allowed people of quality to go to hell like the commonalty? Sir

Harry, of course, repented, and made his will in a proper manner, doubtless received the sacrament and absolution, and left all human infirmities, with his gouty toes, under the family monument, where his body reposed in sure and certain hope of a blessed and glorious resurrection. The finding of his children under such fortunate circumstances was another evidence of the good Providence who watches over the fortunes of the better classes, and does not suffer the steps of good Churchmen to slide beyond recovery.

There were so many reasons of convenience for accepting Madame Kittery's hospitable invitation, it was urged with such warmth and affectionate zeal by Madam Kittery and Miss Debby, and seconded so energetically by Ellery Davenport, to whom this arrangement would secure easy access to Tina's society during the intervening time, that it was accepted.

Harry and I were glad of it, as we should thus have more frequent opportunities of seeing her. Ellery Davenport was refurbishing and refurnishing the old country house, where Harry and Tina had spent those days of their childhood which it was now an amusement to recall, and Tina was as gladly, joyously beautiful as young womanhood can be in which, as in a transparent vase, the light of pure love and young hope has been lighted.

"You like him, Horace, don't you?" she had said to me, coaxingly, the first opportunity after the evening we had spent together. What was I to do? I did not like him, that was certain; but have you never, dear reader, been over-persuaded to think and say you liked where you did not? Have you not scolded and hushed down your own instinctive distrusts and heart-risings, blamed and schooled yourself for them, and taken yourself sharply to task, and made yourself acquiesce in somebody that was dear and necessary to some friend? So did I. I called myself selfish, unreasonable, foolish. I determined to be generous to my successful rival, and to like him. I took his frankly-offered friendship, and I forced myself to be even enthusiastic in his praise. It was a sure way of making Tina's cheeks glow, and her eyes look kindly on me, and she told me so often that there was no person in the world whose good opinion she had such a value for, and she was so glad I liked him. Would it not be perfectly abominable after this to let sneaking suspicions harbour in my breast?

Besides, if a man cannot have love, shall he therefore throw away friendship? and may I not love with the love of chivalry,—the love that knights dedicated to queens and princesses, the love that Tasso gave to Leonora d'Este, the love that Dante gave to Beatrice, love that hopes little and asks nothing?

I was frequently in at the Kittery house in leisure hours, and when, as often happened, Tina was closeted with Ellery Davenport, to took sweet counsel with Miss Mehitable.

"We all stand outside now, Horace," she said, "I remember when *I* had the hearing of all these thousand pretty little important secrets of the hour that now must all be told in another direction. Such is life. What we want always comes to us with some pain. I wanted Tina to be well married. I would not for the world she should marry without just this sort of love; but of course it leaves me out in the cold. I wouldn't say this to her for the world,—poor little thing, it would break her heart."

One morning, however, I went down and found Miss Mehitable in a very excited state. She complained of a bad headache, but she had all the appearance of a person who is constantly struggling with something which she is doubtful of the expediency of uttering.

At last, just as I was going, she called me into the library: "Come here, Horace," she said; "I want to speak to you."

I went in, and she made a turn or two across the room in an agitated way, then sat down at a table, and motioned me to sit down. "Horace, my dear boy," she said, "I have never spoken to you of the deepest sorrow of my life, and yet it often seems to me as if you knew it."

"My dear Aunty," said I, for we had from childhood called her thus, "I think I do know it,—somewhat vaguely. I know about your sister."

"You know how strangely, how unaccountably she left us, and that nothing satisfactory has ever been heard from her. I told Mr. Davenport all about her, and he promised to try to learn something of her in Europe. He was so successful in relation to Tina and Harry, I hoped he might learn something as to her; but he never seemed to. Two or three times within the last four or five years I have received letters from her, but without date, or any mark by which her position could be identified. They told me, in the vaguest and most general way, that she was well, and still loved me, but begged me to make no inquiries. They were always post-marked at Havre; but the utmost research gives no clue to her residence there."

"Well?" said I.

"Well," said Miss Mehitable, trembling in every limb, "yesterday, when Mr. Davenport and Tina had been sitting together in this room for a long time, they went out to ride. They had been playing at verse-making, or something of the kind, and there were some scattered papers on the floor, and I thought I would remove them, as they were rather untidy, and among them I found"——she stopped, and panted for breath—"I found THIS."

She handed me an envelope that had evidently been

around a package of papers. It was post-marked Geneva, Switzerland, and directed to Ellery Davenport.

"Horace," said Miss Mehitable, "*that is Emily Rossiter's handwriting;* and look, the date is only two months back! What shall we do?"

There are moments when whole trains of thought go through the brain like lightning. The first emotion was, I confess, a perfectly fierce feeling of joy. Here was a clue! My suspicions had not then been unjust; the man was what Miss Debby had said,—deep, artful, and to be unmasked. In a moment I sternly rebuked myself, and thought what a wretch I was for my suspicions. The very selfish stake that I held in any such discovery imposed upon me, in my view, a double obligation to defend the character of my rival. I so dreaded that I should be carried away that I pleaded strongly and resolutely with myself for him. Besides, what would Tina think of me if I impugned Ellery Davenport's honour for what might be, after all, an accidental resemblance in handwriting?

All these things came in one blinding flash of thought as I held the paper in my hands. Miss Mehitable sat, white and trembling, looking at me piteously.

"My dear Aunty," I said, "in a case like this we cannot take one single step without being perfectly sure. This handwriting may accidentally resemble your sister's. Are you perfectly sure that it is hers? It is a very small scrap of paper to determine by."

"Well, I can't really say," said Miss Mehitable, hesitating. "It may be that I have dwelt on this subject until I have grown nervous and my very senses deceive me. I really cannot say, Horace; that was the reason I came to you to ask what I should do."

"Let us look the matter over calmly, Aunty."

"Now," she said, nervously drawing from her pocket two or three letters, and opening them before me, "here are those letters, and your head is cool and steady. I wish you would compare the writing, and tell me what to think of it."

Now the letters and the directions were in that sharp, decided English hand which so many well-educated women write, and in which personal peculiarities are lost, to a great degree, in a general style. I could not help seeing that there was a resemblance which might strike a person,—especially a person so deeply interested, and dwelling with such intentness upon a subject, as Miss Mehitable evidently was.

"My dear Aunty," said I, "I see a resemblance; but have you not known a great many ladies who wrote hands like this?"

"Yes, I must say I have," said Miss Mehitable, still hesitating,—"only, somehow, this impressed me very strongly."

"Well," said I, "supposing that your sister has written to Ellery Davenport, may she not have entrusted him with communications under his promise of secrecy, which he was bound in honour not to reveal?"

"That may be possible," said Miss Mehitable, sighing deeply; "but oh, why should she not make a confidante of me?"

"It may be, Aunty," said I, hesitatingly, "that she is living in relations that she feels could not be justified to you."

"O Horace!" said Miss Mehitable.

"You know," I went on, "that there has been a very great shaking of old-established opinions in Europe. A great many things are looked upon there as open questions, in regard to morality, which we here in New England never think of discussing. Ellery Davenport is a man of the European world, and I can easily see that there may be circumstances in which your sister would more readily resort to the friendship of such a man than to yours."

"May God help me!" said Miss Mehitable.

"My dear Aunty, suppose you find that your sister has adopted a false theory of life, sincerely and conscientiously, and under the influence of it gone astray from what we in New England think to be right. Should we not make a discrimination between errors that come from a wrong belief and the mere weakness that blindly yields to passion? Your sister's letters show great decision and strength of mind. It appears to me that she is exactly the woman to be misled by those dazzling, unsettling theories with regard to social life which now bear such sway, and are especially propagated by French literature. She may really and courageously deem herself doing right in a course that she knows she cannot defend to you and Mr. Rossiter."

"Horace, you speak out and make plain what has been the secret and dreadful fear of my life. I never have believed that Emily could have gone from us all, and stayed away so long, without the support of some attachment. And while you have been talking I have become perfectly certain that it is so; but the thought is like death to me."

"My dear Aunty," I said, "our Father above, who sees all the history of our minds, and how they work, must have a toleration and a patience that we have not with each other. He says that He will bring the blind by a way they knew not, and 'make darkness light before them, and crooked things straight;' and He adds, 'These things will I do unto them, and will not forsake them.' That has always seemed to me the most godlike passage in the Bible."

Miss Mehitable sat for a long time, leaning her head upon her hand.

"Then, Horace, you wouldn't advise me," she said, after a pause, "to say anything to Ellery Davenport about it?"

"Supposing," said I, "that there are communications that he is bound in honour not to reveal, of what use could be your inquiries? It can only create unpleasantness; it may make Tina feel unhappy, who is so very happy now, and probably, at best, you cannot learn anything that would satisfy you."

"Probably not," said she, sighing.

"I can hand this envelope to him," I said after a moment's thought, "this evening, if you think best, and you can see how he looks on receiving it."

"I don't know as it will be of any use," said Miss Mehitable, "but you may do it."

Accordingly, that evening, as we were all gathered in a circle around the open fire, and Tina and Ellery, seated side by side, were carrying on that sort of bantering warfare of wit in which they delighted, I drew this envelope from my pocket and said, carelessly, "Mr. Davenport, here is a letter of yours that you dropped in the library this morning."

He was at that moment playing with a silk tassel which fluttered from Tina's wrist. He let it go, and took the envelope, and looked at it carelessly.

"A letter!" said Tina, snatching it out of his hand with saucy freedom,—"dated at Geneva, and a lady's handwriting! I think I have a right to open it!"

"Do so by all means," said Ellery.

"Oh, pshaw! there's nothing in it," said Tina.

"Not an uncommon circumstance in a lady's letter," said Ellery.

"You saucy fellow," said Tina.

"Why," said Ellery, "is it not the very province and privilege of the fair sex to make nothing more valuable and more agreeable than something? That's the true secret of witchcraft."

"But I shan't like it," said Tina, half pouting, "if you call my letters nothing."

"Your letters, I doubt not, will be an exception to those of all the sex," said Ellery. "I really tremble when I think how profound they will be!"

"You are making fun of me!" said she, colouring.

"I making fun of you? And what have you been doing with all your hapless lovers up to this time? Behold Nemesis arrayed in my form."

"But seriously, Ellery, I want to know whom this letter was from?"

"Why don't you look at the signature?" said he.

"Well, of course you know there is no signature; but I mean what came in this paper?"

"What came in the paper," said Ellery, carelessly, "was a neat little collection of Alpine flowers, that, if you are interested in botany, I shall have the honour of showing you one of these days."

"But you haven't told me who sent them," said Tina.

"Ah, ha! we are jealous!" said he, shaking the letter at her. "What would you give to know, now? Will you be very 'good if I will tell you? Will you promise me for the future not to order me to do more than forty things at one time, for example?"

"I shan't make any promises," said Tina, "you ought to tell me!"

"What an oppressive mistress you are!" said Ellery Davenport. "I begin to sympathise with Sam Lawson,—lordy massy. you dunno nothin' what I undergo!"

"You don't get off that way," said Tina.

"Well," said Ellery Davenport, "if you must know, it's Mrs. Breck."

"And who is she?" said Tina.

"Well, my dear, she was my boarding-house keeper at Geneva, and a very pretty, nice Englishwoman,—one that I should recommend as an example to her sex."

"Oh!" said Tina, "I don't care anything about it now."

"Of course," said Ellery. "Modest, unpretending virtue never excites any interest. I have laboured under that disadvantage all my days."

The by-play between the two had brought the whole circle around the fire into a careless, laughing state. I looked across to Miss Mehitable; she was laughing with the rest. As we started to go out, Miss Mehitable followed me into the passage-way. "My dear Horace," she said, "I was very absurd; it comes of being nervous and thinking of one thing too much."

CHAPTER XXI.

Wedding Bells.

The fourteenth of June was as bright a morning as if it had been made on purpose for a wedding-day, and of all the five thousand inauspicious possibilities which usually encumber weddings, not one fell to our share.

Tina's dress, for example, was all done two days beforehand, and fitted to a hair; and all the invited guests had come, and were lodged in the spacious Kittery mansion.

Esther Avery was to stand as bridesmaid, with me as groomsman, and Harry, as nearest relative, was to give the bride away. The day before, I had been in and seen both ladies dressed up in the marriage finery, and we had rehearsed the situation before Harry, as clergyman, Miss Debby being present, in one of her most commanding frames of mind, to see that everything was done according to the rubric. She surveyed Esther, while she took an approving pinch of snuff, and remarked to me aside, "That young person, for a Congregational parson's daughter, has a surprisingly distinguished air."

Lady Widgery and Lady Lothrop, who were also in at the inspection, honoured Esther with their decided approbation.

"She will be quite presentable at court," Lady Widgery remarked. "Of course Sir Harry will wish her presented."

All this *empressement* in regard to Harry's rank and title, among these venerable sisters, afforded great amusement to our quartette, and we held it a capital joke among ourselves to make Esther blush by calling her Lady Percival, and to inquire of Harry about his future parliamentary prospects, his rent-rolls and tenants. In fact, when together, we were four children, and played with life much as we used to do in the dear old days.

Esther, under the influence of hope and love, had bloomed out into a beautiful woman. Instead of looking like a pale image of abstract thought, she seemed like warm flesh and blood, and Ellery Davenport remarked, "What a splendid contrast her black hair and eyes will make to the golden beauty of Tina!"

All Oldtown respectability had exerted itself to be at the wedding. All, however humble, who had befriended Tina and Harry during the days of their poverty, were bidden. Polly had been long sojourning in the house, in the capacity of Miss Mehitable's maid, and assisting assiduously in the endless sewing and fine laundry work which precedes a wedding.

On this auspicious morning she came gloriously forth,

rustling in a stiff changeable lutestring, her very Sunday best, and with her mind made up to enter an Episcopal church for the first time in her life. There had, in fact, occurred some slight theological skirmishes between Polly and the High Church domestics of Miss Debby's establishment, and Miss Mehitable was obliged to make stringent representations to Polly concerning the duty of sometimes repressing her testimony for truth under particular circumstances.

Polly had attended one catechising, but the shock produced upon her mind by hearing doctrines which seemed to her to have such papistical tendencies was so great that Miss Mehitable begged Miss Debby to allow her to be excused in future. Miss Debby felt that the obligations of politeness owed by a woman of quality to an invited guest in her own house might take precedence even of theological considerations. In this point of view, she regarded Congregationalists with a well-bred, compassionate tolerance, and very willingly acceded to whatever Miss Mehitable suggested.

Harry and I had passed the night before the wedding-day at the Kittery mansion, that we might be there at the very earliest hour in the morning, to attend to all those thousand and one things that always turn up for attention at such a time.

Madam Kittery's garden commanded a distant view of the sea, and I walked among the stately alleys looking at that splendid distant view of Boston harbour, which seemed so bright and sunny, and which swooned away into the horizon with such an ineffable softness, as an image of eternal peace.

As I stood there looking, I heard a light footstep behind me, and 'Tina came up suddenly and spattered my cheek with a dewy rose that she had just been gathering.

"You look as mournful as if it were you that is going to be married!" she said.

"'Tina!" I said, "you out so early too?"

"Yes, for a wonder. The fact was, I had a bad dream, and could not sleep. I got up and looked out of my window, and saw you here, Horace, so I dressed me quickly and ran down. I feel a little bit uncanny,—and eerie, as the Scotch say,—and a little bit sad, too, about the dear old days, Horace. We have had such good times together,—first we three, and then we took Esther in, and that made four; and now, Horace, you must open the ranks a little wider, and take in Ellery."

"But five is an uneven number," said I; "it leaves one out in the cold."

"O Horace! I hope you will find one worthy of you," she said. "I shall have a place in my heart all ready for her. She shall be my sister. You will write to me, won't you? Do write. I shall so want to hear of the dear old things. Every stick and stone, every sweetbrier-bush and huckleberry patch in Oldtown, will always be dear to me. And dear old precious Aunty, what ever set it into her good heart to think of taking poor little me to be her child? and it's too bad that I should leave her so. You know, Horace, I have a small income all my own, and that I mean to give to Aunty."

Now there were many points in this little valedictory of Tina to which I had no mind to respond, and she looked, as she was speaking, with tears coming in her great soft eyes, altogether too loving and lovely to be a safe companion to one forbidden to hold her in his arms and kiss her, and I felt such a desperate temptation in that direction that I turned suddenly from her. "Does Mr. Davenport approve such a disposition of your income?" said I, in a constrained voice.

"Mr. Davenport! Mr. High and Mighty," she said, -mimicking my constrained tone, "what makes you so sulky to me this morning?"

"I am not sulky, Tina; only sad," I said.

"Come, come, Horace, don't be sad," she said, coaxingly, and putting her hand through my arm. "Now, just be a good boy, and walk up and down with me here a few moments, and let me tell you about things."

I submitted, and let her lead me off passively. "You see, Horace," she said, "I feel for poor old Aunty. Hers seems to me such a dry, desolate life; and I can't help feeling a sort of self-reproach when I think of it. Why should I have health and youth and strength and Ellery, and be going to see all the beauty and glory of Europe, while she sits alone at home, old and poor, and hears the rain drip off from those old lilac-bushes? Oldtown is a nice place, to be sure, but it does rain a great deal there, and she and Polly will be so lonesome without me to make fun for them. Now, Horace, you must promise me to go there as much as you can. You must cultivate Aunty for my sake; and her friendship is worth cultivating for its own sake."

"I know it," said I; "I am fully aware of the value of her mind and character."

"You and Harry ought both to visit her," said Tina, "and write to her, and take her advice. Nothing improves a young man faster than such female friendship; it's worth that of dozens of us girls."

Tina always had a slight proclivity for sermonising, but a chapter in Ecclesiastes, coming from little preachers with lips and eyes like hers, is generally acceptable.

"You know," said Tina, "that Aunty has some sort of a trouble on her mind."

"I know all about it," said I.

"Did she tell you?"

"Yes," said I, "after I had divined it."

"I made her tell me," said Tina. "When I came home

from school, I determined I would not be treated like a child
by her any longer,—that she should tell me her troubles, and
let me bear them with her. I am young and full of hope, and
ought to have troubles to bear. And she is worn out and
weary with thinking over and over the same sad story. What
a strange thing it is that that sister treats her so! I have
been thinking so much about her lately, Horace; and—do you
know?—I had the strangest dream about her last night. I
dreamed that Ellery and I were standing at the altar being
married, and, all of a sudden, that lady that we saw in the
closet and in the garret rose up like a ghost between us."

"Come, come," said I, "Tina, you are getting nervous.
One shouldn't tell of one's bad dreams, and then one forgets
them easier."

"Well," said Tina, "it made me sad to think that she was
a young girl like me, full of hope and joy. They didn't treat
her rightly over in that Farnsworth family,—Miss Mehitable
told me all about it. Oh, it was a dreadful story! they perfectly froze her heart with their dreary talk about religion.
Horace, I think the most irreligious thing in the world is
that way of talking, which takes away our heavenly Father,
and gives only a dreadful Judge. I should not be so happy
and so safe as I am now, if I did not believe in a loving God."

"Tina," said I, "are you satisfied with the religious principles of Mr. Davenport?"

"I'm glad you asked me that, Horace, because Mr. Davenport is a man that is very apt to be misunderstood. Nobody
really does understand him but me. He has seen so much of
cant, and hypocrisy, and pretence of religion, and is so afraid
of pretensions that do not mean anything, that I think he
goes to the other extreme. Indeed, I have told him so. But
he says he is always delighted to hear me talk on religion,
and he likes to have me repeat hymns to him; and he told

me the other day that he thought the Bible contained finer strains of poetry and eloquence than could be got from all other books put together. Then he has such a wonderful mind, you know. Mr. Avery said that he never saw a person that appreciated all the distinctions of the doctrines more completely than he did. He doesn't quite agree with Mr. Avery, nor with anybody; but I think he is very far from being an irreligious man. I believe he thinks very seriously on all these subjects, indeed."

"I am glad of it," said I, half convinced by her fervour, more than half by the magic of her presence and the touch of the golden curls that the wind blew against my cheek,— true Venetian curls, brown in the shade and gold in the sun. Certainly, such things as these, if not argument, incline man to be convinced of whatever a fair preacher says; and I thought it not unlikely that Ellery Davenport liked to hear her talk about religion. The conversation was interrupted by the breakfast-bell, which rung us in to an early meal, where we found Miss Debby, brisk and crisp with business and authority, apologising to Lady Widgery for the unusually early hour, "but, really, so much always to be done in cases like these."

Breakfast was hurried over, for I was to dress myself, and go to Mr. Davenport's house, and accompany him, as groomsman, to meet Tina and Harry at the church door.

I remember admiring Ellery Davenport, as I met him this morning, with his easy, high-bred, cordial air, and with that overflow of general benevolence which seems to fill the hearts of happy bridegrooms on the way to the altar. Jealous as I was of the love that ought to be given to the idol of my knight-errantry, I could not but own to myself that Ellery Davenport was most loyally in love.

Then I have a vision of the old North Church, with its

chimes playing, and the pews around the broad aisle filled with expectant guests. The wedding had excited a great deal of attention in the upper circles of Boston. Ellery Davenport was widely known, having been a sort of fashionable meteor, appearing at intervals in the select circles of the city with all the prestige of foreign travel and diplomatic reputation. Then the little romance of the children had got about, and had proved as sweet a morsel under the tongues of good Bostonians as such spices in the dulness of real life usually do. There was talk everywhere of the little story, and, as usual, nothing was lost in the telling; the beauty and cleverness of the children had been reported from mouth to mouth, until everybody was on tiptoe to see them.

The Oldtown people, who were used to rising at daybreak, found no difficulty in getting to Boston in season. Uncle Fliakim's almost exhausted waggon had been diligently revamped, and his harness assiduously mended, for days beforehand, during which process the good man might have been seen flying like a meteor in an unceasing round, between the store, the blacksmith's shop, my grandfather's, and his own dwelling; and in consequence of these arduous labours, not only his wife, but Aunt Keziah and Hepsy Lawson, were secured a free passage to the entertainment.

Lady Lothrop considerately offered a seat to my grandmother and Aunt Lois in her coach; but my grandmother declined the honour in favour of my mother.

"It's all very well," said my grandmother, "and I send my blessing on 'em with all my heart; but my old husband and I are too far along to be rattling our old bones to weddings in Boston. I shouldn't know how to behave in their grand Episcopal church."

Aunt Lois, who, like many other good women, had an innocent love of the pomps and vanities, and my mother to

whom the scene was an unheard-of recreation, were, on the
whole, not displeased that her mind had taken this turn. As
to Sam Lawson, he arose before Aurora had unbarred the
gates of dawn, and strode off vigorously on foot, in his best
Sunday clothes, and arrived there in time to welcome Uncle
Fliakim's waggon, and to tell him that "he'd been a-lookin'
out for 'em these two hours."

So then, for as much as half an hour before the wedding
coaches arrived at the church door, there was a goodly
assemblage in the church, and, while the chimes were
solemnly pealing the tune of old Wells, there were bibbing
and bobbing of fashionable bonnets, and fluttering of fans,
and rustling of silks, and subdued creakings of whalebone
stays, and a gentle under-tone of gossiping conversation in
the expectant audience. Sam Lawson had mounted the organ
loft, directly opposite the altar, which commanded a most
distinct view of every possible transaction below, and also
gave a prominent image of himself, with his lanky jaws, protruding eyes, and shackling figure, posed over all as the in-
specting genius of the scene. And every once in a while he
conveyed to Jake Marshall pieces of intelligence with regard
to the amount of property or private history—the horses,
carriages, servants and most secret internal belongings—of
the innocent Bostonians, who were disporting themselves
below, in utter ignorance of how much was known about
them. But when a man gives himself seriously for years to
the task of collecting information, thinking nothing of long
tramps of twenty miles in the acquisition, never hesitating to
put a question, and never forgetting an answer, it is astonishing what an amount of information he may pick up. In Sam,
a valuable reporter of the press has been lost for ever. He
was born a generation too soon, and the civilisation of his time
had not yet made a place for him. But not the less did he at

this moment feel in himself all the responsibilities of a special reporter for Oldtown.

"Lordy massy," he said to Jake when the chimes began to play, "how solemn that 'ere does sound!—

'Life *is* the time to sarve the Lord,
The time *to* insure the gret reward.'

I ben up in the belfry askin' the ringer what Mr. Davenport's goin' to give him for ringin' them 'ere chimes; and how much do ye think 'twas? Wal, 'twas jest fifty dollars, for jest this 'ere one time, an' the weddin' fee's a-goin' t' be a hunderd guineas in a gold puss. I tell yer, Colonel Davenport 's a man as chops his mince putty fine. There's Parson Lothrop down there; he's got a spick span new coat an' a new wig! That's Mis' Lothrop's scarlet Injy shawl; that 'ere cost a hunderd guineas in Injy—her first husband gin 'er that. Lordy massy, ain't it a providence that Parson Lothrop 's married her? 'cause sence the war that 'ere s'ciety fur sendin the gospil to furrin purts don't send nothin' to 'em, an' the Oldtown people, they don't pay nothin'. All they can raise they gin to Mr. Mordecai Rossiter, 'cause they say ef they hev to s'port a colleague it's all they can do, 'specially sence he's married. Yeh see, Mordecai, he wanted to git Tiny, but he couldn't come it, and so he's tuk up with Delily Bar- ker. The folks, some on 'em, kind o' hinted to old Parson Lothrop thet his sermons wasn't so interestin' 's they might be, 'n' the parson, ses he, ' Wal, I b'lieve the sermons 's about 's good 's the pay; ain't they?' He hed 'em there. I like Parson Lothrop—he's a fine old figger-head, and keeps up stiff for th' honour o' the ministry. Why, folks 's gittin' so nowadays thet ministers won't be no more 'n common folks, 'n' everybody 'll hev their say to 'em jest 's they do to any- body clse. Lordy massy, there's the origin—goin' to hev all the glories, orgins 'n' bells 'n' everythin'; guess the procession

must ha' started. Mr. Davenport 's got another spick an'
span new landau, 't he ordered over from England, special
for this 'casion, an' two prancin' white hosses! Ych see I
got inter Boston 'bout daybreak, an' I's round ter his stables
a-lookin' at 'em a-polishin' up their huffs a little, 'n' givin' on
'em a wipe down, 'n' I asked Jenkins what he thought he gin
for 'em, an' he sed he reely shouldn't durst to tell me. I tell
ye, he's like Solomon—he's a-goin' to make gold as the stones
o' the street."

And while Sam's monologue was going on, in came the
bridal procession,—first, Harry, with his golden head and
blue eyes, and, leaning on his arm, a cloud of ethereal gauzes
and laces, out of which looked a face, pale now as a lily, with
wandering curls of golden hair, like little gleams of sunlight
on white clouds; then the tall, splendid figure of Ellery
Davenport, his haughty blue eyes glancing all around with a
triumphant assurance. Miss Mehitable hung upon his arm,
pale with excitement and emotion. Then came Esther and I.
As we passed up the aisle, I heard a confused murmur of
whisperings, and a subdued drawing in of breath, and the
rest all seemed to me to be done in a dream. I heard the
words: "Who giveth this woman to be married to this man?"
and saw Harry step forth, bold, and bright, and handsome,
amid the whisperings that pointed him out as the hero of a
little romance. And he gave her away for ever,—our darling,
our heart of hearts. And then those holy, tender words,
those vows so awful, those supporting prayers, all mingled as
in a dream, until it was all over, and ladies, laughing and
crying, were crowding around Tina, and there were kissing
and congratulating and shaking of hands, and then we swept
out of the church, and into the carriages, and were whirled
back to the Kittery mansion, which was thrown wide open,

from garret to cellar, in the very profuseness of old English hospitality.

: There was a splendid lunch laid out in the parlour, with all the old silver in muster, and with all the delicacies that Boston confectioners and caterers could furnish.

Ellery Davenport had indeed tendered the services of his French cook, but Miss Debby had respectfully declined the offer.

"He may be a very good cook, Ellery; I say nothing against him. I am extremely obliged to you for your polite offer, but good English cooking is good enough for me, and I trust that whatever guests I invite, will always think it good enough for them."

On that day, Aunt Lois and Aunt Keziah and my mother and Uncle Fliakim sat down in proximity to some of the very selectest families of Boston, comporting themselves, like good republican Yankees, as if they had been accustomed to that sort of thing all their lives, though secretly embarrassed by many little points of etiquette.

Tina and Ellery sat at the head of the table, and dispensed hospitalities around them with a gay and gracious freedom; and Harry, in whom the bridal dress of Esther had evidently excited distracting visions of future probabilities, was making his seat by her at dinner an opportunity, in the general clatter of conversation, to enjoy a nice little *tête-à-tête*.

Besides the brilliant company in the parlour, a long table was laid out upon the greensward at the back of the house, in the garden, where beer and ale flowed freely, and ham and bread and cheese and cake and eatables of a solid and sustaining description were dispensed to whomsoever would. The humble friends of lower degree—the particular friends of the servants, and all the numerous tribe of dependants and hangers-on, who wished to have some small share in the prosperity of the prosperous—here found ample entertainment. Here Sam Lawson might be seen, seated beside Hepsy, on a garden seat near the festive board, gallantly pressing upon her the good things of the hour.

"Eat all ye want ter, Hepsy,—it comes free 's water; ye can hev 'wine an' milk without money 'n' without price,' as 'twere. Lordy massy, 's jest what I wanted. I hed sech a stram this mornin', 'n' hain't hed nothin' but a two-cent roll, 't I bought 't the baker's. Thought I should ha' caved in 'fore they got through with the weddin'. These 'ere 'Piscopal weddin's is putty long. What d'ye think on them, Polly?"

"I think I like our own way the best," said Polly, stanchly, "none o' your folderol, 'n' kneelin', 'n' puttin' on o' rings."

"Well," said Hepsy, with the spice of a pepper-box in her eyes, "I liked the part that said, 'With all my worldly goods I thee endow.'"

"Thet's putty well, when a man hes any worldly goods," said Sam; "but how about when he hesn't?"

"Then he's no business to git married!" said Hepsy, definitely.

"So *I* think," said Polly; "but, for my part, I don't want no man's worldly goods, ef I've got to take him with 'em. I'd rather work hard as I have done, and hev 'em all to myself, to do just what I please with."

"Wal, Polly," said Sam, "I daresay the men 's jest o' your mind,—none on 'em won't try very hard to git ye out on 't."

"There's bin those thet hes, though!" said Polly; "but 'tain't wuth talkin' about, anyway."

And so conversation below stairs and above proceeded gaily and briskly, until at last the parting hour came.

"Now jest all on ye step round ter the front door, an' see

'em go off in their glory.　Them two white hosses is imported fresh from England, 'n' they couldn't ha' cost less 'n' a thousan' dollars apiece, ef they cost a cent."

"A thousand!" said Jenkins, the groom, who stood in his best clothes amid the festive throng.　"Who told you that?"

"Wall" said Sam, "I thought I'd put the figger low enough, sence ye wouldn't tell me perticklers.　I like to be accurate 'bout these 'ere things.　There they be! they're comin' out the door now.　She's tuk off her white dress now, an' got on her travellin' dress, don't ye see?　Lordy massy, what a kissin' an' a cryin'!　How women allers does go on 'bout these 'ere things!　There, he's got 'er at last!　See 'em goin' down the steps! ain't they a han'some couple?　There, he's handin' on 'er in.　The kerrige 's lined with blue satin, 'n' never was sot in afore this mornin'.　Good luck go with 'em!　There they go."

And we all of us stood on the steps of the Kittery mansion, kissing hands and waving handkerchiefs, until the beloved one, the darling of our hearts, was out of sight.

CHAPTER XXII.

Wedding After-talks at Oldtown.

WEDDING joys are commonly supposed to pertain especially to the two principal personages, and to be of a kind with which the world doth not intermeddle; but a wedding in such a quiet and monotonous state of existence as that of Oldtown is like a glorious sunset, which leaves a long after-glow, in which trees and rocks, farm-houses, and all the dull commonplace landscape of real life have, for a while, a roseate hue of brightness.　And then the long after-talks, the deliberate turnings and revampings, and the re-enjoying, bit by bit, of every incident!

Sam Lawson was a man who knew how to make the most of this, and for a week or two he reigned triumphant in Oldtown on the strength of it. Others could relate the bare simple facts, but Sam Lawson could give the wedding, with variations, with marginal references, and explanatory notes, and enlightening comments, that ran deep into the history of everybody present. So that even those who had been at the wedding did not know half what they had seen until Sam told them.

It was now the second evening after that auspicious event. Aunt Lois and my mother had been pressed to prolong their stay over one night after the wedding, to share the hospitalities of the Kittery mansion, and had been taken around in the Kittery carriage to see the wonders of Boston town. But prompt, on their return, Sam came in to assist them in dishing up information by the evening fireside.

"Wal, Mis' Badger," said he, "'twas gin'ally agreed, on all hands, there hadn't ben no weddin' like it seen in Boston sence the time them court folks and nobility used to be there. Old Luke there, that rings the chimes, he told me he hedn't seen no sech couple go up the broad aisle o' that church. Luke, says he to me, 'I tell yew, the grander o' Boston is here to-day,' and ye'd better b'lieve every one on'em had on their Sunday best. There was the Boylstons, an' the Bowdoins, an' the Brattles, an' the Winthrops, an' the Bradfords, an' the Penhallows up from Portsmouth, an' the Quinceys, an' the Sewells. Wal, I tell yer, there was real grit there!—folks that come in their grand kerridges, I tell you!—there was such a pawin' and stampin' o' horses and kerridges round the church as if all the army of the Assyrians was there!"

"Well, now, I'm glad I didn't go," said my grandmother. "I'm too old to go into any such grandeur."

"Wal, I don't see why folks hes so much 'bjections to these here 'Piscopal weddin's, neither," said Sam. "I tell yer, it's a kind o' putty sight now; ye see I was up in the organ loft', where I could look down on the heads of all the people. Massy to us! the bunnets, an' the feathers, an' the Injy shawls, an' the purple an' fine linen, was all out on the 'casion. An' when our Harry come in with Tiny on his arm, tha' was a gincral kind o' buzz, an' folks a risin' up all over the house to look at 'em. Her dress was yer real Injy satin, thick an' yaller, kind o' like cream. An' she had on the Pierpont pearls an' diamonds"——

"How did you know what she had on?" said Aunt Lois.

"O, I hes ways o' findin' out!" said Sam. "Yeh know old Gincral Pierpont, his gret-gret-grandfather, was a gineral in the British army in Injy, an' he racketed round 'mong them nabobs out there, an' got no end o' gold an' precious stones, an' these 'ere pearls and diamonds that she wore on her neck and in her cars hes come down in the Davenport family. Mis' Delily, Miss Deborah Kittery's maid, she told me all the partic'lars 'bout it, an' she ses there ain't no family so rich in silver and jewels, and sich, as Ellery Davenport's is, an' hes ben for generations back. His house is jest choke full of all sorts o' graven images and queer things from Chiny an' Japan, 'cause, ye see, his ancestors they traded to Injy, an' they seem to hev got the abundance o' the Gentiles flowin' to 'em."

"I noticed those pearls on her neck," said Aunt Lois; "I never saw such pearls."

"Wal," said Sam, "Mis' Delily, she ses she's tried 'em 'longside of a good-sized pea, an' they're full as big. An' the earrings 's them pear-shaped pearls, ye know, with diamond nubs atop on 'em. Then there was a great pearl cross, an' the biggest kind of a diamond right in the middle on't. Wal, Mis' Delily she told me a story 'bout them 'ere pearls," said Sam. "For my part, ef it hed ben a daughter o' mine, I'd ruther she'd 'a' worn suthin' on her neck that was spic an' span new. I tell yew, these 'ere old family jewels, I think sometimes they gits kind o'struck through an' through with moth an' rust, so to speak."

"I'm sure I don't know what you mean, Sam," said Aunt Lois, literally, "since we know gold can't rust, and pearls and diamonds don't hurt with any amount of keeping."

"Wal, ye see, they do say that 'ere old General Pierpont was a putty hard customer; he got them 'ere pearls an' diamonds away from an Injun princess; I s'pose she thought she'd as much right to 'em 's he hed; an' they say 't was about all she hed was her jewels, an' so nat'rally enough she cussed him for taking on 'em. Wal, dunno's the Lord minds the cusses o' these poor old heathen critturs; but 's ben a fact, Mis' Delily says, thet them jewels hain't never brought good luck. Gineral Pierpont, he gin 'em to his fust wife, an' she didn't live but two months arter she was married. He gin 'em to his second wife, 'n' she tuck to drink and led him sech a life 't he wouldn't ha' cared ef she had died too; 'n' then they came down to Ellery Davenport's first wife, 'n' she went ravin' crazy the fust year arter she was married. Now all that 'ere does look a little like a cuss; don't it?"

"O nonsense, Sam!" said Aunt Lois, "I don't believe there's a word of truth in any of it! You can hatch more stories in one day than a hen can eggs in a month."

"Wal, any way," said Sam, "I like the 'Piscopal sarvice, all 'ceppin' the minister's wearin' his shirt outside; that I don't like."

"'Tisn't a shirt!" said Aunt Lois, indignantly.

"O lordy massy!" said Sam, "I know what they calls it. I know it's a surplice, but it looks for all the world like a man in his shirt-sleeves; but the words is real solemn. I wondered when he asked 'em all whether they hed any objections to 't, an' told 'em to speak up ef they hed, what would happen ef anybody should speak up jest there."

"Why, of course 'twould stop the wedding," said Aunt Lois, "until the thing was inquired into."

"Wal, Jake Marshall, he said thet he'd heerd a story when he was a boy about a weddin' in a church at Portsmouth, that was stopped jest there, 'cause, ye see, the man he hed another wife livin'.' He said 'twas old Colonel Penhallow. 'Mazin' rich the old Colonel was, and these 'ere rich old cocks sometimes does seem to strut round and cut up pretty much as if they hedn't heard o' no God in their parts. The Colonel he got his wife shet up in a lunatic asylum, an' then spread the word that she was dead, an' courted a gal, and come jest as near as that to marryin' of her."

"As near as what?" said Aunt Lois.

"Why, when they got to that 'ere part of the service, there was his wife good as new. She'd got out o' the 'sylum, and stood up there 'fore 'em all. So you see that 'ere does some good."

"I'd rather stay in an asylum all my life than go back to that man," said Aunt Lois.

"Wal, you see she didn't," said Sam; "her friends they made him make a settlement on her, poor woman, and he cleared out t' England."

"Good riddance to bad rubbish," said my grandmother.

"Wal, how handsome that 'ere gal is that Harry's going to marry!" continued Sam. "She didn't have on nothin' but white muslin', an' not a snip of a jewel; but she looked like a queen. Ses I to Jake, ses I, there goes the woman 't'll be Lady Percival one o' these days, over in England, an' I bet

ye, he'll find lots o' family jewels for her, over there. Mis'
Delily she said she didn't doubt there would be."

"I hope," said my grandmother, "that she will have more
enduring riches than that; it's small matter about earthly
jewels."

"Lordy massy, yes, Mis' Badger," said Sam, "jes' so, jes'
so; now that 'ere was being impressed on my mind all the
time. Folks oughtenter lay up their treasures on airth; I
couldn't help thinkin' on't, when I see Tina a-wearin' them
jewels, jest how vain an' transitory everythin' is, an' how the
women 't has worn 'em afore is all turned to dust, an' lyin'
in their graves. Lordy massy, these 'ere things make us
realise what a transitory world we's a-livin' in. I was tellin'
Hepsy 'bout it,—she's so kind o' worldly, Hepsy is,—seemed
to make her feel so kind o' gritty to see so much wealth 'n'
splendour, when we hedn't none. Ses I, 'Hepsy, there ain't
no use o' wantin' worldly riches, 'cause our lives all passes
away like a dream, an' a hundred years hence 't won't make
no sort o' diffurnce what we've hed, an' what we heven't hed.'
But wal, Miss Lois, *did* ye see the kerridge?" said Sam,
returning to temporal things with renewed animation.

"I just got a glimpse of it," said Aunt Lois, "as it drove
to the door."

"Lordy massy," said Sam, "I was all over that 'ere kerridge that mornin' by daylight. 'Tain't the one he had up
here,—that was jest common doin's,—this 'ere is imported
spic an' span new from England for the 'casion, an' all made
jest's they make 'em for the nobility. Why, 'twas all quilted
an' lined with blue satin, ever so grand, an' Turkey carpet
under their feet, an' the springs was easy 's a rockin'-chair.
That's what they've gone off in. Wal, lordy massy! I don't
grudge Tina nothin'! She's the chipperest, light-heartedest,

darlin'est little creetur that ever did live, an' I hope she'll
hev good luck in all things."

A rap was heard at the kitchen door, and Polly entered.
It was evident from her appearance that she was in a state of
considerable agitation. She looked pale and excited, and her
hands shook.

"Mis' Badger," she said to my grandmother, "Miss Rossiter wants to know 'f you won't come and set up with her
to-night."

"Why, is she sick?" said grandmother. "What's the
matter with her?"

"She ain't very well," said Polly, evasively; "she wanted
Mis' Bedger to spend the night with her."

"Perhaps, mother, I'd better go over," said Aunt Lois.

"No, Miss Lois," said Polly, eagerly, "Miss Rossiter
don't wanter see anybody but yer mother."

"Wal, now I wanter know!" said Sam Lawson.

"Well, you can't know everything," said Aunt Lois, "so
you *may* want!"

"Tell Miss Rossiter, ef I can do anythin' for 'er, I hope
she'll call on me," said Sam.

My grandmother and Polly went out together. Aunt Lois
bustled about the hearth, swept it up, and then looked out
into the darkness after them. What could it be?

The old clock ticked drowsily in the kitchen corner, and
her knitting-needles rattled.

"What do you think it is?" said my mother, timidly, to
Aunt Lois.

"How should I know?" said Aunt Lois, sharply.

In a few moments Polly returned again.

"Miss Mehitable says she would like to see Sam Lawson."

"O, wal, wal, would she? Wal, I'll come!" said Sam,

rising with joyful alertness. "I'm allers ready at a minute's warnin'!"

And they went out into the darkness together.

CHAPTER XXIII.

Behind the Curtain.

In the creed of most story-tellers marriage is equal to translation. The mortal pair whose fortunes are traced to the foot of the altar forthwith ascend, and a cloud receives them out of our sight as the curtain falls. Faith supposes them rapt away to some unseen paradise, and every-day toil girds up its loins and with a sigh prepares to return to its delving and grubbing.

But our story must follow the fortunes of our heroine beyond the prescribed limits.

It had been arranged that the wedding pair, after a sunny afternoon's drive through some of the most picturesque scenery in the neighbourhood of Boston should return at eventide to their country home, where they were to spend a short time preparatory to sailing for Europe. Even in those early days the rocky glories of Nahant and its dashing waves were known and resorted to by Bostonians, and the first part of the drive was thitherward, and Tina climbed round among the rocks, exulting like a sea-bird, with Ellery Davenport ever at her side, laughing, admiring, but holding back her bold, excited footsteps, lest she should plunge over by some unguarded movement, and become a vanished dream.

So near lies the ever-possible tragedy at the hour of our greatest exultation; it is but a false step, an inadvertent movement, and all that was joy can become a cruel mockery! We all know this to be so. We sometimes start and shriek

when we see it to be so in the case of others, but who is the
less triumphant in his hour of possession for this gloomy
shadow of possibility that for ever dogs his steps?

Ellery Davenport was now in the high tide of victory.
The pursuit of the hour was a success; he had captured the
butterfly. In his eagerness he had trodden down and disregarded many teachings and impulses of his better nature
that should have made him hesitate: but now he felt that he
had her; she was his,—his alone and for ever.

But already dark thoughts from the past were beginning
to flutter out like ill-omened bats, and dip down on gloomy
wing between him and the innocent, bright, confiding face.
Tina he could see had idealised him entirely. She had in-
vested him with all her conceptions of knighthood, honour,
purity, religion, and made a creation of her own of him; and
sometimes he smiled to himself, half amused and half annoyed at the very young and innocent simplicity of the
matter. Nobody knew better than himself that what she
dreamed he was he neither was nor meant to be,—that in
fact there could not be a bitterer satire on his real self than
her conceptions; but just now, with her brilliant beauty, her
piquant earnestness, her perfect freshness, there was an indescribable charm about her that bewitched him.

Would it all pass away and get down to the jog-trot
dustiness of ordinary married life, he wondered, and then,
ought he not to have been a little more fair with her in exchange for the perfect transparence with which she threw
open the whole of her past life to him? Had he not played
with her as some villain might with a little child, and got
away a priceless diamond for a bit of painted glass? He did
not allow himself to think in that direction.

"Come, my little sea-gull," he said to her, after they had
wandered and rambled over the rocks for a while, "you must

come down from that perch, and we must drive on, If we mean to be at home before midnight."

"O Ellery, how glorious it is!"

"Yes, but we cannot build here three tabernacles, and so we must say, *Au revoir.* I will bring you here again;"— and Ellery half led, half carried her in his arms back to the carriage.

"How beautiful it is!" said Tina, as they were glancing along a turfy road through the woods. The white pines were just putting out their long fingers, the new leaves of the silvery birches were twinkling in the light, the road was fringed on both sides with great patches of the blue violet, and sweet-fern, and bayberry, and growing green tips of young spruce and fir were exhaling a spicy perfume. "It seems as if we two alone were flying through fairy-land." His arm was around her, tightening its clasp of possession as he looked down on her.

"Yes," he said; "we two are alone in our world now; none can enter it; none can see into it; none can come between us."

Suddenly the words recalled to Tina her bad dream of the night before. She was on the point of speaking of it, but hesitated to introduce it; she felt a strange shyness in mentioning that subject.

Ellery Davenport turned the conversation upon things in foreign lands, which he would soon show her. He pictured to her the bay of Naples, the rocks of Sorrento, where the blue Mediterranean is overhung with groves of oranges, where they should have a villa some day, and live in a dream of beauty. All things fair and bright and beautiful in foreign lands were evoked, and made to come as a sort of airy pageant around them while they wound through the still, spicy pine woods.

It was past sunset, and the moon was looking white and sober through the flush of the evening sky, when they entered the grounds of their own future home.

"How different everything looks here from what it did when I was here years ago!" said Tina; "the paths are all cleared, and then it was one wild, dripping tangle. I remember how long we knocked at the door, and couldn't make any one hear, and the old black knocker frightened me,—it was a black serpent with his tail in his mouth. I wonder if it is there yet."

"Oh, to be sure it is," said Ellery; "that is quite a fine bit of old bronze, after something in Herculaneum, I think. You know serpents were quite in vogue among the ancients."

"I should think that symbol meant eternal evil," said Tina; "a circle is eternity, and a serpent is evil."

"You are evidently prejudiced against serpents, my love," said Ellery. "The ancients thought better of them; they were emblems of wisdom; and the ladies very appropriately wore them for bracelets and necklaces."

"I wouldn't have one for the world," said Tina. "I always hated them; they are so bright, and still, and sly."

"Mere prejudice," said Ellery, laughing. "I must cure it by giving you, one of these days, an emerald-green serpent for a bracelet, with ruby crest and diamond eyes; you have no idea what pretty fellows they are. But here, you see, we are coming to the house; you can smell the roses."

"How lovely and how changed!" said Tina. "Oh, what a world of white roses over that portico,—roses everywhere, and white lilacs. It is a perfect paradise!"

"May you find it so, my little Eve," said Ellery Davenport, as the carriage stopped at the door. Ellery sprang out lightly, and, turning, took Tina in his arms and set her down in the porch.

They stood there a moment in the moonlight, and listened to the fainter patter of the horses' feet as they went down the drive.

"Come in, my little wife," said Ellery, opening the door; "and may the black serpent bring you good luck."

The house was brilliantly lighted by wax candles in massive silver candlesticks.

"Oh, how strangely altered!" said Tina, running about, and looking into the rooms with the delight of a child. "How beautiful everything is!"

The housekeeper, a respectable female, now appeared, and offered her services to conduct her young mistress to her rooms. Ellery went with her, almost carrying her up the staircase in his arms. Above, as below, all was light and bright. "This room is ours," said Ellery, drawing her into that chamber which Tina remembered years before as so weirdly desolate. Now it was all radiant with hangings and furniture of blue and silver; the open windows let in branches of climbing white roses; the vases were full of lilies. The housekeeper paused a moment at the door.

"There is a lady in the little parlour below that has been waiting more than an hour to see you and madam," she said.

"A lady!" said both Tina and Ellery, in tones of surprise.

"Did she give her name?" said Ellery.

"She gave no name; but she said that you, sir, would know her."

"I can't imagine who it should be," said Ellery. "Perhaps, Tina, I had better go down and see while you are dressing," said Ellery.

"Indeed, that would be a pretty way to do! No, sir, I

allow no private interviews," said Tina, with authority,— "no, I am all ready, and quite dressed enough to go down."

"Well, then, little positive," said Ellery, "be it as you will; let's go together."

"Well, I must confess," said Tina, "I didn't look for wedding callers out here to-night; but never mind, it's a nice little mystery to see what she wants."

They went down the staircase together, passed across the hall, and entered the little boudoir, where Tina and Harry had spent their first night together. The door of the writing-cabinet stood open, and a lady all in black, in a bonnet and cloak, stood in the doorway.

As she came forward, Tina exclaimed, "O Ellery! it is she,—the lady in the closet!" and sank down pale and half fainting.

Ellery Davenport turned pale too; his cheeks, his very lips, were blanched like marble, he looked utterly thunder-struck and appalled.

"Emily!" he said. "Great God!"

"Yes, Emily!" she said, coming forward slowly and with dignity. "You did not expect to meet ME here and now, Ellery Davenport!"

There was for a moment a silence that was perfectly awful. Tina looked on without power to speak, as in a dreadful dream. The ticking of the little French mantel-clock seemed like a voice of doom to her.

The lady walked close up to Ellery Davenport, drew forth a letter, and spoke in that fearfully calm way that comes from the very white-heat of passion.

"Ellery," she said, "here is your letter. You did not *know* me—you could not know me—if you thought, after *that letter*, I would accept anything from you! *I* live on your bounty! I would sooner work as a servant!"

"Ellery, Ellery!" said Tina, springing up and clasping his arm, "Oh, tell me who she is! What is she to you? Is she—is she"——

"Be quiet, my poor child," said the woman, turning to her with an air of authority. "I have no claims; I come to make none. Such as this man is, *he is your husband*, not mine. You believe in him; so did I,—love him; so did I. I gave up all for him,—country, home, friends, name, reputation,—for I thought him such a man, that a woman might well sacrifice her whole life to him! He is the father of my child! But fear not. The world, of course, will approve *him* and condemn *me*. They will say he did well to give up his mistress and take a wife; it's the world's morality. What woman will think the less of him, or smile the less on him, when she hears it? What woman will not feel herself too good even to touch my hand?"

"Emily," said Ellery Davenport, bitterly, "if you thought I deserved this, you might, at least, have spared this poor child."

"*The truth* is the best foundation in married life, Ellery," she said, "and the truth you have small faculty for speaking. I do her a favour in telling it. Let her start fair from the commencement, and then there will be no more to be told. Besides," she added, "I shall not trouble you long. *There*," she said, putting down a jewel-case,—"there are your gifts to me,—there are your letters." Then she threw on the table a miniature, set in diamonds, "There is your picture. And now God help me! Farewell!"

She turned, and glided swiftly from the room.

*   *   *   *   *

Readers who remember the former part of this narrative, will see at once that it was, after all, Ellery Davenport with whom, years before, Emily Rossiter had fled to France. They had resided there, and subsequently in Switzerland, and she had devoted herself to him, and to his interests, with all the single-hearted fervour of a true wife.

On her part, there was a full and conscientious belief that the choice of the individuals alone constituted a true marriage, and that the laws of human society upon this subject were an oppression which needed to be protested against.

On his part, however, the affair was a simple gratification of passion, and the principles, such as they were, were used by him as he used all principles,—simply as convenient machinery for carrying out his own purposes. Ellery Davenport spoke his own convictions, when he said that there was no subject which had not its right and its wrong side, each of them capable of being unanswerably sustained. He had played with his own mind in this manner, until he had entirely obliterated conscience. He could at any time dazzle and confound his own moral sense with his own reasonings; and it was sometimes amusing, but, in the long run, tedious and vexatious to him, to find that what he maintained merely for convenience and for theory, should be regarded by Emily so seriously, and with such an earnest eye to logical consequences. In short, the two came, in the course of their intimacy, precisely to the spot to which many people come who are united by an indissoluble legal tie. Slowly, and through an experience of many incidents, they had come to perceive an entire and irrepressible conflict of natures between them.

Notwithstanding that Emily had taken a course diametrically opposed to the principles of her country and her fathers, she retained largely the Puritan nature. Instances have often been seen in New England of men and women who had renounced every particle of the Puritan theology, and yet retained in their fibre and composition all the moral traits of the Puritans—their uncompromising conscientiousness, their

inflexible truthfulness, and their severe logic in following the
convictions of their understandings. And the fact was, that
while Emily had sacrificed for Ellery Davenport her position
in society,—while she had exposed herself to the very coarsest
misconstructions of the commonest minds, and made herself
liable to be ranked by her friends in New England among
abandoned outcasts,—she was really a woman standing on
too high a moral plane for Ellery Davenport to consort with
her in comfort. He was ambitious, intriguing, unscrupulous,
and it was an annoyance to him to be obliged to give an account of himself to her. He was tired of playing the moral
hero, the part that he assumed and acted with great success
during the time of their early attachment. It annoyed him
to be held to any consistency in principles. The very devotion to him, which she felt regarding him, as she always did,
in his higher and nobler nature, vexed and annoyed him.

Of late years he had taken long vacations from her society,
in excursions to England and America. When the prospect
of being ambassador to England dawned upon him, he began
seriously to consider the inconvenience of being connected
with a woman unpresentable in society. He dared not risk
introducing her into those high circles as his wife. Moreover, he knew that it was a falsehood to which he never
should gain her consent; and running along in the line of his
thoughts came his recollections of Tina. When he returned
to America, with the fact in his mind that she would be the
acknowledged daughter of a respectable old English family,
all her charms and fascinations had a double power over him.
He delivered himself up to them without scruple.

He wrote immediately to a confidential friend in Switzerland, enclosing money, with authority to settle upon Emily
a villa near Geneva, and a suitable income. He trusted to
her pride for the rest.

Never had the thought come into his head that she would return to her native country, and brave all the reproach and humiliation of such a step, rather than accept this settlement at his hands.

CHAPTER XXIV.

Tina's Solution.

HARRY and I had gone back to our college room after the wedding. There we received an earnest letter from Miss Mehitable, begging us to come to her at once. It was brought by Sam Lawson, who told us that he had got up at three o'clock in the morning to start away with it.

"'There's trouble of some sort or other in that 'ere house," said Sam. "Last night I was inter the Deacon's, and we was a-talkin' over the weddin', when Polly came in all sort o' flustered, and said Miss Rossiter wanted to see Mis' Badger; and your granny and she went over, and didn't come home all night. She sot up with somebody, and I'm certain 'twa'n't Miss Rossiter, 'cause I see her up tol'able spry in the mornin'; but, lordy massy, somethin' or other's ben a-usin' on her up, for she was all wore out, and looked sort o' limpsey, as if there wa'n't no starch left in her. She sent for me last night. 'Sam,' says she, 'I want to send a note to the boys just as quick as I can, and I don't want to wait for the mail; can't you carry it?' 'Lordy massy, yes,' says I. 'I hope there ain't nothin' happened,' says I; and ye see she didn't answer me; and puttin' that with Mis' Badger's settin' there all night, it 'peared to me there was suthin', I can't make out quite what."

Harry and I lost no time in going to the stage-house, and found ourselves by noon at Miss Mehitable's door.

When we went in, we found Miss Mehitable seated in

close counsel with Mr. Jonathan Rossiter. His face looked sharp, and grave, and hard; his large gray eyes had in them a fiery, excited gleam. Spread out on the table before them were files of letters, in the handwriting of which I had before had a glimpse. The brother and sister had evidently been engaged in reading them, as some of them lay open under their hands.

When we came into the room, both looked up. Miss Mehitable rose, and offered her hands to us in an eager, excited way, as if she were asking something of us. The colour flashed into Mr. Rossiter's cheeks, and he suddenly leaned forward over the papers and covered his face with his hands. It was a gesture of shame and humiliation infinitely touching to me.

"Horace," said Miss Mehitable, "the thing we feared has come upon us. O Horace, Horace! why could we not have known it in time?"

I divined at once. My memory, like an electric chain, flashed back over sayings and incidents of years.

"The villain!" I said.

Mr. Rossiter ground his foot on the floor with a hard, impatient movement, as if he were crushing some poisonous reptile.

"It's well for him that *I'm* not God," he said through his closed teeth.

Harry looked from one to the other of us in dazed and inquiring surprise. He had known in a vague way of Emily's disappearance, and of Miss Mehitable's anxieties, but it never had occurred to his mind to connect the two. In fact, our whole education had been in such a wholesome and innocent state of society, that we neither of us had the foundation, in our experience or habits of thought, for the conception of anything like villany. We were far enough from any comprehension of the melodramatic possibilities suggested in our days by that heaving and tumbling modern literature, whose waters cast up mire and dirt.

Never shall I forget the shocked, incredulous expression on Harry's face as he listened to my explanations, nor the indignation to which it gave place.

"I would sooner have seen Tina in her grave than married to such a man," he said huskily.

"O Harry!" said Miss Mehitable.

"I would!" he said, rising excitedly. "There are things that men can do that still leave hope of them; but a thing like this is *final*,—it is decisive."

"That is my opinion, Harry," said Mr. Rossiter. "It is a sin that leaves no place for repentance."

"We have been reading these letters," said Miss Mehitable; "they were sent to us by Tina, and they do but confirm what I always said,—that Emily fell by her higher nature. She learned, under Dr. Stern, to think and to reason boldly, even when differing from received opinion; and this hardihood of mind and opinion she soon turned upon the doctrines he taught. Then she abandoned the Bible, and felt herself free to construct her own system of morals. Then came an intimate friendship with a fascinating married man, whose domestic misfortunes made a constant demand on her sympathy; and these charming French friends of hers, —who were, as far as I see, disciples of the new style of philosophy, and had come to America to live in a union with each other which was not recognised by the laws of France —all united to make her feel that she was acting heroically and virtuously in sacrificing her whole life to her lover, and disregarding what they called the tyranny of human law. In Emily's eyes, her connexion had all the sacredness of marriage."

"Yes," said Mr. Rossiter, "but see now how all these infernal, fine-spun, and high-flown notions always turn out to the disadvantage of the weaker party! It is *man* who always takes advantage of women in relations like these; it is she that *gives* all, and he that *takes* all ; it is she risks everything, and he risks nothing. Hard as marriage bonds bear in individual cases, it is for woman's interest that they should be as stringently maintained as the Lord Himself has left them. When once they begin to be lessened, it is always the weaker party that goes to the wall!"

"But," said I, "suppose a case of confirmed and hopeless insanity on either side."

He made an impatient gesture. "Did you ever think," he said, "if men had the laws of nature in their hands, what a mess they would make of them? What treatises we should have against the cruelty of fire in *always* burning, and of water in *always* drowning! What saints and innocents has the fire tortured, and what just men made perfect has water drowned, making *no* exceptions! But who doubts that this inflexibility in natural law is, after all, the best thing? The laws of morals are in our hands, and so reversible, and, therefore, we are always clamouring for exceptions. I think they should cut their way like those of nature, *inflexibly* and *eternally*."

Here the sound of wheels startled us. I went to the window, and, looking through the purple spikes of the tall old lilacs, which came up in a bower around the open window, I saw Tina alighting from a carriage.

"O Aunty," I said involuntarily, "it is she. *She* is coming, poor child!"

We heard a light fluttering motion and a footfall on the stairs, and the door opened, and in a moment Tina stood among us.

She was very pale, and there was an expression such as I never saw in her face before. There had been a shock which had driven her soul inward, from the earthly upon the spiritual and the immortal. Something deep and pathetic spoke in her eyes, as she looked around on each of us for a moment without speaking. . As she met Miss Mehitable's haggard, careworn face, her lip quivered. She ran to her, threw her arms round her, and hid her face on her shoulder, and sobbed out, "O Aunty, Aunty! I didn't think I should live to make you this trouble."

"You, darling!" said Miss Mehitable. "It is not *you* who have made it."

"I am the cause," she said. "I know that he has done dreadfully wrong. I cannot defend him, but oh! I love him still. I cannot help loving him; it is my duty too," she added. "I promised, you know, before God, 'for better, for worse;' and what I promised I must keep. I am his wife; there is no going back from that."

"I know it, darling," said Miss Mehitable, stroking her head. "You are right, and my love for *you* will never change."

"I am come," she said, "to see what can be done."

"NOTHING *can be done!*" spoke out the deep voice of Jonathan Rossiter. "She is lost, and we disgraced beyond remedy!"

"You must not say that," Tina said, raising her head, her eyes sparkling through her tears with some of her old vivacity. "Your sister is a noble, injured woman. We must shield her and save her; there is every excuse for her."

"There is NEVER any excuse for such conduct," said Mr. Rossiter, harshly.

Tina started up in her headlong, energetic fashion. "What right have you to talk so, if you call yourself a Christian?"

she said. "Think a minute. Who was it said, 'Neither do I condemn thee'? and *whom* did He say it to? Christ was not afraid or ashamed to say *that* to a poor friendless woman, though He knew His words would never pass away."

"God bless you, darling,—God bless you!" said Miss Mehitable, clasping her in her arms.

"I have read those letters," continued Tina, impetuously. "He did not like me to do it, but I claimed it as my right, and I *would* do it, and I can see in all a noble woman, gone astray from noble motives. I can see that she was grand and unselfish in her love, that she was perfectly self-sacrificing, and I believe it was because Jesus understood these things in the hearts of women that He uttered those blessed words. The law was against that poor woman, the doctors, the Scribes and Pharisees, all respectable people, were against her and Christ stepped between all and her; He sent them away abashed and humbled, and spoke those lovely words to her. Oh, I shall for ever adore Him for it! He is my Lord and my God!"

There was a pause for a few moments, and then Tina spoke again.

"Now, Aunty, hear my plan. You, perhaps, do not believe any good of *him*, and so I will not try to make you; only I will say that he is anxious to do all he can. He has left everything in my hands. This must go no farther than us few who now know it. Your sister refused the property he tried to settle on her. It was noble to do it. I should have felt just as she did. But, dear Aunty, *my* fortune I always meant to settle on you, and it will be enough for you both. It will make you easy as to money, and you can live together."

"Yes, my dear," said Miss Mehitable; "but how can this be kept secret when there is the child?"

"I have thought of that, Aunty. I will take the poor little one abroad with me,—children always love me. I can make her so happy; and oh, it will be such a motive to make amends to her for all this wrong. Let me see your sister, Aunty, and tell her about it."

"Dear child," said Miss Mehitable, "you can do nothing with her. All last night I thought she was dying. Since then she seems to have recovered her strength; but she neither speaks nor moves. She lies with her eyes open, but notices nothing you say to her."

"Poor darling!" said Tina. "But, Aunty, let me go to her. I am so sure that God will help me,—that God sends me to her. I *must* see her!"

Tina's strong impulses seemed to carry us all with her. Miss Mehitable arose, and, taking her by the hand, opened the door of a chamber on the opposite side of the hall. I looked in, and saw that it was darkened. Tina went boldly in, and closed the door. We all sat silent together. We heard her voice, at times soft and pleading; then it seemed to grow more urgent and impetuous as she spoke continuously and in tones of piercing earnestness.

After a while, there were pauses of silence, and then a voice in reply.

"There," said Miss Mehitable, "Emily has begun to answer her, thank God! Anything is better than this oppressive silence. It is frightful!"

And now the sound of an earnest conversation was heard, waxing on both sides more and more ardent and passionate. Tina's voice sometimes could be distinguished in tones of the most pleading entreaty; sometimes it seemed almost like sobbing. After a while, there came a great silence, broken by now and then an indistinct word; and then Tina came out, softly closing the door. Her cheeks were flushed, her hair partially dishevelled, but she smiled brightly,—one of her old triumphant smiles when she had carried a point.

"I've conquered at last! I've won!" she said, almost breathless. "Oh, I prayed so that I might, and I did. She gives all up to me; she loves me. We love each other dearly. And now I'm going to take the little one with me, and by and by I will bring her back to her, and I will make her so happy. You must give me the darling at once, and I will take her away with us; for we are going to sail next week. We sail sooner than I thought," she said; "but this makes it best to go at once."

Miss Mehitable rose and went out, but soon reappeared, leading in a lovely little girl with great round, violet-blue eyes, and curls of golden hair. The likeness of Ellery Davenport was plainly impressed on her infant features.

Tina ran towards her, and stretched out her arms. "Darling," she said, "come to me."

The little one, after a moment's survey, followed that law of attraction which always drew children to Tina. She came up confidingly, and nestled her head on her shoulder.

Tina gave her her watch to play with, and the child shook it about, well pleased.

"Emily want to go ride?" said Tina, carrying her to the window and showing her the horses.

The child laughed, and stretched out her hand.

"Bring me her things, Aunty," she said. "Let there not be a moment for change of mind. I take her with me this moment."

A few moments after, Tina went lightly tripping down the stairs, and Harry and I with her, carrying the child and its little basket of clothing.

"There, put them in," she said. "And now, boys," she said, turning and offering both her hands, "good-bye. I love you both dearly, and always shall."

She kissed us both, and was gone from our eyes before I awoke from the dream into which she had thrown me.

.   .   .   .

"Well," said Miss Mehitable, when the sound of wheels died away, "could I have believed that anything could have made my heart so much lighter as this visit!"

"She was inspired," said Mr. Rossiter.

"'Tina's great characteristic," said I. "What makes her differ from others in this capacity of inspiration. She seems sometimes to rise, in a moment, to a level above her ordinary self, and carry all up with her!"

"And to think that such a woman has thrown herself away on such a man!" said Harry.

"I foresee a dangerous future for her," said Mr. Rossiter. "With her brilliancy, her power of attraction, with the temptations of a new and fascinating social life before her, and with only that worthless fellow for a guide, I am afraid she will not continue *our* Tina."

"Suppose we trust in *Him* who has guided her hitherto," said Harry.

"People usually consider that sort of trust a desperate resort," said M. Rossiter. "'May the Lord help her' means, 'It's all up with her.'"

"We see," said I, "that the greatest possible mortification and sorrow that could meet a young wife has only raised her into a higher plane. So let us hope for her future."

CHAPTER XXV.
What came of It.

The next week Mr. and Mrs. Ellery Davenport sailed for England.

I am warned by the increased quantity of manuscript

which lies before me that, if I go on recounting scenes and incidents with equal minuteness, my story will transcend the limits of modern patience. Richardson might be allowed to trail off into seven volumes, and to trace all the histories of all his characters, even unto the third and fourth generations; but Richardson did not live in the days of rail-road and steam, and mankind then had more leisure than now.

I am warned, too, that the departure of the principal character from the scene is a signal for general weariness through the audience,—for looking up of gloves, and putting on of shawls, and getting ready to call one's carriage.

In fact, when Harry and I had been down to see Tina off, and had stood on the shore, watching and waving our handkerchiefs, until the ship became a speck in the blue airy distance, I turned back to the world with very much the feeling that there was nothing left in it. What I had always dreamed of, hoped for, planned for, and made the object of my endeavours, so far as this world was concerned, was gone, —gone, so far as I could see, hopelessly and irredeemably; and there came over me that utter languor and want of interest in every mortal thing, which is one of the worst diseases of the mind.

But I knew that it would never do to give way to this lethargy. I needed an alternative; and so I set myself, with all my might and soul, to learning a new language. There was an old German emigrant in Cambridge, with whom I became a pupil, and I plunged into German as into a new existence. I recommend everybody who wishes to try the waters of Lethe to study a new language, and learn to think in new forms; it is like going out of one sphere of existence into another.

Some may wonder that I do not recommend devotion for this grand alternative; but it is a fact, that, when one has to combat with the terrible lassitude produced by the sudden withdrawal of an absorbing object of affection, devotional exercises sometimes hinder more than they help. There is much in devotional religion of the same strain of softness and fervour which is akin to earthly attachments, and the one is almost sure to recall the other. What the soul wants is to be distracted for a while,—to be taken out of its old grooves of thought, and run upon entirely new ones. Religion must be sought in these moods, in its active and preceptive form,— what we may call its business character,—rather than in its sentimental and devotional one.

It had been concluded among us all that it would be expedient for Miss Mehitable to remove from Oldtown and take a residence in Boston.

It was desirable, for restoring the health of Emily, that she should have more change and variety, and less minute personal attention fixed upon her, than could be the case in the little village of Oldtown. Harry and I did a great deal of house-hunting for them, and at last succeeded in securing a neat little cottage on an eminence overlooking the harbour in the outskirts of Boston.

Preparing this house for them, and helping to establish them in it, furnished employment for a good many of our leisure hours. In fact, we found that this home so near would be quite an accession to our pleasures. Miss Mehitable had always been one of that most pleasant and desirable kind of acquaintances that a young man can have; to wit, a cultivated, intelligent, literary female friend, competent to advise and guide one in one's scholarly career. We became greatly interested in the society of her sister. The strength and dignity of character shown by this unfortunate lady in recovering her position commanded our respect. She was never aware, and was never made aware by anything in our manner, that we were acquainted with her past history.

The advice of Tina on this subject had been faithfully followed. No one in our circle, or in Boston, except my grandmother, had any knowledge of how the case really stood. In fact, Miss Mehitable had always said that her sister had gone abroad to study in France, and her re-appearance again was only noticed among the few that inquired into it at all, as her return. Harry and I used to study French with her, both on our own account, and as a means of giving her some kind of employment. On the whole, the fireside circle at the little cottage became a cheerful and pleasant retreat. Miss Mehitable had gained what she had for years been sighing for,—the opportunity to devote herself wholly to this sister. She was a person with an enthusiastic power of affection, and the friendship that arose between the two was very beautiful.

The experiences of the French Revolution, many of whose terrors she had witnessed, had had a powerful influence on the mind of Emily, in making her feel how mistaken had been those views of human progress which come from the mere unassisted reason, when it rejects the guidance of revealed religion. She was in a mood to return to the faith of her fathers, receiving it again under milder and more liberal forms. I think the friendship of Harry was of great use to her in enabling her to attain to a settled religious faith. They were peculiarly congenial to each other, and his simplicity of religious trust was a constant corrective to the habits of thought formed by the sharp and pitiless logic of her early training.

A residence in Boston was also favourable to Emily's recovery, in giving to her what no person who has passed through such experiences can afford to be without,—an opportunity to help those poorer and more afflicted. Emily very naturally shrank from society; except the Kitterys, I think there was no family which she visited. I think she always had the feeling that she would not accept the acquaintance of any who would repudiate her were all the circumstances of her life known to them. But with the poor, the sick, and the afflicted, she felt herself at home. In their houses she was a Sister of Mercy, and the success of these sacred ministrations caused her, after a while, to be looked upon with a sort of reverence by all who knew her.

Tina proved a lively and most indefatigable correspondent. Harry and I heard from her constantly, in minute descriptions of the great gay world of London society, into which she was thrown as wife of the American minister. Her letters were like her old self, full of genius, of wit, and of humour, sparkling with descriptions and anecdotes of character, and sometimes scrawled on the edges with vivid sketches of places, or scenes, or buildings that hit her fancy. She was improving, she told us, taking lessons in drawing and music, and Ellery was making a capital French scholar of her. We could see through all her letters an evident effort to set forth everything relating to him to the best advantage; every good-natured or kindly action, and all the favourable things that were said of him, were put in the foreground, with even an anxious care.

To Miss Mehitable and Emily came other letters, filled with the sayings and doings of the little Emily, recording minutely all the particulars of her growth, and the incidents of the nursery, and showing that Tina, with all her going out, found time strictly to fulfil her promises in relation to her.

"I have got the very best kind of a maid for her," she wrote,—"just as good and true as Polly is, only she is formed by the Church Catechism instead of the Cambridge Platform. But she is faithfulness itself, and Emily loves her dearly."

In this record, also, minute notice was taken of all the presents made to the child by her father,—of all his smiles and caressing words. Without ever saying a word formally in her husband's defence, Tina thus contrived, through all her letters, to produce the most favourable impression of him. He was evidently, according to her showing, proud of her beauty and her talents, and proud of the admiration which she excited in society.

For a year or two there seemed to be a real vein of happiness running through all these letters of Tina's. I spoke to Harry about it one day.

"Tina," said I, "has just that fortunate kind of constitution, buoyant as cork, that will rise to the top of the stormiest waters."

"Yes," said Harry. "With some women it would have been an entire impossibility to live happily with a man after such a disclosure,—with Esther, for example. I have never told Esther a word about it; but I know that it would give her a horror of the man that she never could recover from."

"It is not," said I, "that Tina has not strong moral perceptions; but she has this buoyant hopefulness; she believes in herself, and she believes in others. She always feels adequate to manage the most difficult circumstances. I could not help smiling that dreadful day, when she came over and found us all so distressed and discouraged, to see what a perfect confidence she had in herself, and in her own power to arrange the affair—to make Emily consent, to make the child love her; in short, to carry out everything according to her own sweet will, just as she has always done with us all ever since we knew her."

"I always wondered," said Harry, "that, with all her pride, and all her anger, Emily did consent to let the child go."

"Why," said I, "she was languid and weak, and she was overborne by simple force of will. Tina was so positive and determined, so perfectly assured, and so warming and melting, that she carried all before her. There wasn't even the physical power to resist her."

"And do you think," said Harry, "that she will hold her power over a man like Ellery Davenport?"

"Longer, perhaps, than any other kind of woman," said I, "because she has such an infinite variety about her. But, after all, you remember what Miss Debby said about him—that he never cared long for anything that he was sure of. Restlessness and pursuit are his nature, and therefore the time may come when she will share the fate of other idols."

"1 regard it," said Harry, "as the most dreadful trial to a woman's character that can possibly be, to love, as Tina loves, a man whose moral standard is so far below hers. It is bad enough to be obliged to *talk* down always to those who are below us in intellect and comprehension; but to be obliged to *live down*, all the while, to a man without conscience or moral sense, is worse. I think often, 'What communion hath light with darkness?' and the only hope I can have is that she will fully find him out at last."

"And that," said I, "is a hope full of pain to her; but it seems to me likely to be realised. A man who has acted as he has done to one woman certainly never will be true to another."

Harry and I were now thrown more and more exclusively upon each other for society.

He had received his accession of fortune with as little exterior change as possible. Many in his situation would have rushed immediately over to England, and taken delight in

coming openly into possession of the estate. Harry's fastidious reticence, however, hung about him even in this. It
annoyed him to be an object of attention and gossip, and he
felt no inclination to go alone into what seemed to him a
strange country, into the midst of social manners and customs entirely different from those among which he had been
brought up. He preferred to remain and pursue his course
quietly, as he had begun, in the college with me; and he had
taken no steps in relation to the property, except to consult a
lawyer in Boston.

Immediately on leaving college, it was his design to be
married, and go with Esther to see what could be done in
England. But I think his heart was set upon a home in
America. The freedom and simplicity of life in this country
were peculiarly suited to his character, and he felt a real
vocation for the sacred ministry, not in the slightest degree
lessened by the good fortune which had rendered him independent of it.

Two years of our college life passed away pleasantly
enough in hard study, interspersed with social relaxations
among the few friends nearest to us. Immediately after our
graduation came Harry's marriage—a peaceful little idyllic
performance, which took us back to the mountains, and
to all the traditions of our old innocent woodland life there.

After the wholesome fashion of New England clergymen,
Mr. Avery had found a new mistress for the parsonage, so
that Esther felt the more resigned to leaving him. When I
had seen them off, however, I felt really quite alone in the
world. The silent, receptive, sympathetic friend and brother
of my youth was gone. But immediately came the effort to
establish myself in Boston. And, through the friendly offices
of the Kitterys, I was placed in connexion with some very
influential lawyers, who gave me that helping hand which

takes a young man up the first steps of the profession. Harry had been most generous and liberal in regard to all our family, and insisted upon it that I should share his improved fortunes. There are friends so near to us that we can take from them as from ourselves. And Harry always insisted that he could in no way so repay the kindness and care that had watched over his early years as by this assistance to me.

I received constant letters from him, and from their drift it became increasingly evident that the claims of duty upon him would lead him to make England his future home. In one of these he said: "I have always, as you know, looked forward to the ministry, and to such a kind of ministry as you have in America, where a man for the most part, speaks to cultivated, instructed people, living in a healthy state of society, where a competence is the rule, and where there is a practical equality.

"I had no conception of life, such as I see it to be here, where there are whole races who appear born to poverty and subjection; where there are woes, and dangers, and miseries pressing on whole classes of men, which no one individual can do much to avert or alleviate. But it is to this very state of society that I feel a call to minister. I shall take orders in the Church of England, and endeavour to carry out among the poor and the suffering that simple gospel which my mother taught me, and which, after all these years of experience, after all these theological discussions to which I have listened remains in its perfect simplicity in my mind; namely, that every human soul on this earth has one Friend, and that Friend is Jesus Christ, its Lord and Saviour.

"There is a redeeming power in being beloved, but there are many human beings who have never known what it is to be beloved. And my theology is, once penetrate any human soul with the full belief that *God loves him*, and you save him. Such is to be my life's object and end; and, in this ministry, Esther will go with me hand-in-hand. Her noble beauty and gracious manners make her the darling of all our people; and she is above measure happy in the power of doing good which is thus put into her hands.

"As to England, mortal heart cannot conceive more beauty than there is here. It is lovely beyond all poets' dreams. Near to our place are some charming old ruins, and I cannot tell you the delightful hours that Esther and I have spent there. Truly, the lines have fallen to us in pleasant places.

"I have not yet seen Tina,—she is abroad, travelling on the Continent. She writes to us often; but, Horace, her letters begin to have the undertone of pain in them,—her skies are certainly beginning to fade. From some sources upon which I place reliance, I hear Ellery Davenport spoken of as a daring, plausible, but unscrupulous man. He is an *intrigant* in politics, and has no domestic life in him; while Tina, however much she loves and appreciates admiration, has a perfect woman's heart. Admiration without love would never satisfy her. I can see, through all the excuses of her letters, that he is going very much one way, and she another; that he has his engagements, and she hers, and that they see, really, very little of each other, and that all this makes her sad and unhappy. The fact is, I suppose, he has played with his butterfly until there is no more down on its wings, and he is on the chase after new ones. Such is my reading of poor Tina's lot."

When I took this letter to Miss Mehitable, she told me that a similar impression had long since been produced on her mind by passages which she had read in hers. Tina often spoke of the little girl as very lovely, and as her greatest earthly comfort. A little one of her own, born in England, had died early, and her affections seemed thus to concentrate more entirely upon the child of her adoption. She described her with enthusiasm, as a child of rare beauty and talent, with capabilities of enthusiastic affection.

"Let us hope," said I, "that she does take her heart from her mother. Ellery Davenport is just one of those men that women are always wrecking themselves on,—men that have strong capabilities of passion, and very little capability of affection,—men that have no end of sentiment, and scarcely the beginning of real feeling. They make bewitching lovers, but terrible husbands."

One of the greatest solaces of my life during this period was my friendship with dear old Madam Kittery. Ever since the time when I had first opened to her my boyish heart, she had seemed to regard me with an especial tenderness, and to connect me in some manner with the image of her lost son. The assistance that she gave me in my educational career was viewed by her as a species of adoption. Her eye always brightened, and a lovely smile broke out upon her face, when I came to pass an hour with her. Time had treated her kindly; she still retained the gentle shrewdness, the love of literature, and the warm kindness which had been always charms in her. Some of my happiest hours were passed in reading to her. Chapter after chapter in her well-worn Bible needed no better commentary than the sweet brightness of her dear old face, and her occasional fervent responses. Many Sabbaths, when her increasing infirmities detained her from church, I spent in a tender, holy rest by her side. Then I would read from her Prayer-book the morning service, not omitting the prayer that she loved, for the king and the royal family, and then, sitting hand in hand, we talked together of sacred things, and I often wondered to see what *strength* and discrimination there were in the wisdom of love, and how unerring were the decisions that she

often made in practical questions. In fact, I felt myself
drawn to Madam Kittery by a closer, tenderer tie than even
to my own grandmother. I had my secret remorse for this,
and tried to quiet myself by saying that it was because,
living in Boston, I saw Madam Kittery oftener. But, after all,
is it not true that, as we grow older, the relationship of souls
will make itself felt? I revered and loved my grandmother,
but I never idealised her; but my attachment to Madam
Kittery was a species of poetic devotion. There was a slight
flavour of romance in it, such as comes with the attachments
of our maturer life oftener than with those of our childhood.

Miss Debby looked on me with eyes of favour. In her
own way she really was quite as much my friend as her
mother. She fell into the habit of consulting me upon her
business affairs, and asking my advice in a general way,
about the arrangements of life.

"I don't see," I said to Madam Kittery, one day, "why
Miss Deborah always asks my advice; she never takes it."

"My dear," said she, with the quiet smile with which she
often looked on her daughter's proceedings, "Debby wants
somebody to *ask* advice of. When she gets it, she is settled
at once as to what she *don't* want to do; and that's something."

Miss Debby once came to me with a face of great perplexity.

"I don't know what to do, Horace. Our Thomas is a very
valuable man, and he has always been in the family. I don't
know anything how we should get along without him, but he
is getting into bad ways."

"Ah," said I, "what?"

"Well, you see it all comes of this modern talk about the
rights of the people. I've instructed Thomas as faithfully
as ever a woman could; but—do you believe me?—he goes

to the primary meetings. I have positive, reliable information that he does."

"My dear Miss Kittery, I suppose it's his right as a citizen."

"Oh, fiddlestick and humbug!" said Miss Debby; "and it may be my right to turn him out of my service."

"And would not that, after all, be more harm to you than to him?" suggested I.

Miss Debby swept up the hearth briskly, tapped on her snuff-box, and finally said she had forgotten her handkerchief, and left the room.

Old Madam Kittery laughed a quiet laugh. "Poor Debby," she said, "she'll have to come to it; the world will go on."

Thomas kept his situation for some years longer, till, having bought a snug place, and made some favourable investments, he at last announced to Miss Debby, that, having been appointed constable, with a commission from the governor, his official duties would not allow of his continuance in her service.

CHAPTER XXVI.

The Last Chapter.

It was eight years after Tina left us on the wharf in Boston, when I met her again. Ellery Davenport had returned to this country, and taken a house in Boston. I was then a lawyer, established there in a successful business.

Ellery Davenport met me with open-handed cordiality, and Tina with warm sisterly affection; and their house became one of my most frequent visiting-places. Knowing Tina by a species of divination, as I always had, it was easy for me to see through all those sacred little hypocrisies, by which good women instinctively plead and intercede for husbands, whom they themselves have found out. Michelet says, somewhere, that "in marriage, the maternal feeling becomes always the strongest in woman, and in time, it is the motherly feeling with which she regards her husband." She cares for him, watches over him, with the indefatigable tenderness which a mother gives to a son.

It was easy to see that Tina's affection for her husband, was no longer a blind, triumphant adoration for an idealised hero, nor the confiding dependence of a happy wife, but the careworn anxiety of one who constantly seeks to guide and to restrain. And I was not long in seeing the cause of this anxiety.

Ellery Davenport was smitten with that direct curse, which, like the madness inflicted on the heroes of some of the Greek tragedies, might seem to be the vengeance of some incensed divinity. He was going down that dark and slippery road, up which so few return. We were all fully aware, that at many times our Tina had all the ghastly horrors of dealing with a madman. Even when he was himself again, and sought, by vows, promises, and illusive good resolutions, to efface the memory of the past, and give security for the future, there was no rest for Tina. In her dear eyes, I could read always that sense of overhanging dread, that helpless watchfulness, which one may see in the eyes of so many poor women in our modern life, whose days are haunted by a fear they dare not express, and who must smile, and look gay, and seem confiding, when their very souls are failing them for fear. Still these seasons of madness did not seem for a while to impair the vigour of Ellery Davenport's mind, nor the feverish intensity of his ambition. He was absorbed in political life, in a wild, daring, unprincipled way, and made frequent occasions to leave Tina alone in Boston, while he travelled around the country, pursuing his intrigues. In one of these absences, it was his fate at last to fall in a political duel.

. . . . .

Ten years after the gay and brilliant scene in Christ Church, some of those who were present as wedding guests were again convened to tender the last offices to the brilliant and popular Ellery Davenport. Among the mourners at the grave, two women who had loved him truly stood arm in arm.

After his death, it seemed by the general consent of all, the kindest thing that could be done for him, to suffer the veil of silence to fall over his memory.

. . . . .

Two years after that, one calm, lovely October morning, a quiet circle of friends stood around the altar of the old church, when Tina and I were married. Our wedding journey was a visit to Harry and Esther in England. Since then, the years have come and gone softly.

Ellery Davenport now seems to us as a distant dream of another life, recalled chiefly by the beauty of his daughter, whose growing loveliness is the principal ornament of our home.

Miss Mehitable and Emily form one circle with us. Nor does the youthful Emily know why she is so very dear to the saintly woman whose prayers and teachings are such a benediction in our family.

. . . . .

Not long since we spent a summer vacation at Oldtown, to explore once more the old scenes, and to show to young Master Harry and Miss Tina the places that their parents had told them of. Many changes have taken place in the old homestead. The serene old head of my grandfather has been laid beneath the green sod of the burying-ground; and my mother, shortly after, was laid by him.

Old Parson Lothrop continued for some years, with his antique dress and his antique manners, respected in Oldtown as the shadowy minister of the past; while his colleague, Mr. Mordecai Rossiter, edified his congregation with the sharpest and most stringent new-school Calvinism. To the last, Dr. Lothrop remained faithful to his Arminian views, and regarded the spread of the contrary doctrines, as a decaying old minister is apt to, as a personal reflection upon himself. In his last illness, which was very distressing, he was visited by a zealous Calvinistic brother from a neighbouring town, who, on the strength of being a family connexion, thought it his duty to go over and make one last effort to revive the orthodoxy of his venerable friend. Dr. Lothrop received him politely, and with his usual gentlemanly decorum remained for a long time in silence listening to his somewhat protracted arguments and statements. As he gave no reply, his friend at last said to him, "Dr. Lothrop, perhaps you are weak, and this conversation disturbs you?"

"I should be weak indeed, if I allowed such things as you have been saying to disturb me," replied the staunch old doctor.

"He died like a philosopher, my dear," said Lady Lothrop to me, "just as he always lived."

My grandmother, during the last part of her life, was totally blind. One would have thought that a person of her extreme activity would have been restless and wretched under this deprivation; but in her case blindness appeared to be indeed what Milton expressed it as being, "an overshadowing of the wings of the Almighty." Every earthly care was hushed, and her mind turned inward, in constant meditation upon those great religious truths which had fed her life for so many years.

Aunt Lois we found really quite lovely. There is a class of women who are like winter apples,—all their youth they are crabbed and hard, but at the further end of life they are full of softness and refreshment. The wrinkles had really almost smoothed themselves out in Aunt Lois' face, and our children found in her the most indulgent and painstaking of aunties, ready to run, and wait, and tend, and fetch, and carry, and willing to put everything in the house at their disposal. In fact, the young gentleman and lady found the old homestead such very free and easy ground that they announced to us that they preferred altogether staying there to being in Boston, especially as they had the barn to romp in.

One Saturday afternoon, Tina and I drove over to Needmore, with a view to having one more gossip with Sam Lawson. Hepsy, it appears, had departed this life, and Sam had gone over to live with a son of his in Needmore. We found him roosting placidly in the porch on the sunny side of the house.

"Why, lordy massy, bless your soul an' body, ef that ain't Horace Holyoke!" he said, when he recognised who I was. "An' this 'ere's your wife, is it? Wal, wal, how this 'ere world does turn round! Wal, now, who would ha' thought it? Here you be, and Tina with you. Wal, wal!"

"Yes," said I; "here we are."

"Wal, now, jest sit down," said Sam, motioning us to a seat in the porch. "I was jest kind o' 'flectin' out here in the sun; ben a-readin' in the *Missionary Herald;* they've ben a-sendin' missionaries to Otawhity, an' they say that there ain't no winter there, an' the bread jest grows on the trees, so't they don't hev to make none; an' there ain't no wood-

piles nor splittin' wood, nor nothin' o' that sort goin' on; an'
folks don't need no clothes to speak on. Now, I's jest
thinkin' that 'ere's jest the country to suit me. I wonder,
now, ef they couldn't find suthin' for me to do out there. I
could shoe the hosses, if they hed any, and I could teach the
natives their catechize, and kind o' help round gin'ally. These
'ere winters gits so cold here I'm e'en a'mos crooked up with
the rheumatiz"——

"Why, Sam," said Tina, "where is Hepsy?"

"Law, now, hain't ye heerd? Why, Hepsy, she's been
dead, wal, let me see, 'twas three year the fourteenth o' last
May when Hepsy died, but she was clear wore out afore she
died. Wal, jest half on her was clear paralysed, poor crittur;
she couldn't speak a word; that 'ere was a gret trial to her. I
don't think she was resigned under it. Hepsy hed an awful
sight o' grit. I used to talk to Hepsy, an' talk, an' try to set
things afore her in the best way I could, so's to git 'er into a
better state o' mind. D' you b'lieve, one day when I'd ben
a-talkin' to her, she kind o' made a motion to me with her
eye, an' when I went up to 'er what d' you think? why, she
jest tuk and mit me! she did so!"

"Sam," said Tina, "I sympathise with Hepsy. I believe
if I had to be talked to an hour, and couldn't answer, I should
bite."

"Jes' so, jes' so," said Sam. "I 'spex't is so. You see,
women must talk, there's where 't is. Wal, now, don't ye
remember that Miss Bell,—Miss Mirry Bell? She was of a
good family in Boston. They used to board her out to Oldtown, 'cause she was 's crazy 's a loon. They jest let 'er go
'bout, 'cause she didn't hurt nobody; but massy, her tongue
used ter run 's ef 't was hung in the middle, and run both ends.
Ye really couldn't hear yourself think when she was round.
Wal, she was a-visitin' Parson Lothrop, an' ses he, 'Miss Bell,

do pray see ef you can't be still a minute.' 'Lord bless ye, Dr. Lothrop, I can't stop talking!' said she. 'Wal,' says he, 'you jest take a mouthful o' water an' hold in your mouth, an' then mebbe ye ken stop.' Wall, she took the water, an' she sot still a minute or two, an' it kind o' worked on 'er so 't she jumped up an' twitched off Dr. Lothrop's wig an' spun it right acrost the room inter the fireplace. 'Bless me, Miss Bell,' ses he, 'spit out your water an' talk, ef ye must!' I've offun thought on 't," said Sam. "I s'pose Hepsy's felt a good 'eal so. Wal, poor soul, she's gone to 'er rest. We're all on us goin', one arter another. Yer grand'ther's gone, an' yer mother, an' Parson Lothrop, he's gone, an' Lady Lothrop, she's kind o' solitary. I went over to see 'er last week, an' ses she to me, 'Sam, I dunno nothin' what I shell do with my hosses. I feed 'em well, an' they ain't worked hardly any, and yet they act so 't I'm 'most afeard to drive out with 'em.' I'm thinkin' 't would be a good thing ef she'd give up that 'ere place o' hern, an' go an' live in Boston with her sister."

"Well, Sam," said Tina, "what has become of Old Crab Smith? Is he alive yet?"

"Law, yis, he's creepin' round here yit; but the old woman, she's dead," said Sam. "I tell you she's a hevin her turn o' hectorin *him* now, 'cause she keeps appearing to him, an' scares the old critter 'most to death."

"Appears to him?" said I. "Why, what do you mean, Sam?"

"Wal, jest as true's you live an' breathe, she does 'pear to him," said Sam. "Why, 't was only last week my son Luke an' I, we was a settin' by the fire here, an' I was a holdin' a skein o' yarn for Malviny to wind (Malviny, she's Luke's wife), when who should come in but Old Crab, head first, lookin' so scart an' white about the gills that Luke, ses he; 'Why, Mistur Smith! what ails ye?' ses he. Wal, the critter was so scared 't he couldn't speak, he jest set down in the chair, an' he shuk so 't he shuk the chair, an' his teeth, they chattered, an' 't was a long time 'fore they could git it out on him. But come to, he told us, 't was a bright moonlight night, an' he was comin' 'long down by the Stone pastur, when all of a suddin he looks up an' there was his wife walkin right 'longside on him,—he ses he never see nothin' plainer in his life than he see the old woman, jest in her short gown an' petticut 't she allers wore, with her gold beads round her neck, an' a cap on with a black ribbon round it, an' there she kep' a walkin' right 'longside of 'im, her elbow a-touchin' him, all 'long the road, an' when he walked faster, she walked faster, an' when he walked slower, she walked slower, an' her eyes was sot, and fixed on him, but she didn't speak no word, an' he didn't darse to speak to her. Finally, he ses he gin a dreadful yell an' run with all his might, an' our house was the very fust place he tumbled inter. Lordy massy, wal, I couldn't help thinkin' 't sarved him right. I tol' Sol 'bout it, last town-meetin' day, an' Sol, I thought he'd ha' split his sides. Sol said he didn't know's the old woman had so much sperit. 'Lordy massy,' ses he, 'ef she don't do nothin' more 'n take a walk 'longside on him now an' then, why, I say, let 'er rip,—sarves him right.'"

"Well," said Tina, "I'm glad to hear about Old Sol; how is he?"

"O, Sol? Wal, he's doin' fustrate. He married Deacon 'Bijah Smith's darter, an' he's got a good farm of his own, an' boys bigger an' you be, considerable."

"Well," said Tina, "how is Miss Asphyxia?"

"Wal, Sol told me 't she'd got a cancer or suthin' or other the matter with 'er; but the old gal, she jest sets her teeth hard', an' goes on a workin'. She won't have no doctor, nor nothin' done for 'er, an' I expect bimeby she 'll die, a-standin' up in the harness."

"Poor old creature! I wonder, Horace, if it would do any good for me to go and see her. Has she a soul, I wonder, or is she nothing but a 'working machine?'"

"Wal, I dunno," said Sam. "This 'ere world is cur'us. When we git to thinkin' about it, we think ef we'd ha' had the makin' on 't, things would ha' ben made someways diffurnt from what they be. But then things *is* just *as* they is, an' we can't help it. Sometimes I think," said Sam, embracing his knee profoundly, "an' then agin I dunno——— There's all sorts o' folks hes to be in this 'ere world, an' I s'pose the Lord knows what he wants 'em fur; but I'm sure I don't. I kind o' hope the Lord 'll fetch everybody out 'bout right some o' these 'ere times. He ain't got nothin' else to do, an' it's his look-out, an' not ourn, what comes of 'em all——— But I *should* like to go to Otawhity, an' ef you see any o' these missionary folks, Horace, I wish you'd speak to 'em about it."

THE END.

PRINTING OFFICE OF THE PUBLISHER.

www.ingramcontent.com/pod-product-compliance
Lightning Source LLC
Chambersburg PA
CBHW051133120726
47905CB00005B/1537